A Logical Lady

JANICE BENNETT

D1405409

ZEBRA BOOKS
KENSINGTON PUBLISHING CORP.

Also by Janice Bennett:

An Eligible Bride
Tangled Web
Midnight Masque
An Intriguing Desire
A Tempting Miss
A Timely Affair
Forever in Time

For Pat

ZEBRA BOOKS

are published by

Kensington Publishing Corp.
475 Park Avenue South
New York, NY 10016

First printing: January, 1991

Printed in the United States of America

A SHOCKING REPUTATION

Lizzie fiddled with the cord that knotted about the bed hanging. "I know you don't like the idea, but it's not as if we'd actually have to go through with a wedding."

He drew a deep breath. "Do you have any idea what you're asking?"

"Of course I do. What's wrong with it?"

"Do you think anyone would believe it? I'm almost twice your age."

She studied the new knot she had added. "There's nothing wrong with that. We're known to be old friends."

"Friends," he repeated, emphasizing the word. "I'll not be accused of seducing a young innocent."

"It's your own fault for earning such a shocking reputation. Have you any other ridiculous arguments?"

"I doubt I have the strength. You'll do as you please, as always, I suppose."

"That's settled, then. We'll hold an engagement party as soon as possible, and I can cry off right after we've captured our murderer."

REGENCIES BY JANICE BENNETT

TANGLED WEB (2281, $3.95)

Miss Celia Marcombe's dark eyes flashed with righteous indignation. She was not a commodity to be traded or bartered to a man as insufferably arrogant as Trevor Ryde, despite what her high-handed grandfather decreed! If Lord Ryde thought she would let herself be married for any reason other than true love, he was sadly mistaken. He'd never get his hands on her fortune—let alone her person—no matter how disturbingly handsome he was . . .

MIDNIGHT MASQUE (2512, $3.95)

It was nothing unusual for Lady Ashton to transport government documents to her father from the Home Office. But on this particular afternoon a gust of wind scattered the papers, and suddenly an important page was lost. A document desperately wanted by more than one determined gentleman—one of whom would murder to get his way . . .

AN INTRIGUING DESIRE (2579, $3.95)

The British secret agent, Charles Marcombe, had done his bit against that blasted Bonaparte. Now it was time to nurse his wounds and come to terms with the fact that that part of his life was over. He certainly did not need the likes of Mademoiselle Therese de Bourgerre darkening his door, warning of dire emergencies and dread consequences, forcing him to remember things best forgotten. She was a delightful minx, to be sure, but it would take more than a pair of pleading emerald eyes and a woebegone smile to drag him back into the fray!

Available wherever paperbacks are sold, or order direct from the Publisher. Send cover price plus 50¢ per copy for mailing and handling to Zebra Books, Dept. 3277, 475 Park Avenue South, New York, N.Y. 10016. Residents of New York, New Jersey and Pennsylvania must include sales tax. DO NOT SEND CASH.

Chapter 1

A muffled voice, indistinct but angry, rose behind the closed oak door of the bookroom. The butler's stately tread came to an abrupt halt, and a spasm of consternation flickered across his normally impassive countenance.

"It would seem my beloved cousin is not alone, Hodgkens." The Honorable Mr. Frederick Ashfield paused just behind the butler, his expression of bored resignation evaporating. He fingered the walking cane he held, and devils of amusement sprang to life in the depths of his lazy blue eyes. "This promises to be a somewhat less dull evening than I feared."

Hodgkens turned his reproving regard on the tall, exquisite figure of the Corinthian who followed him. "Perhaps it would be best if you awaited His Lordship in the Green Salon, Mr. Frederick."

"Oh, undoubtedly it would. But somehow, my dear Hodgkens, I cannot see myself doing it, can you?"

The butler cast him a beseeching glance, encountered that gleam of reprehensible enjoyment he knew of old, and gave an audible sigh. There was no stopping Mr. Frederick when he was in one of his Moods. A gentleman fast approaching his fortieth birthday should have long since abandoned a taste for foolishness and bobbery. Not Mr. Frederick, it appeared.

Hodgkens squared his shoulders, and offered up a silent prayer of thanksgiving that it would be upon Mr. Frederick, and not upon himself, that his master's wrath would fall. Then he knocked.

For a long, pregnant moment, silence reigned. Then the cold, curt voice of John, sixth viscount St. Vincent, bade the intruder enter. Hodgkens reached for the latch, but Mr. Frederick Ashfield grasped it, winked, and gestured for him to take himself off. Hodgkens did so, with alacrity.

Still smiling, Frederick Ashfield let himself into the chill, dimly lit chamber. Only a small fire burned in the hearth, mute testimony to the austere—or more likely parsimonious—hand that prevailed. A single branch of candles—tallow, by the distasteful odor—stood on the corner of the desk.

A gentleman of just above average height stood before the mantel, garbed in dress as inappropriate to the Leicestershire countryside in late November as it was to his stocky build. His coat of dull gold velvet nipped in tightly at his waist and gold thread glimmered across the white satin waistcoat beneath. Black satin trousers disappeared into gleaming calfskin boots with their white tops turned down almost twelve inches. A neckcloth of impossible height and clumsy design completed the costume. His posture mimicked that of an outraged country squire rather than a tulip of fashion.

In a wooden straight-backed chair facing this gentleman sat the slight but ever-erect figure of the viscount. His sober black garb belied the passionate fury that lit his entire countenance, and his great beak of a nose fairly quivered in his thin, angular face. The men glared at each other, neither moving.

Frederick Ashfield raised his quizzing glass and peered languidly at the two combatants. "Am I interrupting?"

"What the devil—?" The viscount half-rose from his chair, irritation patent on his deeply lined face. He

6

turned to the doorway, and recoiled as if encountering a nasty shock.

"Just so, dear Coz." Frederick smiled, though on his cousin it did not produce the stunning effect it regularly had on the ladies. "The devil himself, as you see." He swept the viscount an exaggerated bow.

"Frederick," the viscount breathed in tones of loathing. "In the name of all that's Holy, what brings you here?" He sank back into his chair, pointedly making no move to offer a seat to his unexpected—and unwelcome—visitor.

"Why, to assure you I am still alive and well and infesting the earth. Not, as I am sure you had hoped, gone to my great reward—or punishment." Frederick strolled farther into the chamber and repressed a shiver. He shouldn't have handed his greatcoat into Hodgkens's capable hands; it was damned cold in here. Though it was nowhere nearly as frigid as his beloved cousin's manner.

With deliberation, Frederick lowered his tall frame onto the wooden settle, one of the few, uninviting pieces of furniture the room possessed. Crossing one booted ankle over the other knee, he laid the cane, with its elaborately carved ivory handle, at his side. He smiled benignly at his cousin's livid face.

This took on a darker hue. "I'm occupied at present. I'll deal with you later."

Frederick ignored the hint. Raising his quizzing glass, he subjected the young gentleman before the fire to a thorough scrutiny. That it had been he who shouted earlier, Frederick had no doubts. Nor could he blame him. The viscount could drive a saint to distraction. His effect on an ordinary man was a terrible thing to behold.

"I do not believe we are acquainted." He directed the comment to his cousin.

St. Vincent's thin mouth narrowed even more. "Needham. He's renting the Dower House. My cousin Ashfield," he added, grudgingly.

7

Frederick rose and shook hands with the dandy, for to do so clearly annoyed his cousin. Mr. Needham regarded him with a brooding stare from his gray eyes. The undistinguished features gave away little of his thoughts.

"Pray, do not let me interrupt." Frederick resumed his seat and folded his hands across the subdued brocade of his waistcoat with the air of one waiting to be entertained.

"Mr. Needham is just leaving."

"No, really, m'lord!" Mr. Needham protested. "Not until I have a satisfactory answer. Told you so already." Determination—it was almost belligerent—showed on the young face.

Though not so young, Frederick corrected himself the next moment. The man must be only a few years shy of thirty. Well, that was the perspective of his own eight-and-thirty years.

Needham remained where he stood, his gaze holding that of the viscount. Frederick's interest quickened, though why he could not be certain. It was more, he felt sure, than pleasure at discovering someone besides himself had the gumption to defy the viscount's autocratic decrees. Puritanical to the point of martyrdom—at least everyone else's martyrdom—that was the sixth viscount St. Vincent.

"I gave you the only reason you'll have," the viscount said, his teeth clenched. "Now get out of my house, and I will thank you not to come here again."

"And do not forget to shake the dust from your sandals," Frederick murmured.

Fortunately, neither of the other two gentlemen paid him any heed. Needham remained where he stood. St. Vincent surged to his feet, crossed to the fire, and, with a savage tug, set the bell pull ringing wildly. Hodgkens appeared in the doorway only a moment later, as if he had been anticipating the summons.

"Throw him out!" the viscount snapped.

The butler hesitated, his uncertain gaze straying from Mr. Needham to Frederick's lanky figure, and back again.

"Mr. Needham, he means," Frederick supplied helpfully. "Though to be sure, he'll probably be sending for you in short order to chuck me out, as well."

Anger and chagrin stiffened Mr. Needham's posture as he drew himself up. "You'll regret this, m'lord," he said. Slowly, he transferred his glare to the uncertain butler, who hovered at his elbow. "I will show myself out, thank you, Hodgkens." Suiting action to words, he stalked from the room, the gesture somewhat diminished by his mincing step. Hodgkens hurried in his wake.

Frederick contemplated the oaken door as it closed behind the retreating figures. "The effect you have on people, my dear Coz. It's amazing, you know. Really quite amazing."

St. Vincent's scowl deepened. "What are you doing here?" he demanded for the second time.

Frederick raised a politely reproving eyebrow. "But merely assuring you that your long-lost heir is alive and well. As I was certain you would wish."

"Hah!" St. Vincent grabbed up a poker and shoved the smoldering logs until the fire sprang once more to life. "What has it been, five years? And without so much as a letter. Began to think you might have been killed at Waterloo."

"I merely visited Brussels. I was not, somewhat to my regret at the time as I remember, in the army. But with Bonaparte defeated at last, I found the temptation to roam about the Continent once more irresistible. And when that began to pall, I visited Jamaica, and then India."

"You always were a harum-scarum ne'er-do-well. Not a trace of the fear of God in you. I suppose you finally outran the constable."

"I am sorry to disillusion you." Frederick shook his head in mock sadness. "I am quite flush at present, thank

9

you. I have not come to dip into your purse. Was that young Needham's sin, by the way?"

St. Vincent hesitated in the act of seating himself, then settled primly once more on the edge of his chair. "In a manner of speaking. He had the insolence, to ask my permission to pay his addresses to Georgiana."

"To—Good God, not that fubsy-faced daughter of yours?"

The viscount glared at him. "My girl is thought to be very well favored. 'Her price is far above rubies.'"

"Took after her mother, did she?"

The viscount stiffened. "She's every inch an Ashfield."

"Poor girl." Frederick considered a moment. "Can't say I remember her all that clearly. What's wrong with that fellow Needham? An incipient dandy, of course, and not quite up to snuff. I daresay he could be taken in hand at a pinch, though. Nothing a little seasoning and town bronze wouldn't cure."

St. Vincent's lip curled. "He, who walks in the ways of the world and knows neither righteousness nor repentance. He smells of the shop, as well. Family's in India, making a fortune in trade."

Frederick started in mock horror. "Why didn't you tell me earlier? I should have bestowed your present upon you sooner." He handed over the ebony and ivory cane.

St. Vincent took it, nodding in solemn agreement. "It would have served very well for a thrashing."

"Nothing so coarse." With a deft twist, Frederick turned the ivory, leaving the ebony casing in his cousin's hand. A deadly, needle-sharp blade slipped neatly from its sheath. "You might have run him through for daring to raise his eyes to the ancient lineage of Ashfield."

St. Vincent studied his present with the intentness of a connoisseur. "It is a pity indeed I hadn't known of this before. I might well have put it to its appropriate use." He

10

held it a moment longer, testing its weight, then laid it with care on the floor near his side.

"Does the girl have a tendre for him?" Frederick asked diffidently.

"'A wise daughter maketh a glad father,'" the viscount misquoted only slightly. "She has a level head on her, my girl. She knows better than to fancy herself in love. And certainly not with anyone involved in trade!"

"Certainly not." Frederick rose and crossed to the fire. Only one log remained in the box on the edge of the hearth, and he threw it in. "She must be all of nineteen, by now," he added. "Out for a couple of seasons. Haven't you been able to bring anyone up to scratch?"

The viscount stiffened. "We have not subjected her to the paltry lures of London. Nor is she so vulgar as to be influenced by the materialistic concerns of title or fortune. When the time comes, I shall bestow her upon a suitable man. One of the cloth, I believe."

"What, your local vicar?"

"Indeed not!" The viscount clenched his hands on the arms of his chair. "I would see her wed to that frippery fellow Burnett, first. At least *he* appreciates the finer works of art."

"Meaning religious," Frederick murmured. He considered a moment. "Do I know him?"

"He purchased a hunting box only a couple of miles from here about three years back. Resides here most of the year. Says he can't abide the clamor of London."

"Poor Georgiana," Frederick murmured.

"Oh, it won't come to that. I have my eye on a fellow who's being groomed for a bishop. It's about time we brought a man of God into the family." The viscount nodded, and his expression mellowed. "A man who lays not up for himself 'treasures upon earth, where moth and rust doth corrupt.' Do you mean to stay longer than just the night?" he asked abruptly.

Frederick extended his hands to the meager flames and

11

spoke with a deliberately provoking drawl. "I find myself entirely at loose ends, dear boy. I believe I shall remain for a bit and visit with the tenants."

The viscount snorted. "You are not likely to inherit any time soon." He leaned down, picked up the naked blade, and fingered it.

"No," Frederick agreed smoothly. He took the poker and stirred the embers. "Not unless you obligingly take a regular rasper over some stone wall."

His cousin stiffened. "Ashfield Grange is beyond your grasp."

"So you have pointed out on many an occasion." Frederick kept his voice calm with an effort. The beautiful estate, the old manor with its rambling, historic wings and fertile farm land. . . . "Did you ever shore up the barn?" he asked suddenly, hitting upon a long-smoldering point of contention.

The viscount regarded him down his aquiline nose, as if he were some cockroach that had intruded on pristine ground. "How I keep *my* estate is no concern of yours."

Frederick's hand gripped on the steel rod. His voice, when he mastered it enough to speak, contained the merest purr. "When an estate is entailed, it is also the concern of the heir-apparent."

St. Vincent's lip curled. "I may still produce another son. And damme, see if I don't, just to spite you."

"Lady St. Vincent will be much surprised if you do. Unless you intend to run *her* through and marry again?" He replaced the poker and drew his snuff box from his pocket. "Just how much have you spent on repairs and upkeep since I was here last?"

"That's none of your damned business."

The crackling of fagots settling in the grate filled the sudden silence. Frederick snapped closed the lid of the enameled box and glared at the slight figure of his cousin, who still sat erect in that uncomfortable straight-backed chair. "Do you mean that not so much as one groat has

12

been spent on the tenant farms in the last five years?"

"There hasn't been the need."

"Which means you've spent every cent you could squeeze out of the land on your damned collection, I suppose. Good God, man, how long do you think the estate can remain profitable if you do nothing for it—for your tenants? Do you want to see your income crumble away with the ruins of the farms?"

"They'll last—for my lifetime. I lay up for myself treasures in heaven."

This last was added with an expression of such extreme piety that Frederick almost hurled the box at him. He clutched it a moment, forcibly calming his temper, and returned once more to the settle. He glared across at his companion's self-satisfied smile.

"I'll not let you get away with it," he breathed. "This estate has been criminally mismanaged, as well you know. You'll ruin those poor families who have depended on us for generations!"

If anything, that pasty smirk increased. "Their hope is in God, my dear cousin, as is ours."

"Has your bailiff nothing to say to this?"

"Rycroft?" The viscount gave a short laugh. "He knows it is of more importance to serve God than mammon. He manages very well on what can be spared from God's works."

"God's works! You mean your collection of religious artifacts! You'd rather purchase some thirteenth century reliquary than a new plow!"

"As would any man who seeks to serve a greater Kingdom. As my collection grows, so does my spiritual kingdom."

Foreboding stabbed through Frederick. "Just how large has it become?"

The viscount met his steady gaze with one of sanctimonious triumph. "Thanks to the aid of Mr. Burnett, I have just purchased the one hundred and third piece." A slow, unpleasant smile quirked his thin lips upward. "You needn't look like that, 'dear Coz.' It is quite beyond your power to stop me."

"We'll see." Frederick rose in a slow, fluid movement, drawing himself up to his impressive, threatening height. "We'll see about that. I'll be damned if I let you bleed the Grange into ruination. Or rather, I'll see *you* damned, first."

Chapter 2

The massive hearth in the music room at Halliford Castle blazed merrily, warming the lofty chamber. By the glow of half a dozen beeswax candles, Miss Elizabeth Carstairs studied the ivory keys of the pianoforte before her. With deliberation, she struck a discordant chord. The giant blooded hound at her feet gave tongue to an unearthly howl, and she grinned. A repeat of her ghastly performance brought forth another plaintive yodel.

"Good boy, Cerb." Leaning forward, she praised the hound, scrubbing its squared head and long, flappy ears.

The hound responded by licking her across her freckled face. Lizzie laughed and returned to her unharmonious playing with verve, encouraging Cerb to join in with a baying that could cause the souls of the staunchest to shiver. *That* should put an end to her sister Helena's well-intentioned but sadly misguided attempts to make her perform on this blighted instrument.

Abruptly, Cerb left off his unholy racket and cocked his head, his lip curling and a low growl forming in his throat. Lizzie, too, heard the noise in the hall and stopped her unrhythmic banging on the keys to listen, her curiosity roused. An arrival. A glance at the mantel clock assured her it was much too late for a casual visitor, but still much too early for the duke and duchess of Halliford to be returning from their dinner party. And Cerb never

15

growled at Family.

Slowly the great hound stood, his short hackles rising all the way from his ridiculous ears down to his whiplike tail. The growl deepened and he bared several white teeth, which were in excellent condition.

"That's no way to greet someone come to relieve our boredom," Lizzie admonished. She struck another cacophonous chord and Cerb obligingly howled once more. Whoever had come, the hound had apparently decided, did not pose his mistress a threat.

The door opened, but it was not the butler who stood framed on the threshold. Lizzie's hands dropped from the keyboard as she stared in dawning recognition.

"Frederick?" Even to herself, her voice sounded the oddest squeak.

Cerb bounded forward, barking in a mixture of greeting and defiance, uncertain how to treat this intruder.

"Lizzie?" The tall Corinthian gentleman mimicked her shocked tone exactly. He came forward a step into the room and stooped to offer the back of his hand to the now-snuffling hound.

Cerb subjected it to a thorough sniff, then moved on to the delightful aromas offered by a pair of highly polished Hessian boots, while his tail cleared two sheets of music and a snuff box off a low table.

"Frederick," Lizzie repeated, this time sternly. "What the devil are you doing here? We haven't heard a word from you since Gussie's wedding. And that, in case you've forgotten, was nigh on five and a half years ago."

The piercing gaze of his blue eyes rested on her, unwavering. "No, I haven't forgotten." He advanced several more steps, slowly, so as not to trip over the hound who seemed fascinated by the glove he gripped in his hand. He dropped it onto the now-empty table.

"One glove?" Lizzie regarded him critically.

"I seem to have misplaced the other. Careless of me." He groped at the front of his waistcoat and frowned.

"Frederick, without his quizzing glass?" she murmured, her eyes brightening in mischievous enjoyment.

"I must have left it—" He broke off. "How are you, Lizzie?"

"Devilish glad to see you," she responded in all honesty. "Life's been such a bore, without Gussie or Adrian. There's been no one to *argue* with!"

A slight smile eased the lines of his thoughtful expression. "What, not even the duchess?"

Lizzie rolled her eyes. "Have *you* ever tried to argue with Nell?"

"Once," he admitted, reminiscent. "You are quite right. Were you murdering someone just now, by the way?"

Lizzie shook her head. "Teaching Cerb to sing. Where—oh, there he is. No, sir. Do *not* sit on that sofa. Come here."

Obligingly, the hound uncurled from the satin brocade pillows and came languidly to her side. "Sit, sir. And shake hands."

Immediately, a huge clawed paw batted at Frederick's hand. With a deft move, he caught it.

"This is Cerberus."

"Cer—where on earth did he get his name?"

"Adrian, of course. He brought him home, but was due to leave for Oxford the next week, so he bestowed him on me for company. And Halliford kept calling him 'that Hell-hound,' and you know Adrian."

"Naturally he called him Cerberus. What classical scholar wouldn't?" Frederick released Cerb's paw, only to receive it once more. They repeated this process only twice more before the hound tired of the game. He retired to the hearth with an old shoe unearthed from beneath an embroidered sofa pillow. Frederick seated himself in a chair, staring at Lizzie, his expression unreadable.

She returned that look with open frankness for a moment, then slowly lowered her head to study the ivory keys before her. What was the matter with her? She actually felt *unsettled!* She couldn't be nervous of *Frederick*, of all people! She'd known him forever—well, for the last eight years, at least, since her sister married the duke of Halliford, Frederick's closest friend. It must be the five years without a word lying between them that left her with this peculiar, awkward sensation. She didn't like it.

She glared at him. "Why didn't you write?"

"I've been constantly on the move."

"I—*we*—haven't been."

He didn't answer the accusation. Instead, he rose abruptly. "I brought you a present." Without waiting for her response, he strode into the hall, only to return a moment later carrying an ebony walking stick with a carved ivory handle. He handed it to her without a word.

She ran her fingers along the polished wood. "The perfect thing for tramping through the—" The ivory knob twisted in her hand and she broke off. With a soft cry of delight, she drew the deadly blade from its hiding place. "Frederick! The very thing! I have *always* wanted a sword stick. Thank you."

"Murderous wench," he murmured, and a sudden smile lit his entire countenance. "You haven't changed a bit, Lizzie."

"Well, of course not." She cocked her head to one side and grinned at him. "Why should I?"

"I'm glad you didn't."

The door opened and he turned quickly, almost as if he welcomed the interruption. Winthrop, the elderly butler, wheeled in a tea tray on which stood wine glasses, decanters, and biscuits, but not a single pot or cup. Frederick raised a questioning eyebrow.

Lizzie raised hers right back. "I don't maudle my insides with cat-lap."

A reluctant laugh broke from him. "Now, why did I ever fear you might grow into some simpering miss?"

"Why, indeed?" She glared at him, affronted. "I'm not mawkish."

18

"No, you are altogether as delightful as ever."

His serious tone startled her, but his expression remained unreadable. He busied himself with the decanters, and in a moment handed her a glass of canary.

Lizzie studied him, puzzled by the slight constraint in his manner. "What brings you here so late?"

"My curricle. I'm not reduced to the common stage quite yet."

She stuck her tongue out at him. "Lord, you don't know how *good* it is to—" She broke off, suddenly and uncharacteristically confused. It *was* good to see him again. Strangely good, in a way that seemed totally unfamiliar and just a bit uncomfortable. She shoved the peculiar sensation aside. "Are you staying for a bit or setting off on your travels again?"

He stared for a long moment at the brandy in his glass as he swirled it. "I haven't decided. I meant to stay at the Grange, but half an hour of St. Vincent's company proved more than I could stomach."

"Why on earth did you go there in the first place?"

"A misguided sense of duty, I suppose. Since I am the sole surviving heir, I thought to assure him of my continued existence. But I don't think it pleased him in the least."

"I should think not!"

A half-smile just touched Frederick's lips. "One of these days, I'll probably murder the man." The last was said in a purely conversational tone, but a note of sincerity lay beneath the surface.

Lizzie nodded. "Thereby being proclaimed a hero in Leicestershire for ridding the county of its worst infestation. Why don't you? The prospect of you as a viscount and landlord is irresistible."

"It is, isn't it?"

"You may borrow my sword for the deed," she offered. She ran a hand lovingly down the ebony shaft. "Where did it come from?"

"Delhi. India. They are quite amazingly popular there

among the British."

"Quite useful for any number of things, I should imagine." She drew the blade from its shaft once more and made a couple of tentative passes with it through the air. "Will you teach me to fence?"

"Possibly. Are you considering running St. Vincent through for me?"

"Possibly," she mimicked. "What has he done this time? Or was he merely his usual sanctimonious self?"

"He's letting the estate fall apart. We argued about it—as we always do—and parted, once more, on the worst possible terms. Damnation! Don't get me talking about it. Tell me the news around here, instead. How does Halliford go on as a father?"

The conversation lapsed into a recounting of the safe arrival barely a year before of Lady Sophia Chatham, who even now lay sleeping in the nursery in the Castle's East Wing, a domain she shared with her five-year-old brother, Viscount Grenville. From there Lizzie went on to a description of the twin sons that enlivened the lives of her sister Augusta and her husband, Major Edward MacKennoch, and the three children born to Halliford's brother, Lord Richard Chatham, and his wife Lady Richard, the former Chloe Danvers.

At last, yawning, Lizzie bade Frederick good night and left him in possession of the music room and the brandy decanter. She went first to the kitchens, with Cerb padding at her heels, and turned her pet over to a footman for his evening run. Ten minutes later, with the hound once more restored to her, she made her thoughtful way to her chamber, where she prepared for bed.

She was delighted to see Frederick again. So why did the sight of him produce an unsettled, empty feeling within her? It made no sense. Ever practical, she forced the disturbing but unanswerable question from her mind and concentrated instead on sleep.

She awoke early in the morning, long before the rest of

the household was likely to be astir. Without ringing for her maid, she dressed in her riding habit and boots, and set off for the kitchens to see what could be found in the way of an early breakfast.

Cook provided her with rolls and cheese, and bestowed a meaty ham bone on Cerb. Lizzie stood at the long wooden table and ate in silence, all the while staring moodily at the crackling fire.

She was restless, that must be her problem. The recent rains had kept her too much indoors. She'd soon take care of that; the icy nip in the air beckoned. With her long, mannish stride, she headed for the stable and Patrick, the young Irish hunter purchased for her by Halliford the year before. He needed more schooling if she were to try him with the hunt again next week. He still showed a disconcerting tendency to pass the Master and join the hounds.

An energetic hour passed, divided between a stone wall, a water hazard, and a gate. Cerb kept pace with the colt, frequently getting underfoot, and at last diving through a thicket after a pigeon. He emerged shortly, drenched from a brief foray in a stream, and covered in dirt and twigs.

Lizzie reined in and regarded him with fond exasperation. "This means a bath, I hope you realize."

Cerb sprawled on the grass, lolled his tongue to one side, and panted happily. Obviously, he didn't realize.

She grinned, called him to heel, and turned Patrick back toward the stable. If the hound weren't rinsed quickly, the mud would cake and refuse to come free. At least she felt satisfied the colt was not likely to balk at the first hedge they faced, as he had last time out.

She turned through the arched gateway into the cobbled yard. A closed drag, once an elegant carriage but now in shabby condition, had been drawn up along one side, next to the stone wall. Two mismatched chestnuts stood peacefully in the harness, heads lowered and a back ankle of each cocked. Lizzie slid to the ground and led her mount into a sheltered loose box, out of the growing wind.

She turned Cerb over to three lads, who, grim-faced, dragged the recalcitrant hound toward his fate. Hopefully, they'd be enough, and not need a fourth assistant to keep him in the washtub—as they had last time. She reached for the buckle on her saddle girth, but the head groom hurried forward.

"Someone has called?" she asked. She slid her stirrup up its leather.

The man wrinkled his crooked nose and dragged the saddle from Patrick's back. "Don't know what the likes of them is doing here, miss. Wouldn't sully themselves with talking to me."

Lizzie raised her eyebrows. "Not our usual sort of visitors?"

The elderly groom grinned in spite of himself. "I wouldn't say as they're accustomed to calling at a duke's castle, no, miss."

She glanced at her mount, then across the yard to where the Castle on its knoll rose proud and awe-inspiring. Most unworthy visitors quailed at the gates. The fact these had apparently gained admittance, past the redoubtable Winthrop, intrigued her. She was not one to remain curious for long.

For once, she allowed the groom to tend to Patrick's rubdown. She hurried from the yard, then circled around the Castle and cut through the elaborate formal rose garden. At last, she approached the French windows which led into the library, then hesitated, unsure if she should interrupt.

She could see Halliford's elegant figure seated on the edge of a long table. Frederick stood negligently at his side, his back to her. Beyond him, she could just glimpse a short, stocky figure with flaming red hair and decidedly unfashionable dress. A rather nondescript man stood next to him.

Frederick tensed, and his clenching fists spoke more

eloquently than if Lizzie could hear the words. That decided the matter for her. Abandoning her silly and unproductive scruples, she tried the window, found it locked, and rattled it imperatively.

Halliford turned to regard her over his shoulder. Frederick hesitated, directed a resigned shrug at his host, and opened the glass doors for her.

"Has something happened?" She took a better look at the two men who stood uneasily, facing the imposing figure of the duke, and gained no favorable impression. She didn't approve of people who could be made nervous just by being in Halliford's presence. Nor did these two seem threatening. She glanced up into Frederick's grim face, and decided appearances, in this case, must be deceiving.

"By all means, tell her," Halliford invited. "She'll find out soon enough, anyway. *You* know Lizzie."

"As you say." Frederick drew his snuff box from his pocket and offered it to Halliford, who waved it away. He took a delicate pinch, then dusted a few stray particles from his immaculate neckcloth. "These, my dear Lizzie, are representatives of His Majesty's law-keeping forces. Bow Street Runners, to be exact."

Lizzie perked up. "Are they?" She examined them with interest. "What are they doing here?"

"Ah, now that is the salient point. They have come, my dear, about the untimely demise of my Cousin John, sixth viscount St. Vincent."

Her brow wrinkled. "You cannot mean—"

"I do. They have come to arrest me for his murder."

Chapter 3

"For his—" Lizzie broke off and stared at Frederick, her mouth dropping open. She closed it with a snap. "Oh, no, that's doing it too brown. I'm not falling for that humbug. What *is* going on?"

Halliford fingered the riding whip he clasped. "For once, Lizzie, I greatly fear Frederick is not gammoning you."

"But—" She turned startled and indignant eyes on the two men, who shifted uncomfortably under her accusing stare. "Of all the shimble-shamble, harebrained, *paperwitted*, numbskullish starts! No, really, Frederick, laugh if you want, but what could ever possess them to take such a freakish notion into their heads?"

"I doubt they do it without some cause." Halliford held the gaze of the shorter of the two Runners.

As one reciting a memorized speech, the Runner pronounced: "His Lordship was found stabbed to death shortly after Mr. Ashfield's abrupt and unexpected departure from Ashfield Grange."

Frederick, discovering a lingering speck of snuff on his immaculate sleeve of blue Bathcloth, flicked it off with care. "I am not in the least surprised to hear of my cousin's violent death. But what, I should like to know, made you select me as your—er—villain from amongst

24

his rather lengthy list of ill-wishers?"

"When he was found, he clutched a quizzing glass in his hand," the Runner intoned, still with that stilted formality. "The butler said as it was yours."

"Ah, so that's what became of it. I wondered."

Lizzie directed an assessing glance at Frederick, then thrust out her chin in defiance. "So what if he dropped it? I wouldn't put it beyond that cheeseparing old trout to have stolen it, to save himself the expense of buying one!"

"Now, Missy—," the Runner began uneasily.

Halliford interrupted. "She is quite right. Somewhat sadly outspoken, of course, and her choice of terms must be deplored, but in all essentials she is correct."

"Of course I am," Lizzie averred.

The Runner shuffled his feet and cast an uneasy glance at his partner, a slender man who stared nervously and unhelpfully at his own dusty boots. "Two of the maids and a footman says as how you and His Lordship had a rousing loud argument, sir, and as how the butler never let you out of the house that night."

Lizzie, along with the others, turned to Frederick.

"I let myself out. I have done so upon many occasions, I might add, without raising any comment. In case you were not aware, I lived for a great number of years at the Grange and still consider it my home when I am in England." He straightened his shoulders, reached for his missing quizzing glass, then dropped his hand. Instead, he contented himself with looking down his aquiline nose at the two Runners. "Have you the impertinence to demand that I explain my actions?"

"Aye, sir." The Runner sighed in relief at his comprehension of the situation. "That's the dandy. Just you tell us what happened."

"If you think—," Frederick began, but Lizzie interrupted him.

"Just tell them so they'll go away. I'm sick of looking at

their Friday faces."

"If you could, sir, it would be a help in our investigations, if you sees what I mean." The Runner beamed on him in a conciliatory manner. "It's just that after hearing you argufying with him, no one hears nothing else at all, until the butler goes into the library to snuff the candles and sees His Lordship lying there, run through with that there sword stick you was carrying when you arrived, and no sign of you anywheres."

"Oh, really, Frederick!" Lizzie rested her hands on her hips and regarded him with a pained expression. "Of all the—the *idiotish* things to have done!"

Frederick swung around to stare at her. "Are *you* accusing me?"

She blinked. "Of course not. But really, Frederick, you are getting quite careless. How came you to forget both your quizzing glass *and* your sword stick?"

His eyes narrowed as they remained fixed on her face. "The onset of senility, my dear, I make no doubt. But you do not have your facts correct. I did *not* forget that sword stick. As in your case, I bestowed it upon him as a present. I forbore the temptation of running him through. Someone else, it seems, lacked my self-control." He turned his appraising gaze on the Runner. "Did you question a young gentleman by the name of Needham? Rather dandified? I believe he is currently residing in the Dower House."

The Runner nodded, relieved to be on solid ground. "That we did, sir. Quite shocked was the gentleman, he was. *As* is proper."

Halliford stepped forward, effectively curtailing the interview. "You have now questioned Mr. Ashfield—ah, perhaps I should say the new viscount St. Vincent. He will be remaining here as my guest for several days. If you wish to speak with him again, you may contact my secretary and make an appointment."

Somehow, as he spoke, he ushered the two stammering

Runners from the room and into the waiting Winthrop's hands. As the duke closed the door behind them, their weak protests could be heard, fading as the capable butler escorted them inexorably out.

"They overstepped their authority in attempting to arrest a man who is merely a suspect," Halliford said.

Frederick regarded the duke with a pained expression. "That was apparent from their unease. Really, my dear Halliford, I could have put them to rout quite easily myself, you know."

Halliford inclined his head.

"I'm glad you got rid of them," Lizzie declared, bristling in indignation. "Imagine suspecting *Frederick!* If he'd chosen to dispose of that purse-pinching old humbugger, he would never have been so clumsy about it."

Frederick, whose features had been somewhat drawn, smiled suddenly, his eyes holding a shadow of their usual twinkle. "Just so," he murmured.

"The situation is serious," Halliford pointed out sternly.

"But Frederick—"

Halliford silenced her with a stern look. "Consider the matter from their point of view, for a moment. Frederick is absent for a period of over five years. Then, on the very night of his return, he pays a hurried and unexpected visit to the one man whose death would benefit him the most. They are heard to argue—as they have been heard on many occasions in the past. And then he leaves—but is seen by no one as he does so. Our Runners are obviously asking themselves why."

"And answering themselves, he did not dare be seen because he was covered in his cousin's blood." Lizzie, somber for once, watched Halliford's face intently.

"That is exactly what they think," the duke agreed.

Frederick glared from one to the other. "I suppose you think so, as well."

27

Halliford tugged at the end of the whip he still held. "I know you. The Runners have not that dubious honor."

"It's the most reasonable thing in the world to storm out with no regard for formality when one is furious," Lizzie asserted.

Halliford nodded. "But in this case, unfortunate as well. You cannot deny that from the Runners' point of view, Frederick has indeed behaved in a suspicious manner. They must believe themselves to have a fair amount of evidence against him to have come so speedily and threaten arrest."

"They left, though," Lizzie pointed out. To her intense irritation, she knew a moment's unease.

Halliford glanced at Frederick. "His new status as a peer of the realm would seem to have made them unsure of their authority. Rank has its advantages. Shall we resume our aborted trip to the stables—St. Vincent?"

Frederick blinked, then the next moment his features closed over, betraying nothing of his inner thoughts. "By all means. Lizzie, do you join us?"

She hesitated. "I'll walk out with you, to get Cerb. The vicar is expecting me this morning."

"She organizes the charitable needs of the parish," Halliford explained.

Frederick shuddered. "One can only pity your vicar."

Lizzie let the comment pass. He cast flies, trying to draw a rise from her as he had done many times in the past, but today she didn't feel like responding. Something was wrong. Something *felt* wrong. She couldn't define it, but knew it had nothing to do with this ridiculous charge of murder.

Or did it? No, it was Frederick—or viscount St. Vincent, to give him his new title. He had changed, in subtle ways, over the past five years. And so, she supposed, had she.

At the barn, she collected Cerb, now considerably cleaner, and the two set forth on the well-traveled path through the home farm toward the spinney that eventually led to the vicarage and the edge of the village. That left her nearly two miles in which to think, and her thoughts made uncomfortable companions. Something *had* changed, and with a sinking of her stalwart heart, she knew the easy camaraderie she had shared with Frederick in the past would never be quite the same.

She slowed as they crossed the narrow footbridge over the stream, for once not hurrying on with the task at hand. While Cerb stopped to rid himself of a persistent flea, Lizzie leaned on the rail, listening to the water as it cascaded over the worn and rounded rocks. Her sister Augusta loved this spot. She claimed fairies danced here in the moonlight, to the music of the brook. She'd always been a hopeless romantic. And now that she was married and living abroad with her diplomat husband and twin sons, Lizzie missed her, more than she could believe.

Lord, was that a tear stinging her eye? What a fool she was becoming! Almost as bad as Gussie! But she'd known a strange and wholly unfamiliar desire to behave like a watering pot ever since Frederick walked into the music room last night.

Disgusted with herself, she strode forward, out of the thicket and along the path that led to the vicarage garden, with Cerb padding at her heels.

There, among the neat rows of bare rosebushes, stood the vicar, a floppy hat covering his balding head, protecting it from the rare patch of late fall sun. He gazed away from her, along the lane that wound past his gate, to where two men of meager height, one slightly built, the other stocky, climbed into a waiting dilapidated carriage. As the heavy man entered, a stray beam of light caught his flaming red head. The Runners.

Lizzie waited until the vehicle disappeared around a bend, then hurried forward.

The vicar stared at the pruning shears he held as if he had forgotten what they were for or how to use them.

Cerb bounded gleefully forward to greet him. He looked up, then hastily stepped behind a thorny shrub where the huge hound could do no damage to his frail form.

"Ah, Miss Lizzie." The vicar managed a vague smile. "Is it Tuesday already?"

She took the clippers from him, snipped off an inward twisting branch, then handed them back. "What did those men want?"

"Want?" The elderly clergyman gazed, perplexed, toward the lane. "The oddest thing, my dear. They asked questions about a friend of His Grace's."

Lizzie's throat felt dry, for no reason she could discover. "What sort of questions?"

"What Mr. Ashfield does, if he came here often. I—I don't really remember." He considered a moment, then bristled. "They were quite impertinent, though. I sent them away with a flea in their ears, you may be sure."

Lizzie smiled suddenly. The vicar, old dear that he was, had probably murmured a few rambling uncertainties and regarded them with that hopeful puppy look of his, as if he were uncertain whether he had been of any use or not. It was just as well she was here to take charge of parish matters for him. He'd never manage on his own. Firmly she banished the Runners from her mind and considered instead the question of the harvest festival, and aiding those families who had not gotten their crops safely into their barns before the coming of the early—and torrential—rains.

When she returned to the house in the late afternoon, she learned from her sister Helena that Frederick—she'd have to get used to calling him St. Vincent, she supposed—and Halliford had driven into York to consult with a solicitor over the position of the new viscount.

"Sensible," Lizzie pronounced, though she was sorry she hadn't been able to go along. She retired to the stillrooms where she set about distilling the essences of comfrey, coltsfoot, and other herbs she had gathered and dried during the long summer months. There would be many coughs and inflammations of the lungs this winter, which already promised to be a wet one.

She emerged from the kitchens at last, flushed from the heat of her stove, but satisfied with the progress she had made. She started up the stairs in the Great Hall, then paused. That was definitely the crunch of gravel she heard; a carriage must be pulling up out front. She waited, and a minute later Winthrop sailed into the hall and swung wide the door. Halliford and Frederick—St. Vincent—entered, shivering with the chill air of the early night.

"What did you learn?" Lizzie demanded without preamble.

The new viscount looked up at her. "That our Runners have taken up residence at an inn in the village in order to keep an eye on me."

"What? If that isn't the outside of enough! If they dare come here again, I'll—" She broke off, for once too furious to speak.

"You will do nothing," Halliford said calmly. Excusing himself, he made his way up the stairs.

She glared after her brother-in-law, then returned her attention to St. Vincent. "I warn you, Frederick, I will not tolerate them poking their noses about everywhere. They even had the—the impertinence!—to bother the poor vicar this morning when they left here."

"Accept my humblest apologies. Next time I'm to be accused of murder, I will make certain not to visit you."

She drew a steadying breath. "You should never have behaved in so suspicious a manner."

"My terrible lack of judgment," he agreed. "Or perhaps it was my cousin's. Yes, now I think of it, he should have had the foresight to inform me he was about to be murdered. Then I could have announced my departure to every servant in the Grange and you would not have been inconvenienced by a pair of vulgar makebates."

Lizzie frowned. "I suppose they will haunt us as long as

31

they consider you a suspect, getting underfoot every time we turn around."

The slightest of smiles played about his lips. "I greatly fear so."

She nodded, coming to a decision. "If following an innocent man about is the best Bow Street can manage, I see we shall have to solve this murder ourselves."

Chapter 4

St. Vincent stopped in the act of drawing off his gloves. "And just how do you intend to do that?"

"Go to the Grange, of course." Lizzie folded her arms and regarded him with her candid stare. "We can do nothing from here. Whoever murdered your cousin must be someone from around there, or he could never have arrived and disappeared so quietly."

"I see you have it all worked out. But what do you think Halliford—or Helena, for that matter—will have to say to this scheme of yours?" The amusement, which had been conspicuously absent from his manner since that morning, lit his eyes once more.

It pleased her. It didn't suit Frederick to worry. She dragged her attention back to his words. "They will go with us, of—oh, bother! I forgot. Halliford must go to London at the beginning of the week. Well, Helena and I shall go to the Grange with you, then."

"Will you?" he said softly. "I wonder what your sister will say to that?"

"She'll agree, of course." Though suddenly Lizzie wasn't so sure. Helena had wanted to go to London with Halliford, for she was never happy away from her husband. But surely Nell must see the necessity of aiding Frederick—Lizzie *had* to remember to call him St. Vincent—in this predicament into which he had

33

stumbled. Helena had never the heart to refuse someone in trouble.

"What of your cousin's family?" she asked abruptly.

"Do you mean as possible suspects in his murder?"

"I meant, will it be proper for you to take possession of your estates at once?"

St. Vincent slapped the gloves he held lightly against his leg. "Halliford's solicitor feels it essential, in fact. He dispatched a messenger to carry a letter to—to the dowager Lady St. Vincent." He said the name slowly, as if it felt odd on his lips.

"That settles that, then," Lizzie nodded, satisfied. "When shall we depart? In the morning?"

A slow smile lit his eyes. "I don't suppose the fact that this is November, and the Grange lies in the middle of the best hunting territory in England, has anything to do with your eagerness for this visit?"

"Of course not." Her own eyes twinkled. "The veriest thought hasn't so much as intruded on my mind. How much room does the stable have? And did your cousin keep a string of hunters, or will you wish to borrow one or two of Halliford's?"

"He hunted," Frederick said shortly. "That was the one civilized pastime he allowed himself."

Lizzie caught herself about to lay a comforting hand on his arm, and confused by that impulse, she sought refuge in their familiar teasing. In sepulchral accents, she breathed: "Have no fear. Once we have viewed for ourselves the scene of the heinous crime, we will discover the murderer."

St. Vincent smiled. "Baggage," he said, in tones so much like his old self that Lizzie cheered immensely.

He left her, bent on going to his chamber to change before dinner. Lizzie watched his retreating figure until he disappeared from view. "We'll prove you innocent," she vowed, and the intensity of her words startled her.

Disconcerted, she hurried to her own room. It *was* the hunting that interested her. That, and her natural sense

34

of justice that revolted at seeing an innocent man accused. It had absolutely nothing to do with spending more time in Frederick's company. He amused her, of course, and she *had* missed arguing with someone while he was away.

It actually took two days before they could leave. Much to Lizzie's delight, Halliford agreed to this slight change in plans, to go first to the Grange in Leicestershire before continuing to London. He still had to meet with officials in the government over a labor reform bill he had introduced, but this, he admitted, could be delayed a day or two.

Their arrival late that Thursday afternoon found the ancestral home of the Ashfield family in chaos. A liveried footman stood on a ladder poised precariously on the top step, and attempted to lift the heavy wooden hatchment into position above the lintel. A second footman supported this, but from too low a position to be of any tangible help. Hodgkens scuttled about, peering up, his gestures wholly ignored by his minions.

The curricle, carrying the new viscount and Halliford, swept up the drive only yards ahead of the ducal traveling chariot carrying Lizzie and Helena. Two grooms, each leading two hunters, followed behind. The slow trundling baggage fourgon, which had left Halliford Castle the previous day, had been passed in the lane only minutes before.

As St. Vincent reined to a halt, the butler spun about. So did both footmen. The ladder teetered dangerously, the hatchment crashed to the ground, and the footman grasped the lintel to prevent himself from following. He hung for a moment, then dropped safely to the step.

Hodgkens ignored his minion's expletive. Relief flooded his features as he saw who drove the curricle and he started forward, only to pull up short in consternation. The footman righted the fallen ladder and exchanged an uneasy glance with his companion. Neither seemed certain whether to run to the arrivals' assistance or to repel their advances and send them packing.

The new viscount swung himself off the seat and tossed his reins to his groom who had jumped down from his perch behind. Squaring his shoulders, he strode up the path to the front steps. "Good afternoon, Hodgkens. Was my message received?"

The look he directed at the butler caused that worthy to step back a pace. "Yes, Mr. Frederick—my lord, I mean."

"Good. The duke and duchess of Halliford and Miss Carstairs will be staying with us for a few days. Kindly have Mrs. Hodgkens prepare suitable rooms." He took off his high-crowned curly beaver and handed it to the butler.

That broke the spell that seemed to hold the man. With a quick order, he sent the footmen scurrying for valises and himself went to open the door of the crested carriage that had pulled up behind the curricle.

Lizzie jumped down, leaving Helena to descend gracefully as befitted her position. Already the light faded, allowing her only impressions of the rambling Tudor building before her. A gardener might be profitably employed in cutting back the ivy that covered the upper windows, she decided. On the whole, though, she liked the irregular roof lines and the chimneys sticking up from the oddest spots. It offered a far friendlier welcome than did the imposing façade of Halliford Castle. She could see why Frederick loved it.

She followed her sister inside and stopped dead in the Great Hall. Whoever decorated it had indulged a taste for dark woods and massive furniture with heavy carving. The hangings might once have been of rich colors, but now had faded and become simply dull. Only a single candelabrum burned, and it smoked fitfully.

For a moment, Lizzie regretted not having a fanciful turn of mind, like her sister Augusta. If she had, the oppressive atmosphere might close in about her, fraught with horrors only to be found in the most lurid of novels

Gussie loved. The place simply cried out for murders to be committed by the dozens, along with any other dark and foul deeds that might spring to mind.

She was too practical, though, to indulge in such nonsensical thought. The only murder being committed at the moment was by a pack of moths, their victim a tapestry which should have been tossed on a bonfire a decade or two ago. The deer heads and fox masks had met their fates long since.

"You do not approve of my inheritance?" The new viscount St. Vincent raised his eyebrows in mock hauteur.

She turned from her examination of a second tapestry, which was only slightly less worn than its companion. "Only in your cousin's taste in decoration."

"My uncle's, actually. My cousin never spent a groat on the upkeep of this place." His gaze brushed over the marble tiles of the floor that shone from polishing, moved on to a rusted suit of armor that stood near the wide oaken stairway with its threadbare carpet, then came to rest on a huge painting hanging over a massive, blackened hearth. "It appeared quite elegant in its day. And it will, again."

Lizzie wandered over and looked at the spot. "What it needs is a coat of paint, not just scrubbing."

A slender, silver-haired woman descended the stairs, only to stop and shrink back in a rustle of black bombazine as she saw the group gathered in the hall below. A purple-veined hand fluttered up to cover her mouth. "C-Cousin Frederick? I thought—I mean—you are not alone."

"I have brought visitors, to support you through your sad trial." He stepped forward.

"Celebration, you should say, Cousin." A tall, slender young lady of about Lizzie's age joined the elder on the landing and took her arm. A black veil covered the blond braid which wound about her head in an unbecoming crown.

37

"No, my dear, you must not! What a shocking thing to say." The dowager Lady St. Vincent raised wide, hazel eyes to the other. "Whatever will they think?"

"I don't care! And do not pretend you are not glad, Mamma. I vow I am quite relieved he is dead. As you must be as well, Cousin Frederick." She directed a challenging look at the viscount. Inexorably, she dragged her mother down the steps until they joined the others.

"We would all seem to benefit," agreed the new viscount St. Vincent.

"You must not!" The dowager gripped her daughter's hand, pleading.

"You need no longer be such a timid mouse, Mamma. I might not have been able to stand up for you with Papa, but Cousin Frederick is a different matter. I will not permit *him* to browbeat you!"

Her mother threw a frightened, apologetic glance at the people in the hall. "Hush! Oh, pray, what will they think?"

"That everyone is overwrought from the tragedy." Helena stepped forward, every inch the duchess. "St. Vincent, you will perform the introductions, and then we may all be more comfortable."

The viscount's lips twitched and he swept her an elegant bow. "As you wish. May I present to you my cousins, Isobel, dowager Lady St. Vincent, and her daughter, Miss Georgiana Ashfield? Come make your curtsy, Georgiana. You have the honor of meeting the duke and duchess of Halliford, and Miss Elizabeth Carstairs."

"Oh!" The dowager, quite overcome, tottered forward to sweep a curtsy. "We—we are honored, Your Grace."

Georgiana followed more slowly, eyeing them with open hostility. "It doesn't seem to be quite the thing to be expecting Mamma to entertain at the moment, does it, Cousin? Or could you not wait to take possession of your inheritance and position and show them off? You have coveted them both long enough."

"My love—" Her anguished mother broke off.

St. Vincent strolled forward, his manner languid in the extreme. With one finger under chin, he raised the girl's face so he could look down into it. "You are forgetting your manners, my dear. But I suppose I cannot blame you for rebelling against every tenet drilled into you by your papa. There is no reason, though, to further distress your mamma."

Georgiana pulled away. "Do you expect us to vacate our home on the instant? Oh, excuse me, it is your home now, is it not?" She gave an audible sniff.

St. Vincent regarded her through half-lowered lids. "The Dower House is currently occupied, I apprehend." He turned to her mother. "If you do not mind my moving in, Cousin Isobel, there is no reason why you should not remain."

The woman blinked rapidly, and her soft hazel eyes brightened for the first time. "If you are certain you have no objections—"

"How could he, Mamma?" Yet Georgiana seemed nonplussed by his noncombative attitude.

"How could I, indeed? That is settled, then." He caught Lizzie's speaking glance and smiled. "Except for one thing. My dear Cousin Isobel, would you have any objection to one more guest?"

"This is hardly the time for a party." Georgiana gathered ammunition for renewed hostility.

"Not a party. Merely a hound."

"A—a dog? In the *house?*" The dowager stared at him, aghast.

Georgiana's mouth dropped open, and a sudden gleam lit her large blue eyes. "Papa would never have permitted it! Of course the dog must stay."

"He is quite well-behaved," Lizzie assured the worried dowager. "He will not bother you in the least, I promise. And if he does, I will take him to the stables."

The dowager cast St. Vincent a worried glance. "If—if it is your wish, Cousin Frederick, then of course—"

39

"You've done it, Mamma!" Her daughter enveloped her in an exuberant hug. "You've gone against Papa at last!"

"Oh, dear, I know I should not. But this is Cousin Frederick's house, now, and your papa would want me to do as he wishes."

"He most certainly would not. You know Papa hated Cousin Frederick."

A distinct twinkle entered Cousin Frederick's eyes. "As of this moment, Cousin Isobel, you must please no one but yourself. It will take some getting used to, I make no doubt, but you will come to enjoy it."

A grim-faced woman approached from the back of the house and bobbed a curtsy to the new viscount. Her gaze drifted past him, to the fragile figure of the dowager, and her expression warmed.

"Are rooms being prepared, Mrs. Hodgkens? Then if you will be so good?"

The woman swept a deeper curtsy to Halliford and Helena. "If you please, Your Grace?" She led the way up the main stair.

St. Vincent excused himself to his cousins and offered Lizzie his arm.

She took it with alacrity, and barely waited until they could not be heard before whispering: "Is Miss Ashfield always like that?"

"It's been over five years since I saw her, but I would have thought she was as biddable as her mamma."

Lizzie beamed at him. "She is hiding something, then. We have our first suspect!"

St. Vincent's eyes lit with amusement. "You are forgetting. The murdered man was her father."

Lizzie, who had barely known her own father, shrugged this aside as irrelevant. "She probably couldn't stand him a moment longer. Where does that hall lead?"

"To the family wing."

"Will you be moving into your cousin's room at

once?" She tilted her head, fixing him with her candid stare.

"I think it would be more diplomatic to wait until the estate is wound up. There may be any number of papers that should not be disturbed."

Following the others, they traversed a long gallery as dark as the rest of the house, descended two steps, rounded a corner, climbed another stair, proceeded along a short hall, and, after turning another corner, at last found themselves facing a wide corridor.

"The guest wing," St. Vincent explained.

"It's a regular rabbit warren!"

"You may explore whenever you wish," he promised. Leaving his guests to the care of the housekeeper, he took himself off to the room he normally inhabited on his visits.

Mrs. Hodgkens first escorted the duchess to a large chamber overlooking the front of the house, though Lizzie could see nothing outside except darkness and a few branches of ivy that covered the panes. Halliford she showed to the room next door, then took Lizzie down the hall to a small chamber on the opposite side.

Lizzie entered and greeted her maid, Rose, who looked up from her unpacking. She unfastened her cloak, then examined the apartment with interest. St. Vincent hadn't exaggerated, she decided. The furnishings were of a style popular more than fifty years ago, not at all in keeping with modern taste. She wrinkled her nose.

"I hope you will be comfortable here, miss. It's called the Blue Room." Mrs. Hodgkens cast a dubious glance at the hangings around the bed, which had faded to an indeterminate gray. "The chimney doesn't smoke as badly as most," she added.

"Then I'm bound to be comfortable." Lizzie draped the heavy woolen cloak over a chair. "What time is dinner?"

"His old Lordship dined at eight, miss."

41

Lizzie sighed audibly.

"I could have a maid bring you something," the housekeeper offered, willing but uncertain.

Lizzie bestowed her broadest smile on her. "Famous. I see I shall get along here very well."

Half an hour later, dressed in a forest green evening gown of simple design, and fortified by two rolls and a wedge of cheese, she draped a warm shawl about her shoulders and set off to explore. She wanted to see everything, of course, but one room in particular beckoned her. Ghoulish interest, no doubt, but she wasn't in the least put off by that knowledge. She wanted to visit the library, where the foul deed had been committed.

By dint of trial and error, she located the main stair and made her way back down to the Great Hall. It hadn't improved any in her absence, she decided—not that she'd really expected it to.

Five doors opened off it, and four halls led in different directions. The third door on the second corridor she tried led into a darkened room that smelled of old leather. She stepped inside, and wished she'd brought a taper with her. And a warmer shawl. She shivered in the chill air.

At the far end of the long chamber, soft light from the rising moon seeped in through the French windows. Then something blocked it—not completely, but as if someone stood there, just outside the door. The shape shifted, and a dark, shadowy arm rose and came down on the glass.

Lizzie bit her lip, but no crash followed. Her heart beat fast with excitement. Someone tried to break in! But who—and why? Blood pounded in her ears and a thrill raced along her flesh, leaving goose bumps. She eased herself silently forward, feeling with her slippered toes, groping through the dark to avoid tripping or striking something that would make a sound. A scratching noise reached her and she froze, then started forward once more, curiosity rampant. The noise kept up, uneven but persistent.

She slid her foot another few inches and collided with the leg of a chair. The bump was slight, but the scratching without stopped at once. The meager light flickered, then filled the whole rectangle as the dark figure stole away from the window.

Lizzie abandoned caution and ran. She reached the glass panes, fumbled for a catch, and threw the French window wide. Icy air swirled about her, but the only arms she saw moving were the bare branches of the bushes and trees.

She huddled into the soft woolen folds of her shawl. There *had* been someone there. She spun about and peered through the darkness at the handles. Were those scratches along the painted surface of the wood, as if someone tried to wedge the doors apart?

Frowning, she let herself back in and closed the door against the chill night. It wasn't much warmer within. She checked to make sure the bolt was firmly in place, then went in search of St. Vincent.

She crossed the library with considerably more noise this time, her foot finding not only a chair but a wooden settle and bookstand, as well. She muttered an indelicate word, rubbed her sore toes, and located the door.

She opened it to discover St. Vincent on the other side, on the point of entering. "I was coming to look for you," she declared, pleased. "Where is there a candle?"

He removed one from a sconce in the hall, and lit several tapers in the library. The shadows retreated, allowing Lizzie a view of innumerable books filling the shelves that lined the walls. The desk looked large and useful, but only a very few bare wood chairs met her disapproving gaze. She must have tripped over most of them.

"Have you already solved the murder?" he asked. He placed the candle he held in an empty holder.

Lizzie wrinkled her nose as the unpleasant odor of tallow filled the room. "Someone just tried to break in

43

through the French windows."

"The devil they did." He picked up the candlestick and carried it to the glass paned door and examined it.

"The outside," Lizzie pointed out, ever helpful.

As soon as the doors opened, though, the wind blew out the candle. St. Vincent abandoned the attempt to see, and used his fingers instead. "Something has been used on this," he admitted at last as he came back in.

Lizzie paced to the desk, then turned about to face him. "Why? To steal something? Or to retrieve something lost on the night of the murder?"

A slight frown creased his brow, but his eyes twinkled in the candlelight with his lazy amusement. "That, my dear Lizzie, remains a mystery at present. But I make no doubt you will be the one to solve it."

Frederick rang the bell, and when Hodgkens answered, he told him of the attempted break-in. The butler, sincerely shocked, announced his intention to organize the footmen into a search party, and promised to assure himself not a single door or window remained unbolted where some intruder might enter. Hodgkens bustled off, intent on this errand.

St. Vincent sighed as the door closed behind the butler. "I suppose that will delay dinner even further. Do you think my cousins would mind if we have the meal put forward in future?"

"To six, perhaps?"

He smiled suddenly. "Hungry, Lizzie?"

"Your housekeeper sent something up to me. Nell must be famished, though. We always keep country hours at the Castle."

St. Vincent leaned back against the side of the desk. "Your sister must cultivate your resourcefulness. Why not take something up to her?"

Lizzie folded her arms and stuck out her stubborn chin. "You're trying to get rid of me. I can tell."

44

The smile lines about his eyes deepened. "I am going to see my cousin's bailiff."

She hesitated, as if weighing the entertainment potential. At his suggestion she assist the butler in his investigations, she brightened and took herself off.

The door clicked as she closed it, and the sound seemed to echo deep within Frederick as she left him alone. Alone. The word repeated itself in his mind. He'd spent most of his life that way.

Lord, he was not one to get maudlin! He'd chosen his life. And he'd enjoyed himself.

He strode down the hall to the estate room, where a tall, well-set-up young man stood at once on his entry. The bailiff came around from behind his desk and extended his hand.

"Is it proper for me to welcome you to your estate, my lord?" the man asked.

"Not yet. Not until the solicitors sort out the legal ramifications of my cousin's demise, at least. Rycroft, isn't it? You've been here how long?"

"Four years, my lord. I endeavored to serve His late Lordship to the best of my ability."

"Given the circumstances? That must have proved a challenge."

The man's classically handsome features relaxed into a broad smile. "Indeed it has, my lord. You will want to examine the books. I have them ready for you." He gestured toward the oak desk, where a large pile of account ledgers covered most of the surface.

St. Vincent's heart sank.

The bailiff ran tapering fingers through the longish waves of his golden brown hair. His brown eyes smiled, as if by habit. "I wasn't certain where you would care to begin."

"For now, with the immediate picture, I believe." St. Vincent seated himself, found the chair uncomfortable, and looked around for another. The others looked even worse. The first change he intended to make would be to

45

discover where his cousin had consigned the padded chairs and sofas that had graced the Grange during their childhood.

The bailiff opened the top book and set it before him. St. Vincent took it, and reviewed a number of entries. They made little sense, but that might well be because he had never before had occasion to study estate books. His uncle had not felt it necessary to introduce him to this fine art, and his cousin would rather have set fire to the lot than permit him to interfere.

"Have you listed only expenses?" he asked at last. "I see no entries for income."

Mr. Rycroft studied his hands for a long moment. "The late viscount had his own ideas on how best to run an estate, my lord."

"I am well aware. But I was not, as he, trained for this." He looked up, directly at the other man, inviting explanation.

The bailiff hesitated. "I will only be too glad to assist you in any way I can."

"Then why has there been no income recorded?"

"Because there wasn't any during this period."

St. Vincent's hands clenched. "There—"

"Not for the past two months, my lord."

St. Vincent's teeth clenched, and it was a full minute before he could speak. "I see."

Mr. Rycroft ran his fingers through his hair again and smiled. "If you will permit me to say it, my lord, there isn't anyone on the estate who isn't glad to see it change hands."

"That doesn't surprise me."

The bailiff looked down at the books. "I fear you will find there is much amiss. I could not interest His Lordship in making any improvements—even any necessary repairs."

Frederick held his tongue. Somehow, he doubted Mr. Julian Rycroft had tried very hard.

46

The bailiff's gaze dropped, as if he read St. Vincent's thoughts. "My position would have been forfeited had I spoken my true feelings, my lord."

Frederick grunted, and returned his attention to the books. They appeared to have been meticulously kept, but showed alarmingly few expenditures on the estate. Not a single entry could he find for fertilizers or farming equipment. A great many simply listed "Collection," followed by a combination of letters and numbers.

He flipped through the other books, searching for income. The amounts increased as he went back through time—though not by much. He was lucky there was anything left, he supposed.

One hour and an aching head later, it occurred to him there *wasn't* anything left. He appeared to have inherited nothing but debts, and had not the means of setting anything to rights.

"Did my cousin spend every penny on that damnable collection of religious relics?" he demanded, exerting considerable control over his voice.

"Not quite, my lord." The bailiff didn't meet his gaze. "He gave much away to the Church."

"The Church?" That surprised St. Vincent. "I never knew him to give away so much as a shilling."

"Not locally," Mr. Rycroft explained quickly. "He had some charity of which he never spoke. He sent a great deal to them."

"What was it?"

The bailiff studied his hands. "I'm not certain, my lord. It more than once crossed my mind that the late viscount was being taken in, as it were, but I was never able to learn anything about it."

"Well, if they contact us in the future, you may be damned sure we will learn a *great* deal about them."

He returned his attention to the books, studying entries from earlier years, then comparing them with the most recent ones. Any hopes he had harbored of discovering things were not as bad as he feared evaporated. The neglect of the estate had far-reaching consequences.

"Where are the rents recorded?" he asked suddenly.

The bailiff spread his hands, then clenched them together. "The tenants have been paying only partial amounts, I fear, though His late Lordship threatened to evict them. They simply can't pay. There has been nothing put into the land for so long, it is unable to give anything in return."

"Have you tried experimental techniques?"

Mr. Rycroft hesitated. "I fear I know nothing about them."

St. Vincent stretched his stiff back. "I believe we need Adrian."

"I beg your pardon?"

"Adrian Carstairs. Halliford's brother-in-law. He's just taken Holy Orders, but he's a decent and likeable fellow for all that—at least he was five years ago. I haven't seen him since his sister Augusta's wedding. He was always very keen on experimental agriculture, as I remember."

The bailiff leaned forward, eager, as if sensing hope for the first time. "I would be glad to learn from him. We certainly need more here than the conventional procedures in which I was trained. Do you think he would come?"

"I don't see why not. There's no reason why I can't ask him, at least." He'd check with Halliford that evening, and perhaps write to Adrian Carstairs in the morning.

That decision gave him some encouragement, but not enough. Legally, he was tied, and so Halliford's solicitor had warned him. He might be the sole executor, but he had to do things properly. That meant going through every one of his cousin's papers and settling his affairs before he could begin spending nonexistent funds on salvaging the remnants of a once-prosperous estate. The little matter of his being under suspicion for murder to

48

gain control of the property seemed trifling at the moment.

He emerged from the estate room at last, feeling like Atlas with the weight of the world resting on his shoulders. He could use a glass of wine. That, and Lizzie's cheerful presence. He made his way to his chamber, changed into evening dress, and headed for the Green Salon where the family would be gathering for dinner.

Lizzie wasn't there. Thrusting aside his disappointment, he joined Halliford, who stood near the hearth. On the sofa sat the duchess, quietly elegant in a simple gown edged in delicate embroidery. Beside her, the dowager viscountess in her purple robe looked more than ever like a wilting violet.

Frederick poured himself a glass of Madeira and turned to his cousin, but before he could speak, the door swung wide and Georgiana swept in, defiant, head held high—a head that now boasted a fashionable crop of fluffy curls. Lady St. Vincent gasped.

Frederick set his wine on the table, groped for his quizzing glass, and regarded her for a long moment through the magnifying lens with the knowledgeable eye of the connoisseur. "My dear cousin, I am all admiration," he drawled.

"It's very becoming," Helena agreed, and shot him a quelling look.

He abandoned his half-formed intention to tease the girl. "Your appearance is delightful. Why have you not done this sooner?"

"Papa would not permit it." The girl gave her curls a defiant toss. "I shall no longer live such a nunnish life."

"My love, you must not talk so!" Lady St. Vincent wrung her hands. "Indeed, you should not have done this, not now, with your father barely—"

A scream, muffled by distance, reached them, interrupting the dowager's protest. St. Vincent beat Halliford to the door by inches, and set off toward the Great Hall. Lizzie ran down the last few stairs, her giant hound at her

49

heels. As they reached the bottom, she caught Cerb's collar.

"What happened?" she called.

From the hall leading to the bookroom came Hodgkens, his supporting arm about a weeping maid. The housekeeper bustled in from the servants' hall, and with an air of decided relief the butler handed the distraught girl into his wife's capable hands.

St. Vincent looked from one to the other, and drew himself up. "What is the meaning of this?"

Hodgkens stared at him for a long moment, then slowly raised his hand, in which he clutched a bloodstained glove.

"Well?" St. Vincent demanded.

"Daisy found this shoved beneath a potted palm in the bookroom, my lord," Hodgkens said. "It would appear to have the initials 'FA' intertwined on the cuff."

Frederick Ashfield, newly seventh viscount St. Vincent, drew a deep breath, and realized everyone stared at him.

Chapter 5

"Your missing glove, I believe, Frederick," Lizzie said calmly.

"So it would seem." St. Vincent shook his head. "What my man will say about cleaning it, I dare not think."

Lizzie examined it and wrinkled her nose in distaste. "Quite a bit, I should imagine."

Cerberus pushed past her and sniffed the badly stained leather intently. Affronted, Hodgkens held it high, out of the hound's reach, but the animal rose on his hind legs after it. Lizzie called him sharply to heel, and Cerb sank onto his haunches with a reluctant whimper.

"That—that is blood." Lady St. Vincent's voice quavered.

With deliberation, St. Vincent raised his quizzing glass once more. "Why, yes, I believe you are right, Cousin Isobel. My glove is undoubtedly ruined."

Halliford folded his arms. "Somehow, my dear St. Vincent, this does not seem to be the time to make idle jests."

"Idle? I thought it quite apt. I—" He broke off.

The unmistakable sound of a carriage on the gravel drive reached them. Hodgkens started to straighten his coat, remembered the glove, and stared at it helplessly.

Lizzie took it from him, holding it by the tip of one calfskin finger, and deposited it on a table. Relieved, the butler squared his shoulders and strode across the hall to open the great front door.

"Good evening, Hodgkens. Is Her Ladyship well?" a deep, unfamiliar voice asked.

"Yes, sir." Hodgkens stood aside to admit a gentleman of medium height and wiry build. He removed a voluminous greatcoat to reveal a coat of blue superfine of excellent cut, and a pair of fawn-colored pantaloons encasing a well-muscled leg which disappeared into gleaming Hessians. He handed his high-crowned curly beaver to the butler, then ran a hand over his short, dark auburn hair. He started forward, then stopped at sight of so many people gathered in the hall.

In a moment he recovered, and swept the dowager viscountess a deep bow. "I came to offer my condolences the moment I heard. Dear madam, if there is anything I might do in this hour of need to ease your suffering, you have only to name it."

"It is very kind of you, Mr. Burnett." She cast an uncertain glance at the others. "As you see, my husband's cousin has already come to see to the managing of the estate."

Burnett. So this was the gentleman who took such a great interest in *objet d'art*. St. Vincent's narrowed gaze rested on him, noting the polished manner and elegance of dress. Not a dealer, but a gentleman, possibly a collector as well. Wealth and social prominence spoke clearly in every line of Mr. Burnett's bearing.

That gentleman turned, and Lady St. Vincent performed the introductions to the others. The man acknowledged them, bowing deeply to the duke and duchess. The gaze he directed at St. Vincent could only be described as assessing. He turned to Georgiana, who hovered just behind Lizzie.

"My dear Miss Ashfield. More beautiful than ever,

52

even under such trying circumstances."

Georgiana blushed prettily. The plain black of her mourning gown did suit her, St. Vincent reflected. With those fair curls, limpid blue eyes and that intriguing dimple when she smiled, she might bid fair to become a heart-breaker. What a novel experience it would be for the girl.

He raised a questioning eyebrow toward the dowager, but spoke to their guest. "We were about to go in for dinner, and would be honored if you would join us."

Mr. Burnett disclaimed, but when Miss Ashfield added her entreaties, he agreed. Halliford firmly took his wife's arm, and St. Vincent led in the dowager.

"A delightful predicament. If you will permit, ladies?" Mr. Burnett offered one arm to Georgiana and the other to Lizzie.

Lizzie hesitated a moment before taking it, St. Vincent noted in amusement. He could have told that gentleman that gallantry failed completely where the prosaic Lizzie was concerned.

The dining room loomed as dark and uninviting as the rest of the house. Only single scattered candles burned in the candelabra, and the elaborate chandeliers with their reflecting glass sparklers remained dark. The table could have seated thirty couples with room to spare.

St. Vincent stopped Hodgkens, who had just laid another cover. "There is no need to use the entire table for such a small party. If there are leaves, I want them removed to make conversation possible."

"But—" Lady St. Vincent broke off and gazed up at him in a mixture of fear and consternation.

"There is no need to behave like a timid rabbit, Mamma," Georgiana declared. "Papa is no longer able to give you a set-down, and I am certain Cousin Frederick would not dare." She hurled the words at him, like a gauntlet at his feet.

He didn't pick them up. Instead, he merely smiled, amused. "I would not, indeed. For that matter, I would have no desire to do anything so unhandsome. Do you have an objection, Cousin Isobel?"

"No. That is—you must do as you wish, of course."

"But?" he prodded.

She didn't meet his smiling gaze. "My husband insisted upon it being this way. It has always been so at the Grange, he said."

"Not in my childhood," he informed her. "This was a happy house, then."

Under his direction, the footmen gathered the settings together at one end. St. Vincent seated the dowager at what might be construed to be the foot, and took his own place at the head. The conversation, despite Lizzie's tendency to talk across the table, remained subdued.

"Have arrangements been made for the funeral?" Mr. Burnett asked St. Vincent, under cover of the duchess and the dowager discussing the tapestries that hung on the far side of the room.

"I have not yet had the opportunity to discuss the matter with my cousin to ascertain her wishes."

That lady looked up, surprise patent in her bright hazel eyes. "Surely it is a matter for you to decide."

Georgiana shivered. "Let it be soon."

St. Vincent kept his expression impassive, but his interest piqued. Was she anxious to see her father below ground, or merely to put the whole matter behind her? She was no stranger to funerals; she was the sole survivor of five children, most of whom died in infancy. Death must have been a childhood nightmare for her.

An awkward silence fell, which Lizzie broke. Leaning across the table, she asked Mr. Burnett: "Have you come into the country for the hunting?"

"I reside here most of the year. My family originally came from somewhere hereabouts, I believe, though I

54

have no idea where. The country has always held a fascination for me."

"And the hunting, of course," Lizzie murmured.

The meal drew to a close, and the ladies retired to the drawing room. The gentlemen remained over their brandy and port, but after a bare twenty minutes, St. Vincent rose and suggested they join them.

Mr. Burnett stood at once. "I should not have intruded on this time of grief, but I felt compelled to convey my condolences at once."

"Quite natural," said Halliford.

"I only wish I had not gone away for a few days. If I could have offered any assistance—" Mr. Burnett shook his head.

St. Vincent paused by the door to examine a painting of the martyrdom of St. Stephen. "It's enough to put anyone off his dinner. Did you go to purchase a masterpiece of art?"

"My tastes, I fear, are far more materialistic than were those of your late cousin. Actually," he added with a sudden smile, "I went to purchase a horse."

"Far more sensible," St. Vincent agreed.

They mounted the stairs and traversed the Long Gallery. Turning down the corridor at the end of this, they entered a suite of drawing rooms. In the second of these, Lady St. Vincent and Helena sat near a meager fire.

Georgiana rose from the pianoforte. "Perhaps you will play for us now, Miss Carstairs?"

"I'd be delighted." Lizzie sprang to her feet and Cerb yawned, stretched, and indulged himself in a vigorous scratch.

"No!" Helena cried.

"Don't you like Cerb's singing?" Lizzie asked in feigned innocence.

"Baggage," St. Vincent declared from the doorway, and she grinned at him.

Georgiana took a seat opposite her mother, and Mr.

Burnett drew another chair up at her side. He leaned toward her and murmured something that only she could hear. Soft color flooded her cheeks and she looked away in pretty confusion.

Apparently Mr. Needham was not Georgiana's only suitor, St. Vincent mused. Had Mr. Burnett, also, been refused permission to pay his addresses to her? And would a man kill to obtain the object of his affections?

Really, his education was shockingly incomplete. He had only the vaguest of ideas as to what might motivate one man to do away with another. Money, certainly. But no one stood to gain financially from the old viscount's death except himself. Or anyone who earned a living from the mismanaged estate, perhaps?

He strolled to the hearth, stirred the few sticks back into a blaze, then threw on the remaining logs. Before he retired to bed this night, he would give orders for adequate fires.

He looked up and found that Mr. Burnett remained at Georgiana's side. *Could* he have—but no, that was not a reasonable supposition. It was not as if Georgiana were a great heiress. Her husband would gain naught but a meager dowry—and a surprisingly pretty wife. Her charms, though, lovely as they might be, were hardly a motive for murder.

Her charms, which she only brought into play now her father was dead. His gaze rested on Georgiana's cropped ringlets. They gleamed in the candlelight as she nodded at something her companion said, then she lowered her large blue eyes, pretending to pout. Lady St. Vincent, deep in conversation with Helena, didn't seem to notice her daughter's tentative forays into what was probably her first flirtation. Perhaps Georgiana profited more than he'd realized from her father's untimely death.

This was not a comfortable thought to take to bed with him. To his disgust, none of his others proved any better, either. Someone—other than himself—had good and sufficient reason to want his cousin dead. Of course, it could have been Mr. Julian Rycroft who committed the foul deed, driven to distraction at seeing the once-beautiful estate reduced to poverty by its owner's warped sense of values. As soon as it was decently possible, he decided, he would dispose of that collection of religious artifacts and rebuild the tenanted farms with the proceeds.

He rode out with Halliford the following morning to view, as he phrased it, the remains. Heavy clouds hung low in the sky, turning the prospect bleak and gray. As they neared the rented farm lands, a fine drizzle began.

"We do not appear to be viewing it at its best," St. Vincent said at last.

The duke turned down the brim of his hat against the wind that pelted them with larger drops. "November is hardly the month for scenic tours. I daresay you will be pleasantly surprised come spring."

St. Vincent's gaze ran over a dilapidated barn, with a fence beyond it that would not contain a lamb, let alone a herd of cattle. His hands clenched on his reins, causing his horse to sidle. "*Un*pleasantly surprised, you mean. Confound the man! If someone hadn't already murdered my beloved cousin, I'd do it right now, and cheerfully."

"Beware who might hear you say that," Halliford advised. "It would be wise, in your position, to show a little discretion."

A rueful smile touched St. Vincent's lips, but faded at once. "I seem to possess very little at the moment."

The clouds drifted apart, exposing a patch of blue, but St. Vincent turned his mount back toward the stable. Viewing his inheritance made him long to set it to rights upon the instant, and the fact he could not tore him apart. It was in no good mood that he swung from his saddle in the cobbled yard and handed his reins to a groom.

As they passed the long-neglected shrubbery, a slightly

built gentleman garbed in the black coat of the Church emerged from a path through the thicket opposite them. He saw them and waved, then hurried across, swinging his walking stick with vigor. He stopped before St. Vincent, and his bright green eyes peered at them from beneath a shank of thick, unruly sandy hair. His chin receded, but his beaklike nose more than made up for it. On the whole, the expression on his youthful face was pleasant, if uncertain.

"Do I address the new viscount St. Vincent?" the gentleman inquired.

"You do." St. Vincent inclined his head.

The man nodded, pleased. "I am the Reverend Mr. Montague Winfield." He offered his hand, seemed vaguely surprised and gratified when the viscount shook it, then directed a tentative smile at Halliford.

St. Vincent performed the introduction, and they started once more for the house.

The vicar studied the ground as they strolled, then blurted out: "I understand you used to live here. Before my time, of course. I only came to this parish five years ago. At your predecessor's offering."

St. Vincent repressed a cynical smile. "I am certain you are doing an excellent job, and will continue to do so." Did the man fear to lose his living?

"Thank you, my lord." The vicar fell silent as they entered the house.

Halliford excused himself to go over his notes for his forthcoming meeting with the government officials, and St. Vincent ushered the vicar into the library.

The Reverend Mr. Winfield took a seat, but grasped his stick firmly and tapped a finger on its shaft, as if he could not remain still. He looked up, found St. Vincent watching him, and swallowed. "I have come to offer my condolences," he repeated. "And to welcome you to the neighborhood, of course." He glanced around, a shade too casually.

St. Vincent's interest perked up, along with his curiosity. Definitely, he wanted to know what devils haunted this man of the cloth. He strolled to the table and picked up the decanter. "Would you care for some wine? It's a raw day outside."

"Thank you." The vicar accepted the glass of sherry and sipped it.

Frederick perched on the edge of the large desk. "What most needs doing in the parish?" he asked bluntly.

A rapt expression replaced the vicar's harried one. "There is so much!" he breathed. "So many will suffer this winter, so many have needs that cannot be met." He peered in nearsighted earnestness at the viscount.

St. Vincent knew a momentary, reprehensible urge to offer him Lizzie's aid. But the poor man would never stand up to her energy. Instead, he told the vicar point-blank: "My hands are tied at the moment, but I want to know where the greatest needs are so I can act as soon as I find the means."

The vicar's jaw dropped. "I—we—that is *most* generous of you, my lord. Most generous indeed. 'And we know that all things work together for good to them that love God.' It seems that great good is to come out of this evil murder, after all."

St. Vincent took that to mean he'd been approved. Still, the man cast furtive glances about. Was he morbidly interested in the scene of the death—or anxiously searching for something that was not in sight?

Abruptly Mr. Winfield rose and walked the length of the room. At the French windows, he spun about to face the viscount. "I will make a list of the most pressing needs, my lord, and of the families most desperately requiring assistance."

"I would be grateful."

The man's gaze drifted back to the shelves of books, then with an effort he returned his attention to the viscount. "I must not take up any more of your time. You must have a great deal to do because of this tragedy."

"May I call on you later?" St. Vincent suggested. "We have still the funeral to arrange."

"In the morning, perhaps? I should have that list ready for you by then." Mr. Winfield went to the door. With one last, almost longing glance over his shoulder, he went out.

St. Vincent escorted him to the Great Hall. As the vicar again took his leave, Georgiana ran lightly down the steps. The Reverend Mr. Winfield broke off in midsentence and stared at her; vivid color seeped upward from his clerical collar all the way to his sandy hair. He bolted out the front door.

St. Vincent frowned at it for a moment as it closed behind the man, then he directed a glance of feigned reproof at the surprised girl. "What did you do to frighten him?"

Georgiana thrust out her chin, as if uncertain how to take his teasing. "Nothing. Why should I do anything?"

"Undoubtedly it was your delightful new crop of curls, then. Does every young gentleman in the neighborhood have a tendre for you?"

"You must not—I mean—do you think they do?" Her antagonism crumpled beneath sudden embarrassment mixed with tentative hope.

"Would you like that?"

"Oh, yes. Of all things!" Becoming color flooded her cheeks. She hesitated a moment, then hurried away.

Her step, he noted in amusement, could only be described as sprightly. Shaking his head, he started toward the stairs to put off his riding coat.

Lizzie stood on the landing, watching him, her freckled nose wrinkled in puzzlement.

He stopped and quirked an eyebrow upward. "Is something the matter?"

Lizzie shook her head and came down the last dozen

steps. "She looks quite different with her hair curled, doesn't she? Quite pretty." She sounded puzzled.

He met her forthright gaze and smiled. "You don't approve?"

Lizzie considered, her head cocked slightly to one side. "It suits her. Do *you* like it?"

Instinctively, he glanced in the direction in which Georgiana had disappeared. "Yes, I rather think I do."

Lizzie nodded. "You always did like pretty females, didn't you?"

"All gentlemen do. It's expected of them. But I infinitely prefer to argue with freckles."

That won a half-smile from her. "If your cousin keeps flowering, she's like to turn a lot of heads."

"And I'll be reduced to chasing off lovesick swains. The mere thought is enough to make me return to India on the next boat."

Lizzie looked up quickly. "Will you leave? Once this business is settled, I mean?"

He shook his head. "I have no idea. I've always had an ambition to settle down and be a landlord, but I fear it might become boring. But speaking of 'settling this business,' I have a second suspect for you. Have you encountered a certain Reverend Mr. Montague Winfield, yet?"

"The vicar? I saw him," she admitted. "You don't really think *that* mouse could get up the gumption to run your cousin through, do you?"

"Your phrasing, Lizzie," he murmured, smiling as he shook his head. "But to answer your question, the thought did cross my mind. He was in the library with me just now, and he appeared somewhat nervous. He kept looking about, as if searching for something he couldn't find."

Lizzie's whole countenance brightened. "You think he's afraid he left some Telling Clue to his grievous murder?"

61

A deep chuckle escaped him. "As you say. What have you learned of him?"

"Nothing. Yet," she added darkly.

"Be careful!" To his own surprise, his words came out sharply. "I doubt he's the stuff of which murderers are made, but I'd rather you didn't set up his back, either."

"I'm not so clumsy." Her voice dripped scorn. She started off, then turned back to him. "I think I shall take Cerb for a run. Which direction is the vicarage?"

"Try the path just beyond the shrubbery," he suggested, and went to change from his riding clothes.

The remainder of the day he spent in the estate office, comparing planting charts with harvest reports, and becoming more and more depressed by the minute. He had dispatched a letter to Adrian Carstairs that morning, but had no real confidence his young friend would respond in the near future. "He's traveling," Halliford had explained, adding that Adrian intended to make the most of his time before taking a lecture chair at Oxford in the spring.

The afternoon wore on, and his only disturbance was a maid, who built up the fire. He thanked her absently, lit a branch of candles with a tinderbox he found on the desk, and returned his attention to the farm journal. When at last he stretched and looked out the window, only darkness met his gaze. He rose stiffly from his chair, and grimaced. He would ask Hodgkens about more comfortable furniture at once.

He checked the clock, and with a sense of surprise saw it was after five-thirty. He'd best dress for dinner at once. Shouldn't someone have rung the gong, announcing time to change? Frowning, he made his way to his room, where he found his valet waiting and anxious.

He came back down twenty minutes later, determined to have a word with the butler, but no sign of that worthy could he find in the hall. Frowning, he checked the dining room, but only two footmen were there, laying out the plates and silverware.

"Where's Hodgkens?" he demanded.

The footmen exchanged perplexed glances, and the elder laid down the goblet he held. "If you please, m'lord, Mr. Hodgkens went to change coats before overseeing the laying of the covers, but never returned. And him being so set on everything being just *so* at table."

A sense of unease crept over St. Vincent, though he knew it to be absurd. "I think we'd better find him."

"You think something's happened to him, m'lord?" The second footman regarded him with a ghoulish eagerness.

"I most sincerely hope not."

"M'lord!" The senior footman peered intently out the window. "There's someone out there, running across the yard!"

St. Vincent dashed to the window, and was rewarded with a glimpse of a shadowy figure disappearing in the evening gloom. Whoever it was might have come from the library. St. Vincent broke into a run, with the two footmen at his heels.

He reached the library in minutes, but the door was locked. He stooped to peer through the keyhole, but could see nothing. It appeared to have been blocked.

"Get me a poker—very long and thin."

The second footman took off for the kitchens.

"And you. I'll need a paper." He rattled the knob while the senior footman hurried to the estate room.

By the time the poker arrived, St. Vincent had already slid the sheet of paper beneath the door, positioning it directly below the lock. Taking the poker, he prodded with it through the hole until the key dropped with an audible thud. A moment later he pulled it out, shoved it back into the lock, and dragged the door wide.

The light from the hall illuminated only a short distance into the darkened room. St. Vincent grabbed a candelabrum, lit it from a sconce, and advanced into

63

the chamber.

A dark shape lay stretched on the rug before the hearth. St. Vincent dropped to one knee at Hodgkens's side, and even by the wavering light he could see the blood that oozed sluggishly from a gaping wound on the butler's temple.

Chapter 6

Lizzie reached the head of the stairs in time to hear a piercing shriek. Cerb perked up his ears, gave a tentative woof, and apparently was pleased with the result, for he set up a plaintive barking. Together, they hurried down the several flights and along the hall toward the library.

They were met halfway by a grim-faced St. Vincent.

"Have you ordered the dinner gong to be replaced by one of your housemaids screaming?" Lizzie demanded. "This has happened *both* nights I've been here."

To her satisfaction, that brought a trace of a smile to his lips. "I have been at such pains to procure the sort of entertainment I was certain must delight you the most." He shook his head in mock contrition. "It seems I was mistaken and must apologize."

"What happened *this* time?"

"Someone hit Hodgkens over the head. The screams were the offering of a housemaid who came upon the scene as we were moving him. She assumed—quite mistakenly, I assure you—that he had been murdered."

Lizzie drew in a deep breath and let it out slowly. "Why?"

He brushed a speck of dust from his sleeve. "Because of the amount of blood, my dear, I am quite certain. It does tend to make the most serenely resting body appear quite gory."

"I mean, why did someone hit him?" she snapped.

"That, my dear Lizzie, as yet remains a mystery. Except the second footman—"

"Henry," she supplied.

"Henry," St. Vincent agreed, "saw someone running across the grounds. He *might* have been coming from the library."

Lizzie nodded pleased. "We're getting somewhere. Whoever murdered your cousin wants something from the library. So we have to find it first!"

"Whatever it is," the viscount murmured in agreement.

Lizzie waved this caveat aside. "We'll find out. How is Hodgkens?"

"Recovering, I believe. I have sent a groom for the doctor, and Henry and his companion—what, by the way, is the name of my first footman?"

"James."

"Ah, yes. James. Henry and James are carrying Hodgkens to his room, where Mrs. Hodgkens and three of the parlor maids are even now in attendance—poor fellow."

"Where is everyone else?"

"Hopefully in the Green Salon. Shall we join them? I don't believe there is much we can do here."

Lizzie accepted his offered arm and accompanied him to the long, elegant chamber where the others were indeed gathered. Lady St. Vincent and her daughter sat together on a sofa. Helena sat in a comfortable chair near the fire, setting her beautiful stitches in a shirt for her five-year-old son. Halliford stood at the window, gazing out into the darkness.

Helena looked up. "There you are, Lizzie. You're late."

"I walked Cerb down to the village."

The hound padded over and curled up before the flames near Helena's feet. She stooped and stroked the floppy ears, and he panted happily.

Briefly, St. Vincent told them what had occurred.

The dowager raised her frail hand in alarm, then let it drop. "Will he be all right?"

"He has already regained consciousness," St. Vincent assured her. "But I shall be relieved when the doctor has come."

Dinner, under the circumstances, passed with surprisingly few problems. James, the first footman, might have been a trifle uncertain in taking over his superior's chores as well as his own, but he made a valiant effort and won Frederick's congratulations. The doctor arrived as the meal drew to a close, and both Frederick and Lady St. Vincent excused themselves to consult with this individual over the butler's condition.

Lady St. Vincent reappeared almost an hour later, joining Lizzie, Helena, and Georgiana, where they sat over a desultory game of cards. She brought the cheering news that while the butler would have to remain abed for a se'nnight or more, no lasting damage was anticipated. St. Vincent remained with the butler now, consulting on the management of the household for the interim. She didn't mention the funeral, or how they would manage with so many people in the house without the old retainer's capable aid.

The morning of that somber event dawned two days later, and was anticipated by Lizzie with loathing. She hated funerals, and the body of the old viscount, which had been moved from his room and now lay in state in the black-crepe draped Great Chamber, gave her the shivers. As soon as the vicar arrived, Lizzie slipped outdoors. She remained there until the stately and lengthy cortege, with its carriages and mutes and plumes, departed for the church. She could only be glad she was not required to attend.

By the following day, the house had returned somewhat to normal. The dowager, not much to Lizzie's surprise, raised no more than a token objection to her suggestion that the black be cleared away. Lizzie took charge, and by the time the Reverend Mr. Winfield paid a morning call, the house no longer resembled a mausoleum.

The vicar hesitated in the doorway of the salon where the ladies sat; he looked about, startled. "I came to see how you went on." He managed a timorous smile. "To check on your spiritual strength after your sad duty of yesterday."

Lizzie looked up from her examination of the ruffled shirt her sister embroidered. "As you see, they do better without constant reminder of it."

"I am glad." He bowed to the duchess, then turned to greet the dowager, but his gaze strayed to Georgiana. The young woman continued to hem a handkerchief and paid him no heed.

"Did you hear about the butler?" Lizzie asked.

A soft exclamation escaped Lady St. Vincent. "So terrible," she murmured.

The vicar turned to her in surprise. "Has something occurred? I did notice he wasn't with the other servants at the funeral. Or here, afterwards, for that matter," he added, sudden concern deepening the lines about his eyes.

Either he was an excellent actor, Lizzie decided, or he truly did not know. She decided to reserve final judgment, and told him of the attack.

When she finished, he shook his head. "That this should happen, and at a time when you needed his services the most. I am shocked, deeply shocked. I can only admire the courage with which you have carried on."

"And that of the poor footmen," Lizzie stuck in. "This has left them somewhat busy."

The vicar blinked, then turned abruptly to the dowager. "Perhaps I can be of assistance in this matter. My housekeeper has a nephew who has been in service in London, but prefers the quieter life of the country.

Perhaps he could help you out until Hodgkens has recovered."

Lady St. Vincent glanced at Lizzie. "If St. Vincent does not mind—"

"Of course he won't. He'll be delighted, I'm sure," Lizzie declared. "It's settled, then." But whether the vicar acted out of helpfulness, or out of a desire to have a minion of his own within the house, she looked forward to discovering.

The vicar's gaze returned to Georgiana's lovely face. "You have been very brave throughout this sad ordeal, Miss Ashfield."

Georgiana primmed her lips. Trying not to giggle, Lizzie noted, though the vicar seemed to take her reaction as an attempt to control her emotion.

He patted her hand. "Strain and grief take a terrible toll on people. You should not be ashamed to find relief in a flood of tears, if that is your need."

His implication, obviously, was that he would be delighted if she chose his not-so-broad shoulder on which to cry. Georgiana, though, seemed to be discovering she could take her pick of the local shoulders.

St. Vincent strolled into the room, accompanied by a sturdily built gentleman of unfortunate dandified tendencies. The viscount caught her eye. "Did you meet Mr. Percival Needham yesterday, Lizzie? I just found him in the library."

Her eyes narrowed. "Did you?"

The gentleman laughed, though it sounded a trifle uneasy. Stepping foward, he made a very elegant leg to the ladies. "I was looking for the vicar. His housekeeper told me I would find him over here." He cast a speaking glance at Georgiana, who blushed prettily and looked away.

The corners of Mr. Winfield's mouth drooped as he noted this exchange, and he slumped in his chair. "What may I do for you?" he asked, though without enthusiasm.

"I wished to invite you to join me in a game of cards at the Dower House tomorrow evening. Nothing formal, of course," he added hastily. "And you, my lord? Could you join us?"

He could, and Mr. Winfield also accepted. Frederick slipped out the door, leaving the two gentlemen to arrange the time.

Lizzie rose, ignored her sister's pointed signals to remain, and followed the viscount. "I don't know what to make of the vicar," she told him as they started down the hall. "He lives under the thumb of his housekeeper. Dragon of a woman. Have you met her?"

"I have, when we arranged the funeral. I suppose it's no wonder he's become such a mouse."

Lizzie wrinkled her nose. "I doubt he would have the strength of mind to bring himself to the sticking point of murdering anyone."

"Someone did," St. Vincent pointed out grimly. "Go back in there and observe Mr. Needham with Georgiana. See if you think he'd commit murder to overcome a parental veto to their union."

Lizzie nodded and retraced her steps. As she entered, she saw Mr. Winfield had retired to a corner, where he conversed in subdued tones with Helena and Lady St. Vincent. He left the field—Georgiana—open to his opponent.

A few minutes of listening to both conversations proved enough to convince her that intelligence was not Mr. Needham's strong point. A man of the vicar's greater learning and sense should take the opportunity to display his superiority in Georgiana's presence. A girl brought up in strict seclusion, where sermons were the only permitted reading material, would surely respond. Instead, like some ninny, the vicar allowed Mr. Needham to turn her head with frivolous nonsense.

A few more minutes of concentrated eavesdropping on this conversation was enough to discourage Lizzie. Mr. Needham would not betray himself thus—if indeed he concealed any guilty passions. Not a trace of a single violent emotion did she detect. In short, she decided, she wasted her time.

Nor could she continue to watch with fortitude the two gentlemen casting sheep's eyes at Georgiana. She slipped from the salon and ran up to her own chamber, where she found her hound stretched peacefully before the dying embers in the hearth. Taking her ebony sword stick, she called Cerb to heel and went for a long tramp through the woods. She hated sitting about, accomplishing nothing.

The chill air whipped about her, stinging her cheeks, but today she didn't enjoy it. She wasn't one to indulge in fits of melancholy! Yet the fact she hadn't already uncovered the murderer and cleared St. Vincent nagged at her, like an ill-fitting shoe that rubbed a blister.

She walked for several hours, allowing Cerb to chase anything so unwise as to rustle a leaf, and didn't turn back toward home until midafternoon. When she reached the shrubbery, she paused, glaring at the house. She was cold, but she didn't want to go inside, either. St. Vincent spent all his time with Mr. Rycroft, the bailiff, or going through his cousin's papers, trying to wind up the estate. He'd been too busy so far even to show her how to fence.

She pulled the deadly blade free of its ebony sheath and admired it. Tentatively, she swung the steel in an arc, then tried a lunge.

"Your back foot should be more firmly beneath you," said a deep voice from beyond the shrubs.

She spun about and eyed the newcomer critically. Mr. Burnett must have come from the stables. Chestnut hairs clung to the sleeves of his riding jacket.

He strolled forward, smiling. "With your permission?" He took the blade from her, positioned his feet with care on the frosty grass, and demonstrated a lunge to perfection.

Lizzie watched closely. "No wonder I didn't feel balanced." She accepted her sword back and, with his

71

help, tried again. This time, he applauded her attempt. She regarded him with her open, frank smile. "I suppose you are an expert fencer."

"Not expert, perhaps, but I do well enough."

That was sufficient for her. "Will you show me something more?"

"First," he took the sword from her again, "you must learn how to care for it. The blade should be kept clean. A drop of oil before you return it to its scabbard will help it draw smoothly—should you have the need. Anything more you wish to know I shall be delighted to tell you— inside. I find the wind somewhat daunting."

He held out his hand and she gave him the ebony walking stick. He wiped the blade on his handkerchief and slid the metal easily into the casing.

"I have always wanted to fence," Lizzie said. They started toward the French windows into the library, the closest entry into the house.

"I should be honored to give you any pointers I can."

"Are you expert with a sword stick?"

He laughed. "Not expert. I have used one—my father's, in fact. But I am far more comfortable with a practice foil. Do you suppose there are some here? I can't remember ever seeing any."

Whatever his original purpose might have been in coming to the house, he seemed to have forgotten it. Lizzie, delighted by this turn of events, went in search of James, the acting-butler. He suggested they try the muniments room, directly across the hall from the library. There, he assured Lizzie, along with all the family records dating back to the founding of Ashfield Grange, they would also discover an assortment of guns, fowling pieces, fishing tackle, and swords.

They went there at once, and Mr. Burnett wandered about, gazing at the armament displays on the walls in admiration. Lizzie, ever direct, found the foils after only a brief search.

"Here they are. And their buttons seem firmly

72

attached. Do you think these are safe?"

Mr. Burnett accepted one and ran an experienced eye—and hand—over the blade. "This should do very well. First, I will show you the salute."

He was still explaining the terminology and positions of the blade when the library door across the hall opened and the Reverend Mr. Winfield stuck out his head. He froze for a moment, then emerged, a tentative smile on his pleasant face. He stood at the muniments room door, watching them.

"The blade should be lower," he said unexpectedly, as Lizzie attempted a lunge, hampered by her narrow skirt.

Mr. Burnett's eyebrows flew up. "Do you fence?"

"A little," the vicar admitted.

Lizzie glanced from one to the other. "Show me," she declared, offering Mr. Winfield her foil. "I'd like to see how it's done properly."

The vicar accepted the foil with only a minor show of hesitation, then laid it aside on a long table and stripped off his coat. "I am sorely out of practice," he protested.

Mr. Burnett lowered the buttoned tip of his blade to the floor, a gleam of amusement in his eyes. "I await your pleasure."

Mr. Winfield removed his shoes, and, after a brief salute, they began. The vicar advanced tentatively at first, then grew more sure of himself as he parried Mr. Burnett's attacks with very creditable precision. Lizzie stepped back, watching intently. Mr. Burnett admitted to possessing a sword stick. And Mr. Winfield displayed a very unvicarish ability with the blade. Either one possessed the skill to have killed the old viscount.

But a person didn't run another through simply because there was a sword handy and one knew how to use it. That didn't make sense. There had to be a reason. And offhand, she could think of nothing that either of these two men would gain by the old viscount's death.

Only Frederick, the new viscount, stood to gain. Only Frederick, who hated his cousin, who had wanted him out of the way before the entire estate crumbled from neglect—and who was an expert with a sword.

She banished that thought. There had to be another explanation. The most likely was that the old viscount had surprised a housebreaker, who had then fled, terrified by what he had done.

St. Vincent strolled up behind her and raised his eyebrows. She signaled him to keep silent, and together they watched the fight. The two men advanced and retreated along the length of the room until Mr. Burnett caught sight of the viscount. He lowered his sword at once with a shaky laugh, somewhat embarrassed.

Mr. Winfield, his countenance flushed, strode forward and grasped his opponent's hand. "Well done, sir! I must thank you for an excellent afternoon's entertainment and exercise. I haven't felt so invigorated this age. Nor have I enjoyed myself so much."

St. Vincent drew his snuff box from his pocket and tapped it with one finger. "Is there anything I can do for either of you, or did you just stop in to fence?"

The vicar flushed. "I am sorry, my lord. I succumbed to temptation, I fear. No, I merely popped over to make certain my housekeeper's nephew had arrived and was filling the post to satisfaction."

"Since he has been in the house less than an hour, it is difficult to say," St. Vincent informed him.

The vicar's already heightened color turned a shade redder.

"May I offer you refreshment?"

The vicar stammered his excuses, saying he was neglecting parish duties, but Mr. Burnett accepted with thanks. St. Vincent led his guests across the hall to the library, with Lizzie trailing behind. He let the vicar out with a promise to see him the next evening at the Dower House, then turned back to Mr. Burnett. "I have found some very tolerable Madeira in the cellars," he said. "Ah, Lizzie, if you will excuse us, I should very much enjoy a game of chess, if Mr. Burnett will indulge me."

Lizzie, to her intense irritation, found herself back in the hall, with the door closing in her face. Muttering under her breath, she made her way to the salon where she found Lady St. Vincent and Helena embroidering peacefully. Georgiana was nowhere in sight. Owning to a lively curiosity about the girl, Lizzie started in search of her, but got no farther than the first landing.

A peremptory knock on the front door brought her to a halt. A minute passed and the knock was repeated. The green baize doors into the nether reaches of the house swung noisily and James, struggling to straighten his jacket, burst into the hall. Slowing himself to a decorous pace, he approached the door with what dignity he could muster, and opened it wide. Lizzie, unashamedly, bent down to catch a glimpse of the visitor.

A most unprepossessing sight met her eyes. A short, stocky figure in an ancient greatcoat and unspeakable hat strode inside, shivering with the cold. He pulled off his outer garment to reveal a brown coat of unfashionable cut. He dragged off his disreputable beaver and handed it to James, revealing a straggly shock of vivid red hair.

With a start, Lizzie recognized him as one of the Runners who had come to Halliford Castle to arrest St. Vincent. She started down the stairs, and the man saw her.

His watery blue eyes widened. "Well, now, Missy. Can't say as I was expecting to see you here." He beamed on her, as if her presence added the final panache to a delightful day. "Just dropping in to see how things go on, you know. Is His Lordship at home?"

"I will ascertain," James volunteered, as if suddenly recollecting his current responsibilities.

Lizzie descended to the hall. "Are you in charge of the investigation?"

His smile broadened. "That's the ticket. Coggins is my name. Can't think if we was rightly introduced before."

He seemed in an expansive mood, which suited Lizzie perfectly. She decided to press her advantage. "You'll have to forgive James. He's really a footman, but the butler was attacked three nights ago. I assume you've heard?" She led the way across the Great Hall and into an elegant salon that looked out onto the drive.

"Well, now, Missy. You might say as that's how I come to be here, if you takes my meaning." He looked about the apartment, as if ill at ease in the luxury of his surroundings. "Perhaps maybe you could tell me a little about it?"

"I only know it happened in the library." She sat on the chair nearest the fire and gestured for the Runner to take the seat opposite. "And do you know, the day before that—the day we arrived—I thought someone was trying to break into that room through the French windows."

He had started to sit, but at that he straightened abruptly. "Did you, now, Missy? Why would you go a-thinking anything of the sort?"

"I heard noises, I saw someone outside, and there were scratches about the lock, as if someone had tried to force it."

His eyes narrowed and he sat down. "Were there, now? Perhaps you'd be good enough to show me in a bit?"

"Of course." She smiled on him. "And here is Viscount St. Vincent."

The Runner stood swiftly as St. Vincent paused just over the threshold. The new viscount raised his quizzing glass to better observe the visitor, then turned his lazy regard on Lizzie.

She smiled brightly at him. "I believe you remember Mr. Coggins, Frederick."

"Indeed." He allowed the glass to fall and came forward. "To what do I owe this dubious honor?"

At his haughty tone, a dull flush crept over Coggins's face. "We had word about this alleged attack on one Mr. Hodgkens, who serves as butler here. His nibs, back in Bow Street, thought as it might be a good idea if I was to remain in the vicinity, so to speak. Just to make sure no other little unpleasantness occurs."

St. Vincent stiffened. "Perhaps it would make things easier for you if you simply stayed in the house?"

Coggins stepped backward, collided with the chair, and collapsed into it. "I—"

"An excellent idea! Frederick, I am in awe. It will be the very thing! He should come at once, this evening. I shall summon Mrs. Hodgkens so a room may be prepared for him."

The Runner stared at Lizzie, wide-eyed and alarmed.

St. Vincent eyed her narrowly, then turned back to the Runner. "I shall be delighted to extend the hospitality of my house to you. Mrs. Hodgkens—an admirable woman— will see to your comfort, I am sure."

"I'm putting up at the inn—," Coggins began.

"We won't hear of it, will we, Frederick?"

"Apparently not. Will you need a carriage to fetch your baggage?"

"No." Stunned, the Runner stared at him.

"Then be on your way. I shall have Henry tell Mrs. Hodgkens to expect you in an hour's time." He went to the door and held it open, pointedly.

Coggins, not immune to the subtle air of authority, stammered his thanks and took his leave, though his manner remained markedly suspicious.

St. Vincent closed the door after him. "What, in the name of all that's Holy, possessed you to saddle us with that—that—"

"That representative of the law," Lizzie finished smoothly for him. "Heavens, Frederick, you'd have made a dreadful mull of this. You'd have sent him about his business, wouldn't you?"

St. Vincent drew his snuff box from his pocket. "The thought had occurred to me."

"If he's going to be poking his nose about, it seems best to have him here, where we can keep an eye on him and make certain he doesn't get underfoot." She shook her head, trying to make light of it. "If we're to get this

77

business settled, I can see you're going to need my advice."

To her utter confusion, an unfamiliar gleam lit his laughing eyes.

"Do you know, my dear? I quite agree. Perhaps you will also tell me how I am to prevent him from arresting me after you have departed with Halliford for London?"

Chapter 7

The Runner Coggins duly arrived and moved into an empty chamber next to that of the second footman. His meals, he asserted, he would take with the servants, not wishing to put himself forward unbecoming-like.

Lizzie, who collared him as soon as he emerged from his room, voiced her approval of this plan. "For you never know what you might hear," she told him.

He smiled on her, apparently accepting her services as substitute assistant. "Now, Missy, what was you wishful for me to see?"

She took him down to the library, the whole time giving him a lively account of their arrival, the man she glimpsed trying to break in through the French windows, and ending with the maid screaming when she found St. Vincent's blood-soaked glove.

That last shocked the Runner, and a grim expression crept into his pale blue eyes. "That shuts it, that does," he said.

"It does no such thing," Lizzie snapped. "Why on earth should St. Vincent go to such elaborate pains to *drench* his glove in blood, then leave it where it would certainly be found? If he *had* murdered his cousin, and blood *had* gotten onto his glove, he simply would have taken it with him and disposed of it at the first opportunity."

The Runner stared at her, much struck by her logic. "Aye, so he would. So you thinks as someone set about deliberate-like to make it look as if His Lordship done the deed?"

"Of course!" Lizzie beamed on him as on a bright pupil who had grasped a difficult lesson.

Together, they examined the library, then turned their attention to the French windows and the shrubbery and ivy that lined the rambling house's walls. Though they peered beneath scratchy twigs and examined every tile of the terrace and walkway beyond, not one single tangible clue did they find. At last, they returned to the glass paned door and the scratched lock.

"Those marks prove *someone* tried to break in, don't they?" Lizzie demanded, desperate.

The Runner stuck his thumbs in his pockets and chewed his lower lip. "Well, now, Missy," he said at last, "that's as may be. They don't seem to prove *anything* to me, they don't."

Lizzie fixed him with her disconcertingly penetrating regard. "What do you mean?"

"They might have been made the night you arrived. Then again, they could have been made at almost any other time, they could have." He scratched his ear and tugged at an ivy vine which remained firmly attached to the wall somewhere far above. Shaking his head, he opened the door and stood back for Lizzie to enter.

She went to the fire and held out her chilled hands. "I *saw* someone," she maintained. Behind her, she could hear him prowling about the room.

"What I wants to know, is, why should someone's searching this here library *now* have anything to do with His late Lordship's death? I asks you."

"To make sure he didn't leave any evidence that might point to him!"

"More like to gain access to this here wine."

She glanced over her shoulder to see the Runner had uncorked a decanter and was sniffing the Madeira in an appreciative manner. With a sigh of regret, he replaced the stopper and continued his survey of the apartment.

"This isn't getting us anywhere," Lizzie declared. She considered a moment. "I think we should go to the estate room and examine the books."

"You thinks as there might be something there?"

"Don't sound so dubious. We *might* discover a reason for someone killing him."

"I thought we had," he muttered.

"St. Vincent didn't do it!" Lizzie turned on her heel and marched into the hall, leading the way to the estate room. She threw the door open.

Mr. Julian Rycroft looked up from his desk, startled. She stormed in, Coggins at her heels. Mr. Rycroft rose, eyeing the Runner with no little curiosity.

"This is Mr. Coggins, a Bow Street Runner," Lizzie announced by way of introduction. "He's come to stay for a few days."

"Ah, yes. So I was informed." Smiling, Mr. Rycroft shook hands with the man. "How may I assist you?"

"By letting me have a look at those there books you is keeping, thanking you kindly, sir."

"Pull up a chair." Mr. Rycroft turned to the shelf behind him and selected several thick volumes of bound reports and set them on the table before the Runner. "If you are familiar with the running of an estate, you will find evidence of extreme mismanagement. I fear, though, there was no one to blame but the late viscount."

"Eh?" Coggins looked up. "Bad manager, was he?"

"No manager would be a more apt way of putting it. He did not believe in squandering his money on the farms."

"Well, let's have a look-see." Coggins opened the first of the books and began to study the entries.

Some two hours passed before he closed the final volume. "Charities," he muttered. "Do you mean to tell me he spent all his blunt on *charities?* Didn't he spend nothing on this here land? It's no wonder-like this here estate isn't bringing in no funds."

Lizzie looked up from the racing form she studied. "Don't forget his collection of religious artifacts."

Coggins stared at her, patently revolted. "There, now, Missy, enough of your jokes."

"It's quite true, I fear." Mr. Rycroft laid aside his quill, with which he had been copying a lengthy list. "Here is the record of his donations. I'll find the one of his purchases, if you wish. I am sure the present viscount will himself show you the collection when he returns to the house."

Coggins took the proffered sheet and stared at the entries, stunned. "A monastic brotherhood?" He transferred his bemused gaze to the bailiff. "In France?"

"Devoted to the creation of works of religious art," he explained. "As you will discover, it was the late viscount's passion."

Coggins shook his head.

"Will there be anything else?" Mr. Rycroft picked up the quill once more.

"No, thanking you kindly for your time. I thinks as I'll go talk to the butler. Missy?"

Lizzie, though, had had enough. After delivering the Runner to his quarry, she collected Cerb from his nap before the fire at Helena's side, then strode off toward the stables, depressed. With the Runner in the house, she had hoped for some clue to the identity of the murderer to turn up at once. But none did. If there still were any clues lying about, they must be of an unobvious nature.

She reached the cobbled yard just as St. Vincent and Halliford rode in. They swung off their horses, and the viscount tossed his reins to the groom who ran to meet them. Lines of anger creased his brow, and his piercing blue eyes blazed with a barely repressed fury.

"*Damn* the man," he said, his voice under icy control.

Lizzie folded her arms. "You'd best watch where and how you express yourself, Frederick."

"Why? Has that impudent friend of yours from Bow Street arrived?"

She nodded. "And found nothing."

He gave a short laugh. "I could have told you it would be useless."

"You seemed glad enough to accept the suggestion this afternoon," she shot back.

"Shall we continue this argument inside where it's warmer?" Halliford suggested.

Lizzie hunched a shoulder. "I'm taking Cerb for a run." She called the roving hound to heel and, with him leaping joyfully about her, she set forth in the gathering dusk to work off some of her ill-temper.

She returned a short while later in near darkness, shivering with cold but feeling much more the thing. She was admitted by Arthur, the new footman provided by the vicar, who sprang back in alarm as the hound bounded in.

Lizzie regarded the muddy prints on the tiled floor with disapproval. "He needs his paws wiped."

Arthur backed against the wall. "He does, miss?"

"You might fetch a towel."

"Yes, miss." The lad backed away, eyeing the dog uneasily, then broke into a run as soon as he'd achieved a safe distance.

It was Henry who returned with the cloth.

Lizzie did not encounter Arthur again, in fact, until the following morning. She came upon him in the hall outside the library door, talking to the Reverend Mr. Montague Winfield. The lad murmured something inaudible, excused himself, and hurried away. Lizzie watched him for a moment, then turned to the vicar.

"Good morning, Miss Carstairs." His kindly face broke into an uncertain smile. He clutched nervously at his walking stick. "Arthur just let me in. I hope he's working out satisfactorily?"

"Except for this tendency of his not to announce visitors."

Ruddy color flooded the vicar's countenance, clashing with his sandy hair.

Lizzie relented. "What may we do for you?"

"I just came to collect some parish papers, which His late Lordship had borrowed. I had quite forgotten them until now, with this dreadful business."

"Perhaps Mr. Rycroft—"

"There's no need to bother him. Or anyone, for that matter." The vicar tugged at his collar. "They'll be in the library, probably in the desk. I am certain I can lay my hand on them in a moment. I'll just have a look, shall I?" He darted into the room and closed the door after himself.

Lizzie waited a full minute, which proved the limit of her patience. As quietly as she could, she eased the door open. The vicar bent over the desk, searching through a stack of papers in the top drawer.

"No luck?" she asked.

Mr. Winfield started and spun about to face her. "I—they cannot be far. Have you seen them?"

"It's possible St. Vincent moved them. He's had to go through everything in his role as executor, you know."

The vicar stiffened. Did he actually pale? Lizzie couldn't be certain, but her curiosity now ran rampant.

"Here, let me help." She joined him and dragged another drawer of the great desk open.

"No!" He shoved it closed, almost catching her fingers. "It—it wouldn't be right. I was forgetting the estate has not yet been wound up. It is highly improper of us to be in here, under the circumstances. We must wait upon His Lordship."

"He should be back shortly. He has ridden out with Halliford," Lizzie announced with feigned cheerfulness. "Will you not join us in the morning room to wait?"

Mr. Winfield hesitated, then accepted and followed her up the stairs.

Even in late fall, sunlight filled the chamber they entered, making it an inviting place. Someone—probably Helena—had arranged cuttings of pine and ivy in vases and bowls. The sweet scent filled the air. So did the music of the pianoforte as Georgiana struggled with an unfamiliar melody.

Her mother looked up from the altar cloth on which she set neat stitches, and her hazel eyes crinkled with worry. "That isn't a hymn, my love."

Georgiana kept her gaze on the keys. "It is a ballad. I heard someone sing it once, but I cannot quite remember."

"Papa—"

"I don't care! He isn't here any longer to tell me what I can or cannot play. And I want to play ballads."

"A very lovely one, too," Mr. Winfield said from the doorway, then hesitated. "There is nothing wrong with playing the old ballads," he added.

The girl gazed down at the keyboard, her defiance evaporating. "Mamma is right. Papa would never have allowed it."

"There is much your father did not sanction, Miss Ashfield, that I am certain God himself would not frown upon—or at least would forgive." As if startled by his own vehemence, the vicar turned quickly away. He seated himself at the dowager viscountess's side and picked up a corner of the cloth which she had laid in her lap. "Your work progresses beautifully."

The dowager murmured a response, and Lizzie left the room, thoughtful. Apparently, the vicar had not approved of the late viscount's ways. But that was hardly a reason for murdering the man. With a sigh, she went to see if St. Vincent and Halliford had returned.

As she approached the hall, a light carriage pulled up in the drive. She hurried forward, but it was not St. Vincent's tall, elegant figure who entered the house, but Mr. Percival Needham, resplendent in a costume that would have appeared startling even on Bond Street.

He doffed his sugarloaf hat and swept her a deep bow. "I have come to see how Her Ladyship goes on."

"She's in the morning room. Is that a new coat?" She gestured toward the creation of puce satin.

He turned uneasy eyes on it. "It arrived this morning. Tell me," he added with a rush of candor, "do you think the color quite suits me?"

With difficulty, she kept her face straight. "Oh, yes. It suits you to perfection. Will you come up?" Resigning herself to a boring half-hour watching Mr. Needham flirt with Georgiana while the vicar gazed hopelessly at them, she led the way. She opened the door, and the girl's soft, sweet voice reached them, raised tentatively in the first verse of "Lord Randall."

Mr. Needham stopped just over the threshold, striking a pose as one enraptured. Only as her last note faded to silence did he move forward, applauding.

Georgiana looked about, startled, and soft color flooded her cheeks. "Mr. Needham! I—I didn't know you were here."

"It would have been unforgivable to interrupt such an exquisite performance. Please, I beg of you, sing another."

The girl looked down in confusion—as if she would rather look anywhere than at him. Lizzie's curiosity flared once more. The last time he visited, the girl practically sat in his pocket.

"It is the only ballad I know—and that thanks wholly to Mr. Winfield's kind instruction." She smiled in real gratitude at the vicar.

"Is there no music? You must permit me to obtain some for you."

"There is no need." Lady St. Vincent set another stitch with care. "My own music is packed away in a trunk. I have not had occasion to play it since my marriage."

"May I see it, Mamma?" Her constraint forgotten, Georgiana sprang to her feet, clasping her hands together. "Oh, it is of all things what I should like most."

Mr. Needham strolled up to her and ran his fingers along the keys. "I shall look forward to hearing you play more often, Miss Ashfield." The look he directed at her spoke volumes.

She averted her face and moved a step away. Something *was* going on here, Lizzie decided with a surge of triumph. She glanced at the dowager, but that lady's attention remained focused on her stitches. Apparently, the dowager did not share her late husband's abhorrence for Mr. Needham's interest in their daughter. More likely, Lizzie reflected, she remained oblivious to it.

Georgiana walked to the window, then turned back into the room. "Have you come for some purpose, Mr. Needham?"

A puzzled frown creased his brow. "Only to pay my respects to your mother and see how you go on after the sad trials of this past week."

"As well as can be expected." She bit her lip, then crossed to the bell rope and gave it a tug. "We must thank you for your concern, but we will not detain you. I am certain you must have business elsewhere."

"Georgiana!" Her mother looked up, appalled. "That is no way—"

"It *is*, Mamma. Mr. Needham is a very busy man." She stared at her clasped hands. "I know he has other commitments this morning."

Bewilderment flickered across his face, to be replaced by sudden determination. "There is one place I must be, indeed, Miss Ashfield." He sketched the briefest of bows to the assembled company and took his leave.

In the doorway he almost collided with Helena. He stepped back, bestowed a tight-lipped bow on her, and stormed past. The duchess looked after him, surprised.

Mr. Winfield rose. "I, too, must take my leave. Duchess." He bowed to Helena, then the other ladies, and followed the other man out.

Helena stared after him, then toward Lizzie, who made an expressive face.

"The impudence of that man!" Georgiana exclaimed.

Helena came farther into the room. "Mr. Winfield?"

"Mr. Needham!"

87

Helena considered. "He seems the gentleman."

"Seems, indeed! He is the son of a merchant," Georgiana disclosed in tones of horror. "His family have actually lived in India for at least two generations."

"His manners are all they should be," the duchess responded, unruffled by this dire disclosure. "Somewhat dandified, perhaps, but there is nothing truly amiss. And your father rented him the Dower House. Surely he cannot be that bad."

Lady St. Vincent laid down her embroidery and turned her puzzled gaze on her daughter. "I thought you quite liked him."

"I do not! He—he smells of the shop!"

Lizzie glanced at Helena and quickly looked away. Her eldest sister held her lower lip firmly between her teeth, hard-pressed not to laugh. Poor Nell, what a shocking duchess she made! She would never be cold and haughty. Just impulsive and lovable.

Georgiana drew an unsteady breath. "Excuse me, Mamma, Your Grace." She curtsied to Helena and hurried from the room.

Now what—? Lizzie, a master of the art herself, recognized a hasty retreat when she saw one. Georgiana was up to something. Without compunction, she followed.

The girl hurried up the stairs, and it took Lizzie only a moment to make the connection. She ran to her own room, and donned a heavy wool pelisse to ward off the cold. Then she positioned herself in an unused room near the rear stairs and peeked out her door. A few minutes later, Georgiana hurried down the hall, similarly attired, with a shawl wrapped about her head. Pleased with her deductions, Lizzie allowed the girl to gain a comfortable lead, then followed once more.

Georgiana ran lightly down the steps, cast a furtive glance about the empty hall, then ran down the broad corridor leading to the ballroom. Lizzie, enjoying herself hugely, followed. By the time she inched open the massive door, the vast chamber was empty except for the Holland covers that draped across the furnishings.

Lizzie shivered as she crossed the marble mosaic floor; no fires burned in the gaping hearths. In fact, there was nothing there. The room was empty. She came to a halt, puzzled, then her gaze came to rest on the curtained alcoves.

That was it. The fourth one she checked revealed long French windows which led onto a tiled terrace. They weren't locked. Lizzie slipped out.

Beyond the red tiles lay a shrubbery garden. And beyond that, she caught a glimpse of a dark blue cloak fluttering in the wind as its wearer disappeared into the wood. Lizzie set off in pursuit.

After perhaps two hundred yards, the grove gave way to an expanse of lawn. In the center of this stood a small folly surrounded by shrubs, bare now of their summer foliage. Georgiana ran up the three steps and disappeared inside.

For once, Lizzie decided, the direct approach wouldn't serve. Instead, she crept along the side until she reached a window, then stood on tiptoe and peeked in.

Mr. Needham stood in the center of the room, his hands outstretched toward Georgiana. The girl hung back, uncertainty rampant on her features. He took a step toward her, grasping her upper arms and trying to draw her to him.

She jerked back, pulling free. "No, please don't!"

"Why not? Dash it all, Georgiana, you didn't mind last time."

She shivered. "I shouldn't have come. There is something dangerous about you."

He stiffened. "Dangerous? What the devil do you mean by that? I wouldn't harm you." He approached her again, but she retreated once more.

"Not—not me."

"Whom, then?" He sounded bewildered.

Georgiana's expressive eyes widened with unease.

"Did—did you kill my father?" she blurted out.

"Did I—" Mr. Needham's jaw dropped. "Good God, what sort of question is that?"

"You didn't answer me."

"What makes you think I did?"

"Because you have a sword stick, just—just like the one that killed Papa." Tears slipped down her cheeks.

"If that don't beat the Dutch! Just because of that, you decided I was a murderer?" He ran an agitated hand through his curling locks. "I thought you held me in higher regard than that. I'm surprised you didn't simply laugh in my face when I laid my heart at your feet."

"I—I didn't then know—" She broke off, shaking her head.

"That I was capable of murder?" he finished for her. She nodded.

"*Do* you know it?" He grasped her arms and Georgiana shrank back, her eyes wide with fear. Before Lizzie could react, he thrust the girl from him. The look he directed at her could have killed. "I see. I will not trouble you again, madam." Without another glance at her, he stormed out of the folly.

Without violent emotion, indeed! She'd certainly been wrong about him. Lizzie drew back from the window and exhaled the breath she hadn't realized she held. At that moment, the idea of the dandified Mr. Needham deliberately running the old viscount through with a sword did not seem the least bit ludicrous.

Chapter 8

Without a backward glance, Mr. Needham stomped down the path in the direction opposite from that which Lizzie and Georgiana had come.

A soft wail sounded from the folly, and Lizzie peered back inside to see Georgiana sink onto her knees, convulsed in sobs. Lizzie rolled her eyes. What she needed was to know how much truth lay in the girl's accusation, not to have a Cheltenham tragedy on her hands. She strode around to the door and fixed a reproving eye on her.

"He didn't hurt you," she pointed out.

Georgiana started and raised a tear-streaked face.

"Here." Reaching into the voluminous pocket of her pelisse, Lizzie located a large handkerchief and handed it over. The girl took it and dabbed at her eyes.

"Do you really think he killed your father?" Lizzie demanded.

Georgiana choked on a sob and stared at her. "You— you heard?"

"Of course. Do you really think it?" Lizzie repeated, not to be put off by inanities.

"I—I don't know." Georgiana gulped and patted her eyes once more.

"Blow your nose," Lizzie advised. "You didn't think it the other day when he came to call."

"No. But I didn't know then."

"Know what?"

"About Papa refusing his permission. C—Cousin Frederick only told me this morning."

Lizzie took her arm and pulled her to her feet. "Do you really think that's reason enough for him to murder your papa?" she asked as she guided the girl's faltering steps toward a bench.

Georgiana blinked back the fresh tears that had started to her eyes. "W—what do you mean?"

"He looked capable of murder just now," Lizzie mused, "I'll grant that. But wouldn't it have been more practical to have asked you to elope?"

"Elope? I—I'd never do anything so improper! He must know that."

"Yes, I suppose murder is a much more acceptable alternative," Lizzie muttered. "Do you really believe he did it?"

Georgiana's fingers worked at the serviceable square of muslin. "It—it's just that he loves me, and if Papa refused him permission. . . . Oh, I don't know what to think!" The sentence ended on a rising wail.

"Had he reason to believe you *would* marry him if your father relented?" Lizzie pursued.

Georgiana sniffed. "I—I never actually said so."

Lizzie shot her a disapproving look. "Do you love him?"

"I don't know." Georgiana had recourse to her handkerchief once more. "Papa always said that was a vulgar emotion and I was not to think of it."

Of all the harebrained, scatter-witted—! Lizzie brought her flaring temper under control. "Have you met him here often?"

The girl hung her head. "Only once before. I—I *know* I should not have, but it was so exciting, coming here on a moonlit night. And he behaved in the most delightful manner—so gentlemanly, and not the least bit improper."

Lizzie let that pass. The whole thing smacked of

92

impropriety to her. Not to mention impracticality. It must have been devilish cold and uncomfortable, and involved fabricating any number of lies. "Did he tell you he was going to ask your papa's permission?"

Georgiana nodded. "My first offer." Her lips trembled. "I didn't know he actually had, though—I didn't think there had been time. And now it turns out he did, and on the very night Papa—Papa died."

"Did you want to marry him?"

"I don't know." Georgiana sniffed. "It was so very flattering and exciting! We only had moments together, when Papa's back was turned or he stepped out of the room. Then Mr. Needham would touch my hand or smile at me. It was so romantic! Just like Romeo and Juliet— though Papa would have been furious if he knew I'd read Mr. Shakespeare's work."

"Do you *like* Mr. Needham, or just the romance?"

Georgiana frowned and considered—possibly for the first time. "He's in the first style of elegance," she said at last. "Unlike anyone I've ever met before. And so very handsome. But then, so is Mr. Burnett, and he's a much better rider than Mr. Needham."

"Then you aren't in love with him," Lizzie pronounced. "You just enjoyed having a suitor. Don't worry, you'll have many more. And soon, I shouldn't doubt. Let's go back to the house."

It seemed like such a perfect solution, to have Mr. Needham guilty, but Lizzie regretfully decided she could place little reliance on Georgiana's accusation. The girl possessed a highly developed flair for the dramatic. So far, she had seen her enact defiance and tragedy. She dreaded seeing her in alt.

By the time they returned to the Grange and put off their wraps, Lizzie was starved. It had never been the custom of the house to serve anything in the middle of the day, but St. Vincent, fortunately, had ordered a light meal to be prepared for his guests every day at the noon hour. Lizzie went in search of this.

She encountered only Halliford and Helena in the breakfast room, where a cold collation had been laid out. The two sat near one another, heads bent close, murmuring. Undoubtedly the most revolting endearments, Lizzie reflected. Helena looked up at her entry, but Lizzie waved in a nonchalant manner and went to the sideboard, pointedly turning her back on them.

Love. What a nuisance it must be. Still, both her sisters seemed quite pleased with it. It seemed only *she* experienced no such desire.

With undue force, she tore open a roll, placed a selection of meat and cheese in it, and departed, carrying it with her. Let Helena and Halliford be alone. She'd find St. Vincent to talk to. At least *he* was sensible and not subject to fits of romantic nonsense.

She went first to the estate room, but found only Mr. Rycroft, sitting at his desk and copying figures from one book to another. A tray rested on the corner of the desk, bearing the remains of only one meal.

He glanced at her as she stuck in her head, but made no move to stand. Instead, he set down his pen and left his arm lying over the page. "Can I help you?"

"I was looking for St. Vincent." It still gave her an odd sense of amusement to call Frederick by his title.

"In the library, I believe." He turned back to his work.

Lizzie headed down the corridor, then stopped as the faint clang of metal striking metal reached her. A muffled shout followed, and she broke into a run. The door to the muniments room stood slightly ajar, and the *sotto voce* hiss of steel sliding against steel followed another ringing clash.

Lizzie threw the door wide and came to a stop just over the threshold. St. Vincent, coatless, in stockinged feet, advanced with padding steps on the vicar, who was in a similar state of undress. Both held foils, the practice buttons still in place. The Reverend Mr. Winfield parried the viscount's thrust, countered with an attack at *quarte*, and retreated another step. St. Vincent swept the blade neatly aside and pressed his advantage. Neither paid her any heed.

How well the vicar handled a sword, she noted. But not as competently as his opponent. The thought crossed her mind that St. Vincent might be in the daily habit of using a blade. Firmly, she squelched the unwelcome image that brought to mind.

Mr. Winfield held up his hand and lowered the buttoned point of his sword to the floor. "Enough!" he gasped. "I am sadly out of practice."

St. Vincent leaned on his blade, smiling. "We will have to indulge ourselves more often. I find I grow rusty. Unlike these swords. My cousin seems to have kept them in excellent condition."

"Not His late Lordship." The vicar shook his head. "I believe fencing to have been Mr. Rycroft's hobby."

The viscount frowned. "Was it, now? I had no idea. Perhaps he will oblige me from time to time."

"You will find he has more stamina than I." The vicar seated himself and pulled on his shoes.

St. Vincent restored the foils to their hangers on the wall. He turned, and apparently saw Lizzie for the first time.

His sudden smile sent an unexpected feeling of well-being through her. Unsettled, she strolled across the room, coming to a stop before a display of ancient cutlasses. "It seems everyone around here knows how to use a sword. I should have no trouble finding myself a teacher," she said.

St. Vincent shrugged himself into his coat. "Yes, who would have thought so many competent swordsmen would be gathered together in one place? It is a pastime not so often indulged in these days."

The vicar stood up, dusting off his sleeve. "A gentleman's art, my father called it." He drew out his watch and clicked his tongue in dismay. "I have stayed too long. A delightful morning, my lord. I would not have missed it for the world, but I must be about parish business."

Lizzie and St. Vincent accompanied him across the hall, and saw him out through the French windows in the library. He waved, huddled into his coat as the chill wind whipped about him, and set off toward the path through the shrubs.

Lizzie's frowning gaze rested on the retreating figure. "What do you make of him?"

"He is direct in his attacks."

"But?" she asked, sensing the hesitation in his voice.

St. Vincent shook his head. "I'm not certain. He is not at ease."

She shivered as a gust of icy wind wrapped her skirt about her ankles, and she pulled the long doors closed. "Do you think him direct enough to run someone through with a sword?"

The viscount's lips twitched. "Ever to the point, my dear, are you not? It's very possible."

Very possible. The vicar, Mr. Needham, and just about everyone else. Lizzie strode over to the fire and held out her hands to the flames.

"Go put on something warm. Do you think that hellhound of yours would like to join us for a long walk?"

Lizzie did think so. She hurried, and was back downstairs, huddled once more in a warm cloak, barely five minutes later. The viscount, in a greatcoat and scarf, awaited her by the library door.

They made their way to the kitchens where they discovered Cerberus curled in a corner, his massive paw lying across a meaty ham bone. The hound sprang to his feet at their entry, then looked back at his treasure, torn. With great presence of mind, he tucked it away behind the woodpile, then bounded over to greet his mistress.

The viscount leveled his quizzing glass at him. "Disreputable animal. I suppose we shall find his bones hidden behind every piece of furniture in the house."

"Under the cushions, most like," Lizzie agreed, and opened the kitchen door that led into the vegetable garden. Cerberus thrust past her with a yip of canine delight and tore about the confined area, destroying a cultivated bed and sending a bucket flying with a wave of his whiplike tail.

St. Vincent offered Lizzie his arm. "It still amazes me my cousin permits him in the house."

"It is your house, as Lady St. Vincent will be the first to point out." She tucked her hand through the crook of his elbow. "I doubt she dares make a single rule. Besides, the footmen are growing accustomed to him. I've almost trained him not to jump up on them."

He touched her chilled fingers. "Warm enough?"

Lizzie, disturbed that so simple an act could unsettle her, merely nodded. With Cerb racing in ever-widening circles about them, they headed along a path through the parklands that led, eventually, to the home farm.

For a long while they walked in silence. Crisp air filled her lungs, and aside from the rustling of the few remaining leaves, only the occasional chirp of a sparrow filled the air. The frost would be heavy again this night.

His arm was warm, though. Why had he offered it to her at all?

"What conclusions have you reached?" her companion asked suddenly.

Lizzie returned her thoughts to a more orderly vein— or at least one governed by some logic. "I have no idea *why* your cousin was murdered," she said slowly. "There are far too many people hereabouts who could have done it. No one seems to have liked him—and everyone I meet seems to be adept with a sword."

"Like Mr. Winfield."

"And apparently Mr. Rycroft. Mr. Burnett possesses a sword stick, and according to Georgiana, so does Mr. Needham."

"Does he, now?" St. Vincent looked down at her, his expression arrested. "Damnation. You will forgive my language, of course."

"Of course. I have any time these last eight years."

He frowned. "Has it been that long?"

"Not really. You've been gone for the last five of them."

"For which you should be thankful."

"Why? You always have such a broadening effect on my vocabulary."

"That's precisely what I mean!" He glared at her, suddenly angry. "Hasn't Halliford—or Helena?—ever told you I'm no fit companion for a young lady?"

"Lord, I've known that anytime these past eight years." She managed a casual smile. "I'm not the usual sort of milk-and-water miss."

"No, you're not," he snapped, and started forward.

What the devil was wrong with him? They never argued—not seriously, at least. Puzzled, and more upset than she liked, she looked about for her hound. "Cerb! Here, sir! Leave that poor rabbit alone."

The dog, tail between his legs, came skulking back and cowered at her feet. The next moment, that whiplike appendage wagged frantically again, scattering twigs and fallen leaves with abandon. Lizzie followed Frederick, and the hound, sensing reprieve, bounced merrily at her side.

When she caught up with the viscount, he appeared to have recovered his composure. He glanced at her, his expression his usual well-bred mask that hid any trace of the thoughts behind it.

"Can you think of any reason why Mr. Winfield might want to murder my cousin?" he asked.

She rallied at this return to a less disconcerting topic. "To be a benefactor to the neighborhood? He strikes me as someone who longs to be appreciated."

The viscount stooped, picked up a long branch, and heaved it as far as he could. The ecstatic hound bounded after it. "What about Rycroft?"

"Probably despair over seeing the estate fall into

ruin." She threw him a sideways glance. "The same reason you might kill him."

"Touché," he murmured. Cerb came crashing back through the underbrush, dragging one end of the gnarled oak branch behind him. St. Vincent obligingly heaved it once again. "Mr. Needham?"

"Georgiana seems to think he might have, because her father refused to give his blessing to their marriage."

That stopped St. Vincent. "*Does* she wish to marry him? I hadn't realized."

"I don't think she does, but that's nothing to the point. Why would he want to marry her that much? Enough to commit murder, I mean." She cocked her head, looking up at him, curious about his answer.

"She's turned into a remarkable beauty," he offered.

Lizzie shook her head. "You wouldn't murder a man for that. Is she an heiress?"

"She should have some money from her mother's family. I doubt my cousin left so much as a groat of the unentailed monies he inherited. Every cent he had has gone either to that charity of his or into his damnable collection."

They reached the stone fence that separated the forested land from a pasture. Lizzie leaned against it, staring at the cattle peacefully grazing in the small field. "Where does he keep it?"

"In a locked storeroom. I'll show it to you, if you like."

"Is there anything in there worth murder?"

He shook his head. "I thought of that. But there's been no attempt to break in, and Mr. Rycroft assures me nothing is missing."

Lizzie sighed. "Whom does that leave us with?"

"Mr. Burnett?" A smile sounded in Frederick's voice. "Maybe he killed him when he found out they were vying for the same art treasure."

Lizzie sank her chin onto her folded arms. "Have we forgotten anyone?"

"Not even me."

"What about the servants? Could Hodgkens, for instance, have borne all he could from him?"

He took her arm and drew her away. "Anyone could have. If ever I met someone ripe for being murdered, it was my Cousin John. Possibly his wife couldn't bear another moment of his sanctimonious ways. Or maybe he caught Georgiana trying to crop her hair."

"With the sword stick, of course," Lizzie supplied.

St. Vincent laughed suddenly, an easy sound that did peculiar things to Lizzie's state of mind.

"It's impossible to stay serious when you're around," he declared.

Lizzie remained silent, for once uncertain what to say. Her prosaic heart fluttered as giddily as if she were her romantic sister Augusta! She shook the thought aside. Lord, what made her think of *that* comparison? She'd never had a romantic yearning in her life! Until now?

Around the corner of the path strode a burly individual garbed in the rough garments and leather apron of a gamekeeper. An elderly hound paced at his heels. A low growl started in Cerb's throat, and his lip curled in a threatening manner. He took one step forward, and Lizzie's hand shot down, catching him by the collar. The snarling increased.

The man came a few paces closer, hesitant, but his dog hung back. Cerb gave tongue to a bloodcurdling frenzy of barking. The man stopped abruptly and ran a callused hand through his graying thatch of brown hair.

"Quiet!" St. Vincent silenced Cerb with the sharp command. With a whine, the hound settled on his haunches, though his lip still curled, baring a set of very capable teeth.

The man kept an unwavering eye on the dog. His own animal attached itself to his booted leg, as if seeking protection. "Afternoon, Your Lordship."

"Good afternoon, Treecher."

The gamekeeper looked down, studying the dirt.

"Out with it, man," St. Vincent prodded. "Speak your

100

mind. I'll have no problems or misunderstandings around here."

Treecher looked up, uncertain. "His late Lordship didn't like to be bothered none about what he called trifles, m'lord."

St. Vincent rocked back on his heels. From the depths of his pocket he drew his snuff box and helped himself to a pinch. "I delight in trifles. In fact, I should be very much displeased if they were *not* brought to my attention."

The older man puffed out his cheeks. "Right, then, m'lord. It's this here Runner, like, as has moved into the Grange."

"Coggins," Lizzie supplied.

"Aye, that's his name, miss." He squinted at her, then returned his nearsighted gaze to St. Vincent. "He's poking about, m'lord, upsetting the hounds. Caught him tramping through the parklands, just now, causing a flap and flutter with the grouse."

An amused gleam lit the viscount's eyes. "I will not have my hounds or my birds disturbed. It seems our Runner must be dealt with. Lizzie? Can you call him to heel?"

"Would you have me interfere with the workings of the law?" she demanded, feigning righteous indignation.

He considered. "Do you know, I rather think I would. Do you suppose you could convince him to pursue some practical course, such as finding my cousin's murderer?"

"I'll try to switch him to some harmless line of inquiry, at least."

"I should be delighted if you could succeed." He returned his attention to the gamekeeper. "Have the birds been badly upset? What about the pheasants?"

Lizzie left them in earnest discussion of this all-important matter. Shooting was one pastime she did not enjoy. She could handle a gun, of course—she had wheedled and begged until Halliford had given in and permitted his head gamekeeper to instruct her. And she

101

loved tramping through the muddied underbrush in the chill autumn air. But she found little pleasure in firing upon a living target. She much preferred the hard riding of the hunt, though she tended to fall back near the end, so as not to be in on the kill.

She reached the end of the forested path and gazed across the neatly scythed expanse of lawn to the Grange. It was too beautiful a day to return indoors—all crisp blue sky and nipping breeze. She felt like walking.

With Cerb trotting at her side, she took a paved path leading off to the left. The hawthorns were neatly pruned along this, offering few holes for an enterprising hound to slip through in pursuit of more entertaining game. They ended at last, though, and Lizzie stepped into a wide clearing. The summer folly stood off to the right, backing up against a pond. Directly across from her, the hedged path resumed, leading on to the Dower House. Lizzie started across the trimmed lawn.

"Miss Carstairs—Lizzie!" Georgiana waved from the door of the folly. She clutched a handkerchief of insufficient size in one hand, and a broken sob escaped her. Abruptly, she retreated within.

Not one to be daunted by a few tears, Lizzie promptly changed direction. Inside, she found Georgiana pacing about, wringing her hands, tears slipping down her cheeks.

Lizzie waited, curious, holding Cerb back as the eager hound strained at his collar.

"Oh, Lizzie, it is the most dreadful thing!" She dabbed at her eyes with the lace-edged muslin and sank onto the bench. "I don't know what to do."

"You can begin by telling me what's wrong."

She managed a shaky laugh. "You are always so sensible, dear Lizzie. But this time, I fear, even you will be dismayed."

"Only if you don't cut line and tell me what's toward."

The girl had recourse to her wholly unsuitable handkerchief again. With a sigh, Lizzie handed over her own eminently practical square of muslin. The girl accepted it, blew her aquiline nose, then wiped her tears. Cerb padded forward, nose snuffling as if in commiseration.

"Tell me the worst." Lizzie took the seat beside her.

Cerb bent his huge head and out came his massive, slopping tongue. Georgiana averted her face, just in time, and received the lick on her ear. She dabbed at her cheek.

"It's Mr. Needham. No, not that—that nonsense of earlier. He sent me a note of apology and asked me to meet him here."

"So you did, of course. What did he say to upset you?"

"The—the most *dreadful* thing!" She folded the handkerchief, then shook it out, and Lizzie waited with ill-concealed impatience for her to continue. "He—he claims my papa's estate is being looted."

"Being what?" Lizzie straightened up. Cerb bristled at his mistress's sudden agitation.

"Looted," Georgiana repeated.

"By whom?"

Georgiana shook her head. Her fingers worked on the sturdy muslin of the handkerchief, twisting it in a manner that would have demolished a flimsier material. "He didn't say."

"How, then? Is he accusing Frederick—St. Vincent— of being a dishonest executor?" Cerb punctuated her indignant question with a low growl, menacing, where before he had been merely one hundred and fifty pounds of canine sympathy.

"He didn't say. He just warned me to have a care, or my inheritance would vanish and then I would be penniless, and Cousin Frederick would cast out my mother and me to—to rely on the parish!" She collapsed once more into sobs.

"Rubbish! What utter fustian he's talking! Frederick would never throw *anyone* out, even if they were penniless. And how could you be? Doesn't your mamma have money of her own?"

103

Georgiana blinked watery eyes. "He—he said Papa had been incurring heavy debts, and borrowing money to purchase new pieces for his collection, and they've been disappearing!"

"Being stolen? The collection?" Lizzie jumped to her feet. "What are you sitting here for, then? We'd best tell Frederick—or that Runner, and let him earn his keep! If there's any thievery going on, we'd best tell people at once!"

Georgiana gazed up at her, uncertainty on her woebegone features. "But whom can we tell? What if it is my cousin?"

"Frederick? Why on earth should *he* steal from that silly collection?"

"Because it's *valuable!* It's the only part of the whole estate that's worth any money. And it's not entailed. At least, Mr. Needham doesn't think so," she amended.

That stopped Lizzie. Her eyes glinted, and her voice took on a dangerous undertone. "You think Frederick inherited nothing but a mound of debt, so he's stealing *your* inheritance instead?"

Georgiana quailed. "That—that's what Mr. Needham thinks."

"Fustian. Frederick's trying to save the estate, not deplete it further. What makes Mr. Needham suspect theft, anyway?"

Georgiana stared down at her clasped hands. "He saw one of the pieces—a thirteenth century reliquary, he said—in Leicester, yesterday. He recognized it."

"And how on earth do you think Frederick—confound it, St. Vincent—got it there? He hasn't left the estate since we arrived."

"He—he could have sent someone else with it. Or perhaps he stole it the night my papa died."

"You mean when he killed him." Lizzie drew a deep, unsteady breath. "That's quite enough nonsense, thank you. I think you should instead wonder why your precious Mr. Needham didn't tell you all this when you

104

saw him less than two hours ago."

"That was why he came this morning. Only I—I threw him out. And then when I met him, he was too angry."

That Lizzie could accept. "For that matter, he should not have gone to you at all. It would be far more proper to approach either St. Vincent or your mother with this story."

"What do you mean?" Georgiana regarded her, honestly perplexed.

"That it could have been a deliberate false trail on his part. Perhaps *he* is stealing, and wanted to blame someone else before it was discovered."

"But that might mean— Oh! Did he only want to marry me because I might inherit the collection? What a—a *dreadful* idea!" She stared at Lizzie in growing chagrin. The handkerchief dropped from her fingers and she fled from the folly. In a moment, she disappeared along the hedge-lined path.

Lizzie looked down at the crumpled muslin and picked it up gingerly, her nose wrinkled in distaste. Theft. That was all St. Vincent needed. If only Georgiana were less flighty—but that was a forlorn hope. She had best set about discovering what sense she could make of this new development. And pray Georgiana might meet some sensible gentleman to steady her.

Cerb shoved his cold, wet nose into her hand, and obligingly she stroked the massive head. With a sigh, she set off for the Grange. Hopefully, St. Vincent already would have returned.

As they neared the rose garden, though, she paused, grabbing Cerb's collar to keep him from betraying their presence. Georgiana, hugging her pelisse about her, peered into the library through the French windows; but thick drapes covered the glass. She hesitated, then ran along the path around the corner of the old house.

Why hadn't she simply gone in? Her lively curiosity piqued, Lizzie crept forward, still holding Cerb's collar. Standing to one side of the glass doors, she examined the curtains. They had been imperfectly drawn, allowing a slight crack.

Lizzie fixed her eye to this. Someone moved about within; she could barely make out the figure in the near-darkness of the interior until her eyes adjusted. A man poked among the books, pulling them out at frantic random, clapping them together, then returning them to the shelf. A small pile lay on the table beside him.

He turned, distress patent in every line of his slight body, and with a sense of fascinated delight, Lizzie recognized the beaklike nose and unruly sandy hair of the Reverend Mr. Winfield.

Chapter 9

Lizzie watched as Mr. Winfield looked uncertainly about the room. He hesitated, then crossed to a wall out of her line of sight. She strained her ears, but heard nothing. If only the drapes weren't pulled, she might get a better idea of what he was about. But that, she supposed, was obvious. He looked for something. It seemed a great deal of trouble just for parish papers.

Cerb's tail thumped against her leg and she spun around. St. Vincent stood a few feet away, watching her through his quizzing glass with rapt interest.

"Is this a new game?" He strolled up and peered through the crack in the drapery, then back at her, his eyebrows raised.

"Mr. Winfield is in there, searching."

"Is he, now?" The viscount's brow furrowed in a thoughtful frown, then he nodded. "What a terrible host I am. I ought to be in there helping him." With that, he opened the door, swept back the drape, and ushered Lizzie and Cerb inside.

The vicar jumped and dropped the book he held. He froze, caught in a beam of sunlight, his expression a comical mixture of dismay and fear. Cerb, responding to that latter emotion, offered up his best growl.

Lizzie silenced him with a sharp command, and the

giant hound retreated to the hearth with a chastened mien.

Leisurely, St. Vincent strolled over, retrieved the fallen volume, and handed it back to the vicar. "Have you lost something?"

"Lost—yes!" With an obvious effort, Mr. Winfield recovered. "A sermon. Mine. In—in my own hand. I wrote it," he added, to further elucidate. "His Lordship wanted to read it."

"And now you want it back?"

"Yes." The vicar managed a winsome smile. "Have you come across it?"

"I regret that I have not." St. Vincent raised his quizzing glass once more and surveyed the oak shelf from which several books were now missing. "Really, the appalling state of this room. I'm surprised you haven't suffocated from the dust." He ran a finger along the spotless edge, examined the tip through the magnifying glass, and shook his head. "I shall have it turned out at once, I promise you. Your sermon will undoubtedly come to light."

"No!" Mr. Winfield cried, then tried again, more calmly: "No. Pray, do not put anyone to the trouble on *my* account. I—I am certain it will turn up. Possibly he took it to his chamber, to read before retiring to bed."

"Possibly," St. Vincent agreed smoothly. "Is there any other way in which I might be of assistance to you?"

Mr. Winfield lowered his gaze and a faint flush crept up his face. "No. I should not have intruded like this, but you weren't here, and I was most anxious to recover my sermon. . . ." His voice trailed off.

"Quite natural," St. Vincent agreed cheerfully. "I promise, not a single book shall remain unchecked until it is found."

"No. It is of no great matter, after all. I—I merely wished to save myself the trouble of writing another. If you will excuse me, I—I must get on with it." Mr. Winfield cast one last glance about the room, managed a bright and patently false smile for his host, and let himself out the French window.

Lizzie folded her arms and shook her head in mock reproof. "Really, Frederick, that wasn't at all kind."

He turned his thoughtful gaze on her. "I'm not, sometimes." Before she could react to this unexpected comment, he went on. "What do you suppose he was *really* looking for?" With deliberation, he closed and bolted the doors.

"It *could* be a sermon, like he said. He *is* of a rather nervous disposition." She pulled a strand of brown hair that had loosened from her chignon and absently chewed the end. "I can't imagine a sermon—or even parish papers—being that important to him, though."

"Neither can I."

"If it's something else—" She broke off.

"Yes?"

"It is the opinion of Mr. Needham that someone, probably you, is stealing pieces from your cousin's collection and selling them."

The viscount straightened up. "Why on earth should I steal from myself?"

"Ah, but you miss the point. The collection, since it was purchased during your cousin's lifetime, might not constitute part of the entailed estate. Therefore, since you have inherited nothing but a pile of debts, you are stealing Georgiana's inheritance to make up for it."

The viscount's eyes narrowed, giving him a dangerous appearance. "Since the collection was purchased with funds derived from the estate income, I might debate his claims as to its ownership. As for his accusation—does Mr. Needham actually believe such nonsense?"

"I have no idea. According to Georgiana, he claims to have recognized one of the pieces in a shop while on a visit to Leicester."

"Did he? I wonder if there's any truth in that."

She nodded. "That's what I wondered. The whole thing sounds a hum, to me. A false scent, to distract us from the real crime," she added darkly.

The anger faded from his face. "Just so," he agreed. "Shall we inspect the collection to see if anything is missing?"

Lizzie glanced at the mantel clock. "Or should we wait until tomorrow, when there's more light? The gong to dress for dinner should sound at any minute."

Reluctantly they agreed to put off their investigation until the following morning. Immediately after breakfast, though, they went in search of the bailiff. They found him in the estate office, once more copying over figures from one book to another. He looked up at their entrance, shut the thick volumes, and rose to his feet.

"My lord, what may I do for you?"

Cerb, who padded in Lizzie's wake, thrust his massive head into the room and lolled his tongue out sideways. The bailiff took an apprehensive step back, but the hound ignored him and instead embarked on a thoroughly satisfying scratch.

"You may come with me to examine my cousin's collection," said St. Vincent.

The bailiff, one eye still on Cerberus, came slowly around the edge of his desk. "Go with you, my lord?"

"Yes, I understand I might need a witness to verify I'm not stealing anything. You seem an excellent choice."

A frown flickered across Mr. Rycroft's handsome face. "What do you mean? Is this some jest?"

"A very poor one." Bluntly, Lizzie explained.

Mr. Rycroft straightened up, his brow thunderous. "Steal? From the saferoom? I should think not, my lord! It's impossible. There are only two keys, as you well know. One is even now in your possession."

"And the other?"

"On my own ring. No unauthorized person could have

entered that room, unless another key has been made without my knowledge."

"And would that have been possible?" St. Vincent led the way down the hall, back toward the library. Silence answered him, and he looked over his shoulder.

The bailiff had paused, frowning. "I can see no reason why His Lordship would have done such a thing," he said at last.

"Nor can I." St. Vincent entered the muniments room. At the far end, he stopped before a door. From his pocket he unearthed a ring of keys, sorted through these, and selected one, which he fitted into the lock. The door swung open with a protesting creak.

Lizzie stepped inside, curious. It was a tiny room, no more than a closet, really, for no windows or other doors opened out of it. The two side walls were lined with shelves on which rested a collection of silver, from chafing dishes to epergnes. Against the back wall a number of crates were stacked.

Cerb pushed past her, shoving her aside, and went to sniff out the dark corners. Satisfied that nothing of interest lurked in the recesses, he returned to the doorway and lay down across the threshold, providing an effective block.

St. Vincent strode up to one of the crates and lifted the lid. From inside, he drew a muslin-wrapped package, which he unswathed with care. Slowly, he exposed a small painting in a heavy, gilt frame. He studied it a moment, then held it up for Lizzie to see.

"Raphael," he said. "A thing of beauty beyond its mere monetary value." He replaced it with veneration, then turned to the bailiff. "Where is the catalogue?".

"The what?" Mr. Rycroft came forward a step.

"The listing of his collection. Don't tell me he didn't keep one?"

"Yes, of course he did. It's in the estate room." He turned toward the door, faced the panting hound, and came to an abrupt halt.

"Just step over him," Lizzie suggested in a spirit of pure mischief.

The bailiff regarded the hound, then turned an uncertain eye on her. "Over him, Miss Carstairs? Will there be anything left of my boots if I do?"

"Cerb!" St. Vincent called, and patted his leg.

The hound rose to his feet, indulged in a luxurious stretch, and padded over. Heaving a contented sigh, he lay down on the toes of the viscount's polished Hessians.

St. Vincent eyed the hound with a pained expression. "Have you not succeeded in teaching him even the rudiments of manners, Lizzie?"

"You called him," she pointed out. She glanced toward the door, but Mr. Rycroft had made good his escape while opportunity presented itself.

"He might have brought the listing with him," St. Vincent murmured, following the direction of her gaze.

Lizzie opened another crate and inspected the muslin-wrapped contents. "What will you do if there are items missing?"

"Call in your friend from Bow Street, of course. It's about time he had something constructive to do."

The bailiff returned a few minutes later with a small book, which contained not only a description of each item, but also the date and place of purchase, and the amount paid. While Lizzie drew items from the crates, St. Vincent and Mr. Rycroft tried to match them against the inventory. Cerb retired to the doorway once more where he lay down, head on his massive paws, and kept an intelligent eye cocked on the proceedings.

"Someone should have numbered them," Lizzie said in disgust nearly an hour later, as they tried to identify the third silver chalice.

Mr. Rycroft smiled, and his whole face lighted. "I did suggest it. But His Lordship didn't want to attach anything to these works of art. It *would* be a terrible thing if they were damaged."

"Nonsense. How could they be? I think you should do it at once, then line up the pieces in numerical order. It would be easy, then, to see if anything were missing."

The viscount smiled. "Efficient as ever, Lizzie?" he murmured.

She nodded. "Why waste time doing something in a round-about fashion? Everything just becomes muddled that way."

"I shall strive to remember your advice." His considering gaze rested on her for a moment longer, then returned to the bailiff. "Do you think you can do as she suggests?"

Mr. Rycroft swallowed, and a rueful smile just touched his lips. "As you wish, my lord."

"I'll help," Lizzie said brightly. She leaned over and took the book from the bailiff's hands. "What shall we use as tags? We should do all the silver as well, under the circumstances."

Frederick left them to it. He could trust Lizzie to drive Mr. Rycroft to distraction, but he could also trust her to get the job done, and in the most efficient manner possible. By the time she finished in that room, there would not be the least chance anything could go missing without their being aware of it.

He called Cerb to heel, which seemed easier than stepping over him, and the hound attached himself to his side. St. Vincent had a shrewd suspicion he'd have to bribe him with a ham bone to be rid of him. He could leave him in the kitchen, where he would probably proceed to devour whatever Cook had laid out for their dinner.

As he entered the Great Hall, with Cerb bounding about his feet, Halliford, dressed for riding, came down the stairs. That seemed an excellent way to work off his restlessness, not to mention that of the disreputable hound. Leaving Cerb tugging on the duke's whip, he ran up the steps to change.

Riding over the estate, though, did little to improve his humor. The neglect that everywhere met his eyes could only depress him. Crops rotted in the fields, or worse! in the barns, because of leaking roofs that cried out for repair. And everywhere, the tenants stopped their work to stare at them as they rode by, their expressions cold and accusing.

At the fourth farm they passed, several rough-clad men stood in a huddle, talking. They looked up at the sounds of the approach and one, urged on by the others, stepped forward and waved, gesturing for them to stop.

St. Vincent drew in rein and came abreast of him. He gazed down at the old, weathered face. Cerb trotted up and set up a low growl in his throat, which the viscount stopped with a curt command.

The man's squared jaw thrust out in defiance, and his hands clenched. "Are any repairs going to be made?" he demanded. His voice, surprisingly strong and deep, belonged to a younger man. "My lord," he added, grudgingly, at the viscount's silence.

The appearance of age came early with work and worry, St. Vincent reflected. He studied the other men, and read their tension in their rigid stances. "Repairs will begin as soon as the estate is settled."

"And what until then?" The man took a step closer, his voice more urgent than belligerent.

"Have you food?"

A murmur sounded from the group behind him. "Not enough," one man called out.

St. Vincent met his gaze squarely. "Then hunt. If you haven't ammunition, go to Treecher. I'll give him instructions to expect you."

"There are some people, such as His late Lordship, as would call that poaching," said the man at his side.

114

"Only when it's done without permission."

The man relaxed. "That's good of you, m'lord." He stepped back, permitting them to pass.

St. Vincent called Cerb to heel and spurred his horse forward. For several minutes, he and the duke rode without speaking. Behind them, the men returned to their huddle, but this time the murmur of their voices held excitement, not anger.

"Damnation!" St. Vincent's savage expletive broke the silence. "The devil confound my dearly beloved cousin! How could he let the estate come to such a pass?"

"How much do you need to start repairs?" Halliford kept his gaze focused somewhere between his horse's ears.

St. Vincent glared at him. "I'll not accept a loan."

"It wouldn't be for you. It would be for them."

St. Vincent glanced back over his shoulder, where the men now strode off toward a ramshackle cottage. They would be calling on the gamekeeper within the hour, he wagered. He came to a difficult decision. "I'll do it myself. They're my people."

"As you wish." A slight smile played about the corners of Halliford's mouth. "I always said you were a stubborn, mackerel-backed gudgeon."

St. Vincent nodded, for once awarding such deliberate provocation no more than a smile. He stared out across the land, over the dilapidated farms, the rickety buildings, and experienced a wash of pride. "This is my responsibility," he answered, and was glad. It was his, as he had always wanted. He would make it prosperous once again, and by his own hand.

They neared the boundary hedge and turned toward the home farm. This, alone of all the holdings on the estate, showed any sign of having been kept up. St. Vincent had a shrewd suspicion his cousin had done this under protest—or more likely, that Mr. Rycroft had attended to this without asking. Young Mr. Rycroft seemed an enterprising sort. His manner might be polished and deferential on the surface, but determination similar to the steam locomotive built by Mr. Stephenson lurked just beneath. Probably it took every ounce of that strength to deal with his cousin without—without running him through in a fit of fury, perhaps?

They completed their circuit and turned back toward the stable. By the time they entered the cobbled yard, the massive hound had ceased to bound after hares and contented himself with trotting peacefully at the tired horses' sides.

St. Vincent handed the muddied hound over to the stable lads for grooming, over the dog's vociferous protests. Leaving Halliford to speak to his groom about their fast-approaching departure for London, he set off on his errand.

The path to the gamekeeper's cottage lay through the rose garden, where the thorny bushes were now bare against the coming winter. Dried weeds stuck their unsightly heads through the hard ground. Since the estate obviously didn't boast a gardener, St. Vincent decided he'd set the undergrooms to the job.

He left this depressing sign of decay and pushed his way through an untrimmed hedge. The cottage stood on the verge of the forested parkland, and St. Vincent eyed it with disfavor. A well-tended garden peeked out from behind the dilapidated two-room structure, the only sign of care he could discern. One paned window, he noted as he approached, was broken, and the door did not fit the frame, leaving well over an inch of space on most sides.

The wind must howl through the place in the winter. St. Vincent's hatred for his deceased cousin intensified. Could the man not even see his servants properly housed? The moment he got his hands on some funds—the thought appalled him. How could he make so little stretch to cover so many serious needs?

Thrusting the uncomfortable thoughts aside, he strode

116

forward. Before he could knock, a rustling sounded in the shrubbery and the gamekeeper emerged through a straggly gap. The man came to an abrupt halt and lowered the snare he carried.

"Ah, there you are, Treecher. I wanted a word with you."

"Yes, m'lord?" Treecher eyed him uneasily. "I was checking for poachers, I was. Can't go and have them running rampant."

"Yes we can. But they won't be poachers any more. Anyone who asks may hunt at will."

It took a moment for Treecher to take this in. "Free access to the birds?" he asked at last.

"And to the deer and rabbits, as well. They need the meat. I've told the tenants to ask your permission. I'd like you to go out with them to make certain nothing goes amiss. I believe I can safely leave the matter in your hands?"

"Aye, m'lord. That you can." The gamekeeper nodded vigorously. "That you can, indeed."

"I imagine you will be seeing the first of them shortly. If any problems arise, let me know at once." With a dismissive nod, Frederick started back toward the house.

He had given his tenants some hope, at least. He only wished he could do more. He emerged from the forested path into a clearing, across from which stood the line of hawthorn hedges at the edge of the garden. Beyond that rose the rambling old manor house.

He paused, staring at it. He'd never really expected to inherit. Yet he'd wanted it, all his life he'd loved the Grange, and the knowledge it would not be his had driven him to his useless existence.

Yet it had been an inexplicable—and wholly untenable—longing for something else he could never possess that finally sent him on his travels. He was a man of nearly forty, an experienced rake—a libertine!—who had nothing in common with the prosaic frankness of an

117

*in*experienced chit half his age.

Yet perversely, he continued to enjoy her company. He would miss her when she departed for London, but it would be the best thing possible. He would marry—his position demanded that—but he would select an older female, perhaps a widow, well up to his weight in worldly acumen. Such a woman he could not hurt or disappoint.

He went to his room, where he put off his riding dress and donned clean buckskin breeches and a shooting coat. He dismissed his man, then made his way back downstairs. He wanted to join the shooting party he knew would be forming by now; but his responsibilities lay here. He really should find out how his bailiff and Lizzie went on with their inventory.

He found the saferoom locked, which must mean they had completed their task. He closed the door of the muniments room behind him as he left, and the door across opened.

Lizzie looked out and smiled brightly. "Ninety-seven," she said.

"Ninety-seven what?" Damn it, he wished it weren't such a pleasure just to see her cheerful, matter-of-fact face. It would be unforgivable if he cursed her with his cynicism, or tainted her innocence with his corrupt tongue.

She curled up in a chair before the blazing fire. "Did you have a pleasant ride?"

"Mmmm," he returned, noncommittally. "Are you keeping guard against marauding vicars?"

She nodded. "Or anyone else who wants to search this room. I didn't think it was proper to do it myself until you came back."

"Quite right." He crossed to the hearth and held out his hands, warming them from the dancing flames. "Ninety-seven what?" he repeated.

"Oh. Items in the collection. We put tags on every one of them, and Mr. Rycroft recorded them in his book."

"Ninety-seven," St. Vincent repeated, thoughtful. Somehow, that didn't sound right. Then he had it. He regarded her through narrowed eyes, an unpleasant certainty taking root. "Are you quite sure?"

She directed a disgusted look at him. "Of course I am. Mr. Rycroft didn't seem all that sure, either, but *I* made out the labels and attached them."

"Are you quite positive you didn't miss a few?"

"Is that likely?" she demanded, affronted.

His lips twitched. "No," he admitted. "Not for you. So, there are ninety-seven items in there today, and I distinctly remember my cousin telling me he had just purchased the one hundred and third."

"The—" Lizzie broke off and did some rapid mental arithmetic. "That means there are six missing."

"You always were a wonder at your sums," he murmured, unable to resist.

Lizzie gave him a look, then resumed her musings. "Could they be somewhere else? In his bedchamber, perhaps?"

"It's possible."

Lizzie stood up and shook out the serviceable blue merino of her skirts. "Well, what are you waiting for? Let's check."

He followed her out. Ever direct and to the point, that was his—he squelched that thought. Lizzie was not his, and never would be.

On the second floor, he led the way across the Picture Gallery, down two steps and into another wing. At the third door, he stopped and drew out his ring of keys. After several attempts, he unlocked the room and stepped into an antechamber decorated in depressingly dark greens.

Lizzie wrinkled her nose. "I hope you plan to change the color pattern before moving in."

"You may be sure of it." Though that was likely to take time—and money the estate did not possess. He opened

119

the next door, which was also locked, and let them into a large, low-pitched chamber.

Lizzie shivered. "It's freezing in here." She strode to the window and threw the dark drapes wide, letting a meager light in through the dirty paned window. Ivy clung close, obscuring most of the view. "Didn't he have *anything* done around here?" she demanded.

St. Vincent shook his head. A quick search of the bedside table produced a tinderbox, and with the aid of this he soon had a branch of candles burning. Lizzie took the box from him and lit several more. The unpleasant odor of tallow filled the air.

She looked about the chamber, frowning. "The fire's still laid," she pointed out.

St. Vincent glanced at the hearth where neatly arranged fagots lay. "Set for the night," he said. "Except he didn't need them."

"But we do." Lizzie held a candle to a clump of dried moss. A soft glow rose and spread quickly, kindling the twigs. She turned back and into the room. "Where do we begin?"

St. Vincent dragged his gaze from her forthright figure. "As executor, I have to go through everything in here, anyway. Do you want to do a thorough job, or just look for the missing pieces from the collection?"

She wrinkled her freckled nose. "Why do it all twice?" She set down her taper and pulled open the top drawer of a dresser. "Shall we inventory everything, or look merely for papers?"

They set to work. On Lizzie's suggestion, he rang for a nuncheon tray to be brought to them there. Lizzie made selections from this, heaped them on a plate, and returned to work at once. Though they spent the entire afternoon at their task, not so much as a single document of any importance did they uncover. Nor did they find any trace of the missing items from the collection.

Lizzie, disgusted, shoved the bureau drawer closed.

"Are you certain your cousin had his numbers correct? That he didn't miscount somewhere? Mr. Rycroft had a list of descriptions, you know. There were only ninety-seven of them."

St. Vincent stared thoughtfully at the patches on the dark green bedcurtain. "No. That was one thing about which he would never have made a mistake. There are six items missing. It's possible a few of them—the most recent acquisitions—were just never recorded."

Lizzie drew a deep breath and lèt out a sigh. "Then we have to assume that Mr. Needham knew what he was talking about when he claimed to have seen that piece in Leicester. Who's been stealing them, do you think?"

St. Vincent sat back, watching her serious face as it puckered in puzzled concentration. "Do you mean to tell me you don't have any ideas?"

"Of course I do. Anyone in the house could have borrowed a key at some time, perhaps even had it copied."

"But who would want to?"

Lizzie considered. "I don't think Lady St. Vincent would. She hasn't the nerve. She's showing signs of improving, of course, but that's only been in the last few days."

"So might have been the thefts."

Lizzie cocked her head. "Then why was he murdered, if he didn't surprise the thief?"

"True. All right, for the moment, then, we will eliminate my esteemed Cousin Isobel. What of Georgiana?"

Lizzie picked up her plate and returned it to the tray, then stood staring at it. "She was defiant—almost combative—the day we arrived. She's abandoned that, by the way, in case you hadn't noticed. Now she's indulging in high drama." She considered. "She might well have wanted the money, but I don't think she'd murder her own father. Or anyone else," she added, fairly.

"If the collection is ruled to be *not* entailed, then rightfully it belongs to her and her mother. She'd have no need to steal from it."

"That's in doubt, though. And maybe she needed the money now, and didn't want to wait for the estate to be wound up."

St. Vincent conceded the point. "Then why did she alert you to the possibility of looting?"

Lizzie frowned. "She did make a point of it, too, calling me over to tell me." She bit her lip. "Maybe she wanted to protect herself if the thefts were discovered before she took legal possession of the collection?"

St. Vincent walked over to the window and stared out through the clinging ivy. Before him, the lawn, browning from the frosts of approaching winter, stretched to the edge of a forested copse. "I suppose Hodgkens was a victim of our thief, as well."

"Unless he was helping someone outside to steal, and they had a falling out." She sounded doubtful.

"Not Hodgkens. He was with my family in my uncle's time."

"Who does that leave?" She joined him. "The servants and Mr. Rycroft?"

"I think we should find out what the Reverend Mr. Winfield wanted in the library," St. Vincent said at last.

"I doubt he'll tell us. Unless it really *is* a sermon, and we are making a great deal out of his own penchant for drama."

"No, I—" He broke off.

Below them, in the growing dusk, a cloaked figure slipped away from the wall of the house and ran toward the copse. St. Vincent raised his quizzing glass, but at this distance it didn't help.

"Georgiana," Lizzie stated. "Now, what the devil—"

She broke off as a man stepped away from the trees and

waved a hand. The girl ran straight to him, grabbed his arm, and dragged him back within the shelter of the trees.

"Your cousin seems to delight in holding clandestine meetings with men," Lizzie declared.

"Mr. Needham, again?"

"Couldn't you see? That was the Reverend Mr. Winfield."

Chapter 10

Lizzie made her way downstairs, thoughtful. So many mysteries abounded, and she had to leave with Halliford and Helena in the morning! It just wasn't fair. Frederick *needed* her to help sort out this mess. The Runner Coggins certainly hadn't turned up any answers. But then he didn't know about those six missing items from the collection, either.

Brightening, Lizzie went in search of him to remedy this situation. She ran him to earth at last in the kitchens, eating an apple tart and downing a glass of home-brewed while he had what he called a "right regular jaw session" with the kitchen maid, the potboy, and the cook. With only a bit of persuasion, Lizzie detached him, and led him out into the hall, where she supplied the details of her afternoon's activities.

Coggins listened, his brow creasing as she reached the part of the fruitless search. "Robbery," he muttered, as if the idea were a strange and dreadful possibility. "That never seemed likely, that didn't. You're sure of this, Missy?"

Lizzie nodded, pleased with the sensation her news had created. Maybe *now* the law would get on the right track. "St. Vincent was quite certain his cousin spoke of buying the one hundred and third item," she repeated. "And when I labeled them, there were only ninety-seven."

"St. Vincent it was as told you that, Missy? Well, now, under the circumstances, that does seem to be the sort of thing he would say, doesn't it?" The worry cleared from his rotund face.

Lizzie put her hands on her hips and glared at him. "What the devil do you mean by that?"

The man blinked, taken aback. "Now, Missy, there's no call as for you to be agoing and using that sort of language. What my sister would say if her Janey or Sarah was to talk like that!" He shook his head. "Make her blood boil, it would."

"Then it's a good thing she isn't here, isn't it? Now, kindly stop changing the subject and tell me what you mean."

Under her furious scrutiny, a dull flush crept up his neck and across his face. "Well, Missy, if you was to take and murder someone, begging your pardon of course, wouldn't you want everyone to go and think there might be someone else as had a good reason to do in that gentleman?"

"You mean a—a false trail?"

He beamed at her. "That's right, Missy. Mayhaps our murderer wants us to go haring off after some nonexistent housebreaker instead of closing in on him, like."

Lizzie paced several steps, then spun back to face him. "Or maybe someone stole a few things *after* the murder, hoping we'd think it was before, and that the viscount surprised the thief."

Coggins's features took on a curious expression. "You mean as the things really *might* be missing?"

"Yes. It was Mr. Needham, by the way, who told Miss Ashfield about the theft, and she told me."

"Was it now?" He fell silent a moment, his face screwing in an effort of thought. "Mayhaps I'd just better go along now and have myself a little discussion-like with

125

Mr. Needham."

"Excellent." Lizzie breathed a sigh of relief. "And maybe you should find someone who had seen the reliquary he claimed to have spotted—just to identify it. I'm sure either Mr. Rycroft or Lady St. Vincent would be delighted to go into Leicester with you, if there were a chance of recovering it."

Still, as she watched him stride purposefully off, she could be only partly satisfied with the results of this interview. Even if he did accept the possibility of theft, he would probably just add that to the charge of murder against St. Vincent.

She headed back toward the hall. As she reached it, a gong sounded from deep within the house. Time to change for dinner. Already. With a sigh, she started up the stairs again.

St. Vincent needed her here to keep things moving in the right direction. It chafed at her that she had to leave in the morning. She'd done everything she could—which clearly wasn't enough. Of course, at the rate Coggins operated, both the murder and the robbery might still be unsolved when Halliford returned his family to Yorkshire for Christmas. Undoubtedly, her brother-in-law would want to stop in Leicestershire to see how his friend went on. Somewhat more cheerful, she made her way to her room.

Frederick descended the stairs, dressed for dinner, and glanced into the Green Salon. No one there, yet. Restless, he strode down the corridor. He'd left the *London Times* in the library.

As he reached the Great Hall, the sound of a carriage in the drive caught his attention. This was a somewhat unusual hour to be making a call. Curious, he crossed to the mullioned window and peered out.

A tilbury, pulled by a sweet-stepping bay, rounded the

126

curve of the drive. A well-set-up gentleman, dressed in the black frock coat of a clergyman, drew the animal to a halt. He sat gazing for a moment at the front of the house. Then he set his brake, looped his reins over it, and stepped down.

St. Vincent waited. A minute passed, and then James, still acting for the injured Hodgkens, erupted from the servants' hall and dashed for the front door, tugging at his coat as he went. The lad paused to set his features into a more impassive expression, then opened the door and swept down the stairs with very creditable aplomb.

The gentleman stood with his back to them as he unstrapped a valise from the rear of the tilbury. After freeing it, he handed the case to the waiting footman, then climbed back onto the seat. He drove off in the direction of the stable.

"What's going on?" Lizzie crossed the hall. "Anything interesting?"

Frederick glanced over his shoulder, and his gaze rested on her simple evening gown of deep green muslin. It clung to her well-developed figure in a manner he found very disturbing. She remained oblivious to her own charms; she would probably scorn them if he were ever so imprudent as to point them out to her.

She strode across the marble tiles and joined him at the window. Peering out into the gathering darkness onto the empty drive, she asked: "Has someone come?"

"We appear to be being invaded by vicars," he explained.

The door opened and James reentered the hall, valise in hand.

Lizzie regarded the footman for a moment, pursing her lips. "They would appear to travel lightly, I see. How many?"

"Just one, at the moment."

Lizzie nodded approval. "They're best in small doses, aren't they? Mr. Winfield—" She broke off.

127

The clergyman in question came into view, but no longer alone. Cerberus trotted happily at his heels, his whiplike tail flailing the air and his huge muzzle pushing at the gentleman's hands. With a cry of delight, Lizzie dashed across the hall and out the door.

St. Vincent followed, slowly, and a moment later he was granted the not-so-very pleasing prospect of the ever-direct Lizzie hurling herself into the new arrival's arms. An unwelcome pang shot through him. Confound his attraction to the chit! She could never have belonged to an aging libertine. A young, honorable clergyman with high ideals and principles—nothing could be more suitable for Lizzie. He should be glad for her.

The clergyman set the girl firmly aside. "You're knocking my hat off," he complained, and lifted the shallow curly beaver to reposition it on the thick waves of his light brown hair. "Now, what's going on here?" He looked up, straight at St. Vincent.

Frederick languidly raised his quizzing glass, and the aching emptiness seeped out of his stomach, to be replaced by an immense relief. "Adrian?" He dropped the glass and his smile of welcome broadened.

Mr. Adrian Carstairs strode forward and clasped his hand. "It's good to see you again—St. Vincent." He hesitated only a moment over the use of the title. "What is going on here?"

"You got my letter? I hadn't expected it to reach you so soon."

The young Reverend Mr. Carstairs shook his head. "I went to the Castle and was met by old Winthrop. He told me some garbled tale of your being taken up for murder and Halliford and Lizzie dashing off to rescue you. I must say, I'm glad it wasn't true."

"Oh, it is. Quite true, my dear boy. Come into the house, though. Would you care to dress for dinner?"

He led Adrian inside and to the salon, where so far only the dowager viscountess had come down. St. Vincent introduced his guest, then stood back in sardonic amusement, watching as the young gentleman proceeded to charm his timid Cousin Isobel.

Lizzie stood near, her hands resting on the back of a chair, gazing fondly on her only brother. Frederick studied them. Adrian's hair might be the lighter and curlier, but he lacked the mischievous expression that danced in Lizzie's eyes. His seemed graver, though always kind.

Adrian looked up, and his sudden warm smile flashed. His resemblance to Lizzie, Frederick realized with an odd pang, could be striking.

"If you'll have someone show me to a room, I'll only take a moment. I promise, Lady St. Vincent. I won't delay your meal."

"Take as long as you need, Mr. Carstairs."

To St. Vincent's further amazement, his normally retiring Cousin Isobel patted Adrian's hand as he bowed to take his leave. St. Vincent escorted him out, and took the opportunity to fill him in on all that had happened. By the time they returned downstairs, it was settled between them that Adrian would take charge of the farms, thus indulging his avid love for experimental agriculture.

"In the morning I'll escort you about the estate, with Mr. Rycroft, so you may see what you are up against."

Adrian waved the warnings aside. "I'll enjoy it, you know that. I'm only too pleased for the opportunity."

And to be of assistance, St. Vincent guessed. Just like his sister.

By now the others had gathered, and by the time Adrian had greeted Helena and his brother-in-law, and been introduced to Georgiana, James waited to announce dinner. The meal was livelier than usual, and St. Vincent did not look forward to the quiet of the morrow, when three of his guests would be gone.

"I do wish we didn't have to leave in the morning,"

Helena declared, looking across the table to where her husband and Adrian discussed the arrangements her brother had made at Oxford for the coming term.

"There is no reason why *you* must go, my love," Halliford said. "Would you rather stay with Lizzie and Adrian?"

"You are welcome for as long as you wish." St. Vincent suppressed a surge of longing. It would be best if Lizzie left; then he couldn't be tempted by her. He would miss her damnably, though. He'd already learned that during the last five years.

"Why don't we stay? Someone has to keep that Runner from making a mull of everything." Lizzie looked from her sister to her brother-in-law and back again, and her face fell.

"If you don't mind, Lizzie, I would rather go with Halliford," Helena said.

"I haven't seen Adrian this age," Lizzie protested.

Of course she didn't want to stay to see *him*, Frederick reflected. Well, that was the way he wanted it—that it had to be.

"If Her Grace permits?" The dowager viscountess clutched her napkin, as if she gathered courage to put forth some bold suggestion. "You may stay in my care, Miss Carstairs. Georgiana and I should be delighted to have your continued company." She raised timid eyes to the duchess, then lowered her gaze to her plate.

"An excellent suggestion," the duke declared. "Adrian may make certain she doesn't cause any mischief."

Lizzie threw a darkling look at her brother-in-law, but refrained from comment. Instead, she leaned across the table and grasped the dowager's hand, giving it a grateful squeeze. "Thank you! I won't be of the least trouble to you, I promise."

Halliford made a strangled sound, but managed to keep his countenance. "It seems the matter is settled, then."

The duke and duchess of Halliford departed in the

morning, amid much hugging and ordering to behave. The last, directed solely at Lizzie, St. Vincent had a shrewd notion would be promptly ignored. If he knew his Lizzie, she would charge full force into solving the burglary and murder, and without a thought for her own welfare or comfort—or that of anyone else, for that matter. Single-mindedness and determination were traits she possessed in spades. Coupled with the intense loyalty that characterized all the Carstairs siblings, it turned her into a formidable ally.

The traveling chariot emblazoned with the Halliford arms disappeared around the bend in the drive. St. Vincent glanced at his two charges, who had linked arms and now strolled back into the house. They weren't his charges, though; he wasn't left taking care of two children. Adrian was all of five-and-twenty, now, and had been the virtual head of his household since getting out of leading strings. And Lizzie—

He broke off that thought. Lizzie was no longer the amusing child who had entertained him so thoroughly in the past. She was a young woman, and a very capable and straightforward one, at that. And one he intended to protect from his baser instincts. His honor demanded he behave to her as a gentleman—and his pride dreaded her reaction if he did not.

To his mingled pleasure and discomfort, she chose to accompany them on their ride about the estate, listening as intently as Adrian to the never-ending list of problems and needs that met their searching gazes. They returned to the house almost three hours later, and Adrian, after putting off his riding dress, went at once to the estate office with Mr. Rycroft. St. Vincent left them together with a strong sense of relief. He had made at least one step in the right direction. Now, if only he could come up with some money.

He strolled down the hall to the library, poured himself a glass of wine, and settled in an overstuffed chair that

131

had been brought down from an attic. For a very long while, he stared into the flames in the hearth. He was tempted to claim that damnable collection as his, for it was purchased with the proceeds from the estate that should have gone into its upkeep. Yet where would that leave Georgiana and Cousin Isobel? They needed something on which to live. But the tenants needed it, too. And now.

He should hear from his solicitor any day. Then, at least, he would know how much of his own funds he could gather at once. Just how far he could stretch his limited resources, though, remainded a mystery.

The door opened. He slid farther down in the chair and ignored it.

A slight cough sounded. After a moment, Hodgkens announced: "Mr. Burnett has called, my lord."

St. Vincent looked up, surprised to see the elderly retainer. "Are you sure you should be back to your duties, Hodgkens?"

"Yes, m'lord. Thank you." The butler stood back to permit the visitor to enter, then retreated, closing the door once more behind him.

St. Vincent nodded a greeting, then crossed to the table where a selection of decanters stood, and held one up; his guest accepted. Frederick filled glasses and they both retired to chairs before the fireplace.

"To what do I owe the pleasure?"

Mr. Burnett smiled. "Plain vulgar curiosity. That, and boredom. If you had not noticed, the ground has been too hard to exercise my hunters."

"So you came to see whether or not our tame Runner has hauled me off under guard?"

"Or someone else. You don't seem a likely choice to me, somehow."

"Don't I?" St. Vincent studied him through narrowed eyes.

Mr. Burnett shook his head. "You don't strike me as

being clumsy. Had you wanted to murder your cousin, I am quite certain you would have accomplished it in a much neater manner, with not one trace of suspicion resting on yourself."

"You flatter me." In spite of himself, he smiled. "You also share the opinion of Miss Carstairs. She, too, thinks I would have been far more devious. Which returns us to the question of who *did* do it."

"You have made no progress? That Runner has certainly been poking his nose about the neighborhood. I doubt there is anyone he hasn't questioned at least twice." A slight frown formed between his brows. "This must be uncomfortable for Her Ladyship and Miss Ashfield."

"As you say. You know more about my cousin's activities during the last few years than I. Have you not any ideas?"

Mr. Burnett studied the amber wine as he swirled it in his glass. "Some, perhaps. But nothing definite."

"*Any* ideas are being welcomed," St. Vincent said dryly. "Do you know anyone local who might bear a grudge?"

Mr. Burnett shook his head. "I fear he wasn't very well liked, but I haven't heard of any specific fights. I'd be of more help to you on ancient history. My family lived around here until about seventy-five years ago, you know. I've only been in England for three years, myself. I was born in America—Virginia, to be exact." He kept his eyes on the flames. "Are you well acquainted with your cousin's bailiff?" he asked presently.

"Mr. Rycroft? He has not been here more than four years, I believe."

Mr. Burnett nodded. "It probably has nothing to do with anything, but I don't quite trust the man. Ham-fisted when he rides."

St. Vincent raised an amused eyebrow. "I noticed his horse seemed docile. But that is hardly a reason to

133

murder someone."

"There's something a little too polished about him."
Mr. Burnett rose abruptly. "I should not be speaking
thus of one of your employees."

"Did you ever do so before my cousin?" St. Vincent
remained where he was, though his eyes rested on his
visitor.

Mr. Burnett hesitated, then nodded. "Once. Only a
few days before he was—he died."

"Did you, now." St. Vincent spoke softly, to himself.
"I doubt he took any heed. But if he did—" He broke
off and gazed down at the viscount, his expression
troubled.

St. Vincent nodded. "I take your point."

They settled down for a hand or two of piquet, and
worries temporarily vanished before this all-consuming
occupation. Several hours passed before his visitor at
last rose to leave, and St. Vincent found himself
strangely refreshed for having laid aside his problems for
a good portion of the day.

He did not see Lizzie again until dinnertime. She was in
the salon before him, staring moodily out the window
into the darkness. Cerb stretched out on the sofa
cushions before the fire. He regarded the hound through
his quizzing glass, but forebore to protest.

"Have you spent an enjoyable afternoon?" he asked,
every inch the concerned host.

She didn't even look over her shoulder. "I haven't
learned a thing," she said in disgust. "What did Mr.
Burnett have to say?"

He didn't bother asking how she knew about his
visitor. Somehow, Lizzie always knew everything that
went on. "He told me to beware Mr. Rycroft, and that his
own family used to live around here—about seventy-five
years ago."

Lizzie turned to face him, her freckled nose wrinkled in
thought. "Mr. Rycroft is a possibility, if he were caught

134

stealing from the collection. As for Mr. Burnett's family—" She considered a moment, then shook her head in regret. "An old family grudge makes a pretty poor reason for murder, I suppose."

"Very true." St. Vincent shook his head, his regret only half-mocking. "I fear we shall have to look for our guilty party elsewhere."

Adrian stalked into the salon, unhesitatingly ordered the hound off the sofa, and took his place. Cerb padded to the hearth, circled three times, and sank down with a heavy sigh.

"To be perfectly blunt, St. Vincent," Adrian said, the anger in his voice carefully controlled, "it's a lucky thing your cousin was murdered when he was, or there'd be nothing left of the estate at all."

"It would hardly be felicitous for me to agree."

"Or for me to have said it in the first place." Adrian shook his head, mute apology in his expression.

St. Vincent poured a glass of Madeira and handed it to him. "Oh, no. Think nothing of it. Lizzie, I am sure, can tell you how furious I have been with my dear cousin." He poured some for himself. "I might even have gone so far as to threaten him with violence. Did I ever, by the way, offer to murder him?" he asked Lizzie.

She lowered her gaze, for once not meeting his with that frank regard he so much enjoyed. Good Lord, did the chit think him capable?

The next moment, though, she looked up squarely. "No. *I'm* the one who offered to run him through with the sword stick—if you'd teach me how to use it."

"So you did."

"And I still think it was a good idea." She took the glass St. Vincent had just filled for himself and sipped it. "This really is an awkward situation. When we find the murderer, do we turn him over to Bow Street or praise him as a public benefactor?"

Adrian tried to frown, but amused understanding

glinted in his eyes.

St. Vincent's spirits lifted. "Bye the bye, did you mention the matter of the looting to our beloved resident Runner?"

Lizzie nodded, and glowered.

"Dear me." He drew his snuff box from his pocket, flicked it open with a deft movement, and offered it to Adrian. That gentleman waved it aside with a word of thanks, so St. Vincent helped himself to an infinitesimal pinch.

"He had the—the *affrontery* to suggest you made up those missing six items." Lizzie's brow puckered in concern. "I'm afraid he has his heart set on arresting you, Frederick, and the devil's in it that I don't know what we're going to be able to do to stop him."

Chapter 11

St. Vincent hesitated, then replaced the chased silver box in his pocket. "I believe we had best mention those six pieces to Mr. Rycroft," he said at last. "He might be able to recall them."

Lizzie snorted. "Not he. I doubt he cares a fig about that collection, except for the money it represents that might have been better spent. And *that*, he told me, he'd rather not dwell on." She tugged at a loose strand of hair, and returned to an earlier question that still vexed her. "Do you think Mr. Needham really saw one of them in Leicester, or do you think he was trying to make us fly from the scent?"

"That depends." St. Vincent strolled over to the fire, then turned back to face her. "He might have deliberately drawn attention to the looting so we wouldn't suspect *him* of being responsible."

"But we do," Lizzie, ever practical, pointed out.

St. Vincent's lip twitched. "He has not the felicity of being familiar with the manner in which your mind works, my dear."

She beamed at him, accepting this as a compliment.

"We know my Cousin John was murdered for a reason," he pursued. "Either because he discovered the thefts, or—?" he looked from Lizzie to Adrian and back again, a questioning eyebrow raised.

137

Adrian shook his head. "He doesn't appear to have been a popular gentleman. But to murder a peer of the realm—! There would have to have been a very compelling reason."

"You don't think someone just lost their temper and used a weapon readily at hand?" Lizzie regarded her brother with what was for her an unusual respect.

Adrian glanced at the viscount. "Could he anger someone to that extent?"

"Easily."

Adrian stared thoughtfully at his hands. "Did no one except yourself stand to gain from his death?"

"I would hardly call this pile of debts a gain."

"There is the title—and the estate, debt-ridden as it may be."

St. Vincent acknowledged the point. "The only others to gain would be his widow and daughter. His wife might well have reached a point where she could tolerate him no longer—but a sword stick does not seem to be quite in Cousin Isobel's style."

"And what of his daughter?" Adrian leaned forward, intent on the answer.

"She might have longed for freedom. He was domineering—and in a particularly nasty sort of way. Made her do penance for the slightest offense—" He broke off, his brow creasing. "As I remember, he beat her quite often when she was a child."

Lizzie drew in an audible breath. "Public benefactor," she muttered.

St. Vincent nodded. "One does find it difficult not to sympathize with his murderer, whoever that may be."

Georgiana and her mother entered the salon, putting an abrupt end to their discussion. Nor were they able to return to it that night. Lizzie retired to her bed at last, dissatisfied with the way things stood, but unable to think of a single idea to help.

The following morning dawned cold and crisp, beckoning her outside, to escape from mysteries and indulge in a gallop across the fields. St. Vincent needed her, though, and she would not let him down. She put on a warm woolen gown and went down to the breakfast parlor.

Lady St. Vincent sat at the table, sipping her tea. The remains of a slice of toast lay on a plate before her. The viscount stood at the window, staring across the lawn toward the expanse of forest as if he, too, longed to slip away and escape in vigorous activity.

"It is your house, now," the dowager declared. For once, she did not sound timid. Nor did she sound as if the thought were in the least distasteful to her.

St. Vincent turned to regard his cousin over his shoulder. "Under the circumstances, and while you reside in the Grange, it might be considered in bad taste."

"And that was never one of your faults." Lizzie strode forward, announcing her presence.

The dowager viscountess looked up and focused her vague gaze on her. "St. Vincent wishes to change the furnishings in the Blue Drawing Room."

"Do you wish to?" Lizzie asked, coming directly to the point.

The dowager hesitated a moment. "Yes." She sounded somewhat surprised.

"Then by all means, make it more comfortable." Lizzie selected a hearty breakfast and joined the woman at the table.

Lady St. Vincent stared at her, mouth slightly open, as if the thought of doing something merely to please herself were unheard of. After several minutes of silence, she offered: "I believe the original furnishings have been stored on the upper floor of the South Wing."

Lizzie wrinkled her nose. "With luck, they won't have succumbed to mildew. May I help you select which pieces are to be brought down?"

"You mean—now?" Lady St. Vincent cast a frightened glance toward her cousin, encountered his disarming smile, and dropped her gaze to the napkin she

139

crumpled with nervous fingers. "That is, of course, up to St. Vincent."

"Devil a bit," the gentleman said cheerfully. "You two will know better than I what is fit and what isn't. I give you a free hand. I intend to go shooting this morning."

"Oh dear, and without a gamekeeper! Will you be able to manage with just a groom to help you?"

St. Vincent, who had started toward the door, turned about to face her. "What do you mean?"

"It was dreadful about Treecher."

He fingered the shaft of his quizzing glass. "Was it? What happened?"

"His being dismissed like that. Did Mr. Rycroft not tell you?" The habitually frightened expression crept back into her face. "My husband had no interest in shooting for himself, but he could not tolerate the idea of theft."

Lizzie opened her mouth, caught St. Vincent's commanding eye on her, and fell silent.

"What did he do?" the viscount asked. "Was he discharged?"

The dowager clutched her cup of tea. "Yes. On the very day my husband—" She broke off, then continued. "My husband caught him with a snared rabbit and a partridge. Poor man, I daresay he was only trying to supplement his food, but he was dismissed on the spot."

"Was he," St. Vincent murmured. "Yes, I shall have to look into that. Make the most of your morning," he said, holding Lizzie's gaze.

She glared at him, but recognized his seemingly casual words as an order. She nodded, and he winked at her and strode out of the room.

"All right," Lizzie said with a measure of determination as the door closed behind him, "let's get started."

She'd much rather go with Frederick than waste her morning indoors. She couldn't see how her projected activity would help her uncover the murderer—and probably thief, as well—unless she took the opportunity to gain the dowager's confidence. Yes, if she set her mind to it, she might well learn something about the servants and inhabitants of Ashfield Grange.

Frederick emerged from the corridor into the Great Hall just as Adrian, already wearing one of his host's shooting jackets, ran lightly down the stairs. He looked his guest up and down, and winced.

Adrian laughed. "You're only two inches taller than I am. I should have thought this would be a better fit."

"It's the color, dear boy. Never mind. It seems we have another little mystery on our hands." He started for the game room.

"Oh?" Adrian fell into step beside him. "What is that?"

Briefly, St. Vincent related the incident of the dismissed gamekeeper, who was still very much at his job. Adrian listened in silence as they selected their guns and loaded ammunition into their pouches.

"Then why is he still here?" he asked at last.

"Offhand, I would say he doesn't realize my Cousin Isobel knew of his dismissal, and hoped to continue as normal. Instead, she simply doesn't know he is still here."

"And what of Rycroft?"

"I doubt he knows, or he'd have stopped his wages."

In silence, Adrian checked his fowling piece once more, then lowered the barrel to the ground. "Being dismissed is hardly a motive for murder," he said at last.

"Isn't it? I wonder. I believe we will speak with Treecher."

Slinging their weapons over their shoulders, they set off for a morning's sport. They headed first to the gamekeeper's cottage, and Adrian's mouth set in an angry line as his comprehensive gaze took in the appalling state of decay. Frederick rapped sharply; there was no answer. After a minute, he knocked again.

141

"Probably he's checking the grounds," Adrian suggested.

Hoisting their guns once more, they set off down a path toward the coverts St. Vincent had spotted on one of his surveying walks two days before. As they circled around the clearing near the folly, Georgiana's raised voice reached them. St. Vincent stopped at once, but Adrian cast an uncertain glance toward the folly.

"If you think I'm going to let overly polite scruples interfere, you can think again," St. Vincent said affably.

Adrian, after a brief struggle, grinned. "You don't think she knows anything, do you?"

"I don't think she's guilty of anything herself, if that's what you mean. But yes, I do think she has her suspicions. I'd like to know how well-founded they are."

But try as he might, he could hear nothing more. The next moment, hearing became extraneous. Georgiana stormed out of the folly, followed at once by Mr. Percival Needham, and their actions spoke eloquently. He grabbed her arm, drawing her back toward him. The girl pulled away, shaking her head, and broke into a run. Mr. Needham started after her, then stopped at the edge of the clearing. Georgiana fled down the trail, the snapping of twigs and rustle of brush punctuating her flight.

St. Vincent's eyes narrowed as they rested on Mr. Needham's furious face. "Thwarted love?" he murmured.

Adrian shook his head slowly. "Thwarted something. But I wouldn't call it love."

"Do you think him afraid?"

Adrian cast him a curious glance. "Of what?"

"According to Lizzie, Georgiana fears Mr. Needham may have murdered her father because he forbade him to marry her. And had him thrown out of the house," he added, reminiscent.

The man in the clearing grabbed up a broken branch and slammed it against a tree. The branch cracked in his hand. Throwing it aside, he stormed back into the folly.

142

St. Vincent shifted the weight of his shooting pouch, but as he started forward once more, Mr. Needham reappeared in the doorway and ran down the shallow steps, clasping a fowling piece in his hands. St. Vincent exchanged a comprehending glance with Adrian.

"I wouldn't have thought our incipient dandy would shoot."

"Or is his dandyism mostly for show?" Adrian countered. "On the whole, I think I'd rather he joined us."

St. Vincent nodded and stepped forward, hailing him. "Needham!"

Mr. Needham stopped dead, then turned slowly to face them. "What?" he demanded, his face still a mask of fury.

"Care to come with us? We're going to check the coverts."

Mr. Needham hesitated a moment, then nodded, and fell into step at Adrian's side. St. Vincent performed the sketchy introduction.

The next several hours passed in the pursuit of grouse, with the beating of the bushes, the sudden flap of wings, and the infrequent gunshot the only sounds. They reloaded for themselves and carried their own birds. At last, Mr. Needham, in a far better mood, took his leave of them.

Adrian and St. Vincent remained where they were for perhaps another half-hour, until Treecher, the game-keeper, found them. He regarded the new viscount, considerably put out.

"You didn't tell me as you was wishful to shoot today, m'lord."

St. Vincent checked his gun, then measured in a small amount of powder. "I only decided this morning. We stopped by your cottage, but you weren't there."

"No, m'lord. I was out with a party of tenants—as you requested."

"Excellent." St. Vincent studied his string of grouse,

then looked directly at the gamekeeper. "I understand poaching used to be quite a problem in the past."

Adrian rose abruptly and strolled away. St. Vincent's gaze remained fixed on his gamekeeper.

Treecher didn't meet that look. "Not now, m'lord, thanks to your generous offer."

"In fact," St. Vincent continued as if there hadn't been an interruption, "I have been informed you were dismissed from my cousin's service for that very crime."

Treecher's complexion paled. "It weren't for myself, m'lord."

"Wasn't it? I don't think I'd have blamed you if it had been. For whom, then?"

"Mr. Kelling, as was butler at the Grange a'fore Mr. Hodgkens."

"Yes, I remember. Where is he?"

"In one of the cottages, m'lord." Treecher shuffled his feet, uncomfortable. "His pension weren't enough for him to get along on. Living in squalor, he is, and that sick as is pitiful to see. Since His Lordship didn't shoot none, I didn't think he'd miss the stray pigeon or rabbit. But he did."

The venom in the man's tone didn't surprise St. Vincent in the least. He drew a deep breath. "What would you have done if my cousin had not died?"

Treecher kicked at a broken twig. "I don't know, m'lord."

"It would not have been easy for you?" he pursued, relentless.

"No, m'lord." Treecher looked up at last. "I'm an honest man, m'lord, what was driven to desperate measures. But not murder, if that's what you're a-hinting at."

"It's not. Very well, then. I already told you any tenant on this estate is welcome to whatever game he can get. That goes for you and any of the other workers, as well."

Treecher eyed him, his expression uncertain. "Aye,

144

m'lord. And me job?"

"I suggest you keep doing it—with care. We can't have the tenants firing on each other by accident, can we?"

"No, m'lord." He sounded a trifle dazed.

"You may begin by taking these birds and giving them to whoever needs them most."

"Aye, m'lord." He accepted the birds and stared at them, uncertain.

"Go along then. You will remain in my employ unless there is some *just* cause to let you go." Pointedly, St. Vincent turned his back on the man and checked his gun. After a long minute, he heard Treecher's retreating footsteps.

"He probably can't believe his luck." Adrian, grinning, strolled up.

St. Vincent looked after the gamekeeper as he disappeared through the underbrush. "Damn my cousin," he breathed. He rammed his loader down the barrel of his fowling gun. "And damn what he has done to this place."

"I rather think your wish concerning the late viscount will have been granted," Adrian said, solemn. "I—"

A muffled shot sounded from behind them, and something whistled past St. Vincent's ear. A number of soft thuds announced the entry of a round of shots into an elm, directly behind where his head had been only a moment before.

Chapter 12

The ricocheting explosion of the gunshot almost over her head brought Lizzie, who had at last escaped the Blue Salon, to an abrupt halt. She ducked low and shouted: "There are people here!"

Some distance away, someone crashed through the underbrush. Lizzie sprang to her feet and started in pursuit, then drew to a halt, scanning the wood. She couldn't make out anyone. Whoever it was must have been horrified to realize he might have hit a person. That, of course, and afraid of getting caught out in such criminal carelessness. She turned back, and, shielding her eyes, searched for the place where only a minute before St. Vincent had stood with her brother.

Slowly, the viscount rose from his crouch. Adrian did likewise, and turned to examine the holes that peppered the tree trunk just behind their heads.

Lizzie ran up to them. "There's some idiot out here with a gun!"

"I'd noticed," St. Vincent remarked dryly. "I don't suppose you saw who it was?"

"No. One of the tenants, most like. They came very close to killing you." She ran a finger over the holes in the tree, and, to her consternation, found her hand trembled.

"They didn't, though." He caught her hand in his.

"Did it frighten you?"

"Of course not!" She pulled free. "Lord, what sort of milk-and-water miss do you think I am?" She turned away, back toward the house. The other two fell into step with her. After a moment, she added, in a tight voice: "You really can't get yourself killed in some silly accident when there's no heir to Ashfield Grange, you know."

Silence followed her words for a very long time. Then: "No, I suppose not," St. Vincent mused. "What a frightful prospect lies ahead for me."

A slight smile tugged at the corners of her reluctant lips. "What would happen to the estate if you died without an heir?"

Frederick considered. "I'm not certain. I believe I may break the entail, and will the property as I wish."

"Then if I were you, I would do so at once."

"Perhaps I shall. Though I have no immediate intention of following my cousin to the grave. Perhaps I should assign someone to help our good Treecher with the tenants. I don't want that little bit of carelessness repeated."

As they continued, he told her of the gamekeeper's explanation for having been fired. "Yet I cannot believe either Kelling or Treecher guilty of his murder," he finished.

"No, however justified it might have been," she agreed with a sigh. "And that leaves us back where we were. I wonder if our Mr. Coggins has spoken with Mr. Needham, yet?"

He had, but the results were not quite what Lizzie had hoped. Mr. Needham had expressed himself more than willing to accompany the Runner and either Mr. Rycroft or the dowager Lady St. Vincent into Leicester to identify the stolen reliquary. Lizzie, disgruntled by this candid willingness to help, settled down to await the results.

Not until the following evening, though, did she learn them. The shopkeeper in Leicester admitted to having had a reliquary recently, and the description might or might not fit several of the items from the collection. With regret, he informed them he was unable to furnish the direction of the man who purchased it three days before. A traveler, he believed, for he was certainly not local. He himself had obtained the box from a clergyman. A Catholic gentleman, who had prized the reliquary highly. No, no one local, he added, all smiling apologies for not being more helpful. If he again encountered either the priest or the purchaser, he promised, he would obtain their directions and notify Bow Street at once.

"And o'course, there's no saying as this here reliquary was ever in the late viscount's possession," Mr. Coggins added darkly as he finished his recitation to St. Vincent.

Lizzie groaned. "Did you accomplish nothing?"

The Runner regarded her with a pained expression. "For all we knows, Missy, that there box might have been brought to that shop with the hopes that His Lordship might buy it to *add* to his others."

Lizzie nodded, not at all pleased.

Mr. Coggins took his leave, and St. Vincent and Lizzie traversed the halls to the Green Salon where the others would be gathering for dinner. As he opened the door, a man's deep voice reached them.

"It will be the perfect day, with luck, Miss Ashfield." Mr. Burnett turned as they entered. He stood at once, and made an elegant leg. "Miss Carstairs. St. Vincent. I have called to invite you all to join a hunt on the morrow."

Georgiana tossed her head, setting her golden curls bouncing. "I shall be delighted to ride, even if the others do not."

"Why shouldn't we?" St. Vincent strolled to the side table and poured glasses of wine, which he handed to the others.

Mr. Burnett accepted one, then directed a deprecatory smile at the dowager. "There is no disrespect meant to your husband, I assure you."

148

"I never thought—that is—" Soft color flooded that lady's pale cheeks. "Of course you must hunt, if that is your wish. All of you."

"Then we accept your invitation. Ah, there you are," St. Vincent added as Adrian entered. "There is to be a hunt tomorrow."

A slight smile touched Adrian's lips. "It's bound to be safer than shooting," he agreed.

Mr. Burnett looked up from his wine. "What do you mean?"

"Some careless fool came within a few inches of hitting me this morning," St. Vincent said with studied casualness. "It was of no great moment, merely somewhat startling. It is not likely to happen again."

Mr. Burnett's brow snapped down. "Poachers?"

The viscount nodded. "And with my full permission, at that. Dear me, I have no one to blame but myself."

Hodgkens entered to announce dinner, and St. Vincent invited Mr. Burnett to join them. That gentleman declined, with many thanks, saying he was pledged for a card party and would already be late. St. Vincent saw him to the door, then joined the others in the dining room.

Lizzie waited for him. Under cover of the first course being removed, she asked the viscount the question that had suddenly popped into her mind, and left her shivering. "What if it *wasn't* an accident this morning?" she whispered.

He frowned. "What else could it have been? No one has anything to gain by my death. I doubt the tenants are accustomed to shooting, that is all. They will be shortly."

Lizzie studied her plate for a moment, then raised her candid gaze to his. "You are quite certain, I suppose, you *don't* have an heir?"

"None of whom I've ever heard." He brushed the back of her hand with his finger. "You may be very certain if an heir did exist, my Cousin John would have long ago seen to *my* murder to allow someone else to inherit. Even

149

he, though, recognized the need to have an Ashfield at the Grange."

Lizzie accepted this, and fell silent.

In the morning, they breakfasted at a time when the servants were barely up and about. Their mounts were brought round, and long before eight they set forth for the home of Squire Stellings, the local hunting master.

Georgiana engaged Adrian in polite conversation, and Lizzie fell back beside St. Vincent. His attention remained far from her, though. He gazed out over the land—his land. There was a new set to his shoulders, Lizzie noted. Pride, that's what it was. It showed in every line of his body, in his expression, even in his eyes. This was *his* estate.

Her brow lowered, thoughtful. How long had this sense of possessiveness existed? As a child growing up here, he would never have expected to inherit. But about what did he think as he saw his cousin's sons die of childhood diseases, one by one, until no more were born? Did he begin to hope—

Lizzie broke off that thought in disgust. To think, even for one moment, that Frederick might actually have *killed* someone for the sake of the estate was unworthy of her. And of him.

They rounded a curve in the lane and came in sight of a lone rider ahead of them. As they trotted closer, Lizzie recognized Mr. Needham.

He turned, drew in rein, and greeted them warmly. With very little effort, he maneuvered his horse so that he rode beside Georgiana. The girl lowered her gaze, steadfastly not looking at him. Adrian dropped back, allowing them to converse in private.

Lizzie frowned at her brother in reproof, and urged her own horse forward. If either of these two said anything of interest, she wanted to know. Georgiana no longer seemed upset by Mr. Needham's presence—but neither did she flirt with him. Instead, they spoke in low, even tones.

Their conversation, much to her disgust, covered only the merest commonplaces; she gave up eavesdropping long before they entered the gates of the sprawling Stellings estate. Lizzie rode moodily down the drive, but her ill humor vanished as she caught sight of the other riders who gathered near the stableyard. She could not remain depressed with a hunt in the offing.

Mr. Burnett waved, then detached himself from the others and headed toward them. "I'm glad you were able to join us," he called. "Come, St. Vincent. Have you met the master, yet? Mr. Carstairs? Allow me to introduce you." He took the two gentlemen under his wing.

Mr. Needham turned to Georgiana. "Will you ride with me?" he asked.

"Not if you intend to retire after the second fence and leave me alone."

Mr. Needham flushed. "My boots—"

"No one cares a fig if your boots become muddied."

"*I* care!"

Georgiana shook her head. She urged her chestnut gelding forward and joined a group of young people. After a moment, Mr. Needham followed.

Mr. Burnett rode up to Lizzie, but his frowning gaze followed the couple. He sat in silence for a minute.

"Is something wrong?" Lizzie asked.

He shook his head. "Forgive me. I don't quite trust him."

"Mr. Needham?" She bristled, all attention. "Why?"

"I just wonder how ardent his attentions would be to her if he thought she wasn't an heiress."

"She isn't," Lizzie responded. "If anyone is counting on her inheriting that collection of her father's, they are fair and far out. It was purchased with the proceeds from the estate, at its expense. It will be awarded to St. Vincent."

Mr. Burnett nodded. "I'm glad, for his sake. I wonder if someone ought to drop a hint in Needham's ear?"

Lizzie grinned. "Go right ahead. But I thought his own

fortune sufficient to permit him a poorly dowered bride."

"It might be."

They fell silent, but before it could become awkward, the houndsman came forth with his pack, and their thoughts took another, and all-consuming, direction.

They returned from the hunt tired but much refreshed. Mr. Needham, true to his reputation, had dropped at once to the back. Lizzie had no idea when he left the others, but would have been much surprised to hear he had jumped as much as a single fence.

She, on the other hand, had enjoyed every one of them. The exercise had done her a world of good, clearing her mind, and Patrick had behaved just as he ought, only balking at one stone wall. Her only regret was that she couldn't bring Cerb with her. She'd make it up to him that afternoon with a long walk through the parklands.

Mr. Burnett, much to Georgiana's obvious pleasure, accompanied them back to the house. They turned their horses over to their grooms in the stable, and started along the shrub-lined path toward the drive. Adrian remained in the cobbled yard, feeling his mount's near front tendon and discussing a possible poultice with St. Vincent's groom.

"I should be getting home," Mr. Burnett murmured, but his gaze rested on Georgiana.

"Not until you have paid your respects to Mamma. She will so like to hear about the hunt."

The butler admitted them to the house, and Georgiana paused only to hand him her whip and gloves. Mr. Burnett removed his hat, and Georgiana led him inexorably away.

Hodgkens laid the hat aside and turned to the viscount. "Mr. Winfield has called, my lord. He is awaiting you in the library."

St. Vincent stiffened. "Is he? Has he been here long?"

"A little more than half an hour, my lord."

St. Vincent nodded. "Then I shall not keep him waiting a moment longer. Lizzie, do you care to change, or

152

will you come with me?"

There was no need for an answer. She cast him a derisive look and led the way down the hall.

When she opened the door, the vicar was kneeling on the floor, shaking out a book. He stood abruptly, dropping the volume, and stared at her in horror.

Lizzie directed her appraising scrutiny over her sapphire blue habit. "Dreadful, isn't it?" she said cheerfully. "I always seem to come home covered in twigs and mud and horse hairs."

"No, you—it's quite delightful, I'm sure." The vicar collected the book, replaced it on the shelf, then stood.

"What may I do for you?" St. Vincent inquired. He gestured toward a chair, invitingly.

The vicar declined. "I only came to see if you had as yet discovered my sermon."

St. Vincent glanced at Lizzie. "No, we haven't. But since you are here, I suggest we subject this room to a thorough search. Where have you already looked?"

"No!" Mr. Winfield swallowed. "There—there's no need. I've looked everywhere, now. He—he must have placed it in another room. It's really no matter, no matter at all. Nothing you should concern yourselves over. I shall simply write another, and be done with it." He managed a shaky smile. "I shall probably do better with it this time, anyway. Now, you must excuse me. My housekeeper will be expecting me back for nuncheon." He bolted to the long French windows, unlocked them, and scuttled outside.

Lizzie stared after him in silence for a long moment. "Whatever it is he's looking for," she said at last, "he doesn't want us to find it."

"That thought had occurred to me. You do not believe it to be a sermon, then?"

She cast him a withering look. "He acted as if we had just caught him in some disreputable act."

He smiled. "I don't think I believe him, either. Shall we find out?"

153

Lizzie turned slowly about, scanning the innumerable volumes that filled the shelves lining the walls. "It would help if we knew where he really *had* searched."

"I don't think we can expect him to tell us, somehow. Shall we begin?"

A slight cough caught their attention, and they turned to see Hodgkens standing in the doorway. "Her Ladyship's compliments, my lord, and will you and Miss Carstairs join her for nuncheon?"

St. Vincent muttered something under his breath, which Lizzie, much to her regret, couldn't make out.

"I'd forgotten. Burnett is here. Tender our apologies, Hodgkens, and we'll be down as soon as we've changed."

Less than half an hour later, Lizzie ran lightly down the main stairs to the hall, dressed now in a simple walking gown suitable to sustain the onslaught of dust promised for the afternoon. St. Vincent, to her amazement, was before her, looking no less his usual polished self for having hurried. She'd always known him to be a capable gentleman. With a smiling apology for holding up the meal, she made her way to the sideboard and made her selections.

Mr. Burnett appeared to be at pains to make himself even more agreeable than usual. Lizzie's suspicions flared at once, only to vanish beneath the obvious explanation. Georgiana positively bubbled in her pleasure at his solicitous and wholly admiring presence at her side.

Adrian sat in silence at the far end of the table, watching the others, somehow detached. He'd become more solitary of late, Lizzie realized, and that thought disturbed her. If he weren't careful, he'd fit too well into the almost monastic life of an Oxford don, and bury himself in his books, his reasearch and learned writings. He needed someone to keep him alive and laughing. She cast a speculative look toward Georgiana, and shook her head, abandoning that idea.

"Unhappy reflections?" St. Vincent murmured.

154

Lizzie shook her head, for once not wanting to share her thoughts with him. Marriage wasn't for everybody. Not for Adrian, not willingly for St. Vincent. And not for her, either. So why did she feel depressed?

They finished eating and Lady St. Vincent rose. Mr. Burnett followed suit at once, and thanked her for her kind invitation. He took his leave of the assembled company, and Georgiana offered to walk him to the stable. As an afterthought, she included Adrian in the suggestion as well. He declined, and disappeared in the direction of the estate room with the expressed intention of planning possible winter crops.

St. Vincent watched the others depart, then offered Lizzie his arm. After a moment's hesitation, she took it. She'd thought it great fun when he'd treated her like a lady when she was still, for all intents and purposes, in the schoolroom. Even the last time they met, for Augusta's wedding, when she'd been only fifteen. He'd been gallant, and she thought it a great game. So why now, when she was of an age to merit such considerations, did they upset her? Because his manner remained avuncular, but she was now an adult?

They entered the library and she pulled free, deciding this matter needed further consideration.

She dove into the search with determination, glad to have something practical with which to occupy her mind. It wasn't like her to dwell on imponderables. She liked action, and she liked to have things obvious. Ferreting out a murderer suited her taste to perfection—much more so than wondering why St. Vincent's company, which before she had enjoyed wholly, now made her self-conscious and left her feeling gauche. She didn't like that sensation.

More than three hours passed in the fruitless search. Lizzie at last shoved the final volume back into place, then stood and glared about the room in disgust.

"What a waste of a day!" she declared.

St. Vincent frowned. "We're done here. Run along

155

and play. You've earned it."

She glared at him. "Lord, Frederick, I'm not a child."

"No, you're not," he snapped. Abruptly, he turned on his heel and left the room.

Lizzie stared after him, startled. Was that the matter? She'd grown up—and he felt he'd lost the "niece" he had long indulged? The worst of it was she didn't want things to go back to the way they had always been between them. What she was beginning to want from him was the one thing he would never give. He reserved his admiration for worldly ladies and avoided unfledged chits untutored in the art of dalliance. Depressed, she went upstairs, collected a thick cloak, and searched out Cerberus.

She discovered him in the estate room, his head resting forlornly on his front paws as he watched Adrian work. He leapt to his feet at her entrance, greeting her with yips of delight mingled with a growling insistence that she devote some time to his entertainment.

Adrian laid down his pen and regarded the hound with fond exasperation. "He *was* being quiet."

"Don't worry, I'm taking him out." To her surprise, she almost snapped at her brother. Things had her more upset than she realized. This would never do!

She set off for a long, rousing walk, hoping to work off her ill temper and unsettled emotions.

Her steps took them through the forest beyond the Dower House, and only when she stumbled over an unseen branch did she realize the light was failing. The sun must have sunk behind the line of poplars long ago, for dusk gathered about her, making huge shadows of the shrubs that lined the path. Recalling Cerb from where he burrowed after a rabbit, she turned and began the long tramp back to the house.

It would be quicker, of course, if she could find the short cut that led through the clearing by the folly. After a bit of investigation, which involved cutting across the Dower House gardens, she found an arched entryway similar to that on the Grange side. She set off through this, whistling slightly off key.

Darkness surrounded her by the time she reached the clearing, but she didn't let that bother her. She'd been down this path any number of times; it would be impossible to get lost.

As she started past the folly, though, a raised voice stopped her and she glanced at the structure.

"How dare you?" Georgiana cried.

A muffled voice answered, and Lizzie sighed. Why on earth did Georgiana continue to meet Mr. Needham in the folly? Really, she was getting quite tiresome with her dramatics.

"No! You cannot say that!" the girl cried.

That gave Lizzie pause. She honestly sounded distressed—possibly afraid. Without compunction, she headed to the folly window.

"I know you don't want to believe it, Miss Ashfield, but he stole it from me!" a deep male voice answered.

"He paid you—"

"One tenth of what it was worth, as he knew well at the time. He was fully aware I needed the money or I never would have been induced to part with it in the first place. It belonged to my father! He cheated me."

"Is that why you murdered him?"

Silence answered her. At last, in an odd, cracking voice, the man breathed: "What do you mean?"

Lizzie silenced Cerb's low growl, then stood on tiptoe. She could barely discern the figures in the darkness inside. They stood several feet apart, which relieved her. If he'd had his hands about the girl's neck, Lizzie wasn't certain how she would have intervened.

"I know you were at the Grange the night my papa was murdered. Was that why you came? To demand more money from him? Did he refuse, and did you kill him with that sword stick Cousin Frederick gave him? Don't try to deny you were there. I saw you! It was well after Mr. Needham left. I suppose Cousin Frederick had gone already, too. Is that when you killed Papa,

157

Mr. Burnett?"

The sturdy shadow that was the man turned away from Georgiana, and he seemed to droop. "He was dead when I got there," he said at last. He sounded calm—drained, really, as if he had kept that knowledge to himself for too long.

"A likely story! You may be sure I shall inform that Runner of the matter at once."

"Miss Ashfield—Georgiana—" He broke off and ran an agitated hand through his hair. "Do you honestly believe I killed him? What chance would I have of getting my money, then? As much as I hate to admit it, getting my hands on the ready is of far more import to me than some paltry revenge."

Georgiana pressed her palms over her face. "Then who did kill him?" she cried.

Mr. Burnett hesitated, then caught her wrists gently. "For your sake, my dearest Miss Ashfield, I hope that can be determined soon."

A shaky sob escaped the girl, and Lizzie groaned inwardly. Of all the lachrymose wet gooses—! Didn't she know most gentlemen detested a weeping female?

Mr. Burnett, though, did not appear to be of their number. Tenderly, he gathered the girl into his arms, whispering softly into her ear. She drew back, murmuring something of which the only word Lizzie caught was "improper." Lizzie couldn't agree more.

Mr. Burnett caught her hand and raised it to his lips. "Forgive me. In my present circumstances, I have nothing to offer you. My desire to comfort you overcame prudence."

Lizzie didn't know whether to be glad or sorry the darkness obscured his expression from her. Georgiana, though, drew back, and a half-sigh, half-giggle escaped her.

"I—I must be getting back." With a last, tentative glance over her shoulder at him, she fled from the folly and across the clearing, moving with ease by the light of the crescent moon that rose above the trees.

Mr. Burnett strode after her, but slowed to a halt a half-dozen paces from the structure. The dim glow fell clearly on his smiling countenance. Whistling a reel, he turned on his heel and walked with a springing step in the direction of the Dower House.

Chapter 13

Lizzie remained where she stood, puzzled, her hand gripping Cerb's nose to prevent him from barking. The animal set up a low growl, and hastily she retreated with him toward the pond.

Did Georgiana make a habit of accusing everybody of murdering her father? That might be her way of trying to help. If she expected an instant confession, though, she had been sadly disappointed on both occasions. Mr. Needham had been furious. And Mr. Burnett—? Her brow creased. He'd been distressed. But whether it was because Georgiana thought him capable of murder or for some other reason, she couldn't be certain.

She'd have to find out which piece in the collection the old viscount had purchased—at apparently a shockingly low price—from Mr. Burnett, and when. It would also be interesting to discover if it were among the items missing from the collection. Would he, she wondered, try to steal it back since basically it had been stolen from him in the first place?

She peeked around the edge of the folly, but Mr. Burnett was no longer in sight. He must have left a horse somewhere; it was too far to walk back to his own home. She eased her grip on the protesting Cerb, and the hound fell silent. Together, they started for the path Georgiana had taken, back to the Grange.

A man *might* kill another if he thought he'd been cheated. The proper procedure would have been to challenge him to a duel, of course. But duels were illegal, and she had a shrewd notion the old viscount would have refused. If Mr. Burnett had only just learned of the viscount's villainy, and gone to him in a passion, he might well have struck out in fury. Definitely, she needed to learn about this particular item, and the sooner the better.

She placed no real reliance on Georgiana's carrying out her threat to tell Mr. Coggins. Therefore, she decided to do it for her. Such an interesting bit of information should not be kept to herself—particularly if there were any chance it could help Frederick. She proceeded with a jaunty step.

She found St. Vincent in the library, frowning at the cases of books. "Still searching for that sermon?" she asked.

He turned thoughtful eyes on her. "What have you been up to?"

Cerb flopped down before the hearth, panting contentedly. Lizzie turned a fond eye on him. "He really behaved quite well today. Didn't you, Cerb?"

"Lizzie—," the viscount began, his tone threatening.

She relented. Briefly, she told him about Mr. Burnett and whatever piece of the collection he claimed the viscount had swindled out of him.

St. Vincent listened, and the fine creases in his brow deepened. "You think this is really the solution?"

"It seems the most likely, doesn't it? I never could believe Mr. Needham murdered your cousin just because he wouldn't let him marry Georgiana." She made a face. "Who in their right mind would murder for such a paltry reason?"

"True. Love is certainly an overrated emotion, is it not?" He turned away. "I take it you have acquitted Mr. Needham of having any possible monetary motive? You are quite certain his own fortune has not been greatly exaggerated, or perhaps lost?"

"If Mr. Needham counted on marriage to Georgiana to save his finances, he'd have ditched himself."

"I believe you are right. He would hardly murder the one man he thought stood in his way unless he were certain of the fortune attached." He smiled suddenly. "It seems as if you may have discovered the solution after all, my dear Lizzie."

She smiled. "I told you I'd solve the problem. Shall we tell Mr. Coggins about Mr. Burnett?"

"Let us first consult with Mr. Rycroft," St. Vincent decided. "It will make a greater impression on him if we can identify the object, the exact price paid, and its ostensible value."

Pleased with this suggestion, Lizzie headed for the estate room. They found the bailiff hard at work, with Adrian at his side carefully scrutinizing several closely scrawled sheets.

Mr. Rycroft looked up at their entry, then rose. "You must think me a poor excuse for an estate agent for not long ago having implemented ideas similar to those Mr. Carstairs has suggested."

Adrian glanced up, embarrassed. "Why should you have thought of them? This form of agriculture is still considered experimental, though we have had great success with it. With a bit of hard work, we can have the fields ready for spring planting. We even might be able to get a crop from your succession houses, if we fertilize properly."

"Good work, Adrian. What will we need to do?" St. Vincent, his original purpose in coming to the estate room apparently forgotten, joined Adrian in the examination of the sheets.

Lizzie let out a sigh of exasperation. She couldn't blame him, of course. The estate was his ruling passion. But he seemed to forget he was still under suspicion of murder for that very reason.

"You would have been justified in seeking legal action

against the late viscount, my lord," Mr. Rycroft declared.

"He probably should have." Lizzie picked up a list of farming equipment. A description of necessary repairs followed almost every item. She dropped it back on the desk. "Would it have done any good?"

Mr. Rycroft hesitated. "I don't know. The estate *could* have been removed from the viscount's control, but there would still have been the problem with money. Every year we receive less, as the farms produce so little the tenants are unable to pay."

Lizzie set her jaw. If St. Vincent *had* murdered his cousin, she really couldn't have blamed him. If— Good Lord, did she actually entertain that as a possibility? *Could* Frederick be guilty of murder?

To her further dismay, she found her normally logical thinking severely impaired. Despite the motive and evidence, she simply could not believe Frederick capable of so fundamental a wrong. Besides, she had another candidate for her villain. That only left her to wonder whether Mr. Burnett, as well as having both a motive and the opportunity, had it in him to commit murder in a fit of anger.

She had best concentrate on this possibility. "Do you know which pieces of the collection came from where?" she asked abruptly, and somewhat incoherently.

Mr. Rycroft blinked. "Oh," he said after a moment. "He kept records, with a description of the pieces and a record of the transaction."

That was what she wanted. Lizzie nodded. "I need to know everything about the piece he purchased from Mr. Burnett."

"From—" He broke off, frowning. "I'll have to look that up. Which item was it, do you know?"

Lizzie shook her head, and with an audible sigh, Mr. Rycroft went to a shelf and pulled out a thick record book. "He listed them by item, not seller," he said, somewhat pointedly.

"There are only ninety-seven items. It shouldn't be

too hard."

Mr. Rycroft directed a half-comical look at her, and returned his attention to the book. "Yes, here it is. I thought it would be recent. A chalice, Italian, from the fifteenth century. Purchased at the beginning of September from Mr. W. Burnett, for five hundred pounds."

"How much is it worth, though?" Lizzie peered over his shoulder as he closed the book.

"I must assume five hundred pounds."

"Could it be worth more?"

Mr. Rycroft replaced the book carefully on the shelf. "I am not an expert on art objects, Miss Carstairs. It conceivably could be worth more. It could also be worth less."

"I believe I shall take it to Leicester tomorrow and have it appraised." St. Vincent joined them. "Which number is it?"

"I'll get it for you." The agent fumbled among his keys.

"No need. Where is that book where you recorded the numbers?" He picked a small volume from the table, glanced at it, then found another. He leafed through the pages until he came to the last with writing. For a long moment he frowned at it. "You were wrong, Lizzie. There are only ninety-five items listed here."

"There can't be. I distinctly remember ninety-seven." She peered over his shoulder.

"Ninety-five?" Mr. Rycroft, too, studied the book. "He's right, Miss Carstairs. That's odd. I, also, had the number ninety-seven in my mind. I wonder what made us think there were more?"

"I counted them," Lizzie persisted.

He frowned. "You also numbered the tags. You must have made up two more than there really were, and gotten confused."

"I don't get confused," Lizzie muttered, but to herself. She pulled the book where she could see it, also. "Here's

Mr. Burnett's—number seventy-six. Fifteenth century Italian chalice, five hundred pounds. Seventy-six," she repeated, and headed out the door.

St. Vincent caught up with her as she strode down the hall. "Upset, Lizzie?"

"I don't make mistakes." She looked up at him, frowning. "I was *certain* there were ninety-seven pieces."

He patted her shoulder, then withdrew his hand abruptly. "Old age, Lizzie. It plays havoc with the memory."

She didn't smile at his sally. It was almost as if she and St. Vincent stood on opposite sides of a windowpane. She could see him clearly, yet there was this unprecedented obstruction that kept them from interacting in their old, comfortable manner. He resented her growing up.

In the storeroom, they quickly discovered Item Number Seventy-six, one Italian Chalice, right in its place. Lizzie turned it over, subjecting it to a thorough examination.

"Is something the matter?" St. Vincent turned from the wall where the silver and gold serving pieces were arranged.

Lizzie handed him the chalice. "It just doesn't look worth committing murder for."

A deep chuckle escaped him. "Disappointed, Lizzie? But remember, it wasn't the chalice but the money—or perhaps the principle."

"True." She brightened. "Will you really go into Leicester tomorrow?"

"I think so. And I will take Coggins with me."

She brightened. "You *do* think it possible, then?"

"I do. Georgiana saw Mr. Burnett approach the house, and he was convinced this was worth ten times more than my cousin gave him for it. If he really is in straitened circumstances, he might have come here in a fury. My cousin's endearing graces might well have led to murder."

Lizzie watched him lock the storeroom behind them.

165

"Going to Leicester is really a formality then, isn't it? It doesn't matter what the piece is *actually* worth—only what he believes."

"Yes. I think your Mr. Coggins is going to be very pleased."

"Not likely. He has his heart set on arresting you, remember."

The following evening, Lizzie joined St. Vincent and Mr. Coggins in the library upon their return. The dealer in Leicester, the viscount told her, asserted that the piece was worth no more than three hundred pounds, which price Mr. Burnett had paid him for it last August.

"Then why—" Lizzie broke off, assimilating that information. "Mr. Burnett said he'd *inherited* it!"

"One cannot believe everything someone says." St. Vincent shook his head, mocking. "I never thought you to be so trusting, Lizzie."

She glared at him. "I'm not. I'd say Mr. Burnett is trying to swindle Georgiana!"

Frederick nodded. "So it would seem. But that also removes his motive for murder."

Lizzie stared at him, crestfallen. The next moment, though, her fighting spirit resurfaced. "Unless he tried his swindle on your cousin. What would have happened, then?"

St. Vincent raised a questioning eyebrow and looked at Coggins.

The Runner, who had remained silent throughout the recitation of the day's gleanings, leaned back in his chair before the fire. "Well, now, Missy, that's a right good question, that is. Would His Lordship take it unkindly-like? Enough to maybe attack Mr. Burnett?"

"I'd say it was very likely."

Coggins leaned back in his chair and nodded meditatively. "No telling what these here collectors will be a-doing. Fanatics, they are. I remembers a case a half-dozen years or so ago, wheres some young cull goes and tries to sell a faked painting to an expert." He shook his head

166

reminiscently. "Spotted it at once, of course. Fellow was transported."

"A lesson to us all," St. Vincent said dryly. "But as far as we know, my cousin was not offered a fake."

"No, there was nothing fake about that chalice," the Runner admitted. "Which leaves us back right where we was, begging Your Lordship's pardon."

Right back where they were. Lizzie looked from the Runner's skeptical face to St. Vincent's frowning one. Deep lines creased his brow and etched about his eyes. She had seldom seen Frederick worried in the past. It distressed her, made her want to set everything to rights for him. And so far, she had failed.

"I suppose you see this whole episode as my desperately trying to throw false trails at you," the viscount declared with uncharacteristic heat.

"Well, now, my lord, it *does* seem to have led us nowheres, as you might say."

"Damn you," he said, with relative calm, and strode out of the room.

Coggins threw an anxious glance at Lizzie. "What my sister would say," he muttered, "if anyone was to go and use such language in front of her Sarah or Janey, I just don't know."

Lizzie glared at him. "Why don't you make yourself useful and figure out what Mr. Winfield keeps searching for in here?" she demanded, and stormed out.

It was time and past she changed for dinner. With Lady St. Vincent always so neatly turned out, and Georgiana developing a flair for elegance, it would never do for her to appear— She stopped dead in her tracks. What in heaven's name was she thinking? Why *shouldn't* she appear as she normally did? What was wrong with it?

Everything, an irritating voice in the back of her mind answered. St. Vincent admired attractive women—not ramshackle hoydens who behaved and dressed as if they were brought up in a stable.

That stopped her. Did she want him to *admire* her—or

167

merely accept the fact she was no longer a child? She might as well find out. That was one question she could settle, at least.

In her chamber, she searched among her few gowns, and finally settled on an amber crepe that her sister Helena had almost ceased to hope she would ever wear. A pelerine of blond lace cascaded off her shoulders, almost reaching her elbows. A matching edging peeped up from the low-scooped neckline.

The maid, encouraged by Lizzie's unprecedented interest in her appearance, dared to unbraid the thick brown hair and brush it up to the crown of her head. From there, under Lizzie's critical eye, she arranged several ringlets to fall down her back and teased the hair about her face into a halo. Lizzie drew the line at ribands or artificial roses, but when she at last regarded her reflection in the mirror, she barely recognized herself.

Well, why shouldn't she try something new? Her sister Augusta always enjoyed looking her best. Gussie was a beauty, of course, which Lizzie was not. She made a face at herself and strode determinedly out of the room. What did that matter? She was Lizzie.

She reached the hall, started for the Green Salon, but stopped as the butler hailed her.

"Miss! Begging your pardon, but His Lordship's compliments, and will you join him in the library?"

A flutter of nerves attacked her stomach as she reversed directions and headed for the other corridor. What a—a ninny she was being! At least she could judge his reaction to her appearance without a crowd of others about. It might be less embarrassing that way if he disapproved.

But he wasn't alone. He stood beside the fireplace with Mr. Coggins, who broke off in midsentence as Lizzie entered the room.

"Ah, there you are now, Missy." The Runner threw her a smile of triumph. "You see? I did just what you asked me to do."

168

Lizzie blinked. "You mean—"

"I found me a hollow panel, I did. I'll wager you weren't expecting nothing like that, now were you?"

"No, I don't think I was." She hurried forward, eager. "What's in it?"

"Now, that's the rub, Missy."

"He means we haven't yet discovered the opening mechanism," St. Vincent stuck in.

She looked up to find Frederick's gaze resting on her, a gleam in his eyes that had nothing to do with their discovery. Emotion surged through her, startling and more than a bit frightening. To her further amazement, she found she liked it.

The next moment, his brow snapped down and he turned away. Well, she had her answer. He found her attractive—but not up to snuff. And yes, it mattered to her. Not that it would make any difference. Appearances were not enough where Frederick was concerned. He preferred his ladies experienced and flirtatious—which she could never be.

"Any suggestions, Missy?"

The Runner's words recalled her, and with an effort, she returned her attention to the matter at hand. Lord, here she was faced with a secret panel, yet she would rather sort out this emotional muddle.

Forcing it to the back of her mind, she eyed the carved oak paneling. Obligingly, St. Vincent sounded the boards for her. One, indeed, echoed as if a hollow space lay beyond.

"It would have to be something that could be found easily," Lizzie decided, entering into the spirit of the hunt. "Have you tried all these little knobs and curlicues?"

"We had just begun."

"How far down does it go?" She knelt and tapped near the floor, but could detect no difference in sound. "There must be something in there! It certainly isn't empty. Do you suppose we'll find a body?"

"Bloodthirsty wench." St. Vincent poked at what might have been a cherub but more closely resembled a gargoyle. When that didn't work, he reached for a carved pineapple.

An eerie creaking made Lizzie jump. She stood back, watching in fascination as a small cupboard door opened up just below eye level.

"It's only a *little* one!" Her face fell. "I was hoping for a priest's hole, at the least."

"Or maybe a secret stair that leads to the dungeons?" St. Vincent suggested.

Lizzie brightened. "Is there a dungeon?"

"No," he admitted.

She threw him a darkling glance. "Well, we shall just have to make do with what we have. Though a secret stair *would* have been something like. How does this work?" She peered inside, trying to see the working mechanism.

"I think what is in here is of more importance." St. Vincent set her firmly aside and reached in. He brought out only a small handful of papers.

"No stolen jewels." Lizzie sighed. "Really, such a promising start as a secret compartment, yet it turns out to be nothing but a big disappointment."

St. Vincent groped for his quizzing glass and read the top sheet through the magnifying lens. After a moment, he set it aside and studied the next. "Well, well. The old dog," he murmured. "Or do I mean 'young' one?"

Lizzie looked up, hopeful. "Have you found something?"

"I have indeed. Letters."

"Is that all?"

"From Mr. Winfield, to a certain married lady in the district. They appear to be of a highly eloquent and poetic nature—though indiscreet, under the circumstances."

"Are they?" Lizzie reached for one, but St. Vincent, by virtue of his superior height, removed them from her reach.

"I think not, my dear. I shall spare your blushes. Now

170

we know what he has been trying to find in this room."

"And what he didn't want *us* to find," Lizzie agreed, though a trifle wistful. She *would* like to know what they said.

St. Vincent examined the next and his eyebrows rose. "I believe I have wronged our good vicar by thinking him paltry. I wonder how my dear cousin got hold of these?" He turned to the next letter with verve.

Coggins coughed. "I believe, m'lord, that is less important-like than whether His Lordship was blackmailing Mr. Winfield."

"Of course he was," Lizzie declared scornfully. "Why else would he have kept them?"

St. Vincent nodded. "I quite agree. But what form would it take? He may have been greedy when it came to his collection, but demanding money—" He shook his head, and his expression was far from pleasant. "I believe it would have taken a far subtler—and crueler—form."

Chapter 14

St. Vincent stretched his long legs and shifted his position in the uncomfortable chair. Despite the bright morning sun, little light penetrated into the study at the vicarage. Mr. Coggins, his expression set in grim determination, sat opposite him. Neither had spoken since the austere Mrs. Dunstan ushered them in fifteen minutes before.

Restless, St. Vincent rose and crossed to the bookshelves, where he subjected the volumes of sermons to an unenthusiastic scrutiny through his quizzing glass. Behind him, the door opened and someone hesitated on the threshold. Slowly, deliberately, he turned around.

The Reverend Mr. Winfield peered from one to the other of his visitors. "My lord? Mr. Coggins? My housekeeper said you had called to see me. I'm sorry I was from home." He advanced into the room. "How may I be of service to you?"

The Runner rose. "I'd like you to answer a few questions if you don't mind, sir."

"Certainly." The vicar shivered and crossed to the fire to warm his coattails. "A raw morning," he explained with a faint smile.

"About some letters," Coggins pursued. "Written by you to a certain Mrs. Dorothea Stellings. Wife, I believe, of Squire Stellings."

172

For a long moment, Mr. Winfield gazed at his walking stick; his knuckles whitened on it. At last, he raised his head and looked directly at the Runner. "What—what letters?"

"These." St. Vincent held out two of the sheets he had discovered in that secret compartment in the library.

Mr. Winfield made no attempt to look at them. His eyes misted with bleak hopelessness. A shattering sigh escaped him, and he sank onto the nearest chair. His cane clattered to the floor at his side, unheeded. "You found them."

A grim smile just touched Coggins's lips. "We—"

St. Vincent signaled him to silence. He took the chair across from the vicar and leaned forward. "Do you want to tell us about them?"

"You won't believe me, I know." Mr. Winfield shook his head, then lowered his face into his hands. His muffled voice could barely be heard when he forced himself to continue. "No shame whatsoever attaches to the lady. I beg of you, for her sake, do not let this come out. She must not be ruined by any touch of scandal."

"She knows nothing about this, does she?" St. Vincent asked, his tone gentle.

Mr. Winfield looked up, horror reflected on every feature. "You asked her?"

"No. It was a guess." St. Vincent rose and stared at the fire. "Forgive me, but I glanced at a few. The emotion—" He broke off.

"It was all in the letters." The vicar stared at his hands. "To act on my feelings would have been a sin against the Almighty God. To approach the lady herself, even under the guise of friendship, would have been to insult both her and her husband. Her virtue is unquestionable. So I—"

"You enacted an eloquent and romantic attachment in your mind, and expressed it through a poetic correspondence you never sent."

Mr. Winfield nodded, not looking up.

173

"How did the late viscount obtain these here letters?" Coggins asked, his tone brisk.

"He stole them. They were in a drawer—I kept it locked, of course—" He broke off, directing a nervous glance over his shoulder. "My housekeeper likes to straighten things for me, you see. But this one day, I'd been called away suddenly to a villager who had been taken ill, and I must have dropped the key. When I returned, I found it lying on my desk. The—the letters were gone. He'd called to see me, my housekeeper said—and he left after half an hour."

"How soon did he start to blackmail you?"

The vicar rubbed a trembling hand over his ashen face. "A month. For four long weeks, he let me suffer. Then he sent for me."

"And?" Coggins tapped impatient fingers on the arm of his chair.

Frederick glanced about the ancient furnishings, which could be described as adequate rather than comfortable or even homey. "He could hardly have expected to obtain money from you."

"Hardly." A shaky laugh, devoid of any humor, escaped him. "He demanded I do penance. In sackcloth and ashes. He was a sanctimonious old—" The vicar broke off, horrified by what he'd been about to say.

"In many ways, he resembled some of the less likeable of the medieval monks," St. Vincent explained to the Runner, who merely snorted. "What else did he want?"

"Services."

"What kind?" St. Vincent watched him intently. The vicar kept something back, but what— "Georgiana?" he asked, hazarding a sudden guess.

Mr. Winfield's head jerked up, his eyes wide. "How—did he—?"

"He mentioned he intended her to marry a bishop. Did he desire you to groom her for the position?"

The vicar nodded. "She has no interest in marrying a man of the cloth, though her father refused to see it." A

174

touch of wistfulness crept into his voice. "Her heart, young as it is, is set on wedding a man of fashion."

"And did you do as he ordered?" Coggins asked.

A dull flush spread across the vicar's face. "I could not permit those letters to be shown about."

"Did my cousin not guess the inevitable result of forcing you to spend time in Georgiana's company?"

"What—what do you mean?"

"That you became aware of her—er—charms?"

"It would be most improper, under any circumstances—"

St. Vincent tapped the letters. "I could not help but notice when you began to liken the divine Mrs. Stellings's dark hair to spun gold. It was Georgiana you wrote about, was it not?"

The vicar bit his lip, then slowly nodded. "Not at first. She was still in the schoolroom when I came to take up my living and met— Then one day she came to church dressed as a lady. She was only seventeen, so innocent and sweet, and she had been raised in the ways of our Lord."

"The perfect wife for a vicar," St. Vincent agreed.

Mr. Winfield looked up quickly. "She is! Only—"

"Only Mr. Burnett and Mr. Needham also noticed her, and their fashionable air and talk of London turned the poor girl's head," St. Vincent finished.

Mr. Winfield nodded mutely. "How could I approach an angel when she was so young and had no experience of any other way of life? And her father intended her for a man high up in the church. Higher than I could ever rise. He knew how I felt, and forbade me to speak to her."

"At least that freed you from teaching her to be a bishop's wife," Coggins said.

"Oh, no." The vicar's jaw clenched. "I had to go on seeing her, almost every day, and guard my feelings from her. He warned me what would happen if I engaged her affections, even inadvertently."

Coggins muttered something beneath his breath.

"What other services did His Lordship demand of you?" he asked abruptly.

"Only to pacify the tenants. They wanted repairs, reductions in their rent, but he—he made me exhort them to seek penance for desiring worldly things instead of encouraging the work of God."

"Did you believe in this 'work' of his?" St. Vincent asked, curious.

"No!" Mr. Winfield appeared to startle himself with his vehemence. "Objects of art are nothing more than worldly wealth, even if they portray heavenly images. How could I reconcile the acquisition of that when it caused such suffering?"

"Which makes this all a very tricksy case, it does, m'lord," Coggins declared in disgust as they took their leave a few minutes later. "Wasn't there no one hereabouts as had a good word to say for your cousin?"

"Not that I've ever met."

Coggins strode on in silence for several minutes. "Mind you, now, I don't know as how I believe your good vicar told us all he could, not by a long shot I don't."

"He'd hardly admit to anything worse unless we already knew about it," St. Vincent agreed. He rubbed his hand over his smooth-shaven chin. "Odd. I never would have thought Georgiana capable of inspiring such devotion. She was quite fubsy-faced when I saw her five years ago."

Coggins snorted. "She's a well-enough favored young lady. But I don't see as how *you* should be so all high and mighty pleased about the results of our little talk with Mr. Winfield. Came off sounding innocent, he did. I'd of thought you'd be wanting him to look as guilty as could be. Yet there you was, all sympathy and understanding-like."

St. Vincent shook his head. "I rather like our vicar. I can't say I'd personally hold it against anyone who saw fit to rid the world of my cousin, but the law must take its course, I suppose, and I wouldn't particularly want it to

176

take Mr. Winfield."

"He does seem a peaceable sort of gentleman. Met a fellow like him once," Coggins mused. "All nice and quiet and proper as you please, till one day he run amuck with an iron rod and bashed in the heads of his entire family."

"Delightful. Have you any more stories of a similarly edifying nature?"

"Many's the tale I could tell, m'lord. Many's the tale."

Fortunately, though, Coggins chose to keep them to himself. They traversed the remainder of the shaded path to the Grange in silence. At the library French windows, Coggins took his leave to pursue his inquiries, as he said. With a nod, he strode off in the direction of the stables.

St. Vincent, frowning, unlatched the long-paned glass door and entered. Cerb, who lay stretched out before the hearth, thumped his tail in acknowledgment, then closed his eyes once more.

Lizzie sprang up from her chair where she had awaited his return. "What did he say?"

St. Vincent poured himself a glass of wine, then settled on the sofa across from her and related the results of their morning's interview. Lizzie listened in frowning intensity, until he came to the part about the vicar's attachment to Georgiana. She broke into highly uncomplimentary laughter.

"Does *everyone* want to marry her?" she asked at last.

"Not quite everyone," St. Vincent demurred.

Lizzie cocked an eyebrow at him. "There is nothing wrong with wedding your cousin, you know. It would be quite suitable."

"You mistake. We should not suit in the least. My taste runs—in quite a different direction."

Lizzie nodded knowledgeably. "To ladies of experience. *I* know."

"The devil you do." His brow snapped down. "Where did you get that idea?"

"From you." She reached out with one toe and

177

dragged a footstool in front of her. She arranged her feet on this and grinned at him. "Don't you remember? When we were in Brussels, you were quite taken with that—"

"*Damn* my wretched tongue! You just listened, didn't you, and took it all in. I'm surprised Halliford hasn't demanded my hide!"

She tilted her head. "He might if he knew how freely you talked," she admitted.

He ran a hand through his curling blond hair, chagrined. If that didn't prove just how unsuitable a companion he was for her. . . . "The devil's in it, my girl, that I forget to guard my tongue when I'm with you. If I were to treat you as I ought—"

"It would be damnably dull." She rose abruptly and paced about the room. A crease just formed in her brow.

Of old, he recognized plans brewing behind that delightful face. "Spill it, Lizzie, what schemes are you weaving?" he demanded.

"Nothing. What do you mean?"

"That mind of yours is at work—and that invariably spells trouble for someone."

"I—not this time." She strode toward the door, but stopped just in front of it, her hand resting on the knob. Slowly, she turned back to face him.

"We found—and eliminated—a motive for Mr. Winfield to have murdered your cousin. Have we done the same for Mr. Needham and Mr. Burnett?"

"It's very possible. As you pointed out, Needham isn't likely to murder someone just because he refused permission to marry his daughter. Nor is Burnett likely to have murdered him when it was in fact *he* who was the swindler. No, the most likely reason was that my cousin caught someone in the act of stealing."

"Such as Mr. Rycroft?"

St. Vincent reached into his pocket and drew out his snuff box, giving himself a moment to consider. "The thought has crossed my mind," he admitted at last. "But

Rycroft would have been taking a terrible risk. It would have only been a matter of time before he was caught."

Lizzie stared into the fire for a long moment. "It does seem rather foolhardy, doesn't it?" She sighed. "Will you invite them all for dinner tomorrow night? I wish there were a way we might include Mr. Rycroft, too, without making him suspicious. It's a pity your cousin didn't permit him to join the family."

St. Vincent regarded her from beneath lowered brows. "I don't think I entirely trust you, my dear. What are you planning?"

"Nothing, really. I'd just like the opportunity to see them together."

"You are not to turn the meal into an inquisition."

She shook her head, and that delightfully mischievous smile flashed. "You may direct the talk," she offered magnanimously. "I just want to see their reactions when you make it clear the collection will be sold to finance improvements on the estate rather than going into Georgiana's dowry."

"That should be somewhat interesting," he agreed. "But sometimes a man just might wish to marry a lady for a reason other than money."

She threw him a scornful look and took herself off.

Lizzie made her way up to her bedchamber, lost in thought. Frederick must have begun to contemplate marriage. It was inevitable—but unwelcome to her. What could she possibly have in common with the worldly, fashionable bride he would choose? And what would that nebulous beauty do when faced with the Grange, in all its glorious decay? Turn around and return to London?

Lizzie would not have that. Frederick's bride must love his estate as much as he did, or he would never be happy. Lizzie nodded to herself, coming to a decision. The place needed a few improvements before it would be ready to

179

welcome the sort of wife Frederick would choose. To start with, Lizzie would round up two of the grooms and see to the removal of the ivy that blocked the lower windows.

She headed toward the stairs, but the sound of St. Vincent's voice, coming from the dowager viscountess's parlor near the landing, stopped her. Unashamedly, she peeped in just as that lady drew back, flustered.

"Of course you may invite whom you wish to dine. That you should even think to consult me—" She broke off, distressed. "But is it—are you certain it is quite the thing for us to be entertaining so soon after my husband's death?"

"And inviting his possible murderer to the house?" Lizzie asked brightly.

The dowager, startled, turned to face her. "What do you mean?"

"That we are trying to discover who it might be."

St. Vincent directed a quelling glare at Lizzie, which she ignored.

"We want to Learn What We Can." Her tone capitalized the words, and she turned her most beseeching look on the dowager. "You *will* lend us your support, will you not?"

Lady St. Vincent studied her face for a long moment, as if seeking to gather courage, then turned to St. Vincent. "What do you wish me to do?"

"Merely play hostess."

With that, the dowager agreed, and Lizzie marched St. Vincent off to the library to write the notes of invitation. These were dispatched by way of a groom, and within an hour, three acceptances arrived back at the house. Lizzie, pleased with the success thus far of her scheme, set off to find the grooms.

The following evening, she reached the drawing room ahead of the others and poured herself a glass of canary while she waited. Adrian joined her shortly, and a few minutes later the others also came downstairs.

Mr. Burnett was the first of their guests to arrive. He

180

greeted his host and hostess, then sought out Georgiana as if the path to her side were the only one available to him. Lizzie folded her arms, watching the couple with interest as Mr. Burnett bent his auburn head near the girl's golden ringlets. Was his attraction for her real or feigned? she wondered. Mr. Needham's and Mr. Winfield's arrival only a few minutes later broke up this *tête-à-tête*, and the conversation turned naturally to the hunt which would gather at the Grange on the morrow.

Whether out of mischief or kindly intentions, Lizzie couldn't be certain, but St. Vincent arranged for Mr. Winfield to partner Georgiana at dinner. She herself went in on Mr. Needham's arm.

"Pleasant to be having a meal without that curst Runner of yours peering at every mouthful I take," Mr. Needham declared.

"Has he been?" St. Vincent served himself from the platter of herring in cream and waved the footman James to continue his round.

Mr. Burnett looked up from his conversation with the dowager. "Has he been at the Dower House, as well? I thought he had taken up residence at my hunting box."

Mr. Winfield, with an uncharacteristic spark of humor, shook his head. "He couldn't have. He's taken more than one meal of late at the vicarage."

"Blasted impertinence!" Mr. Needham declared. "I can't think why you tolerate the man, my lord. I simply can't understand it at all."

"I don't believe I have much choice." The viscount took a sip of wine, and the hovering Henry instantly refilled his glass.

"He had the infernal cheek to question my servants!" Mr. Burnett added.

Mr. Needham skewed his entire upper body around in his chair to look at the man; the height of his shirt points made it impossible for him to turn his head. "My man threatened to quit! Subjecting himself to the questions of a—a vulgar makebate is not what he is accustomed to."

"Dear me," St. Vincent murmured. "Lizzie, it seems

181

you must call him to heel. Or do you think he is following a lead?" He met Lizzie's gaze and held it, meaningfully.

Lizzie took the hint. "I'm certain of it. Whatever else our Mr. Coggins may be, it isn't a slowtop. I'll wager one of the servants said something without realizing it might be important, but Mr. Coggins caught on! Frederick, do you think this means he might arrest your cousin's murderer soon?"

The footman Henry sloshed wine onto the table as he refilled Georgiana's glass. With a horrified apology, he mopped at the dripping mess with a napkin.

Lizzie looked quickly about the assembled diners, but could detect no other reaction to her words. She couldn't envision the second footman as a murderer, though. The spilled wine must have been a simple accident. She had learned nothing. She'd have to let St. Vincent try again later over the brandy and snuff.

When the meal drew to a close, Lizzie departed reluctantly with the ladies. She would much rather remain and help Frederick draw out the gentlemen on the subjects of his cousin and the murder. Well, she could trust Adrian to do his share. She slumped into a chair and watched with no enthusiasm whatsoever as Georgiana played a sonata on the pianoforte.

The gentlemen joined them in a surprisingly short time, and the three guests all headed directly for the musician. It seemed Helena had a point, all those years she tried to force Lizzie to practice. Gentlemen were indeed captivated by musical accomplishment. More fools they.

She cast a sideways glance at St. Vincent, but could gain no clue from his expression whether or not he shared the others' enjoyment.

Rather she should wonder if one of their guests had betrayed himself! Of course, the guilty party might not have been there; Mr. Rycroft had been absent.

Georgiana finished, and at once the gentlemen begged her to play more. She fluttered long lashes and begged them to select her next piece. Somehow, the other two elbowed Mr. Winfield out of the way, and while Mr. Needham placed a sheet of music before her, Mr. Burnett moved the candles to provide her with more light. Really, she'd have to warn the vicar not to abandon the field so quickly. That left the other two in free and direct competition for Georgiana's favors.

Lizzie shifted her position, trying to hazard a guess as to who might be successful. Mr. Needham played off the airs of an exquisite—almost to perfection. Mr. Burnett, though, sneering at these efforts, brought the conversation around to the sport planned for the morrow.

"You may assure your gamekeeper we'll rid him of those foxes. Nothing like a hunt! Excellent day's exercise, and all to the good. Can't have your birds being savaged."

Mr. Needham shuddered. "It's a pity there must be such a ghastly end to such an entertaining ride."

"Do you find it entertaining?" Mr. Burnett feigned surprise. "I thought you wouldn't—or perhaps that should be *couldn't*—go beyond the second fence. Though to give you credit, at least you take the field. I never could trust a man who didn't." He allowed his gaze to stray momentarily to where Mr. Winfield sat with Lady St. Vincent and Adrian.

In this tactic he erred, for Georgiana bristled in the vicar's defense. "Not all take pleasure in encouraging the hounds to kill a fox."

"Cruel, when one considers it, you know," Mr. Needham declared, playing to this advantage. He gave an exquisite shudder. "Now, *I* ride for the joy of the chase, but retire before the poor fox—" With delicacy, he let the sentence fade. "Besides, some of us don't choose to present ourselves to the ladies in a muddied state. So vulgar. And others are involved in more noble pursuits." He turned to St. Vincent. "Are you aware, my lord, that only recently our good Mr. Winfield sold several pieces of silver plate and used the proceeds to help the village poor?"

Lizzie opened her mouth, caught St. Vincent's warning glance, and shut it again.

"Did he?" The viscount directed his searching scrutiny on Mr. Winfield's flushed countenance. "That was very generous of you."

"Not in the least." The discomfitted vicar rushed into speech. "When one sees the—the shocking conditions under which some of these people must live—no man of conscience could do less. I do not consider it of any great moment. Rather, I blame myself for not doing more." He fell silent, uncomfortable.

Mr. Burnett promptly changed his tactics. "An excellent thing to have done. You are only to be commended," he declared, thus causing the poor vicar's flush to deepen. "It is only a shame others in this neighborhood have not his sense of *noblesse oblige.*"

"Really?" Mr. Needham languidly raised his delicately carved quizzing glass to his eye. "Do you consider yourself noble?"

Mr. Burnett flushed. "I know as much of my family background as do you."

Mr. Needham's lip curled. "Do you?" He dropped his eyepiece and turned to St. Vincent.

He barely had asked at what time the hunt would assemble in the morning when Hodgkens entered with the tea tray. Lady St. Vincent settled behind this with an audible sigh of relief. Georgiana giggled, caught her mother's pleading gaze, and subsided.

It was not until their guests had taken their leave, and Lady St. Vincent and Georgiana had gone upstairs, that Lizzie found the opportunity to speak with Frederick. She trailed him into the library, where he offered her a glass of wine. She settled in one of the comfortable chairs.

"Well, Lizzie?" St. Vincent sipped his Madeira. "Which of them committed the murder?"

She ignored his deliberate provocation. "What I want to know is where Mr. Winfield got that silver plate."

184

"The Grange?" St. Vincent lounged back in the overstuffed chair, tented his fingertips and regarded her over their peaked top.

"Why not?"

The viscount drew a deep breath and let it out slowly. "You believe my cousin caught Mr. Winfield stealing?"

Lizzie considered. "He might have admitted to the blackmail so easily because he hid a far greater crime." Pleased with this bit of reasoning, she looked up at the viscount, but he responded with less than enthusiasm. "You don't agree?" she demanded.

"Which greater crime?" St. Vincent rose to his feet. "Murder or theft?"

"Both," Lizzie responded promptly.

"So Mr. Winfield is currently your prime suspect."

She hesitated. "It *is* hard, isn't it, to choose just one. I don't think I've ever before known of someone hated by so many."

"He mastered the knack," St. Vincent assured her.

A sharp rap sounded on the door, and the butler strode in, his expression harassed. St. Vincent set down his glass with a click. "What is it, Hodgkens?"

"Two pieces of the gold tableware are missing, my lord."

Lizzie's jaw dropped, but she bit back her cry of excitement.

"Missing?" St. Vincent repeated.

"Yes, my lord. I always count them as I put them away in the storeroom. We are definitely short two."

"Had the lock been forced?"

"No, my lord. Nothing appeared to have been disturbed in the least. But two large serving spoons are not there."

"One of the guests could easily have pocketed them," Lizzie pointed out.

St. Vincent directed an amused glance at her. "Before we go accusing our guests—a shocking breach of etiquette, I fear—we would do best to check our own

185

household. We will begin with the servants' hall, I believe."

A thorough investigation of these quarters, though, produced nothing of interest until they tapped on the door of an under parlor maid. The sound of frantic movement followed, and Hodgkens nodded grimly. St. Vincent threw the door wide.

Lizzie, standing on tiptoe to see over his shoulder, caught a glimpse of a bearded man—the gamekeeper, before St. Vincent turned and shoved her back.

"Go to your room, Lizzie."

"But Frederick—"

"Go!" His tone brooked no argument.

Unwilling, yet knowing she had no choice, she retreated. Behind her, she could hear Hodgkens's outraged demands that the errant couple be fired on the spot, and St. Vincent's calm orders for him to be quiet. Lizzie's trailing steps took her out of earshot, and with a sigh, she headed for the library.

Twenty minutes crept by, which Lizzie spent pacing about the room in ever-increasing impatience. At last, the door opened and St. Vincent entered.

Lizzie went to him at once and grabbed his arm. "What happened?"

His brow snapped down, accenting the lines of exhaustion that marked his face. "You shouldn't have waited up. I told you to go to your room."

Lizzie poured him a glass of wine, but he waved it aside. "Frederick—," she began, threatening.

"All right. Treecher denies the theft, and I'm inclined to believe him. He certainly didn't have those damned golden spoons on him."

"Will you fire Lily?"

"How—" He broke off and Lizzie just smiled. "I don't care to discuss it. Go to your room, please."

Lizzie tilted her head to one side and frowned at him. "Are you going to ignore their—"

"Lizzie!" He drew a deep, ragged breath. "It's been a

long day, Lizzie. For once, do as you're told." He grasped her elbow and propelled her toward the door. "I—" A frenzy of barking broke across his words.

"Damn it!" He took off at a run, with Lizzie at his heels. He burst through the door to the servants' hall, but halfway down the corridor he stopped and continued at a slow walk.

By the wavering light of the candle held by Hodgkens, Lizzie could make out the housekeeper and a potboy, newly returned from taking Cerberus for his walk. The hound crouched low, yelping. The trio stood behind him, staring down at a crumpled figure lying on the floor, with a long, slender shape protruding from it. With a sense of sick horror, Lizzie recognized the handle of her sword stick.

Chapter 15

St. Vincent strode forward and dropped to his knee beside the fallen figure. Lizzie bit her lip, for once hanging back. It wasn't that so much blood upset her; it was just that there was obviously nothing she could do. She called Cerb to heel, and he slunk to her side.

St. Vincent rose at last, his expression grim. By the light of that flickering candle held in the butler's trembling hand, the viscount's face appeared ashen.

"My lord—?" Hodgkens reached out a shaking hand, then let it drop.

"Summon Coggins," the viscount directed.

The butler glanced at the potboy, who nodded and fled as if relieved to escape the scene.

"Frederick?" Lizzie came a hesitant step closer and Cerb whined.

"Stay back!" he ordered.

"Who—?"

"Henry," he said shortly.

Lizzie nodded, feeling ill. The murder of the old viscount had been one thing. She hadn't known him—and she hadn't been around to see his body. But the second footman—

The image rose in her mind of Henry spilling wine at the dinner table. She'd been saying perhaps one of the servants had revealed something about the murder to

Mr. Coggins. . . .

A hand gripped her shoulder and she opened eyes she hadn't realized she'd closed. She looked up, shaking off the wave of nausea.

St. Vincent gazed down at her, his expression an odd mixture of gentleness and anger. "I want you to return to Halliford Castle."

She shook her head. "I'm all right, now." To prove this, she peered around him. "What can I do to help?"

"Nothing. Except leave."

"That won't help anything." She swallowed, feeling more her usual capable self, though she welcomed the reassurance of his touch. "I'm not one to turn missish on you."

He shook his head. "I want you to go."

"Well, I won't."

"St. Vincent? Lizzie?" Adrian, garbed in a deep blue dressing gown and nightcap, strode toward them. "I thought I heard Cerb—" He broke off as his gaze focused on the inert form of the footman. For a long moment he stood still as his lips moved in silent prayer for the dead. When he finished, he looked at St. Vincent

The viscount identified the young man. "I want you to take your sister home in the morning," he added.

"I already told him I'm staying right here."

"Of course you are. Both of us. We won't leave you in the lurch," Adrian asserted. "We'll stand buff."

"So you can quit wasting your efforts trying to convince me," Lizzie informed the viscount. "We have made up our minds."

"Ever determined," St. Vincent murmured.

"Naturally. So instead of arguing, which will get us nowhere, let's try to discover what happened." Though horribly, she thought she knew.

"Just what I'm thinking we should be doing, Missy." Coggins strode toward them, yawning cavernously. "Sorry, m'lord. I'd of been here a mite sooner, but I was sleeping like a newborn babe. Didn't even hear the dog

189

barking." He knelt down, straightened the body so he could get a clearer view of the wound, and shook his head.

Lizzie bit her lip, refusing to succumb to any vaporish fits. St. Vincent's hand tightened on her shoulder, and she moved a step closer to him and shivered.

"Nasty weapon, this," Coggins said. "Not the same one as killed His late Lordship, is it? The carving on the handle looks different."

St. Vincent shook his head. "This one belongs to Miss Carstairs."

The Runner directed a reproving look at her. "Now, Missy, what would you be wanting with the likes of this? It ain't ladylike, not a bit of it."

"Neither am I," she retorted.

Coggins rose. "And where did you acquire such a weapon?"

"You know perfectly well," St. Vincent snapped. "I gave it to her. I brought two of them back from India with me. But I believe I have already told you that."

"Aye, m'lord, that you did." The Runner regarded him from beneath his bristly eyebrows. "And where was you, if I may make so bold as to asks, when this here poor lad was a-getting hisself run through?"

"Talking with Miss Carstairs in the library."

The Runner blinked. "Is this true, Missy?"

"Yes. We spoke for—what?" She looked up into St. Vincent's rigid face. "About five minutes before Cerb started barking?"

"About five," he agreed.

Coggins perked up. "Only five minutes you was talking, was it? And how do you know as he wasn't dead afore His Lordship went and joined you in the library?"

Lizzie opened her mouth, then closed it with a snap.

St. Vincent drew his ever-useful snuff box from his pocket and helped himself to a pinch. "I believe I am being accused of a second murder in a round-about fashion," he said to no one in particular. "But I fear I can

190

prove my innocence, my poor Coggins. In this instance, at least. Hodgkens himself walked down this very hall with me as far as the library door. There were no bodies there at the time to clutter our path."

Coggins spun to face the butler. "Is that true?"

Hodgkens blinked. "Of course it is. Do you doubt Master Frederick—His Lordship, I should say?"

Coggins's jaw set in a belligerent manner. "Master Frederick, is it now," he muttered. "Are you so certain His Lordship went *into* the library, or could he have followed you back up this here hall?"

Hodgkens's features took on a pained expression. "He could not have followed me, Mr. Coggins. I saw him open the door and I heard Miss Carstairs ask him what happened. He could not have left without her knowing after that."

"And what *had* happened?" Coggins ignored the last of the speech and focused on what promised to be the most interesting. He settled once more on the viscount.

St. Vincent glanced at Lizzie, shrugged, and told the Runner briefly of the missing gold tableware and the incident with the maid and the gamekeeper. Coggins's already florid complexion took on a darker hue. He clicked his tongue in disapproval, but whether at the events of the evening or at St. Vincent's word being corroborated, Lizzie couldn't tell.

When Frederick finished, the Runner heaved a sigh. "Well, I suppose we'd best get on with this." He turned a kindly eye on Lizzie. "There's no call for you to be staying awake any longer, Missy. Why don't you just go on up to your bed?"

She stood her ground. "I want to know what's happening."

The Runner shook his head, as if dismayed by her unseemly determination to be in the thick of things, and turned to the butler. "Will you go over the house, Mr. Hodgkens, and see as if there ain't any way as someone could of slipped out all quiet like?"

191

The butler hurried off, apparently glad to have something constructive to do. Coggins nodded to himself, then drew out his Occurrence Book and began to make painstaking notes.

Lizzie shivered again, and Adrian put an arm around her shoulders. "If you'd rather—?" he began.

She shook her head. "I'm fine. But can't we help? We could look, too. What if the murderer is still in the house?"

"I rather think that is what our beloved Runner believes," St. Vincent murmured.

Lizzie shook her head. "You couldn't have killed Henry." She swallowed hard, and forced down the lump in her throat. Emotion only got in the way, disrupted her thinking. "Let's look, too."

"I'd rather as you didn't, Missy," Coggins said without so much as looking up. "Mr. Hodgkens and his staff will know better than you if anything's been disturbed. We shouldn't have long to wait."

In fact, they waited for less than five minutes. Arthur, the footman provided by the vicar, ran down the hall toward them, sketchily clad in breeches dragged on over his nightshirt. Coggins, much to Lizzie's interest, drew a pistol from his pocket.

"There's a door left on the latch!" the lad called as he neared. "At the back of the house, it is. I—"

He got no further. Coggins set off, with St. Vincent and Adrian right behind him. Lizzie gritted her teeth, inched past the body without looking, then also broke into a run.

The door, when they reached it, was indeed unbolted, but nothing further could be learned from it, despite the Runner's thorough examination. Slowly, they trooped back down the hall.

"Did young Henry catch someone thieving?" Coggins muttered.

"Or did he know something?" St. Vincent suggested, meeting Lizzie's worried gaze.

Coggins glared at him. "First thing we got to do is

gather the servants," he decided.

Lizzie didn't hold out much hope for this plan, but she soon found herself wrong. They discovered them already assembled in the kitchen, where a wide-eyed maid boiled water for tea. Mr. Coggins called the footman James into the hall and asked if he had seen anyone.

James thought for a moment, then shook his head. "No one, Mr. Coggins. Excepting the vicar, of course. Sorry I can't be of no help."

"The vicar?" Coggins stopped writing. "When?"

"About a half-hour after he left, I reckon."

"Why did he return?" St. Vincent demanded. "I had no idea."

"Says as he forgot his walking stick. You know the one what he always carries, m'lord. We didn't see it right off where he thought he left it, so I took him to see Mr. Rycroft."

"Mr. Rycroft, next, I think," Coggins said as they allowed the footman to rejoin his fellow servants.

"Did you know that the footman who found the door on the latch is the nephew of Mr. Winfield's housekeeper?" Lizzie asked.

Coggins fixed her with a stern eye. "Now, what are you implying, Missy? That young Arthur wanted hisself a permanent position here so he done in the second footman?"

"I don't believe even Miss Carstairs's fertile imagination could have come up with that one," St. Vincent protested. "I believe she wished you to be aware of the possible connection between the vicar, and that door being found on the latch."

Coggins's brow cleared. "You mean as he might of let Mr. Winfield out *after* he killed Henry?"

Somehow, Lizzie didn't think she quite meant that, but she let it pass. It was late, she was tired, and despite her determination, her mind did not seem to be functioning with its usual efficiency.

The procession made its way to the main wing of the

house, then up the carpeted stairs to the third floor where the bailiff had his rooms. The man, when he finally answered their knocks, yawned and blinked in sleepy surprise at being disturbed.

"No, I didn't stay with the vicar the whole time," he answered in response to the Runner's question. He turned to St. Vincent, concerned. "We separated and searched on our own."

"Did you find his walking stick?" the Runner asked.

"Yes, we did, and the merry devil of a time we had of it, too," he added. "It had rolled under a chair in the Green Salon."

"And what time did you show Mr. Winfield out?"

Mr. Rycroft frowned in an effort of memory. "I'm really not certain. After we found his stick, of course." His disarming smile flashed in apology.

Mr. Coggins clicked his tongue and jotted a few notes into his book. "Did you bolt the door after him?"

Mr. Rycroft turned to St. Vincent again. "Has something occurred, my lord?" The viscount told him, and the bailiff's jaw dropped open. "Murdered?" he repeated when he found his voice.

"Yes, sir. So if you wouldn't mind answering my question about the door?" the Runner pursued.

Mr. Rycroft rounded on him. "Of course I bolted it. What do you take me for, my good man?" He glared at Coggins.

With a hasty word of thanks, the Runner beat a strategic retreat, leaving Mr. Rycroft to return to bed. Lizzie shivered in the chill night air, but set off in determined pursuit.

St. Vincent caught her by the arm, then turned to Adrian. "Take her to her room and stay with her." He held Lizzie's gaze for a moment, commanding her obedience, then marched off after the Runner.

She experienced a sensation of loss at his departure, but fought it back. She was tired, that was her problem. A

194

few hours of sleep would restore her mind to its usual efficient order. She made her way to her room, assured her brother she would be all right, and set about preparing for bed.

She must have drifted off to sleep at last, for she awakened at an early hour to find her maid Rose bending over her. Lizzie yawned, eyed the mantel clock with disfavor, then memory of the night's tragedy flooded back. She sat up at once. "What is going on?" she asked.

"Mr. Coggins is that anxious everything goes as normal, Miss Lizzie." The woman held up a dressing gown for her. "He says as you're all to hunt, just as planned."

"Hunt!" It didn't seem proper, somehow, yet she knew their riding to hounds could not possibly disturb Henry in any way. Very likely the Runner had hopes of catching his murderer. If that were the case, she would help in any way she could. She did not approve of someone going about killing conscientious young footmen.

She dressed quickly in her sapphire blue riding habit, and ran down the stairs to see what she could find by way of a sustaining breakfast. The hunt gathered at the Grange this day, she remembered; their guests would be upon them all too soon.

By the time their party had eaten and made their way out to the stable, Mr. Needham, mounted on a placid black, had already arrived. He circled the cobbled yard while St. Vincent threw Lizzie lightly onto Patrick's back. Adrian had already assisted Georgiana onto Elmo, her favorite gelding. The girl moved off at once to join Mr. Needham.

Lizzie turned a jaundiced eye on that gentleman. He had chosen to wear a riding coat with a pinched-in waist, topped by impossibly high shirt points. It was dangerous to ride that way, with his head held stiffly forward. She doubted he'd venture far enough for it to become a problem, though. White tops gleamed on his riding

195

boots; he would never run the risk of muddying them. She wagered he'd retire before he even reached the first fence.

The others began to arrive in small groups of three or four. Mr. Coggins roamed the yard, watching everyone with that penetrating gaze that made even the most innocent of hearts experience a twinge of guilt. Mr. Burnett rode in, and Georgiana excused herself to Mr. Needham and brought Elmo up to greet the newcomer. Mr. Needham, momentarily alone, fell prey to the determined Mr. Coggins, who strode up to him in a purposeful manner.

Lizzie spared the discomfited Mr. Needham only the briefest glance. Without compunction, she spurred Patrick forward to hear what passed between Georgiana and Mr. Burnett. She was in time to see that gentleman flash his most charming smile at the girl.

"There was no opportunity to speak to you last night," Georgiana declared in an undervoice that just carried to Lizzie. "I wanted to tell you I think it the most dreadful thing. I do not understand why you remain on civil terms with my family, considering how shockingly my father behaved toward you."

He covered her hand with his own, fleetingly. "I would not have you distressed for the world. It was unforgivable of me to mention it to you, with him so recently—" He broke off, as if delicacy forbade him to mention the subject.

She gazed earnestly into his eyes. "I do not grieve for him—you must not think I do. What I have learned of him since that night has filled me with the greatest shame. I only wish I had the means to make it up to you at once. As soon as Cousin Frederick comes into proper possession of his inheritance, I shall see to it we make amends."

With a sense of surprise, Lizzie realized Georgiana did not yet know Mr. Burnett's tale of swindling was false.

She determined to set the girl straight on the matter as soon as possible.

No time like the present. A sense of propriety flitted across her mind, but she dismissed it and brought her huge chestnut closer.

"That is a very interesting story, Mr. Burnett." She smiled brightly at him. "Why is it that the shopkeeper told Mr. Coggins he sold that chalice to you only a short while ago, and for less than the viscount paid you?"

Mr. Burnett's jaw clenched. "I see you have uncovered my shame, Miss Carstairs. That chalice was one of the few things I inherited from my father, but I fear my lack of funds drove me to sell it. I never thought to have it appraised, first. Then when I discovered His Lordship possessed a keen interest in such works of art, I purchased it back and offered it to him. He knew its worth, but pretended to accept the price I set as fair. Not until a couple of weeks later did I learn of the price *he* was offered for it."

"It is the most shocking thing, is it not, Lizzie?" Georgiana's lovely color burned brighter.

Lizzie caught Patrick's head as it swung toward Georgiana's Elmo with teeth bared. "Who wanted to buy it?"

"Another collector. He offered the viscount ten times what I received for it, but he turned it down, saying it was worth far more than that."

"And how did you learn of this?"

"The collector wrote to me, to discover if I had any other items that might be of interest to him. I was only sorry I did not."

"You must have been furious," Lizzie declared, all righteous sympathy.

"I was probably mad enough to murder," he admitted, though a trifle ruefully. "I came over here that night with the intent of—er—what your brother, Miss Carstairs, might call 'supplying him with a little of the

197

home-brewed.' "

"Darkening his daylights?" Lizzie suggested. "Milling his canister?"

A reluctant laugh escaped Mr. Burnett. "Shocking, Miss Carstairs."

"Yes, isn't it? Why didn't you, by the way?"

"He was already dead when I got here."

"Thus depriving you of the opportunity to vent your spleen?"

He chuckled once more. "As you say. Lord, how improper this conversation has become. Miss Ashfield, I do most humbly beg your pardon."

Georgiana shook her head, but did not meet his earnest gaze. "Your sentiments were entirely justified. I can only feel shame—"

"Nonsense!" Lizzie broke in. "It had nothing to do with you. You suffered at your father's hands as well. As did your mother, and apparently everyone else with whom he came into contact. Why didn't you tell someone he was dead, Mr. Burnett?"

He had the grace to look sheepish. "I didn't dare! Forgive me, Miss Ashfield, I must seem the greatest coward alive to you. I had come, you understand, with the intention of doing him a violence—though not that much of one. My only thought was to escape."

"One cannot—" Lizzie broke off, seeing a gentleman somewhat uncertainly astride a plodding gray mare she recognized as belonging in St. Vincent's stable. "Good Lord, is that Mr. Winfield?"

Mr. Burnett turned, and his shoulders shook in silent mirth. "Our good vicar is going to hunt? He has never done more than watch! Whatever can have possessed him?"

"How very daring of him!" Georgiana cried. "I knew him to be a man of excellent good sense, but I had no notion he might also have such spirit! I must speak with him." She turned Elmo and in minutes wended her way through the milling horsemen to the vicar's side.

Mr. Rycroft strode out of the house, looked around, and headed directly toward St. Vincent, who sat astride his raw-boned bay. The viscount leaned down to listen, then swung from the saddle. The two spoke for several minutes, then St. Vincent hailed a groom and handed over his reins. He accompanied the bailiff back into the house.

"Problems?" Mr. Burnett asked.

"Yes. Our second footman was murdered last night."

Mr. Burnett's neatish chestnut sidled as his hands clenched on the reins. "What?"

"Run through with a sword stick. Don't speak of it, though. Coggins—our Runner, you know—wanted everything to proceed as normal today. Except, of course, he insists on behaving like a vulture and making everyone nervous. I don't know what he hopes to accomplish."

Mr. Burnett stared at her, his expression a mingling of shock and uncertain humor. "You are certainly taking this calmly, Miss Carstairs. I should have expected you to succumb to a fit of the vapors."

"I'm not missish."

"No, I see you cannot be. Why did your Mr. Coggins not cancel the hunt and subject us all to a thorough inquisition?" His eyes widened. "There were three of us invited to dinner last night. Does he suspect one of us? Or does he believe it to have been another of the servants?"

"He hasn't informed me—yet. You have heard of the possible looting, have you not?"

Mr. Burnett drew in a deep breath. "You mean that poor footman might have caught a housebreaker in the act?"

"Possibly. There is also a chance he knew more of the late viscount's murder than he admitted, and tried to blackmail someone. Do you remember how he spilled the

199

wine at dinner as we talked about some such possibility?"

Mr. Burnett opened his mouth, then closed it with a snap. "I do," he said at last. "This is appalling!"

"Mr. Coggins is like to make life very uncomfortable for everyone until he settles on his victim. He is just aching for a bit of solid proof against St. Vincent."

"Miss Carstairs, you have my deepest sympathy. It is clear we must rid ourselves of his pestilential presence. I suppose we shall not succeed until he has arrested someone, though." His gaze swept the assembled company, as if seeking out the guilty party.

Lizzie left him lost in contemplation, and urged Patrick forward. She located Adrian, and together they drank their stirrup cups. The chill wind promised a brisk morning's ride. Her horse shook his head and stamped at the ground, impatient to be off. Lizzie didn't blame him.

St. Vincent emerged from the house a quarter of an hour later, and remounted only moments before Squire Stellings arrived, accompanied by two houndsmen and his pack. The party set forth, headed through a fallow field, then leapt the fence and crossed the road. The hounds scrambled over the stone wall on the other side, caught a scent, and the chase erupted.

Lizzie, riding near the rear with Adrian, glanced back in time to see the vicar's borrowed gray mare clear the wall. Mr. Winfield, somewhat unceremoniously, landed with arms and legs wrapped about his mount's neck. The gray came to an abrupt halt, calmly lowered her head to crop a mouthful of weeds, and the vicar slid to the ground, almost landing on his nose.

Lizzie reined in. "I'll go back and help," she called to her brother.

By the time she reached the vicar, he had picked himself up and stood brushing the dirt and weeds from his borrowed hunting coat. "Are you all right?" she called as she pulled up at his side.

Mr. Winfield sighed. "I believe so."

"Did the angels forget to 'bear thee up in their hands, lest thou dash thy foot against a stone'?"

"I'm afraid so." The vicar shook his head. "It's really true that 'Pride goeth before destruction, and an haughty spirit before a fall.'"

Lizzie grinned. "Do you continue?"

"No, I think I shall return. I was never an intrepid horseman, I fear." Somewhat gingerly, he eased himself back into the saddle. The mare grabbed a last mouthful of weeds and allowed him to collect the reins.

"You can ride around that way." Lizzie pointed helpfully toward a long line of yew trees. "There's a bridge over the stream, and only a shallow ditch before you reach the road."

With fervent thanks, the vicar turned the mare in that direction. Lizzie watched their departure for only a minute. What fools men made of themselves over ladies. At least, over particular ladies. No gentleman would ever go to such extremes to please *her*. She frowned. Two weeks ago, she'd have been smug about that fact. Now, it bothered her.

She spurred Patrick forward and set off in pursuit of the others, who already had disappeared through the woods beyond. Fortunately, Patrick was a hunter worthy of the name—and every guinea Halliford paid for him. He flew over the uneven terrain, clearing every ditch, hedgerow, and fence in his path. In less than twenty minutes she caught up with the trailers, then passed even such neck-or-nothing riders as Mr. Burnett and Georgiana.

Mr. Needham, she noted, must already have departed the field. She urged Patrick ahead, waved merrily to Adrian as she passed, and closed in beside St. Vincent, who rode just behind the master.

"I didn't think you'd remain long in the rear!" he shouted.

"Of course not!" Exhilaration filled her, banishing the

201

worries of the looting and murders. Here, on the back of a flying horse, she controlled her world.

She raced neck and neck with St. Vincent, and enthusiasm welled within her. They neared another stone wall, and a laugh escaped her. She leaned low over Patrick's neck, urging him on, feeling his mighty hindquarters bunch for the takeoff. Then they flew, and St. Vincent—

Her laugh died, replaced by a scream. St. Vincent, tangled in his broken saddle, landed in the mud, and his head struck the base of the wall.

Chapter 16

Trembling, the blood draining from her face, Lizzie reined in, jerking Patrick's head about so the animal reared. She had to block where Frederick lay. . . .

The riders cleared the wall and thundered past, swerving to avoid her, somehow not trampling the unconscious viscount. Then Adrian pulled up, waving frantically to those who followed, and the trailing riders slowed, then stopped.

"What happened?" one of them called.

"St. Vincent's been thrown," Adrian shouted back.

The man laughed. "Took a regular rasper, did he? Stand clear."

Lizzie paid them no heed. With the frenzy of horsemen no longer flying by her, she leapt from her saddle and knelt at Frederick's side. Adrian joined her as the other riders cleared the wall and continued.

"Why didn't they help?" Lizzie cried. "Adrian, he's bleeding dreadfully!"

Her brother jerked at the viscount's neckcloth, muttered a very unclergymanlike oath, and at last pulled it free. "Head wound. They always bleed like the very devil. Here, Lizzie, stay with him. I'll ride for help."

She nodded, panic for once overcoming her normal practicality. She couldn't go to pieces like this! She *never* did. And Frederick needed her.

That thought helped steady her world, and she began to take stock of his injuries. He bled horribly, but as Adrian pointed out, that was from the gash where his head struck the sharp edge of the stone wall. Already, the area swelled. She had better not move him until assistance came. If he'd injured his back, or even broken a limb, she would not be doing him any good.

Never before had she felt so completely useless. She *wanted* to do something—anything!—but until Adrian returned with help, she could only assure herself he still breathed—though none too steadily.

She swallowed hard, fighting back an impulse to behave in a very missish manner. Good Lord, was she about to become a watering pot? Disgusted, she wiped the back of her hand across her cheeks.

The rumble of voices reached her, along with the creaking of boards and wheels. Several farmers in the next field ran in her direction, leading a horse harnessed to a rough-hewn cart. Adrian rode at their side. As they neared the hedgerow, they veered off to the left. One of the men dragged open a gate, and Adrian galloped through, though the others didn't follow.

He reached her side and swung down. "How is he?"

"I don't know." With difficulty she kept her voice level. This was *not* the time to succumb to a fit of the vapors! She could indulge in that mawkish pastime after she handed Frederick over to the care of a doctor.

Adrian subjected the viscount's arms and legs to a cursory examination, and nodded in satisfaction. "No obvious injuries," he declared.

Lizzie bit her lip. Her brother seldom used that tone of forced cheerfulness.

The farmers led the cart horse as close as possible and unloaded the gate which they'd removed from its hinges. Under Adrian's direction, they laid it next to the sprawled viscount.

Adrian stripped off his coat and cast it over the gate, then turned to the men. "Can you ease him over?"

"Aye, sir, we've picked up the likes of His Lordship afore, we have," one said.

With surprising care, he and his companions maneuvered St. Vincent onto the gate. Lizzie grabbed a clinging stirrup and pulled it free of his boot.

Adrian let out a sigh of relief and looked about. "Where's your horse, Lizzie?"

"I don't—no, he's grazing over there. Frederick's followed the pack." She returned her gaze to the viscount's face. Why did he have to be so pale? Damn the man, he'd survived for almost forty years. A simple tumble from a horse shouldn't cause him more than a few bruises. Yet she'd feel better if only he would regain consciousness.

She bit her lip and looked up at her brother. "Will you lead Patrick back, Adrian? I'm going to ride with Frederick."

Without waiting for his response, she scooped up the fallen saddle and scrambled into the cart, then directed the farmers to slide the gate in beside her. Not until the viscount was in position did she sink down beside him. One of the farmers went to the cob's head, and they moved slowly—and jerkily—forward.

She grasped St. Vincent's right wrist, which was near, and placed her fingers over his pulse. She could feel it—but surely it should be stronger than that.

Behind them, Adrian, mounted once more, trotted up with her horse in tow. He met her wide-eyed look with a smile meant to instill confidence. It failed miserably.

He came alongside and tossed her Patrick's reins. "I'm riding for the doctor," he called. With a wave, he took off.

Lizzie, with Cerberus at her feet, glared out the multipaned library windows at the unoffending terrace beyond. Adrian and the doctor had firmly excluded her from the room while the latter examined the viscount.

She wouldn't have minded so much if they hadn't allowed Lady St. Vincent to enter at one point. The *least* that lady could have done was to tell her what went on in there. But all she would vouchsafe was an unhelpful, "Don't worry."

The door opened and she spun about as Adrian entered. She ran to him and grabbed his arm. "What does the doctor say?"

He squeezed her hands, then disentangled them from his coat sleeve. "He has concussion and a few cracked ribs, but he is otherwise unharmed."

Lizzie let out her breath in a ragged sigh. "May I see him?"

This Adrian permitted, and accompanied her up the stairs and down the maze of corridors that led to the best guest chamber the viscount occupied. Lizzie entered on tiptoe, realized her behavior was worthy of her overly romantic sister Augusta, and resumed her normal determined stride. Cerb paced beside her.

St. Vincent lay on the bed, the coverlets folded back so his arms rested on top of them. The doctor had positioned his head so she could only see his left cheek and temple— with their bulky bandage. She swallowed and came to a halt.

"Is he conscious yet?" she whispered.

"Yes. The doctor brought him round. He may be asleep, though. He swallowed a pretty hefty dose of laudanum."

Lizzie dragged a chair up beside the bed and seated herself. "What can I do?"

The hound whined softly, then circled twice and flopped on the floor at her feet. He laid his giant muzzle on his front paws and fixed his worried canine gaze on the viscount's inert figure.

There was nothing she could do but wait, and hope. She remained at his bedside with Cerb either at her feet or stretched out before the hearth, whimpering occasionally in response to her worry. For perhaps the first time

206

in her life, she regretted she had no hobby with which to occupy her hands—and mind.

She would take care of him, nurse him back to health, never leave his side. He needed her—or was that the other way around?

She gazed at his beloved face as full understanding dawned on her at last. Her heart didn't flutter, her senses didn't reel, she didn't feel giddy or romantic or foolishly ecstatic. Instead, a flood of deep emotion washed through her, leaving her content just to be at his side.

No wonder she hadn't realized the full extent of her feelings before. Love wasn't the silly nonsense she'd always believed it to be. It was much more wonderful and sane and *right*. It hadn't burst upon her, but crept up gradually, seeping through every part of her until it was impossible to doubt its reality or the happiness it brought her. She belonged with Frederick.

But she wasn't what he wanted. She had seen for herself the sort of lady who captured his fancy, and anything farther from her own prosaic self would be impossible to imagine. Well, she would devote herself to him until such time he chose to wed. Then she'd marry some vicar and concentrate her energies on good works— Lord, she was becoming maudlin!

Lady St. Vincent, her soft, pale brow lined in concern, peeked in to see how St. Vincent went on. Lizzie banished her unproductive thoughts and gave her report, though she had little to tell. She resumed her silent vigil. Shortly after nuncheon, which she had been unable to eat, she was again interrupted, this time by Georgiana. The girl announced that Mr. Needham and Mr. Burnett had heard of the accident, and had called to pay their respects and wish him a speedy recovery.

Lizzie welcomed these diversions, brief as they were. One, though, she did not. Toward late afternoon, Mr. Winfield crept into the room, somewhat defiantly and over the butler's protests, saying he had come to pray for the afflicted man. In this endeavor, he was joined by Lady

St. Vincent and Georgiana. Lizzie, despite being a good Anglican at heart, found this more than she could bear. "Almost as if he were a Papist saying the Last Rites!" she complained to Adrian.

Her brother soothed her as best he could, which was notably unsuccessful, and went upstairs to hurry this visitor on his way. With a groan, Lizzie fled the house and spent the remainder of the afternoon ruthlessly directing the grooms in the weeding of the rose garden. Cerb helped, too, digging frantically at several long-abandoned gopher holes until he at last set off in pursuit of a rabbit.

The evening chill at last drove Lizzie back indoors. Stopping only to shed her pelisse and scarf in the hall— and to turn Cerb over to James to have his massive, muddied paws wiped—she ran up the stairs and down the wide corridor to St. Vincent's room. She tapped lightly and peeped in without waiting for a response.

Adrian, who occupied her abandoned chair by the bedside, looked up from his untranslated copy of Thucydides.

"Safe to come in?" she asked, "or are there any vicars lurking in the corners?"

He smiled and rose. "Only me."

She waved that aside. "You're not a vicar. Lord, you're not going to become one, are you? I can't really see you puttering around among mildewed roses in a tiny garden."

"Nor can I. I fear it's the life of an Oxford don for me."

Lizzie regarded the recumbent figure on the bed, and her teasing mood evaporated. "Is he—?" She didn't like the looks of the large purplish red bruise that spread across his temple and cheek.

The wide-set blue eyes opened slowly and St. Vincent's gaze settled on her with some difficulty. "Not dead yet, my dear. Sorry if that disappoints you."

Relief surged through her, and she sank down on the covers beside him and clasped his hand, which closed over hers. "What a devil of a scare you gave us,

Frederick," she declared. Despite her attempt at a normal tone, her voice trembled, and she fought back tears.

"Pray accept my humblest apologies. Adrian told me you actually sat in here for awhile. Whatever did you do to occupy yourself?"

"I thought what a bore needlework must be." She rallied, glad he appeared not to notice her uncharacteristic emotion. "Can you imagine doing nothing but sitting around all day, setting stitches? How do you feel?"

He groped at his neck, and managed a frown which was accompanied by only the slightest wince. "Adrian, where is my glass?"

Adrian found it on the dressing table and handed it over. St. Vincent thanked him, raised it to his eye, and directed a piercing look through it at Lizzie. The strain of focusing appeared to be too much, though, for he dropped it at once. "As always, my dear, I am in the pink of health."

"Purple, you mean." She smiled at him, cheered by such normal behavior on his part. "Contrary to how you must feel," she added, "we did not permit the entire hunt to run over you."

He inclined his head. "You have my deepest gratitude for your quick thinking."

"Unlike yours. I should have thought you'd know better than to mount without inspecting your girth. You're not one to leave that to your groom."

St. Vincent glanced at Adrian.

"I didn't tell her, yet," her brother said.

"Tell me what?" She looked from one to the other, quickly. "What are you hiding from me?"

"Not hiding. I only found out a little while ago."

"Found out what?" Her voice took on the threatening tone for ages adopted by sisters to their elder brothers.

"My girth had been cut," St. Vincent said.

"Had been . . . ," Lizzie's voice trailed off. She swallowed hard. "Do you mean—*deliberately?*"

"It would be a difficult thing to do *accidentally*," St. Vincent informed her, somewhat waspishly.

Adrian laid a hand on Lizzie's shoulder, but spoke to the viscount. "Now that you're better, perhaps we should leave you to get some rest. I'll just ring for your valet." He suited action to words, then started for the door. "Are you coming, Lizzie?"

She glared at him. "You tell me casually that someone may have tried to—to kill St. Vincent, then just *drop* the subject?" She looked from her brother to the viscount, who lay amongst the pillows, his eyes once more closed.

Adrian took her arm and propelled her from the room. "He needs rest, Lizzie. I'll tell you what I know downstairs. Though it's not very much."

A dapper little man hurried along the hall toward them, then slowed to a more decorous pace as he neared, as befitted the personal valet of St. Vincent of Ashfield Grange. Cummings, even more than his master, appeared to know what was due to his new-found consequence. The haughty half-smile faded from the man's thin lips. "Is His Lordship—?"

"Resting," Adrian assured him. "Keep an eye on him." He caught the valet's gaze and held it.

The little man nodded, and Lizzie had the distinct impression he intended to stand over his master with a pistol. The intensity that radiated from him increased her own sense of unease. He honestly seemed to believe drastic action might be called for.

They saw him inside, then Lizzie grasped her brother's arm and marched him toward the stairs. "How could St. Vincent's girth have been cut? Was it done on purpose for the hunt, or just for the next time he rode?"

Adrian hesitated, then continued down the steps. "The girth was in good condition when his groom saddled up."

"Or did he just say that, to protect himself?"

Adrian shook his head. "St. Vincent checked it before he mounted. Of that he was certain."

Lizzie frowned in an effort of memory. "But not before he mounted the second time."

Adrian glanced over his shoulder. "What do you mean?"

"Didn't you see? He got off to talk to Mr. Rycroft. They went into the house together, leaving a groom holding his horse. There were any number of people about," she added, frowning. "Oh, this doesn't make sense! *Why?* Who would want to kill him?"

"I wish I knew, Lizzie."

They reached the hall and she headed toward the library. Adrian followed. She went directly to the sideboard and poured them each a small glass of Madeira, then settled near the fire, staring into it without seeing.

"Someone did a very good job of making him appear guilty of his cousin's murder," she said at last.

Adrian sipped the wine and gazed into the flames. "Lord, Lizzie—" He broke off and the two stared at each other. "That—no, that's not reasonable."

"I know it isn't. But the possibility has occurred to you, too. Hasn't it?" Deliberately, Lizzy voiced the question that hovered, unwelcome, in each of their minds. "What if St. Vincent was more than just a convenient victim to take the blame for his cousin's death? What if someone wanted to be rid of *both* of them?"

"But there's no reason!"

"What better way, than to make it appear that one had murdered the other?" she pursued.

"But *who?*" Adrian slammed his empty glass down on the tray. "The only person who would have anything to gain would be St. Vincent's heir, but he has none! He's the last of his line."

"Are we *certain* of that?" Lizzie regarded him intently.

Adrian rose to his feet in one fluid movement. "Perhaps we'd better see just how much Frederick really knows of his family background."

"After he's slept," Lizzie said, though with regret.

They did not visit St. Vincent until later that evening, after dinner. Lizzie, with Adrian at her side, tapped lightly on the viscount's door, and Cummings, his expression harried, stepped into the hall.

"How is he?" she asked.

"He has consented to swallow a bit of gruel, miss. A good sign, I assure you."

"Without complaint?" Lizzie demanded at once. "He must be sicker than we thought!"

The valet regarded her with an understanding eye. "No, miss. *Not* without complaint."

"Well, that's a relief, at any rate. May we see him?"

But Lizzie's hopes of St. Vincent's remembering some forgotten branch of his family died as soon as they put the question to him. He shook his head as firmly as he could manage while it still throbbed.

"I told you before. I have no heir," he said, somewhat thickly.

Lizzie frowned. "It must be your will, then. You have made one now, haven't you, Frederick?"

St. Vincent directed a pained gaze at her. "That is hardly a question to ask a man in my condition, Lizzie."

"It's exactly the question. Who stands to gain?"

He regarded her through sober eyes. "Your brother-in-law is mentioned."

"I believe we can eliminate Halliford as a suspect," she said dryly. "Who else?"

"There is an elderly cousin of whom I was quite fond as a child. She lives in Harrowgate. To be near the doctors. She suffers from gout and rheumatism, I believe."

"That's it? Who is *her* heir, then?"

"An orphanage, I fear. My will leads us nowhere."

"There is no reason for someone to try to kill you!" Lizzie declared in disgust.

"I suppose I have imagined the whole?"

"You haven't," she snapped. "And neither have I," she added, but only to herself.

No matter how hard she tried, she found herself unable to abandon the notion of an unknown heir. The conviction that one really existed took firm and unshakable possession of her mind. Leaving Adrian with St. Vincent, she made her way to the drawing room, where Lady St. Vincent worked on the altar cloth by the light of a dozen candles—beeswax, Lizzie noted, not tallow. Georgiana sat at the pianoforte, practicing.

Lady St. Vincent looked up, her expression anxious. "How is he?"

"He'll probably be up tomorrow. He's never one to let a mere tumble from a horse bother him."

The dowager smiled in honest relief. "I'm so very glad."

"So am I." Lizzie knew a moment's irrational desire to burst into tears on the woman's shoulder, but fought it off. "What do you know of the Ashfield family?" she asked, instead.

The dowager viscountess set another stitch with care. "Their history? It's been long and distinguished. What would you like to know?"

"If there could possibly be an heir of whom no one knows anything."

Lady St. Vincent lowered her embroidery into her lap and stared at Lizzie, her gentle face a picture of alarm. "You think St. Vincent's fall—?"

"It wasn't an accident."

"How dreadful." The woman stared at the embroidered cloth in silence for a moment, then tucked her needles into the work with trembling hands. "We had best go to the muniments room, I believe."

Leaving Georgiana to her painstaking study of Mozart, the dowager led the way to the chamber where records had been stored for generations. She hesitated in the doorway, looking about. "I am quite certain it's kept in here."

"What is?" Lizzie walked to the center and turned about, as if expecting to spot something obvious.

"The family Bible. It's very old, and every birth and marriage has been recorded in it for generations."

Lizzie brightened. "The very thing!"

After a brief search, she discovered the large leather and wood bound volume on the mantel above the fireplace. She handed it to the viscountess, who opened it and leafed through the Book. A frown creased her fine brow, and she turned the pages back again, one by one.

"It's missing," she said at last. "The page with the family tree. It's been torn out!" She held out the Bible, where the ragged remnants of a sheet could barely be discerned.

"*That's* what we've needed!" Triumphant, Lizzie grasped the Book. "Have you seen Mr. Coggins?"

The dowager didn't appear to hear. Misting tears filled her large, still-lovely eyes. "How could someone? To tear a page from a Bible!"

Lizzie murmured in sympathy, then drew her gently back to her altar cloth and the tender ministrations of her daughter. She saw them settled, then went in search of the Runner. Encountering Hodgkens in the Great Hall saved her a wasted trip to the servants' quarters; Mr. Coggins, the butler said, was in the viscount's room. That meant she could give everyone her news at once. She ran lightly up the stairs.

She entered the bedchamber to find what could only be termed a Confrontation taking place. Coggins stood at the side of the bed, his face a full crimson, his chin jutted out in anger. Pillows propped St. Vincent in a sitting position, but Lizzie, after one glance at the fury in his face, doubted he would remain abed much longer. Adrian stood between the two, as if his presence were all that prevented the two men from coming to blows.

Coggins swung around as the door closed behind Lizzie, and the scowl faded from his face. Without a word, she held out the Bible to him.

He took it with reluctant hands. "What is this, Missy?"

"The family Bible. Lady St. Vincent and I found it in the muniments room. The page with the family tree has been torn out."

"Has it?" St. Vincent, who had sunk back, eyes closed, sat up straight. "Let me see, Lizzie."

Over the Runner's protests, she snatched back the heavy volume and handed it to the viscount. "There."

"I see." He sounded grim.

"I don't," the Runner protested.

Lizzie turned to him with all the patience of one explaining a simple fact to a child who refused to listen. "Someone wanted to keep their connection with the Ashfield family secret. There *must* be another heir."

Coggins's heavy brow creased, and she could almost see his mind working within. At last, he asked: "Why?"

Lizzie blinked. "If St. Vincent is blamed for his cousin's murder—," she began.

The Runner waved that aside. "The Reverend here," he gestured to Adrian, "has been telling me all about this here idea of yours, Missy. But what I wants to know is, what good would it do this here mysterious heir of yours? If it's someone who's been seen around here, and he comes forward and claims the estate, he's going to look mighty suspicious-like." He beamed at Lizzie. "We're not addle-pated up in Bow Street, Missy. Long-headed, we are, no matter what some folks may care to say."

"The heir could have hired someone to—to do away with the old viscount and throw the blame on Frederick," Lizzie pointed out.

"What, and have someone about to blackmail him? He'd be mighty foolish to do that, Missy, mighty foolish indeed."

Lizzie glared at him. "What do you think, then?"

The Runner ran a finger along the ripped remains of the page. "It *could* be as you suggest, Missy. Or His Lordship here might be awanting us to go thinking just that."

"What do you mean?"

215

"He means, my dear Lizzie, that he thinks *I* tore the family tree out in the hopes you'd think exactly what you do."

"But—" She stared at him, shocked.

"I've been out to the stable, now, Missy, and His Lordship's groom swears as no one could have cut that there girth without his knowing. It seems mighty possible to me that mayhap His Lordship might have gone and done it hisself, 'cause he knew the long arm of Bow Street was closing in about him."

Chapter 17

Lizzie almost spluttered in her fury. When she mastered her voice, she cried: "Of all the—! No, Adrian, I will not be silent. This—this nincompoop has—" She broke off, for once bereft of words sufficient to describe her feelings.

"A first," St. Vincent murmured. "Remind me to mark this in my diary. Lizzie is unable to express her mind."

She swung around to face him. "I suppose you're just going to make a joke out of this, as you do out of everything!"

St. Vincent raised an eyebrow. "Am I laughing?"

"Go ahead and lie there. And you," she spun to face Coggins. "You go and accuse an innocent man and let the *real* murderer escape. I'm not so craven!" She stormed to the door.

"Lizzie!" Adrian started after her, but a soft—and infuriatingly amused—word from St. Vincent stopped him.

Lizzie slammed the door behind her, then took several deep, steadying breaths. There had to be a reasonable, logical explanation. It wasn't just *anybody* who wanted St. Vincent out of the way. Nor could it be just anybody hired for the job. It had to be someone who could have come close to the viscount's horse that morning without arousing suspicion. A groom? His *own* groom, perhaps? She started slowly for the drawing room.

Georgiana still played, but this time a flawless performance; she had an audience. Mr. Burnett and the Reverend Mr. Winfield sat with her mother. Mr. Rycroft hovered attentively in the background, though he appeared to be doing nothing, as far as Lizzie could tell.

He looked up as she entered, and a slight frown creased his classically handsome brow. He moved to join her. "I was looking for Mr. Carstairs. Have you seen him?"

"He's with St. Vincent."

"Then I won't trouble him. If you could just mention, next time you see him, that I would be glad to have a word with him?" He bowed over her hand, smiling, and excused himself to return to his work.

Mr. Burnett, his expression puzzled, watched him leave. "Did anything strike you as strange in his manner?" he asked of the others in general.

"Mr. Rycroft?" Lady St. Vincent glanced at the door which had closed behind the bailiff. "He seems less worried than usual, does he not? I am so glad, for his sake. Such a dreadful burden as he has had to bear. Perhaps Mr. Carstairs has discovered some way in which we may make the lands more profitable this year. Lizzie, my love, how does poor St. Vincent go on?" The dowager turned to the more important question.

"Better, if our beloved Runner would leave him in peace." She eyed the other two men with speculation, but refrained—with what for her was amazing tact— from asking point blank if either of them had just happened to take a knife to the viscount's saddle.

"We may thank God for his deliverance," Mr. Winfeld declared. "Our prayers, dear Lady St. Vincent, have been answered."

218

"We may all be glad," that lady responded.

"Someone isn't," Lizzie muttered.

Mr. Winfield looked at her, troubled. "Do you mean Mr. Rycroft? The suspicion did cross my mind that perhaps the accident did not displease him."

"Did it, now." Mr. Burnett looked at him sharply. "I thought only I entertained that idea."

Mr. Winfield, the picture of misery, shook his head. "Such a very un-Christianlike thing for a man of the cloth to permit to cross his mind. Forgive me, dear Lady St. Vincent."

That lady said nothing. She merely stared at the closed door, her finely lined brow furrowed in dismay. "It cannot be true," she murmured.

Maybe it was, but at the moment Lizzie had another problem to keep her awake. She spent a sleepless night contemplating how best to discover whether or not an heir might really exist. She came down the stairs in the morning, determination marking her every movement. After a hearty breakfast, which she shared with Cerb, the two set off for a brisk walk through the chill woods along the path to the vicarage.

The steeple of the ancient stone church pierced high into the brilliant blue sky. She paused, struck by its beauty, but only for a moment; her nose felt like an icicle. Frost lingered on the ground in the shaded patches.

Mr. Winfield emerged from a side door of the church into a neatly laid out courtyard. Cerb bounded forward in greeting, and the vicar ducked strategically behind a bench.

"Good morning!" Lizzie strode up to join him.

The exuberant hound leapt up, front paws on the man's narrow shoulders, and proceeded to lick his face with enthusiasm. Lizzie latched onto Cerb's collar and dragged him down. The vicar retreated a pace farther.

"He's just glad to see you," Lizzie explained,

219

scrubbing the massive hound's ears. Cerb lolled his tongue out sideways and panted happily.

"Er—always such a pleasure to see you, too," Mr. Winfield managed.

"Do you keep the church records in there?" she gestured toward the sanctuary.

"The records? No, indeed not. We have an office." Pride in this possession replaced his nervousness. "Would you care to see it?"

"Very much."

The vicar eyed Cerb uncertainly. "Would your dog perhaps care to—"

Lizzie took pity on him. She reattached the lead she carried to the hound's collar and tied it to the door handle on the church. The door looked solid enough. With a firm adjuration for her pet to sit, and remain just where he was until she returned for him, she turned back to the vicar. Cerb's frenzied yelps followed them into the low building across the court.

The records were there, all right—hundreds of years of them. Lizzie regarded the shelves of aging volumes containing lists of births, marriages, and deaths, and stifled an inward groan.

"If I could be of any assistance to you?" Mr. Winfield peered at her myopically. "What did you wish to find?"

She smiled brightly. "I'm just interested in the Ashfield family history."

Mr. Winfield drew a pair of spectacles from his pocket, polished them, and placed them on the bridge of his beaklike nose. "Would not the muniments room at the Grange provide you with more information?"

"Not enough for vulgar curiosity." To prevent his asking more questions, she drew the last volume from its shelf and opened it. A mishmash of entries greeted her reluctant eyes. Nothing, it appeared, transpired in the parish without being recorded. Gritting her teeth, she wended her way back through time, checking each entry for the Ashfield name.

The vicar lighted several candles and placed them at her side. She thanked him absently, without looking up from her work. With a murmured apology, he at last departed for business of his own, his exit from the room being marked by Cerb's renewed yelps. These quieted eventually, and Lizzie returned her concentration to her search.

Working backwards made it difficult. A quick rummage through a desk, though, produced pen, ink, and paper, and she made a separate recording of each death and marriage, then checked it off against the mention of the birth as she reached it. The Ashfields appeared to have been a prolific family, though many of the children died in infancy.

Hunger finally intruded on her, and she set the volume back on its shelf. She'd recorded every Ashfield who had either been born, married, or died between 1820 and 1723, and had earned nothing for her diligence except a severe headache. She snuffed the candles, glared at the silent rows of volumes, and strode out to retrieve the restless Cerb.

She didn't return until late that afternoon, when her determination overpowered her loathing of the task. It had to be done, and no one but she was likely to do it. So she might as well get on with it.

In April of 1703, she found the record of the birth of one Samuel Ashfield. She stared at the name for a long moment, then checked her list. No mention of any Samuel's marriage or death appeared anywhere. Her fingers clenched on her pen as a thrill of exultation raced through her, and she reread the entry again. Samuel Ashfield, third son of the second viscount.

A younger son. A possible heir to inherit . . . The record was over a hundred years old, long enough for everyone to forget his existence.

Her hands trembled with elation. She had to be sure, though. This was too important for a casual error. Carefully, she went over the records once more. He might never have married. But he had to have died,

221

even if only recently. She inched her way forward through the innumerable names and listings, reading every line with care, until she returned once more to the record of the sixth viscount's death less than a month before. The Honorable Mr. Samuel Ashfield's name did not appear again.

Lizzie closed the book and stared thoughtfully at the black cover, then went in search of her brother.

She found him in St. Vincent's room, with the patient out of bed and seated comfortably in an overstuffed chair before the fireplace. Her heart lifted at sight of Frederick; then she noted his elaborate dressing gown, which was of such outlandish pattern as to instantly win her disapproval. She regarded it with a baleful glare.

"Do you know, one might almost think it does not meet with her approval," St. Vincent declared of no one in particular.

"It does not." She closed the door and joined them at the table, and looked instead at her brother's hand of cards. "Frederick, have you ever heard of a Samuel Ashfield? Born in 1703?"

St. Vincent shook his head. "Should I have?"

She gave him an enigmatic smile. "There is no mention of his death in the parish records, that's all."

"A long-lived gentleman?" he suggested.

Adrian looked at her sharply. "What do you think happened to him?"

She sank onto a chair, twitched a card from her brother's hand, and played it. St. Vincent tossed down one of his own, and she took the trick. "I'm hoping Frederick can give us an idea. He was a third son," she added helpfully.

St. Vincent subjected the matter to serious consideration. "Over one hundred years," he mused. "How do you intend to find out what became of him?"

She selected another card, and Adrian, smiling slightly, offered her the entire hand. Absently, she

222

shook her head. "Obviously, he left the area, and most likely he broke contact with the family."

St. Vincent's eyes gleamed. "Of a certainty. Undoubtedly he committed some vile and fiendish crime and they packed him off to the Colonies with the sincere hope he would die in the crossing."

Lizzie glared at him. "I'm trying to help," she pointed out, her expression hurt.

"And I'm trying to be practical. Do you really think you can trace him? His descendants—if he had any—probably have no idea our branch of the family exists."

"Unless they've been plotting vengeance for their ancestor's being cast out," Adrian suggested, mischievously.

Lizzie regarded him with fond exasperation. "Well, why not? Have you a better idea?"

St. Vincent ran a finger along the top of his cards, picked one and made his play. "He might have been killed at any time, and word simply not brought back."

"Or he might have settled somewhere and raised a family," Lizzie countered. "He might have had any number of sons, and a descendant ready to claim the title."

St. Vincent studied his remaining two cards. "You have my full permission to investigate any black sheep you may find in my familial cupboard. Or do I mean skeletons?"

Adrian selected a card, Lizzie nodded approval, and he played it. His expression, though, was serious as he turned to her. "Do you really think this idea of yours is likely, Lizzie?"

"I don't know," she said after a moment. "If there *is* another heir, then he might well be glad to see Frederick dead."

St. Vincent frowned. "It's a possibility, of course, but I don't see how it can be a viable one. If an Ashfield came into the district, everyone would be aware of it."

"I know." She sank her chin into her cupped hands.

"And if he came under a false name, to remove the obstacles between himself and the title, he could never come forward to claim it, or he'd be recognized and exposed."

"This is all nothing but speculation," Adrian pointed out. "But for St. Vincent's sake, we'd best find out for certain what became of this Samuel."

"My protectors," St. Vincent murmured, shaking his head, but his tone did not mock. A sad smile just touched his lips as his gaze rested on Lizzie.

She stood. "Where should we begin?" She looked from one to the other of them. "The muniments room?"

St. Vincent nodded, albeit cautiously.

Adrian cast him a considering look. "Why don't you stay here? Lizzie and I can go over the records."

"It should only take you about a week," the viscount informed him, his smile one of encouragement.

"A week?" Lizzie regarded him in horror.

"About that. The Ashfields have a long history."

"Which may come to an abrupt end if we don't get to work," Adrian pointed out under his breath as he and Lizzie departed.

Lizzie met his serious gaze and nodded. "We'll have to discover this heir—"

"If one really exists," Adrian inserted.

"—as quickly as possible," she finished, sounding, she knew, daunted. "Let's get some help."

The bailiff would be the obvious choice, but Lizzie rejected him out of hand. Mr. Rycroft *had* seemed somewhat pleased over St. Vincent's accident. On the whole, she'd rather he didn't learn of their suspicions. Why, she couldn't quite be certain. Lady St. Vincent, though, would make an admirable helper.

She found that lady once more engaged in her embroidery, her daughter at her side setting delicate stitches into the hem of a shawl. Quickly, Lizzie explained her idea.

Georgiana stared at her in wide-eyed amazement. "A

224

missing heir?" she asked, incredulous.

The dowager viscountess clutched her embroidery frame. "Oh, how very distressing this all is. I had hoped it could not be true."

"Someone murdered Papa and wanted Cousin Frederick accused," Georgiana breathed. Excitement animated her lovely countenance. "Oh, of all things it would be the most exciting! Do you really think it possible?"

"You sound as if you would be glad if someone killed St. Vincent," Lizzie accused.

Georgiana stared at her through limpid blue eyes. "Of course not. I *like* Cousin Frederick."

"This is only speculation, remember," Adrian said.

Lady St. Vincent rose. "Cousin Frederick has always been so very kind to us. I should like of all things to help. Shall we begin at once?"

With four of them working, their labor progressed more quickly than Lizzie had expected. They set aside records prior to 1703 and concentrated only on the later ones. But though they poured over the thick volumes and scanned every document, the name Samuel did not appear.

"Apparently he did nothing to further the interests of the family," Georgiana said as she closed the last book the following evening.

Lizzie glared about her at the piles of documents and records in disgust. "Nothing! Not a single clue! More than a day wasted!"

The dowager lowered her lorgnette and rubbed her strained eyes. "Might he not have furthered his own interests, though?"

"What do you mean?" Adrian turned from where he had begun to restack the books on their shelves.

"If you left home to make your fortune, wouldn't you want those you left behind to know if you succeeded?" A diffident smile just touched her gentle mouth. "I don't know, of course, but it would seem

225

likely, would it not?"

"*If* he succeeded," Lizzie stuck in, but she watched the dowager closely. "Wouldn't any letters that were kept be in here?"

"Oh, no. Not unless the main branch of the family were enhanced in some way. A younger son, succeeding on his own, would have been ignored, I fear." Lady St. Vincent shook her head. "The Ashfields have always been so very single-minded, you see. Other letters would either have been burned or eventually stored in the attics."

"There are lots of things up there," Georgiana agreed. "We used to play among them. I remember bundles and bundles of yellowed sheets, all done up with ribands and smelling of lavender and pennyroyal."

"The attics," Adrian repeated. Instinctively, he glanced upward.

"Are there many?" Lizzie asked, trying very hard to sound enthusiastic.

"I'm afraid so." This time, the dowager smiled with real warmth, and the habitual nervousness that marked her countenance evaporated.

"Lord, it's late." Adrian stifled a yawn. "Shall we continue in the morning?"

"Please." Lizzie rubbed her strained eyes. "What a job this has been! If there's any danger to St. Vincent, though, we've got to find it."

When they gathered at the breakfast table the following morning, the viscount himself joined them. Lizzie threw down her napkin as he hesitated on the threshold, and hurried to his side.

"Are you sure you should have come down?"

He raised a humorous brow. "I thought you detested people who lay abed coddling themselves."

She waved that aside. "Adrian, should he—"

"I can manage very well."

226

He took her hand, which she had rested on his arm, and raised her fingers to his lips. A warm glow spread through her, which slowly changed to sadness. Of course he was fond of her; he'd always regarded her as a niece. He wouldn't be comfortable with any other relationship between them.

She freed herself and turned away. "At least the work will go faster with someone else to help."

He followed her to the sideboard, only a slight limp marring his progress. "Do we begin at once?"

"It's very good to see you up." The dowager viscountess rose uncertainly to her feet and held out her hand toward him. "You must not strain yourself, though."

He kissed her fingers. "I doubt Lizzie will permit it."

"Nor will I." Georgiana went to him, stood on tiptoe and planted a kiss on his cheek. "I wouldn't like it at all if you were killed."

St. Vincent patted the girl's hand and smiled at her. He was fond of Georgiana, too, Lizzie noted. She regarded the girl with critical appraisal. There wasn't much *not* to like, she decided at last, and returned to her chair. The girl's figure was ethereally slender. Fairylike, Augusta would have called her, with that cloud of lovely golden hair, that tiny uptilted nose, those lips as red as if she had been eating berries. And not a freckle in sight. What did men have against freckles, anyway? *She'd* never given them a thought. Before.

Lizzie finished her meal in silence, then pushed her chair away from the table. "I'm going to get started. Adrian, are you ready?"

The others came also, with St. Vincent trailing at the rear, carrying a plate on which rested a tankard and a roll stuffed with several juicy slices of beef.

They paused on the top floor, and Lizzie threw open the first door on their right. Little light filtered through

227

the grimy panes into the low-pitched chamber. It was sufficient, though, to illuminate the dust motes that floated through the air. Lizzie wrinkled her nose and sneezed.

"My apologies," St. Vincent drawled. "My dear Cousin Isobel, I thought you had issued instructions that the attics were to be turned out every other decade or so."

"Oh, dear, it is dreadful, is it not?" She wrung her hands. "But my husband said there was no need to waste a maid's time—" She broke off, honestly distressed.

He laughed softly and caught her agitated hands. "My dear Cousin, you must know I delight in teasing. You may order the servants exactly as you please from now on."

Georgiana touched the top of a trunk, then regarded her fingers with distaste. "I doubt there has been anyone in here for upwards of a dozen years!"

"Very probably more, I should think." St. Vincent dusted his own fingers with his voluminous handkerchief.

"Let's not waste time." Lizzie strode across the room, fumbled with the window latch, and threw the sash wide. Sunlight streamed in and she shivered in the chill breeze. "There, at least we can breathe, now. Well?"

She fixed the others with a determined eye and Georgiana and Lady St. Vincent each turned to a trunk. Adrian pulled open a drawer of a chest and began to sort through the contents.

"Efficient as always," St. Vincent murmured, and seated himself on the edge of a chair.

Lizzie turned her back on him and opened another trunk.

Nearly two hours later, she sank down on a teetering stool. "Has your family never tossed *anything* into the

228

fire?" she demanded. Nine thick bundles of letters lay on the floor at her side, and she held another in her hand. She shoved it down with the others, and closed the lid of the trunk. Similar piles lay near each of the others.

"If this Samuel of yours ever did write, the chances of his letter having been kept are very good," St. Vincent said, and smiled at the quelling glare Lizzie directed at him.

"If we can *find* his letter among all these," Georgiana said with a sigh.

"We will." Lizzie allowed no trace of the dismay that crept over her to enter her voice. They would find it because they had to, to ensure Frederick's safety. It might all be nothing but a false trail, but then at least they'd know the danger to him lay in another direction. And they would take appropriate precautions.

"Why don't we read through the ones we've found?" Adrian asked. "That should take us a day or two. And it might save us further searching in here."

"An excellent suggestion." St. Vincent rose stiffly to his feet and gathered his collection of yellowed sheets. "Shall we repair to the library?"

Lizzie located a hatbox, dumped its ancient contents into the rummaged trunk before her, and shoved the bundles of letters into it instead.

The air in the library might be cleaner, and the light from the multitude of candles made the decipherment of the cramped, spidery hands possible, if not easy, but Lizzie soon grew restless. She had passed too many days inside, poring over records. She needed to get out, to get some exercise, to enjoy the icy air. She hated this stifled feeling. The others, though, kept doggedly at their chore, reading each letter with care, searching for any mention of the missing Samuel. She would not desert her post.

"I feel like I'm prying," Georgiana said as she laid a

sheet aside. "Could we not just look at the signatures until we find one from Samuel?"

"Someone else might mention him," Lizzie said. She set aside several sheets dated after 1750. She'd come back to them later.

Hours passed, with their only diversion a cold nuncheon. They returned to their task almost at once. Fortified by a glass of wine, Lizzie once more perused what loomed like a never-ending pile of correspondence.

Early evening already closed about them when the dowager viscountess looked up from the scribbled sheet she studied through her lorgnette. "Samuel married in 1741," she exclaimed. She peered at the page again. "A Mary Lincott, living in Boston." With an air of timid triumph, she handed the missive to St. Vincent. "He apparently wrote to an aunt, who wrote to his mother."

St. Vincent gripped the letter, scanning it quickly until he found the names. "We can now dispense with anything prior to 1741," he announced. "And see if you can find anything signed 'Hester.'"

Silence fell once again, punctuated by the crackling of the flames in the hearth and the crinkling of ancient papers as they were unfolded and scanned. A maid entered and rebuilt the fire, cast them a curious glance, then withdrew. They continued their search.

Almost two hours later, Frederick's soft laugh made Lizzie look up. "Well?" she demanded.

"I've found it!" he declared. "Lizzie, you were right."

"Of course I was. Stop being so provoking and tell us."

"It's to Cornelius, fourth viscount, from someone who identifies himself as Samuel's eldest son Joseph."

"Eldest," Lizzie repeated, leaning forward, eager. "What does he say?"

"That his younger brother quarreled violently with

230

him. So much so that the boy changed his name and moved away. Joseph has no idea where the boy was going, nor does he seem to care, according to this."

Lizzie joined him and took the sheet. "No," she said at last. "Not a clue as to where his brother went—or even what his name is." She sighed, returned to the letters, and silence engulfed them once more.

This time, only half an hour passed before St. Vincent spoke again. "Joseph's daughter wrote to Aunt Lavinia, begging permission to come to England to be presented. It appears that Joseph is furious that his only child is not a male, and he will have nothing to do with her education."

Lizzie set down the uninformative letter she deciphered. "Then if there is a rightful heir, he will be descended from Joseph's nameless brother who moved away!"

"Nameless, indeed, if he changed it."

Lizzie stared at St. Vincent, aghast. "It could be anything!"

"Then we had best see if we can find any clues," Adrian said.

St. Vincent stared at the diminished pile before him. "Do you think it likely he kept in touch with the family—after going to such an extreme as changing his name?"

Lady St. Vincent laid aside the letter she had just finished. "Oh, dear. It doesn't, does it?"

Lizzie gazed into the fire, unseeing. "This must be the answer! We would be wasting our time looking for an Ashfield, for he will have a different name! Why, the heir might be in the district now!"

"Whom do you suggest?" A warm light touched St. Vincent's tired eyes. "One of your suspects? Mr. Needham, whose family has been in India? Or Mr. Burnett? I believe he was born in America. Or would you rather have Mr. Winfield? His name is so very similar to ours. Ashfield could easily have become Winfield."

Lizzie shook her head. "It must be Mr. Burnett, for he even admitted his family originally came from Leicestershire!"

Georgiana opened her mouth to speak, then closed it tightly again. "Do you really think so?"

St. Vincent shook his head. "Mr. Burnett *might* prove to be a legitimate heir, but he could hardly be the villain of our murder."

"Why not?" Lizzie regarded him, somewhat daunted.

"He would need a motive, and I cannot believe, if he *is* the one, that he knows the nature of his connection with the Ashfield family."

Lizzie considered a moment, then nodded in reluctant agreement. "If he did, he would pretend to know nothing, wouldn't he? He'd never have mentioned the circumstances of his people coming from Leicestershire."

"It does indeed seem a foolhardy thing to do, if he were guilty," Adrian agreed.

Lizzie sighed. "No, he cannot be the murderer. But it did seem so perfect!"

St. Vincent smiled. "We cannot even be sure Mr. Burnett really is my heir—if one exists."

"It could, indeed, be anyone," Lady St. Vincent said, dismayed.

Lizzie threw down the sheets that remained in her lap. "We are no closer to solving this problem than we were before," she declared in disgust.

St. Vincent refolded the pertinent letters and set them aside. He then turned his attention to shoving the others back into their boxes to be returned to the attics.

"Are we done, then?" Georgiana asked. "Are we not to look for anything else?"

St. Vincent shook his head, absently. "I don't believe there's any need. We will present these to Lizzie's

Runner, I think, and see what he makes of them. They should at least provide something to occupy his mind other than accusing me of slicing my own girth."

Lizzie shoved her stack of letters back into the hat box. "But will you be safe? We still have no idea who it might be—or if this is even the reason behind your accident."

Chapter 18

After handing the letters over to the skeptical Coggins, St. Vincent seemed to lose all interest in the matter. The Runner sent instantly to London to begin tracing the possible missing heir, but St. Vincent paid no further heed to the mystery of his cousin's murder. He spent his time with Adrian and Mr. Rycroft, going over account books or riding about the estate.

Lizzie watched him in growing confusion. Why didn't he care? It was almost as if he didn't expect anything to come of this line of inquiry. But why shouldn't he, unless—unless he already knew the murderer could not be this missing heir?

She closed her eyes, trying to think logically, which had become difficult of late. Frederick had been the one who found the letters. . . . The image of his slashed girth rose in her mind. Confound it, he hadn't cut it himself! Nor had he planted those letters to throw suspicion away from him! St. Vincent was *not* a murderer! She knew him too well to be able to suspect it for even a moment. Yet the question of his possible guilt remained in her mind, unbanishable, haunting her.

She might as well get on with her investigations. With the intention of discovering whether Mr. Winfield's family had ever lived in America, she set forth through the frost-laden woods toward the vicarage. Cerb barreled ahead through the underbrush, to the accompaniment of crashes and fluttered squawks as wood pigeons made their frantic escape.

Lizzie followed, her steps dragging. Her forthright soul protested this line of inquiry. It was too sublte, too convoluted, to work. If no one suspected an heir, then one would not be looked for upon Frederick's death. If he were someone known to them, the heir himself could not come forward to claim the title and estate, for that would immediately throw suspicion onto him. Unless, of course, St. Vincent could be made to look guilty of his cousin's murder—or his death appeared to be an accident.

She caught up with her exuberant pet where the trees gave way to shrubs and the path led down a slight incline to the hedged garden surrounding the vicarage. Grabbing Cerb's collar, Lizzie convinced him to leave off his exploration of a small burrow amidst the tangled roots of a tree and accompany her.

As they neared the church, she glimpsed two people amid the bare rosebushes, standing stiffly, almost combative. Arguing? Lizzie's interest perked up. The slight man in black she identified at once as Mr. Winfield. The dark green pelisse on the lady with him belonged to Georgiana. The girl said something Lizzie couldn't quite catch, but its effect on the vicar was immediate. His erect back slumped, his head hung, and he nodded as if admitting to some mortal sin. Georgiana stared at him, and her anger visibly evaporated. She moved toward him in a fluid movement, clasped his hands between her own, and gazed into his face with an expression of abject adoration.

Mr. Winfield made no move to extricate himself. He patted her hand with all the ineptitude of one acutely embarrassed and unaccustomed to having a lovely young lady hanging on him.

Cerb strained against her hold, and let out a yelp of

protest as Lizzie refused to let go. Georgiana and the vicar looked up, startled, and he stepped back, dropping her hands as if they suddenly burned him. Lizzie released the hound and he bounded forward, loudly vociferating his greeting.

Lizzie reached them while Georgiana attempted to hold the hound, his exuberant tongue licking at top speed, at arm's length. Lizzie called him to heel, and reluctantly he sank to his haunches.

Mr. Winfield managed a shaky smile. "Good morning, Miss Carstairs. I see your Cerberus enjoys his usual excellent health."

Lizzie agreed, then realized she hadn't the faintest notion how to proceed. She liked to ask questions point blank. This going about things in a subtle manner was not in the least to her taste. She regarded the vicar's worried countenance as he gazed at the giant hound, and decided she had nothing to lose.

"Has your family ever lived in America?" she asked.

He blinked, bewildered by her question.

"Lizzie!" Georgiana stared at her, aghast. "How can you even suspect such a dreadful thing? A man of the cloth?"

Mr. Winfield turned his mild gaze on her. "There is nothing in the least reprehensible in having lived in America, my dear Miss Ashfield. On the contrary, I believe the rigors of life there might be held to improve one's soul."

Lizzie's mouth dropped open, and she closed it with a snap. "You mean they *did?*"

"No. If they had, I am certain I should even now be pursuing my calling on those distant shores." He shook his head, not without a certain measure of regret. "A challenging prospect, but alas, not for me. No, my people are from West Sussex, where we have resided for generations."

"Oh." *If* that were true. Fortunately, it was one of those things that could quite easily be discovered.

236

The vicar waited a moment, as if expecting her to elaborate, but she did not. "If you will excuse me?" he asked. "Parish business, I fear."

Lizzie nodded absently, murmured her goodbyes, and turned back the way she had come. Georgiana fell into step beside her, but Lizzie paid her no heed. The vicar was still a likely candidate for having murdered the old viscount, she reminded herself. There was that business of blackmail. But she could honestly think of no reason why he should want to do away with Frederick. Perhaps that was someone else entirely.

"I don't think I ever realized how kind Mr. Winfield is," Georgiana said, breaking across Lizzie's thoughts.

"Kind?" She glanced at the girl. "In what way?"

A soft flush stole into Georgiana's cheeks. "I—I overheard something Mr. Rycroft said to Hodgkens, about the gamekeeper carrying on a—a liaison with one of the maids. Hodgkens wanted them both dismissed, it seems, but Cousin Frederick refused."

"And what did Mr. Winfield have to say about that?"

"Well, it occurred to me, from something Cousin Frederick said—" She broke off, her color deepening. "That is—I asked Mr. Winfield—"

"What on earth are you getting at?" Lizzie demanded, exasperated.

"It was all a secret, for Papa would have dismissed them both if he had known, but Mr. Winfield says he performed their marriage several months ago."

Lizzie stopped and stared at her. "Your father would have sent Treecher and Lily packing for *marrying?*"

Georgiana nodded. "And they both needed to work, Mr. Winfield says, so he told no one. Isn't it romantic? I never would have thought he would dare defy Papa."

Apparently, that had elevated the man to hero status in Georgiana's eyes. Lizzie fell silent, considering. Yes, she could well imagine the old viscount firing a servant who dared have a life of his or her own. Frederick wouldn't, though.

She caught a loose strand of soft brown hair and chewed meditatively on the end. Would that be a motive for killing the old viscount? What if he found out, perhaps caught the gamekeeper on a nocturnal visit to the maid? The gamekeeper had already been dismissed! she remembered suddenly, and only that morning! She had never met the old viscount, but from everything she had heard, he might well have flown into an uncontrollable rage at encountering the man sneaking into the house.

Some murders, she decided, were justified. If only that fool Runner hadn't selected Frederick as his prime suspect, she would be more than ready to let the matter drop. Henry, though, was also dead, and his murder could *not* be thought a public good. She would not let herself forget that.

She parted from Georgiana as soon as they entered the house, and made her way to the library. There, somewhat to her surprise, she found St. Vincent and Adrian playing piquet rather than concerning themselves with estate business.

She eyed them with disfavor. "Why didn't you tell me the gamekeeper was married to Lily?" she demanded.

St. Vincent's elegant brow rose a fraction. "I felt the least said about the matter, the better. What ever made you think they were *not* married?"

"The way everyone behaved, as if their being together was shocking."

"But you were not shocked?"

She shrugged and sat down at her brother's side. "What has the outcome been?"

"I have ordered the preparation of quarters for them until Treecher's cottage can be made livable." He played a card, and waited for Adrian's response.

Lizzie was taken aback. Always, she prided herself on her ability to cull information everywhere. Always, she was the first to know everything. She was slipping!

It was Frederick's fault. She let his troubles preoccupy her to the exclusion of all else. Or more likely, the fault lay in her, for letting love cloud her judgment.

Silently, she watched as the game ended. Adrian checked the score and St. Vincent gathered the cards, shuffled, and dealt once more. If only he hadn't become a viscount ... but no, his elevation in status had little to do with his taste in feminine companionship. She amused him at the moment, but he would marry a woman whose worldly wisdom would keep him from growing bored. A sinking sensation filled her stomach, as she recognized she wanted something she could never have.

Quietly, she left the room.

She didn't see Frederick again until she entered the Green Salon before dinner. He looked up from his position on the sofa before the fire, and a humorous smile lit his bright blue eyes. She made her way to a chair set at some distance from him.

His gaze narrowed. "What's bothering you, Lizzie?"

"What should be? After all, we've only had two murders." She managed a cheerful, but false, smile.

"Forced brightness," he murmured, as if adding this to a catalogue of symptoms. "Normally, you would join me and tell me what mischief you and Cerb brewed today. And undoubtedly you'd take me to task for some little oversight about the estate."

"You're doing all you can."

"How do you know? You're not asking. This isn't at all like you not to involve yourself in everything. Are you sickening for something?"

"Don't be ridiculous. I'm never ill." She prodded at the fire with a poker, and wondered how long she had with him before he decided to begin his search for a bride.

Lady St. Vincent and Georgiana entered, interrupting her troubled thoughts, and resolutely Lizzie embarked on a lively discussion with Georgiana on the entertainments to be found in Leicestershire in the depths of winter. This resulted in their decision to invite Mr. Burnett, Mr. Needham, and the vicar for an evening of cards. Frederick evinced little interest, and instead embarked on a discussion with Adrian on how best to stop the decay of the estate.

Lizzie threw herself wholeheartedly into plans for the gathering, with the result that a surprising array of refreshments awaited the guests who gathered two nights later.

St. Vincent, resplendent in a coat of deep blue velvet, greeted the arrivals, and accepted their congratulations on his safe recovery from his riding accident. He turned these aside with a joke, though Lizzie watched closely to try and detect any hint as to who might have cut his girth.

Her gaze swept the room, coming to rest on Mr. Needham; he stood before the hearth, deep in conversation with Mr. Winfield. The vicar's gaze strayed frequently toward Georgiana, as if he longed to go to her side. So did Mr. Needham's. They would probably both join her in a minute, Lizzie reflected.

Mr. Needham, she decided, did not look happy. Did he sense that, despite the dandified beauty of his appearance, he was being cut out in Georgiana's affections? Or was he merely sorry St. Vincent was still alive?

The door opened and Hodgkens stood aside to admit Mr. Burnett. That gentleman strolled in and looked the viscount over, a touch of amusement in his eyes.

"I hope this will not keep you from riding to hounds as soon as your bruises mend," he said.

St. Vincent led him to the refreshment table and handed him a glass of wine. "They are well on their way already. When is the next hunt?"

Mr. Burnett laughed. "The end of the week, my dear fellow. Will you join us, then?"

"Of a certainty."

Lizzie glared at Frederick, but he merely directed an enigmatic smile at her. She turned away, annoyed. Did he openly court death? The next attempt on his life was likely to be more successful, she feared. Unless, of course, he knew no such attempt would be made.

An uncomfortable knot tightened in her stomach once more. *Did* anyone really want St. Vincent dead? Coggins didn't think so—and she had developed a grudging respect for the Runner's abilities. Confound it, did St. Vincent make a May-game of her, letting her try to pin the murder on someone else? She went to one of the card tables and began to thrust chairs ruthlessly into position.

Still, her gaze strayed back to Frederick, uncertain. As much as she hated to admit it, she had changed during those five years since she had spent so much time with him in Brussels. He had roamed the world, seeing the Continent, Jamaica, and India. Had he changed, too?

No! the answer rushed to fill her mind. He was still very much the same, capable of sardonic humor but never murder. Honesty, though, compelled her to admit she could no longer trust her instincts where he was concerned.

Their gathering, she noted an hour later, was a huge success. Only Mr. Needham appeared to be in less than a jovial mood. He retired to a corner with a glass of wine, and seemed lost in dismal thoughts of his own. Not even Georgiana could coax him into a more cheerful frame of mind. Had he abandoned his much-professed desire to marry her? Or did his sullen mood lie in jealousy?

As soon as the girl rose from her game of piquet with the attentive Mr. Burnett, relinquishing her place to St. Vincent, Lizzie intercepted her and drew her aside. "Have you any idea what might be bothering Mr. Needham?" she asked.

Georgiana pondered a moment, then shook her head.

"You once accused him of murdering your father," Lizzie pursued, her tactics blunt as always.

Georgiana bit her lip. "I know I did, but I don't think I ever really believed it. This possible missing heir is a *much* better chance, is it not?" She turned once more to regard Mr. Needham. "His manners are so very polished, I truly cannot envision him killing someone."

"He doesn't lack the backbone," Lizzie said slowly. She moved on, and a minute later joined Mr. Winfield for a game of piquet; the two slipped comfortably into talk of parish matters.

To her relief, the party broke up early, their guests claiming the frigid night and heavy cloud cover made travel dangerous. Lizzie, along with the others, trailed into the hall while the footmen produced cloaks, gloves, and hats. St. Vincent stood to one side with Mr. Burnett, discussing the upcoming hunt.

Mr. Needham, Lizzie realized suddenly, was not with them. She turned about, in time to see that gentleman on the far side of the Great Hall, studying his reflection in a huge gilded mirror. Lizzie's lip curled. A simpering tulip. What ever made—

The thought broke off. Was Mr. Needham talking to himself? Or to someone who stood just out of her sight? Suspicious, Lizzie strolled in her most casual manner toward him. A hand protruded from a doorway beyond Mr. Needham. That gentleman drew something from his pocket and handed it over; then, with a final touch to his neckcloth, he turned to rejoin the others. He saw Lizzie and hesitated a moment, then swept past her with a nervous smile.

Lizzie peered through the doorway into the drawing room. A tallish, well-set-up gentleman with wavy golden brown hair slipped out the door on the far side. Mr. Julian Rycroft. Now, what would Mr. Needham be giving the bailiff in so surreptitious a manner?

Her first impulse, which was to tell St. Vincent at once, she banished. She didn't want to give him such a golden opportunity to make jokes about her playing Bow Street Runner. Undoubtedly a simple explanation would shortly present itself, and then he would tease her unmercifully for being so suspicious.

In silence, she made her way to her room. She could remember a time when she would have laughed at St. Vincent's lighthearted banter, and have given in return even better than she got. But now she'd gone and complicated everything. Had he been aware of her changing sentiments, even before she? If so, it was no wonder he had begun to put a distance between them.

She had barely donned her robe and dismissed her maid, when a crash resounded down the hall. Her troubled thoughts vanished, and she ran into the corridor. Adrian, shielding a candle with one hand, burst from his room and headed toward the other wing. Lizzie followed, her heart beating far too hard for such mild exertion. The sound had come from the vicinity of St. Vincent's bedchamber.

Adrian reached it first and jerked open the door. He stopped just over the threshold. Lizzie clutched his arm, standing on tiptoe to see over his shoulder.

The fire in the hearth illuminated the chamber, obviating the need for the candle Adrian held aloft. Her gaze riveted at once on the splintered mass that only minutes before had been St. Vincent's great, curtain-hung bed.

Chapter 19

"Frederick!" Lizzie pushed forward past her brother, her gaze never wavering from the wreckage. The blood drained from her face, leaving her cold and trembling. Adrian grabbed ~~the sleeve~~ of her dressing gown, but she pulled free.

"Somewhat of a mess, isn't it." An almost calm voice spoke from the vicinity of the fireplace.

Lizzie spun about. "Frederick," she breathed.

He stood in the shadowed recess of the hearth, garbed in his richly patterned dressing gown and slippers. He came a step into the room, and the flickering light of the flames danced along the brandy glass he clutched in one hand.

Lizzie took an unsteady step toward him, then forced herself to stop and take a deep breath. He was safe. And she mustn't embarrass him with an emotional display.

"What happened?" Adrian climbed the single step to the dais and studied the broken timbers atop the mattress.

"I believe the beams that supported the top gave out." Frederick located his quizzing glass on the top of his dresser and regarded the mess through the lens. After a moment, he crossed to the bell pull and tugged it.

Lizzie, recovering from her shock, joined her brother. She traced a finger along the twisted curves of the eight-inch-thick pillars. "Why would anyone make a bed canopy out of anything so heavy? If you'd been lying under that—" She broke off and shuddered.

"In another minute, I would have been." Frederick picked up a torn fold of the blue velvet bed curtains. "It shouldn't have collapsed," he added.

They waited in silence until Cummings hurried into the room. The little man stopped short and stared. After a moment, he turned wide, horrified eyes toward his master.

"It would seem my inheritance is now falling about my ears," Frederick informed his valet.

"How—?" Cummings broke off.

"An excellent question," St. Vincent agreed. "How, indeed?" He shoved aside an armful of curtains and bent to examine the splintered mess on the mattress.

Lizzie picked up a candle and held it close to the severed base of one of the posts. "Can you see what happened?"

Adrian nodded, his expression grim. "It's been cut."

Frederick examined the top end, which until recently had connected with the canopy. "Someone took a saw to it," he confirmed.

"Let me just summon the footmen, m'lord," Cummings said.

St. Vincent met Adrian's frowning gaze. "I think not. It will be best if we leave this for our Runner to inspect."

Lizzie swallowed hard and her free hand closed about Frederick's arm. "You mean it was done on purpose? But—wouldn't you have seen the sawdust?"

"Not if whoever did this covered the bed with a sheet, then took it away with him." St. Vincent covered her hand with his own, and squeezed gently.

"When?" she asked, dragging her gaze from his face.

"After the bed was turned down, I should imagine, or it would have collapsed on the housemaid." He turned to his valet. "Do you know when that would have been?"

"Early, m'lord," Cummings said, still shaken. "Before

245

the guests arrived. She was needed in the kitchens. The staff here is hardly adequate."

"I suppose your climbing in was supposed to shake it enough to bring it down," Lizzie said. Somehow, she kept her tone purely conversational.

"Only instead I leaned against one of the posts for a moment before going to pour a brandy." St. Vincent regarded the mess, his expression solemn. "Do you know, I have begun to get the distinct impression someone would be glad to see me dead."

Lizzie clenched her teeth and fought the lurching in her stomach. Determinedly, she concentrated on the practical aspects of the situation. "If we cannot clean this up, you'll have to find somewhere else to sleep tonight. Are there any other beds made up?"

"There's a daybed in my room," Adrian said. "You'd be—comfortable—there."

St. Vincent smiled, though somewhat dryly. "Thank you, my boy. Though I doubt there are any more traps set for me in this chamber."

"No, this one should have done the trick quite effectively." Lizzie didn't look at him. "I know it's a silly notion, Frederick, and quite unworthy of me, but I think I would sleep better if you shared Adrian's room—just for this one night."

"Very well, Lizzie, though I doubt I'm in any danger here except from splinters." He picked up a fragmented board and turned it over. "I think, though, we had best solve this little mystery of ours. Life will quickly become a bore if I must constantly be examining my girth or reins or carriage or anything else I touch for signs of cutting."

They left, locking the room behind them, and Cummings hurried ahead to arrange such comforts for his master as could be found. Lizzie accompanied them as far as her brother's door, where she bade them good night, and continued on to her own chamber.

Once inside, she took off her dressing gown and crawled between sheets. She was far from sleep, though;

246

nor did fluffing her pillow and snuggling beneath the comforter help. St. Vincent had been lucky—again. She shivered, only partly with the cold. Would Mr. Coggins consider this another "staged" accident? For that matter, did she?

If not—and, of course, it wasn't!—Frederick was in very real danger, and she—or anyone else—might not be able to save him. That knowledge frustrated her, leaving her with a sense of helplessness she found intolerable.

She rose early the following morning, despite her disturbed night, donned her riding habit and a warm cloak, then she strode across to her brother's room. The door remained securely locked, which Lizzie hoped was a good sign. Unless she intended to stand guard outside, there was nothing she could do for him at the moment.

Restless, she made her way down to the kitchens, where she cajoled a hearty breakfast from the indulgent cook. Cerb and Patrick could both use a good run this morning, and so could she. Later she would collect the grooms and tackle the ivy that still blocked the windows at the back of the house. Satisfied with this decision, she set out for the stableyard, shivering in the icy breeze and enjoying its stimulating effect.

As she crossed the rose garden, a flutter of red caught her eye, and she turned to see the tail of a scarf protruding from behind a thick oak. It wasn't hanging there on its own, either. She could just glimpse the muddied heel of a top boot resting on a tangled root. What the devil—?

She started toward the intruder, then opted for discretion. She turned aside, into a shrubbery, and circled back. By careful maneuvering, she managed to come up behind the greatcoated figure just as he darted off. He cast a furtive glance from side to side, and with a sense of interested surprise she recognized the undistinguished countenance of Mr. Percival Needham.

Now, why was he sneaking about the grounds on such an icy morning, hiding behind trees? It wasn't at all the sort of behavior she expected of him—and it followed so soon after his odd action of the night before. Her curiosity rampant, she followed as he crept from oak to elm, always taking great care to keep himself hidden—from someone in front of him, at least. Whom did he follow?

She kept up her own pursuit, her curiosity growing. They passed the gardens of the Dower House with only the briefest pauses and continued their unorthodox progress. They were heading in the general direction of the vicarage, it dawned on Lizzie. Yes, now they were definitely skirting the path. She knew a strong impulse to hurry ahead to discover just what was going on and who led them this merry dance, but she stifled it. They were almost there; she would learn in a few minutes.

She peered ahead, but Mr. Needham was no longer in sight. Where—? Puzzled, she hurried forward, only to collide with that dandified gentleman as he emerged from behind a bush. She took a steadying step backwards, and he glared at her, rubbing his arm where she had hit.

"I lost him," he said in disgust.

"Who?"

"Mr.—" He broke off. "What the deuce are you doing? Following me?"

"Yes. Who were *you* following?"

Mr. Needham seemed to consider the question for a moment, then shrugged. "Mr. Rycroft, of course. Who else?"

Who else, indeed. "Why?" Lizzie hazarded.

"I went up to the house to speak with St. Vincent, but—"

"At this hour of the morning?" She raised skeptical brows. "He rarely leaves his chamber before ten."

"Doesn't he?" The self-styled dandy frowned.

"What happened?" she prodded.

"Oh. I was just nearing the house when I saw Mr. Rycroft coming out of the ballroom. I'd never seen a man look so suspicious. He kept glancing over his shoulder.

248

So naturally I followed."

Lizzie chewed her lower lip. "Why should Mr. Rycroft go to see Mr. Winfield so early in the morning?"

"And in so peculiar a manner?" Mr. Needham nodded, his expression puzzled.

She tugged at a loose strand of her hair and came to a decision. "The top of St. Vincent's bed collapsed during the night. If he'd been in it, and not still getting ready, he would have been killed." She studied his face for any clue to his reaction.

Mr. Needham shuddered. "Dreadful. And so soon—" He broke off, then shook his head. "No, of course not," he murmured. "Just a frightful run of experiences for him. I hope it doesn't give him a distaste for his inheritance."

"Oh, no. Only for allowing the estate to remain in such ill repair. What did you give Mr. Rycroft last night?"

"What—oh." He gave her a rueful smile. "You saw, did you? I had asked him for some information."

"But you were giving something to him, not the other way around."

He straightened up, affronted. "I paid him, of course, for his trouble. Now, if you will excuse me, I still wish to speak with St. Vincent."

"What did you want to know?"

He flushed. "That doesn't concern anyone but me."

Lizzie allowed the subject to drop, though she would have given a great deal to know the answer. Together, they returned to the house, with Lizzie disgustedly convinced she had gained nothing by her morning foray.

St. Vincent entered the breakfast parlor at what for him was an unseasonably early hour. Somehow, this morning he had experienced absolutely no desire whatsoever to lie abed.

Georgiana, looking lovelier than ever in a pale green muslin, looked up and smiled as he entered. "Good

249

morning, Cousin Frederick."

Adrian turned from the sideboard where he'd been heaping ham on his plate. "Ah, you're awake. Did you pass a pleasant night, St. Vincent?"

The viscount cast him a pained glance. "Oh, tol-lol, dear boy. Is your sister not down?"

"She's gone riding, I believe. Oh, and I set Coggins on that little job we talked about last night." Adrian seated himself at the table, then looked back at his host. "Do you know, I believe we should concentrate our efforts on repairs to the house and carriages at present."

Georgiana glanced from one to the other, her lovely blue eyes betraying nothing but mild surprise. "Is anything amiss?"

St. Vincent smiled blandly at her. "Some of the furniture is falling apart."

She exclaimed in dismay. "Mamma will be so upset. I hope no one was hurt."

"As you see." He availed himself of a tankard of ale and several slices of rare beef, then stared moodily out the window. Leave it to Lizzie to hit upon exactly the right activity for this morning. She was so full of energy, so—so young, her life not cluttered with regrets. He downed the tankard and poured a second, then found he didn't really want it.

He glanced back at Georgiana to see her unconcernedly dipping dry toast into her tea. Apparently, she had no idea of what occurred during the night. That wasn't surprising, though. She and her mother occupied the family wing of the old, rambling house, a long distance from where his guest chamber was situated. It would have been odd if they *had* heard anything. Perhaps it was time he moved into the master's chamber.

He was just finishing his breakfast when Hodgkens entered the salon and announced that Mr. Needham had called to see him, and awaited his pleasure in the library. He rose and set his napkin beside his place. "Will you tell Mr. Rycroft I will join him in half an hour's time, Adrian?" He went to join his visitor.

He entered the room to find Lizzie perched on the arm of a chair, her freckled cheeks becomingly flushed from the chill wind outside. His heart constricted in his chest, forming an icy lump that dissolved into a vast emptiness.

Youth hadn't faded from him; he'd flung it away in reckless disregard, as one blind to its value—and with it, any chance for his happiness.

He shied from the loneliness that stretched before him. Instead, he turned to Lizzie's companion—or more correctly, he mused, her current opponent. Mr. Percival Needham turned hurriedly from her to face him as he strode into the room.

St. Vincent's gazed narrowed. Normally, the young sprig aped the dandy set with painstaking care, taking the greatest effort over his appearance. This morning, he bore every indication of having dragged himself through the shrubbery. St. Vincent raised his quizzing glass and studied a leaf that rested on the would-be tulip's shoulder.

Percival Needham followed the direction of that pointed stare and brushed the offending object away.

"You wished to speak with me?" St. Vincent advanced into the room, allowing the glass to drop. "Whatever have you been about?"

Mr. Needham waved that aside. "I do wish to speak with you, my lord. In private."

St. Vincent directed a look of inquiry at Lizzie. "Is this a problem?"

She sighed. "We are queuing for your time, it seems. I'm next."

He opened the door, and she exited, though she bestowed a speaking look on him as she did. A sad smile just touched his lips as he turned back to his other visitor. "What may I do for you?"

Mr. Needham abandoned the mirror in which he'd

251

been studying his cravat with concern. He patted it uneasily. "I came to ask how the investigation is progressing."

"As well as can be expected, I make no doubt." St. Vincent drew his snuff box from his pocket, flicked it open with his thumb, and offered it to his guest. Mr. Needham helped himself to a too-large pinch and went off in a fit of sneezing. St. Vincent took a more judicious amount, then closed the box and settled in a chair. "Is there any particular reason you ask?"

Mr. Needham made use of his handkerchief, then tucked it away. "Your Runner hasn't been to the Dower House in several days." He managed an almost convincing laugh. "Surely that is remarkable enough in itself to warrant curiosity."

St. Vincent inclined his head, unhelpfully. "I am not in Mr. Coggins's confidence. Miss Carstairs might better be able to tell you what goes on in his mind."

"Yes, Miss Carstairs." He ran a finger about his collar, as if it had become too tight. "She tells me you had another accident—your bed collapsed."

Just what, exactly, had Lizzie told him? Enough to make him nervous, that was obvious. Had she mentioned the saw marks? He kept a pleasant smile on his lips, but watched the man intently.

"Yes, the estate has fallen into dreadful repair. We must hope nothing else falls."

"Then you don't think—no, of course not. Silly idea, really." Mr. Needham managed a sickly smile.

"Think what?"

"Ridiculous suspicion. With your cousin's being murdered, though—" His voice trailed off.

"Ah, I see." St. Vincent feigned enlightenment. "You are wondering if my two accidents were, in fact, attempts by some nefarious person to—er—rid the world of my presence? But who would want to?"

"No one! I mean, why should someone? I said it was a ridiculous notion."

"As for the absence of our Runner, I should rather think that would be an occasion to cause rejoicing on your part."

"On my part? *I* don't mind him! He can come around all he chooses. I don't have anything to hide. I—I just thought maybe it meant he'd learned something?" He ended on a note of half-hope, half-fear.

"Not to my knowledge," St. Vincent said gently.

Mr. Needham nodded, hesitated a moment, then took his leave. He passed Lizzie, who waited in the corridor, with no more than a pathetic smile.

St. Vincent watched this departure through the open doorway, and sighed. "Next!" he called, and she entered without any signs of embarrassment at having been caught listening.

"Have you blighted his troth?" she asked cheerfully.

"Blighted his—oh. No, there was no need. He had not come to offer for Georgiana."

"What, then?" She curled into an overstuffed chair.

"To discover how the investigation progresses. I couldn't tell if he were more distressed by your Runner's no longer haunting the Dower House, or at the prospect of his learning something. Now, about what did *you* wish to see me?"

She grinned. "Oh, I've had the most entertaining morning. I followed Mr. Needham, who was following Mr. Rycroft, who was visiting Mr. Winfield." Briefly, she told him of her surreptitious journey through the wood, and that equally surreptitious meeting in the Great Hall the night before. "I feel quite certain we have a significant clue in there somewhere, but I just don't see how it all fits."

St. Vincent tried to stop a choke of laughter, but failed utterly. She directed an injured glare at him.

"My dear Lizzie," he said when he could speak again. "Never could I have imagined you without some theory. Do you not think them all bound together in some conspiracy against me? Perhaps Mr. Needham hired Mr.

Rycroft to saw through the bedposts."

"I doubt he'd have such a clever notion. Really, Frederick, you aren't taking this in the least bit seriously," she accused. "It would serve you right to be charged with murder."

That sobered him. "I already have been," he pointed out.

"Not formally!" she countered.

She took her leave to resume her aborted trip to the stableyard, and he followed her to the window. For a long while, he gazed after her.

He had made disturbingly little progress toward solving this whole convoluted, dangerous affair. He had ideas, of course, but too many of them and, at this stage, all conflicting. His mysterious ill-wisher might well succeed in removing him before he ever came to the right conclusions.

A gentle rap on the door interrupted his thoughts. The dowager viscountess entered, for once not waiting for his response. She stood uncertainly in the middle of the room, and only on his invitation did she sit down. She was silent for a long moment. "These chairs are quite comfortable," she said at last.

"I'm glad you approve. They had been stored in one of the attics."

The dowager studied her clasped hands, awarding him an excellent view of her soft, silvery-white hair, braided into its customary coronet. When she looked up, her hazel eyes avoided his gaze. From her reticule, she drew a handful of papers and handed them over.

With a sinking sensation in the pit of his stomach, he accepted them. "More bills?" It wasn't really a question.

"They have only just been delivered—I suppose I should have let Hodgkens take them to Mr. Rycroft, but I wanted to speak to you . . ." Her voice trailed off. She came to her feet and stood for a moment, gazing down into the fire. "I hate to see the estate any more grossly encumbered than it is."

St. Vincent leafed through the stack. "Local tradesmen. They must be paid, of course."

She clenched her delicate hands together. "How much longer before the estate may be wound up and we know where we stand? There are so many bills to settle—things we need to purchase. We don't even know if Georgiana will be left with any dowry!"

"She will be!" St. Vincent forced his temper back under control. "You may be sure she will not suffer for her father's distempered freaks."

"Will you sell my husband's collection?"

"The moment those damned—forgive me, those dashed—solicitors grant permission."

"But that won't be until someone is officially charged with my husband's murder, will it?" She breathed the last, as if reluctant to put her fears into words.

"It will not."

She nodded, then straightened as if forcing herself to broach a distasteful subject. "Will you be able to advance us any funds?"

He crossed to the desk. With the small key that hung on his chain, he unlocked the bottom drawer. In there rested all that remained of the notes he had with him. He had already written to his banker, but as yet had received no answer. A gentleman rarely possessed much actual cash. His fortune, such as it was, remained securely invested on the 'Change. He handed her a small purse, and she took it with an air of apology he well understood.

After she left, he studied the bills once more, adding them up—and knowing he had not the wherewithal to cover them. In disgust, he went to join his bailiff and Adrian.

He found them poring over the books, trying to decide on the most pressing repairs, which would also provide the greatest benefit to the estate at the minimum expense. By the sober expressions on their faces, it did not appear they fared well. St. Vincent sank into a chair and prudently decided not to ask.

There was another matter he could broach, about which Lizzie would be quite pleased to discover the truth. "I understand you visited the vicarage this morning," he said to his bailiff without preamble.

The man started, then a slow smile spread over his features. "It concerned a matter with which His late Lordship refused to become involved. I did not believe you would care to be disturbed by it at the moment, either."

"Ah, but I interest myself in every aspect of estate life." St. Vincent leaned back in his chair, his eyes half-shut. "What was this matter?"

"Mr. Winfield is seeking aid for the poor, again."

"I see. Which poor in particular?"

Julian Rycroft fingered the wide lapel of his coat, not quite meeting St. Vincent's compelling eye.

Adrian spared him the trouble of answering. "He hopes to aid the tenants with some repairs before the coming of the snows."

St. Vincent rose abruptly and paced several angry steps across the room. "*My* tenants. I see. And why has no one thought to mention Mr. Winfield's intent to me?" This time, it was Adrian upon whom his furious gaze fell.

"Because their predicament is in no way your fault, and until the estate is wound up, you are in no position to do anything to help."

"The devil I'm not!"

He slammed from the room, seething. He should have seen his cousin dead years ago, before everything came to this pass. At this moment, he could almost wish him alive again, so he could enjoy the exquisite pleasure of strangling him.

By the time he reached the library, he had regained partial control of his volatile temper. *Damn* his well-meaning friends. The tenants were his responsibility, and he would make certain his helpers did not forget this again. Since he couldn't touch a single piece of that blasted collection, he'd sell out of the funds. His future was now linked to that of Ashfield Grange; he had no need of monies outside of this, his land and his people.

He dashed off a note to his man of affairs, dusted it with sand and sealed it with the St. Vincent crest pressed firmly into the hot wax. The symbolism of this act was not lost on him, and his old cynical amusement rose once more at his new, idealistic self.

After he dispatched a groom to deliver the letter to the mail, though, the near futility of his defiant act struck him. His private funds were limited; they didn't approach the vast sums necessary to restore the Grange to a thriving estate once more.

Unquiet, he paced out to the stableyard. He hadn't ridden since that hunting accident; if he wasn't careful, he'd grow stiff. He might as well enjoy riding while he still could. He'd probably be reduced to selling his cattle next. As soon as they were legally his, of course.

If he had any sense, he should go to London and hang out for a rich wife at once. He must marry and beget a legal heir for the sake of the estate and the title. Yet he couldn't discover in himself any desire to install in his home the sort of female whose company he had enjoyed in the past.

There was only one female he wanted here. Yet he could never inflict this pile of debt—and his own, aging, cynical, far-too-worldly-wise self—on the one unspoiled girl who had long held his heart.

She was with the horses, as he had known she would be, with that ridiculous hound bounding at her side as she took that young Irish hunter through his paces in the large paddock beyond the stableyard. Her brother-in-law could afford to buy her horses worthy of her. He could not. She had known abject poverty and emerged unscathed and optimistic. He had known affluence and become jaded. She deserved the best—and that was certainly not he.

He turned away from the rail, struggling against his frustrations. The land—he had to concentrate on the land. If only this were a duel, where he could face an opponent and come to blows!

Or was it? His determination to fight filled him with a sense of purpose, and his spirit rose to the challenge. He might not have money, but he had his wits. He would not be defeated. His grooms, whether they liked it or not, were about to become carpenters. And he would lead them.

He strode toward the cobbled yard, where he passed the remainder of the day with his horrified employees. He didn't rest until darkness forced him to quit his inventory-taking of building supplies.

He returned to the house at last, where only a deeply ingrained sense of propriety caused him to contemplate the dinner hour with any degree of patience. He wanted to return to the estate office and begin scheduling repairs.

This, he discovered only a few hours later, did not take long, and he retired to the library with Lizzie for a quiet game of piquet. Cerb, curled on the hearth rug, worked on a beef bone and paid them little heed.

They were disturbed from an argument over strategy less than an hour later. There was a peremptory rap on the door, and Coggins entered. Cerb set up a low growl, but apparently decided the newcomer posed no threat to his treasure. He resumed his systematic demolition of the bone.

St. Vincent, fresh from a bantering argument with Lizzie, eyed the Runner with disfavor. "I thought we'd gotten rid of you. I haven't seen you around all day. Did you take a look at my bed?"

Coggins huffed. "That I did, m'lord. And it was just as Mr. Carstairs said it would be. As to why I haven't come to see you sooner, I've been active in the pursuit of my Duty."

"How about in the pursuit of murderers?" Lizzie asked.

His face broke into a reluctant smile. "That's the

258

ticket, Missy. I've received this here letter from London. Delivered by special messenger, it was."

"Does it say anything?"

The Runner cast a reproving eye on St. Vincent. "It would hardly have been sent by special messenger if it didn't, m'lord."

"Of course it wouldn't." Lizzie made a face at Frederick. "What *does* it say, Mr. Coggins?"

He nodded in approval at her. From his pocket, he drew a folded sheet and handed it over.

St. Vincent took it and scanned the closely written sheet, and a sense of satisfaction oddly mingled with anger filled him as he folded it at last once more. "You will be delighted to know, Lizzie, that our Mr. Needham's father has been employed by the East India Company only since 1791."

Lizzie did some rapid mental arithmetic. "How old is he?"

St. Vincent glanced at the Runner.

"Seven-and-twenty, he is, Missy. Born in Calcutta."

"And his father?"

"As always, my dear, you are hot in pursuit of the scent. He came from America."

She nodded, as if that clinched matters for her. "We'll have to watch him carefully," she decided. "As soon as he makes another attempt on your life, we'll have him."

"Thank you," he responded coolly. "But if it doesn't interfere with your plans too much, I would just as soon catch him *before* he murders me. If you don't mind, of course." He turned back to the Runner. "Has there been any word on Mr. Burnett, yet?"

"No, m'lord. That'll take longer, that will. No one seems to know anything of him here in England—which is to be expected, seeing as he comes from America. Can't see as we have any choice but to wait for an answer from there."

Lizzie frowned. "Perhaps we can—"

The footman James burst into the library, interrupting

the rest of her idea. "M'lord, there's an intruder on the grounds. Begging your pardon, Miss, but Mr. Hodgkens thinks as it would be a good idea if we could borrow your hound, to scare him off, like."

Coggins's brow snapped down. "An intruder, is it?"

St. Vincent stiffened, but when he spoke, it was in his habitual drawl. "Hodgkens has made an excellent suggestion. Take the useless animal at once." He gestured to where Cerberus, the splintered remains of his bone at his side, snored peacefully before the blaze.

"He's not useless!" Lizzie declared, staunchly if somewhat untruthfully. "Besides, I have a much better idea. You won't mind being used as bait for a trap, will you, Frederick?"

Chapter 20

"Bait for—" Fortunately, further words failed St. Vincent. After a brief struggle, he declared, with considerable heat: "I should mind very much, Lizzie." He turned to the footman. "Where is this intruder, James? Near the house or in the woods?"

"Sneaking through the rose garden, he was, m'lord."

St. Vincent strode toward the door. "Lizzie, stay in here. We'll get to the bottom of this."

"Not without me, you don't," she muttered, and hurried after the men.

By the time they reached the hall, the butler had recruited two grooms and a potboy, who had armed themselves with pokers and fire tongs. Julian Rycroft and Adrian joined them as Coggins, taking official control, ordered his troops to slip quietly out the various doors and search. That should cover near the house, Lizzie reflected. With both the Runner and Adrian sticking close to St. Vincent, over his irritated objections, he should come to no harm.

She stopped on the edge of the terrace, considering. If she had hoped to enter the house to do bodily harm to the owner, she would not remain in the vicinity once a hue and cry had been raised. She would either retreat in good order, or simply retire to a quiet location where she could await events in comparative comfort—perhaps a place where she might have an excuse to be if she were found. And there was just such a location. She struck out along the well-trodden path that led through the neatly trimmed shrubs.

Five minutes later, she emerged into the clearing before the folly. Behind it, moonlight reflected off the pond, illuminating the scene—but not nearly as well as did the carriage lamp that hung in the doorway. Someone was there.

Using every ounce of the limited stealth she possessed, she inched her way closer. Two people could be glimpsed inside, and in the hands of the gentleman rested a valise. Not dangerous murderers, but dangerous elopers.

Abandoning her caution, she strode up the steps and stopped in the doorway, arms akimbo, glaring at the couple. "Have you any idea how much trouble you've just caused, Georgiana?" she declared. "What the devil do you think you're about?"

"We were so desperate, Mamma and I." The girl sniffed and groped for her handkerchief.

Mr. Burnett handed her his. "It might be a little irregular, Miss Carstairs, but I assure you—"

"Irregular! You have the entire household out beating the bushes for a potential murderer. I doubt anyone will be pleased it was no more than you bent on the most ridiculous piece of folly it has ever been my misfortune to encounter."

"It—it isn't folly," Georgiana cried. "We saw the butcher this afternoon in the village, and the look he directed at us made us long to sink into the ground! Mamma was mortified."

Lizzie blinked, but before she could demand an explanation, Mr. Burnett interrupted.

"What did you mean, a potential murderer?" he asked.

"Housebreaker, I should have said," Lizzie hedged. "What is going on? I take it you are *not* planning an elopement?"

"An elopement? Lizzie, how could you think it? I'd never do anything so—" Georgiana broke off and had the grace to look shamefaced. "Well, I suppose this isn't quite—quite *proper*, but nothing as dreadful as a flight to the border."

"What *are* you doing, then?"

"I asked Mr. Burnett to sell one of the pieces of Papa's collection so we could pay the rest of the local tradesmen. The money Cousin Frederick gave Mamma won't go nearly far enough."

"Good Lord!" Lizzie stared at her, aghast. "You mean you broke into the strongroom and just took something without telling St. Vincent?"

"I didn't 'break in,' I borrowed Mr. Rycroft's key. He always leaves it hanging where anyone could find it. And don't look so accusingly at me! I wasn't *stealing*. If there were any available funds in the estate, they would be advanced to us for just this sort of problem. But there aren't, so I did the only thing I could think of."

"You could have discussed it with Frederick!"

Georgiana sniffed. "He'd never have agreed—he wouldn't have dared, with that horrid Runner just aching to find an excuse to arrest him. This way we'd have the money, and no one would be able to blame him."

"What about you? And Mr. Burnett? You'll only bring even more suspicion down on him this way."

"Just what the devil do you mean by 'even more'?" he demanded.

"There have already been thefts from the collection."

Mr. Burnett stared at the valise he still held. "The thief—someone who knows how to dispose of valuable works of art—" He broke off.

Georgiana stepped back a pace, away from him, and her hand fluttered up to cover her mouth.

"I have *not* been stealing!" he snapped at her.

"N—no, of course you would not," she said, though a trifle uncertainly.

"I suppose you also think I murdered your papa

263

because he caught me," he continued.

"Oh, this is dreadful!" Georgiana cried. "It *will* make it look as if he's taken and sold things before, won't it, Lizzie?"

"It will. It was a kind thought to want to help, Georgiana, but this will do more harm than good. Let's go back to the house and see this safely restored to the strongroom."

Mr. Burnett hesitated. "May I escort you ladies?"

"Only if you care to explain this episode to Mr. Coggins."

He did not. He handed Lizzie the valise, and Georgiana thanked him for having been willing to help her in her hour of need. With a stiff bow, he took his leave of them.

Lizzie extinguished the lantern. By the dim moonlight they started back, walking single file along the narrow path between the clipped hedges.

"I suppose Mr. Winfield was right," Georgiana said presently.

"About what?"

"Not acting upon impulse." Georgiana sighed. "I just wanted to help, though."

"Mr. Winfield seems a very wise man."

"He does, does he not?" Georgiana brightened. "He's so very kind, too."

They neared the rose garden, and Georgiana hesitated. "Why are there so many lights?"

"I told you. You were seen leaving, and James raised a hue and cry about intruders."

Georgiana giggled nervously. "Well, I must say, it will make it difficult to get back without anyone knowing. Have you—" She broke off and drew farther into the shadows.

Lizzie peered over her shoulder in time to see Mr. Rycroft crossing the lighted terrace. He cast one long, searching gaze about the shrubbery, then let himself into the library.

"Come on." Lizzie gave Georgiana a push between the shoulder blades, and they headed for the same door. Lizzie entered first, found the room empty, and signaled Georgiana to join her. She tucked the valise under the huge desk.

Georgiana went to the fire and warmed her chilled hands. "You won't tell anyone, will you?" She threw a beseeching glance over her shoulder at Lizzie.

"You won't do anything so silly again?"

"No," she said at last. "I'll find another way to help Cousin Frederick and Mamma." She looked up, then, directly at Lizzie. "Do you think Mr. Burnett might have murdered my papa? Because of the collection?"

"Do you?" Lizzie countered.

Georgiana gazed into the dying flames for a long minute before answering. "No. He was so very angry about Papa swindling him over that chalice, but he must have known he'd never recover any of the money if he let his temper get the better of him."

"Whom do you suspect, then?"

Georgiana bit her lip, her eyes widening with a secret and reprehensible pleasure—the picture of one about to indulge in gossip. "Mr. Rycroft," she breathed. She selected a poker and stirred the smoldering remains of the fire.

Lizzie drew a chair closer to the warmth and settled herself comfortably. "Why?"

"I don't trust him." The girl added another log to the coals. "He watches people, and in the most calculating manner. I have no idea what he is up to, but it cannot be any good. I'll bet Papa caught him at whatever it is and Mr. Rycroft murdered him. I've seen the way he stares at Cousin Frederick, too."

"Why didn't you say something about this before?" Lizzie demanded.

"It's all so vague, isn't it? But it is better than believing Mr. Needham or Mr. Burnett capable of it."

"I don't know. I've known some dandies with a very

nasty streak in them," Lizzie said, considering.

Too many motives were turning up. Frederick— He was still out searching for a possible assailant, she remembered. She had better call off the hunt. She sent Georgiana off to bed, then turned back to the French windows.

She did no more than open them. The men had gathered on the far side of the terrace, cold and grim, to report their lack of findings to Mr. Coggins. Sticking her head out the door, she called: "It was all a mistake."

The Runner spun about to face her. "What do you mean, Missy?"

"I mean James saw Miss Ashfield, who had gone for a walk because she was restless."

St. Vincent drew out his snuff box and fingered it thoughtfully. "There is no need, then, for us to be crawling through the shrubs in the freezing darkness?"

"None whatsoever," Lizzie responded cheerfully. "Are you coming in?"

"We are." The viscount regarded the circle of grumbling men. "I would recommend you repair to the kitchens for a glass of something before retiring. Mr. Coggins? You may remain in charge." With a dismissive nod to the others, he strode toward the French windows, which Lizzie obligingly opened wide for him.

"Georgiana?" he demanded as soon as the door closed behind him. He crossed to the hearth to warm himself.

Briefly, she told him what had occurred. He swore softly but fluently, to her amused interest.

"I'll lock that up before going to bed," he promised. "And maybe I should see to having a new lock installed."

Lizzie nodded absently, having thought of a new idea and therefore already having lost interest in the collection. "Has it occurred to you how many possible reasons there are for people wanting your late cousin dead?"

"It has. Beginning with my own. Why, have you thought of more?"

266

She poured them each a glass of Madeira and brought one to him. "In all the excitement of thinking there might be a missing heir, I completely forgot your cousin's penchant for blackmail."

Frederick paused with the glass halfway to his lips, then took a thoughtful sip. "Has something else occurred?"

"No. Only that we know Mr. Winfield was one victim. Might there not have been others?"

St. Vincent swirled the dark red liquid in his glass. "Whom did you have in mind?"

"Well, there is Mr. Needham. Blighted love never seemed a reasonable motive, but why did your cousin object to him so strongly?"

St. Vincent raised an amused eyebrow, and Lizzie grinned. "All right, aside from the way he apes the dandy set. Don't you think it possible your cousin learned something to his discredit?"

"We have enough viable motives on our hands without your fabricating more."

She shrugged. "How about Mr. Burnett? He must need a great deal of money to support that hunting box. He's admitted to not having much."

St. Vincent ran a meditative hand along his chin. "They were both present that night the gold serving pieces went missing and Henry was murdered, were they not? So was Mr. Winfield, for that matter."

"And don't forget Mr. Rycroft."

"You're incorrigible, Lizzie," he said, but his expression was rather sad instead of teasing. "Come, it's past time we sought our beds."

The following morning, Lizzie went straight to the great desk in the library, where she worked for over an hour. The result was one list of everyone who might have wanted to murder the old viscount and why, and another of everyone who had the opportunity to murder the hapless footman. A third enumerated those who could have both cut St. Vincent's girth and damaged his bed. When she finished, she sat back and studied them with care. All three looked depressingly similar.

On the whole, she decided, her morning's labor hadn't helped clarify things in the least. In disgust, she made her way to the breakfast parlor to see what could be found in the way of a sustaining nuncheon.

Lady St. Vincent was there before her, standing at the sideboard, adjusting a large and hideous silver epergne. She glanced up as Lizzie entered. "I cannot find its partner," she said.

Lizzie eyed the piece with disfavor. "Good."

The dowager fluttered her hands in dismay, then resumed her contemplation of the heavy wrought silver with its curling embellishments and gargoyle faces. "They were a wedding present from my parents, but my husband thought them heathen."

"Not hideous?" Lizzie murmured.

Lady St. Vincent didn't seem to hear. "He had them locked away in the sideboard. I wonder what ever became of the other?"

"Probably in the bottom of a cupboard, somewhere." Lizzie crossed to the buffet, on which only empty plates stood. "Am I too early?"

"No, we're awaiting our guest. Did I not tell you?"

Lizzie brightened. "Who?"

"Mr. Winfield. We need to make some definite plans for the church fund, but what I shall tell him, I don't know."

"He knows why you can't help."

That fact did not appear to relieve Lady St. Vincent's worry. Her response, though, was cut off by Hodgkens announcing the vicar's arrival. The butler stood back to usher in Mr. Winfield, who bowed low to the dowager viscountess. St. Vincent and Adrian followed shortly with Georgiana, somewhat subdued, entering last.

Mr. Winfield went to her at once, led her to a seat at the table, and positioned himself at her side. His gentle conversation worked its inevitable effect, and her

268

artificial smile soon became genuine.

"At least you needn't worry about his remembering the church fund," Lizzie murmured to the dowager as Hodgkens and his minions entered, bearing trays of thinly sliced meats and cheeses and piles of fruit and rolls.

That lady regarded her daughter in surprise as the vicar left her to fill their plates from the waiting trays. "He's the nicest man, of course, but—oh, dear, she should be brought out."

Lizzie shook her head. "She wouldn't like it, you know. It would go against everything she was raised to believe in. She'll enjoy an occasional visit later, but *ton* life would be too frivolous for her."

The dowager squeezed her hand. "You are so very right, Lizzie. Now that she is trying her wings a little, she will soon want to settle—" She broke off.

Lizzie followed the direction of her puzzled glance. Mr. Winfield stood as if transfixed, his horrified gaze resting on the silver epergne. Lizzie bit her lip to keep from laughing. "It is horrible, you know."

Lady St. Vincent sighed. "Perhaps I will abandon the search for the other."

The vicar recovered from his start and turned to her. "The other?"

"There were a pair of them, but one is missing," Lizzie explained.

The vicar regarded the epergne once more and a shudder shook his slender frame. Hurriedly, he filled the plates, but it was clear his composure had deserted him. He returned to Georgiana, but continued to cast occasional, distressed glances at the offending object.

That epergne meant something to the Reverend Mr. Montague Winfield, Lizzie decided, and she intended to find out what.

As soon as the meal drew to a close, Mr. Winfield excused himself, and apologized for not discussing the church fund as they had planned. "Another time?" he suggested, bearing every appearance of a fox in search of a hole. "Yes, another time. Just send for me, my dear Lady St. Vincent." He bowed quickly to the dowager and Lizzie. "Miss Ashfield." He grasped the girl's hand, raised it briefly to his lips, thereby drawing a startled but pleased gasp from her, and took his abrupt leave.

"Was it something I said?" St. Vincent asked, amusement vying with surprise.

"More like something from which he ate," Lizzie suggested. "Excuse me."

There was no time like the present, and all that. Lizzie hurried to her room, changed her flimsy slippers for a pair of stout walking boots, and donned her warmest pelisse. Ever practical, she added a woolen scarf, then set off for the long, cold tramp through the woods to the vicarage.

Twenty minutes later, she crossed the barren rose garden and strode up to the vicar's study. She could see him inside, standing motionless before his battered old desk. On the surface before him lay a crumpled cloth, and from within the folds shone something large and silver.

Lizzie drew a deep breath and exhaled slowly; a cloud formed before her. It was too cold to stay out here. She rapped on the French windows.

Mr. Winfield started, and spun about to face her. Every trace of color drained from his face.

Philosophically, Lizzie let herself into the room.

"Miss—Miss Carstairs—" He regarded her in horror.

Lizzie moved past him and peered at the hideous silver epergne that rested on his desk. It matched, detail by excruciatingly awful detail, the one that even now stood on the sideboard at the Grange.

"I—I didn't steal it!" he protested.

"No one in their right mind would."

A shaky laugh escaped him. "This—this is dreadful. I never dreamed—" He broke off.

"No, this is a figment from a nightmare," Lizzie assured him.

270

"It is certainly that!" A touch of color returned to his face, leaving his complexion less ghastly.

"Where did you get it?"

"Mr. Rycroft brought it to me yesterday. He said St. Vincent—the old viscount, that is—told him to give it to me to aid the poor, but with the murder it slipped his mind. Understandable, of course. But Her Ladyship seemed to know nothing of it." He turned his harried gaze on Lizzie. "There has been looting from the estate, I've heard."

"And you think you've just been caught with one of the stolen pieces?"

"Yes. I mean, no! I didn't steal it! But that *is* how it looks, isn't it?"

"Not in the least. Mr. Rycroft will confirm what you said."

Lizzie took her leave and marched back along the now-familiar path, intent on settling this one matter at once. The vicar's distress was obvious. Did he think himself the recipient of stolen goods? Or, if he stole it himself, had not known there was a match and it would be easily identified?

She found the bailiff at work in the estate room, copying figures neatly from one book to another. He looked up as she entered, then closed one ledger and laid it neatly over the other. His smile of greeting spread across his handsome countenance.

"An excuse to take a break for a few minutes. Miss Carstairs, I welcome you. How may I be of service?"

"Are you familiar with Lady St. Vincent's silver epergnes?"

He laughed. "Does she have you searching for it, too? I assure you, I have not seen that blighted piece. She had me go through the storeroom, you must know."

"Actually, Mr. Winfield has it. Don't you remember the late viscount asking you to give it to the vicar?"

"Give it to the vicar?" he repeated, perplexed.

"Yes, I'm sure you must remember. It was just before

271

he died," she added helpfully.

Mr. Rycroft ran his fingers through his orderly golden brown hair. "No. I have no memory of that at all. What ever gave you that idea?"

"Mr. Winfield."

Mr. Rycroft stared at her blankly. "Why—" He broke off, frowning. "Did he tell you he had it, or did you catch him with it?"

"I saw it," she admitted.

Mr. Rycroft shook his head, the creases in his brow deepening. "Why would he tell you something so easily proved a lie?"

"Because he lacks imagination?" Lizzie suggested.

Which one of them really lied, though? The little matter of the silver plate Mr. Winfield had sold before intruded forcibly on her mind. Nor could she believe the old viscount ever would have requested anything to be given to the poor. Had not the vicar already admitted being ordered to preach to them to turn their thoughts to Heaven and abandon hopes of worldly help? Still, her Anglican soul recoiled at thinking ill of a man of the cloth.

What about the bailiff, though, who had constant access to the valuable treasures of Ashfield Grange? That didn't make sense, either. It would be too obvious—and why would he give it away if he'd gone to the trouble—and danger—of stealing it? Mr. Rycroft did not strike her as lacking in intelligence.

There was one way to find out, of course; she could always set a trap.

Chapter 21

"You're out of your mind, Lizzie," St. Vincent set the decanter back on the tray too hard, causing the remaining glasses to rattle.

She didn't say anything. She merely regarded him with a pained expression.

He ran a harassed hand through his waving blond hair and tried another tack. "Do you really think you'll fool anyone?"

"That's up to you, isn't it? No, listen, Frederick. All you have to do is be jubilant, and no one will doubt your desire to celebrate. It's no secret from anyone around here you've been moving heaven and earth to find some funds."

He stared down into the earnest, determined face and stifled a desire to cradle it between his hands. She trusted him—as an uncle. He would do nothing to damage that innocent frankness that undermined his good intentions.

Damn the country squire who would eventually win her! He picked up his glass and stalked to the fireplace, where he stared down into the flames. "We'll need something of real value, something everyone will believe."

"I've given that some thought."

Of course she had. He fought against his rush of warm amusement, and lost. "And?"

"Do you think you could persuade Lady St. Vincent to loan us some jewelry?"

He swung about to face her. "You expect me to ask her to hand over one of the few valuable things she still possesses? So that I may show it to the neighborhood, then leave it out in some highly accessible location in the hopes someone will try to steal it?"

"Yes."

He stared at her, speechless.

"Well, how else are we to catch our thief? Only consider, Frederick. Everyone knows your cousin already sold everything of value so he could buy religious art for his collection. And they also know you can't touch *that* until the estate is wound up—"

"Which won't be until I'm proved guilty of his murder. Thank you, I'm well aware of that."

"What do you think I'm trying to prevent?" she demanded, exasperated. "We have to prove someone *else* guilty. And we might well do that if we can discover who has been stealing. We *have* to set a trap." She settled on the edge of a chair and fixed her serious gaze on him.

He closed his eyes, mostly to block out the sight of her engaging and wholly delightful countenance. "You want me to invite your list of suspects to a dinner and a card party tomorrow night?"

"Well, everyone except your gamekeeper. We'll have to figure out another way of letting him know."

"To be sure. We want everyone to have an equal opportunity to steal poor Cousin Isobel's jewelry, don't we?"

"Of course."

He shook his head, fighting back his smile. Sarcasm did not phase Lizzie. From long experience, though, he knew her thinking to be clear and her hunches accurate. If he could only catch someone in the act of theft. . . .

"If this *does* work—and mind you, I said *if*—can you be certain your thief will be your mysterious looter, and not someone just tempted by my seeming carelessness?"

She blinked. "Do you think *everyone* is basically dishonest?" She sounded surprised.

A wave of shame washed over him. To Lizzie, there was either right or wrong, yes or no, with few—if any—gradients between. Either one was honest, or one was thoroughly dishonest.

"You think your looter may have murdered my cousin because he was caught in the act. What makes you think he won't have a try at me when I spring the trap?"

She considered this a moment, frowning. "I don't know if the thief *is* the murderer," she said at last. "Besides, you won't be alone. I'll be there."

"You will not! I'll have your tame Runner to assist me, thank you, and you'll be safe in your bed."

"I will not!" she declared in fair mimicry of his tone. "This is *my* plot!"

He glared at her for a moment, then gave up. If he had to sit up half the night waiting for someone who in all likelihood wouldn't be fool enough to come, then he might as well enjoy her company. There were limits to altruism.

"Can you be quiet?" he shot at her, then sipped his wine, enjoying her loud assertions that she could be quieter than a mouse, which everyone knew made a dreadful racket with all its rustlings and scamperings.

After she departed to give Cerb his morning constitutional, he went upstairs to his Cousin Isobel's sitting room to put Lizzie's outlandish request to her. To his surprise, that lady listened to the plan in silence, then nodded.

"I believe I have just the thing—a set of emeralds. They were my mother's." She cast an apologetic glance at him. "I saw no need to tell my husband of them."

St. Vincent held up his hand, disturbed. "I don't want you making any sacrifices. There is a chance they might be lost."

"It is a chance worth taking." She led the way into her bed chamber. "Things cannot go on the way they are."

She burrowed into her clothes cupboard and emerged at last with a hatbox. After untying the fastening bow, she removed the lid and lifted out a disreputable and shockingly ugly affair of black curled plumes. She turned this over, pushed aside the aged lining, and removed an emerald and diamond necklace. She weighed it in her hand for a moment, then passed it over.

"I don't like doing this," St. Vincent said.

"It will be quite safe. You did say this was Miss Carstairs's idea, did you not?"

The twinkle in her eye surprised him. His own lit with an answering, if somewhat reluctant, smile. "I only hope the results are worth the effort."

"I do not see Miss Carstairs permitting them to be anything less. If you will issue the invitations for tomorrow night, I will speak with Cook."

St. Vincent went next door to the master chamber he had moved into only the previous day, then hesitated. He would have to announce the supposed discovery immediately to the household, which left the necklace vulnerable at once to a little looting on the part of the staff. Unlike Lizzie, he believed the gold, diamonds, and emeralds to be a tempting combination to even the most honest of servants.

Forcing himself to whistle a cheerful tune, he headed downstairs to display the prize to Adrian and Julian Rycroft. Until he baited the trap, he determined, he would keep it on his person at all times.

Mr. Burnett arrived first the following evening, dressed with studied negligence. He greeted his host and hostess warmly, and directed a sheepish smile at Georgiana. Mr. Winfield arrived next, and retired to a corner with Adrian and Lizzie.

Mr. Needham was the last to arrive. St. Vincent's position by the fireside, where he stood talking to Julian Rycroft, awarded him an excellent view of that gentleman's appearance. His clothes would have attracted attention anywhere, for it was obvious he had been at pains to create a stunning effect. The lime velvet coat and green silk breeches were a startling thing to see in late November in the depths of Leicestershire. His manner, though, proved of far more interest to St. Vincent. Mr. Needham cast a nervous glance about the room as he advanced farther into it, then approached his hostess with reluctance and exchanged a brief greeting.

St. Vincent swirled the sherry in his glass and watched Lizzie. She sat up straight in her chair, watching Mr. Needham intently, then appeared to recollect herself. She visibly relaxed and turned to say something to Mr. Winfield, which St. Vincent couldn't overhear. She wouldn't give away their trap.

He poured Mr. Needham a glass of the excellent sherry and strolled over to his side. That gentleman started and drew back, then forced a wide smile of greeting that appeared more grotesque than pleased.

"Good evening, St. Vincent," he said, obviously not meaning it.

"So glad you could come." St. Vincent turned on the full charm of his own smile and awaited the response to his comment.

It took a minute to come. Mr. Needham sipped the wine, cleared his throat, and ventured another ghastly grin. "A card party, you know. Of all things the most pleasant—especially when one is buried in the country. A—a celebration, I understand?"

"Yes, a most welcome one. And one in which I believe our good vicar will join us." He spoke the last words louder, and was rewarded by the Reverend Mr. Montague Winfield looking up. "We will soon have enough funds to begin repairs on the tenants' cottages."

The vicar peered over the wire rim of his spectacles. "Will we, my lord? That is indeed cause for celebration. Have you—er—"

St. Vincent took pity on him. "No, we have not yet wound up the estate. But as you may be aware, I have recently moved into my predecessor's bedchamber.

Something came to light which I believe will suit our purposes to admiration." He paused for dramatic effect, then from his pocket he drew the glimmering necklace.

Georgiana caught her breath in an audible gasp. "*Papa* had that?"

He smiled, well pleased by the reaction of the others. "It is not entailed. Therefore, one can only assume it belongs to your mother and is not part of the disputed estate. And Lady St. Vincent has graciously bestowed it upon me to begin the necessary repairs."

Mr. Burnett took the necklace, raised it to the candlelight, and ran an expert eye over it. "This should bring a considerable sum. I congratulate you, St. Vincent. Your tenants should be suitably grateful." He handed the gems to Mr. Needham, who accepted them with reluctance. Almost at once, he passed them to Mr. Rycroft, who stood behind him.

"In the morning I will take it into Leicester and sell it. By tomorrow evening, Mr. Winfield, work will have begun."

The vicar sat speechless for a moment, then rose unsteadily to his feet. He clasped St. Vincent's hand. "It is an excellent thing you do. You will be rewarded in the next life, I promise you."

"I intend to remain in this one a good deal longer, you may be certain."

"So many plans." Mr. Winfield returned to his chair, but further conversation with him proved impossible. He stared off into space, an expression of dreamy delight on his amiable countenance.

When Hodgkens entered to announce dinner, Georgiana was forced to shake the vicar's arm before he roused himself from his pleasant reverie. Beaming at her, and with no regard for any seating order, he offered her his arm and escorted her to the dining room.

After St. Vincent seated his cousin-in-law at the foot of the table, Wesley Burnett caught him. "Do you have the thing safe?" he asked softly. "I don't like to think ill of

278

anyone, but there has been looting."

St. Vincent raised his eyebrows. "It will be quite safe, I assure you. Everyone has seen it here this night. Who would dare take it? Besides, you have all become such good friends, I feel quite certain none of you would serve me such a backhanded turn." He spoke the last loudly enough so that all might hear.

Lizzie frowned at him as if warning he overplayed his role, but he merely smiled back. The comment did well enough. Only Mr. Needham appeared to squirm in his chair.

That dandy's uneasiness remained throughout the meal. St. Vincent kept an eye on him while he pretended interest in Mr. Burnett's conversation. What he really wanted was a moment of privacy to question Lizzie, who sat next to Mr. Needham. What did she make of his manner? Knowing his Lizzie, she would have answers for him later, while they waited to see if anyone stumbled into their trap.

When the ladies at last retired from the dining room and the covers were removed from the table, he drew the necklace from his pocket once more. Brandy and port decanters made the rounds, and he, with Adrian's assistance, made quite certain they kept circling. He wanted the company about half-sprung, so no one would think it odd when he hid the jewels in the epergne that Hodgkens had removed to the sideboard.

The conversation turned naturally to hunting, and with every round of the decanters, the stories became wilder and funnier. He found himself relating with humor his own recent fall, and the resulting indignities suffered at the hands of his valet and household of self-appointed caretakers.

The distant gong of a clock recalled him to a sense of the time, and he rose. "We had better join the ladies before they think we aren't coming." He took an unsteady step from the table, and found to his irritation it was not wholly assumed. Confound this weak head of his.

It had never been so before. The quiet life bore certain penalties, it seemed. With deliberate clumsiness, he allowed the necklace to fall to the floor.

"Careful with that," the vicar cried. He bent down and retrieved it.

"Thank you." St. Vincent achieved an exaggerated bow and accepted the necklace into his hands. He attempted to shove it back into his pocket, but luckily the elaborate tracery of metal and stones caught and refused to be neatly inserted. "Needs a hiding place," he announced, slurring his words.

He looked about vaguely, pretended to spot the epergne, and nodded wisely. He leaned forward until his face was mere inches from the vicar's. "Don't tell anyone," he hissed. He staggered to the sideboard, lifted the carved silver lid, and stowed the necklace safely inside.

Now, all he had to do was pretend to be castaway for the rest of the evening, and everything should go well. He'd best confine his card games to either Lizzie or Adrian, though. It would never do for him to show any shrewdness, but neither would it do for him to lose any great sums.

The guests remained for a little over two hours, then took their leave. Mr. Rycroft, after thanking the viscount for including him in the enjoyable evening of celebration, departed for his own rooms. St. Vincent cast a hazy glance about the chamber, noted that only the intimates with the plot remained, and relaxed his pose.

"Lord, that was a strain. Lizzie, if your Runner has not been hiding in the dining room all this time, keeping an eye on those dashed emeralds, I really will commit a murder." He stood and stretched. "Cousin Isobel, Cousin Georgiana, my sincerest apologies for my abominable behavior this night."

Lady St. Vincent inclined her head. "You would have made an excellent showing on the boards, Cousin Frederick. I was all admiration."

"You have never played piquet worse," Lizzie stuck in. "I was bored to tears."

He grasped her hand and raised it to his lips. "Accept my apologies." He held her fingers a moment longer, then dropped them abruptly, knowing he enjoyed the contact more than he should. "I would suggest we all go upstairs and prepare for bed. I doubt anything will happen for at least an hour or two."

"I'll just check on Mr. Coggins." Lizzie hurried to the dining room, while the others trooped into the hall where they collected their candles. She joined them as they started up the stairs, and nodded brightly in response to St. Vincent's quirked brow. She accepted her taper from him and they made their way to their various bed-chambers.

At the corridor where they separated, she caught his arm. "Half an hour?" she whispered.

The glow of the candlelight washed over her, and eagerness shone in her eyes. He nodded and turned quickly away, and all the way to his room he lectured himself sternly on proprieties in general, and on his own errant and wholly untenable desires in particular.

He prepared for bed, dismissed his valet, then leisurely pulled on his clothes once more. Settling in a chair, he allowed another half-hour to pass. Then silently, without so much as a candle to betray his movements, he crept into the hall and toward the Main Stair.

As he neared it, the shadows against the wall wavered, and a shape detached itself and took a step toward him. By the faint gleam of a low-burning oil lamp on the steps below, he saw the paleness of Lizzie's face against the mass of brown hair. He gestured for silence, and wondered if she'd seen. She continued toward him, appearing to float through the eerie darkness, a ghostly figure wrapped in a deep blue dressing gown against the chill of the drafty hall.

Laying one hand on his arm, she stood on tiptoe to whisper in his ear. "I thought you'd never come."

Unable to stop himself, he reached out, tenderly touching the wisps of hair that fell about her eyes. Her mouth was so close to his—

She hugged his arm, pulling him toward the steps. "Who do you think will come? Mr. Needham?"

Excitement filled her voice, but not the same kind that rushed headlong through St. Vincent. He gritted his teeth, called himself several of the ripe names that came to mind, then hushed his eager companion.

"The more I think about it, the less this trap seems likely to succeed." The next moment, he regretted his words. Her fingers tightened on his forearm, and he had to fight back the desire to cover them with his own.

"It must!" she whispered.

"I know. If it doesn't, I am like to have one very tired and irritated Runner in the morning, who will think this is naught but a diversion to take his mind off arresting me."

"He cannot be such a fool!"

At least her faith in him should please him. Unfortunately, he wanted much more from her, more fool—or was that rogue?—he. She shivered in the chill draught, and he cast prudence to the winds and slipped a protective arm about her. That much, at least, he could have.

She snuggled against him—then abruptly pulled away. Had he betrayed his feelings? He longed to throw something in frustration. He wasn't ready yet to lose her friendship. But for her sake—and his own—perhaps it would be best.

Blackness stretched out before them as they reached the bottom of the illuminated steps. Not a sound reached their straining ears. Lizzie tugged at the arm she gripped and drew him across the Great Hall. They moved cautiously; careless footfalls on the marble tiles tended to echo throughout the vast chamber, and the slightest noise could ruin their carefully baited trap.

St. Vincent reached out, feeling the wall, and located

the corridor leading to the formal dining room. Here a thickly woven carpet muffled their steps. He had paced the route that evening, keeping careful count, under the guise of befuddled stumbling. Another three steps. . . .

"Where is Coggins?" Lizzie's whisper sounded loud in the silence.

"Here, Missy. There's no call for you to be here. Dangerous, it might be."

"Then I had best be here to keep an eye on you two."

"I take it there has been no one yet." St. Vincent interrupted what he feared would become a lengthy argument.

"No, m'lord." Coggins sounded grudging. "It's still early, though. If anyone *does* try to steal this here necklace of Her Ladyship's, he'll want to make very certain as no one is still awake."

"What do you mean 'if'?" Lizzie whispered.

St. Vincent patted her shoulder, caught himself caressing it, and shoved her toward the doorway into the dining room. "You keep watch out here," he ordered the Runner. "Miss Carstairs and I will stand behind the drapes. Don't make any move until you hear me call."

"And what, my lord, if you isn't able?"

"Come when you hear a fight," Lizzie suggested brightly. She ducked into the room before St. Vincent could push her again.

"And mind, not a word out of you," he breathed as he positioned her behind the floor-length velvet hanging that lined the outside walls of the room.

"It's cold in here," she protested.

"Then go back to your bed."

"As if I would! I—"

"Quiet!" he muttered. He should stand on the opposite side of the room, but no cover offered there. Telling himself he really had no choice, and they would be much warmer together, he slid in beside her and twitched the drapes back into position.

"How long do you think we'll have to wait?" she

283

asked presently.

"Tired?" He could think of far better ways to pass a night. A delicate scent—violets—surrounded him, assailing his senses, making it difficult to remember he was a gentleman. A rake of his experience would have no trouble seducing the girl. If it were anyone else, he might give it a try. But *not* Lizzie. She deserved better.

Then the implication of that delightful scent dawned on him. "Are you wearing perfume?" he demanded, incredulous.

"No." He could hear the disgust in her voice. "Your laundry maids confused my things with Georgiana's and drenched them in violet."

"I like it."

"You do?"

"It makes me think of warm spring days and meadows filled with flowers."

"*Al fresco* luncheons?"

A soft chuckle escaped him. "You're incorrigible, Lizzie. Have you not a single romantic bone in your body?"

"I shouldn't think so. Augusta got the lot for the whole family, you know."

He shook his head. "One of these days, my girl, you'll fall in love, and then you'll see."

"Will I?" Her voice sounded muffled. "Love doesn't *have* to be all silly romantic nonsense, you know."

"Most people like it that way."

"Do you?"

"It can be enjoyable. How did we get onto this topic, anyway? It can't be the least bit proper."

"Since when did that ever bother us? And you started it."

"I know." He gritted his teeth. "As soon as this business is settled, I'm going to London."

"To find a wife?" She didn't pretend to misunderstand.

"The sooner I have an heir, the better."

She was silent a moment. "Have you anyone in mind?"

He drew a slow, steadying breath to keep from yelling "Yes!" Instead, he merely said: "I've been out of the country for too long."

"Nell might know of someone," Lizzie said presently, "though if you want her to have beauty as well as some fortune, it might be more difficult. Your title will help, of course."

"Thank you. You can have no idea how glad I am that I have *something* that makes me acceptable."

"Perhaps a widow—"

"Shall I just leave the selection of my bride to you?"

"You never had any trouble finding flirts before," she pointed out.

They lapsed into silence, and his thoughts drifted back over the past five years, to his constant search for diversion, his attempts to drive from his mind the conviction that the only female for him was a prosaic young lady with a disconcertingly candid stare and not an ounce of romance in her soul.

He had failed. And now he was with her once more, how could he ever let her leave? He—

A scuffing noise sounded in the hall and Lizzie tensed at his side. Her hand crept into his, squeezing it for an instant before retreating. He couldn't see anything, but he knew, as a certainty, they were no longer alone in the room.

He eased himself toward the break in the drapes and peered out. Only blackness met his searching gaze. He strained his ears, listening for any betraying sound.

Wood scraped against wood as someone bumped into a chair and knocked it against the table. A muffled oath followed, then a minute later the clink of metal against metal as the intruder lifted the heavy silver lid from the epergne. St. Vincent could just make out the dim figure against the darker background.

There could be no mistaking the clanking that followed

285

as the thief drew forth the emerald and diamond studded necklace. St. Vincent emerged from cover and inched closer, bracing himself, and his foot caught the chair leg, ramming it against the edge of the table.

The figure whirled, oriented, and landed the viscount a heavy facer.

Chapter 22

St. Vincent staggered back, caught his balance, and swung a nasty right hook that floored his opponent. Blood pounded in his ears as hatred for this looter filled him. He grabbed the man by the coat lapels, dragged him to his feet, and swung a punishing bunch of fives that landed the intruder on his back.

Dimly, he was aware of shouting; candles flickered and suddenly he could see. Julian Rycroft staggered to his feet and St. Vincent, losing the last shred of his control, closed with murderous intent. Before he reached him, the bailiff dropped like a brick. St. Vincent stopped in his tracks, taken aback.

Beside Rycroft's fallen figure stood Lizzie, the dented epergne in her hands. She nodded in satisfaction. "I knew this had to be useful for something," she said.

Coggins pushed past her, pulled up the man's eyelids, and shook his head. "No need for you to go a-hitting him like that, Missy," he said in tones of reproach.

"There certainly was not," St. Vincent agreed. "What the devil do you mean by interfering? Don't you think I could have handled him myself?"

"Too well. In another minute you'd have had a second murder charge hanging over you." She stepped aside to allow the Runner to bind the bailiff's wrists. "I've never seen you that furious."

St. Vincent drew an unsteady breath. "Damn the scoundrel! Stealing from the estate that gave him his livelihood."

"I didn't say I blamed you, did I?"

A low groan drew their attention to the bailiff's prone figure. His head rolled to one side and his eyes opened. He tried to reach out, struggled against the rope, and his disorientation evaporated. "What's the meaning of this?"

"I am placing you under arrest," Mr. Coggins intoned, adopting a suitably impressive manner, "for the theft of certain items from this household."

Mr. Rycroft stared hard at him for a moment, then turned to St. Vincent. "What is he talking about?"

"Looting." His fist clenched, and he felt Lizzie's restraining clasp on his arm. "I imagine Lady St. Vincent's emeralds are only one of a considerable number of things you have taken."

Mr. Rycroft struggled to a sitting position. Coggins helped him to stand, then shoved him unceremoniously into a chair. "I haven't stolen anything!" he declared.

St. Vincent scooped up the necklace that had fallen to the floor during the fight, and raised an eyebrow.

Mr. Rycroft flushed. "I remembered you putting it into the epergne after dinner. It didn't seem safe, when every man in the room saw you do it. I intended to keep it for the night where it couldn't be stolen and return it to you in the morning."

"Then why didn't you use a light? There is no need to sneak about in the dark if your intentions are honorable."

"Forget that silly necklace," Lizzie interrupted. "I think it would be more practical to discover what he did with all the items he stole from your cousin's collection."

"I never stole—"

"Oh, cut line!" She silenced him with an impatient gesture. "You copied over the list of items, eliminating a couple of them. I imagine you also changed the labels on several pieces, too, to make it hard to detect. And I have no idea how many things you took before St. Vincent insisted on a numbered inventory."

"Mr. Winfield—"

"No." St. Vincent rocked back on his heels. "Had he taken things, the tenanted farms would be in far better condition. Did you give him that epergne to deliberately throw suspicion on him?"

"I never had it! He must have panicked when you caught him with it, and offered the first excuse he could think of."

"More like he told the truth," Coggins said.

Lizzie nodded. "That's what I think. You did your best to make him look guilty, and make us think he murdered the old viscount when he was caught, but it won't work."

Mr. Rycroft glared at her. "I didn't murder anyone! And you can't prove I stole anything."

"Don't you go a-worrying yourself none about that, now. We'll find the place where you sold things. You don't looks to me like the type what has a confederate. Can't trust nobody these days, you can't. No, you probably went somewheres close at hand to dispose of things."

"Like that shop in Leicester where Mr. Burnett did his business," Lizzie suggested.

The flicker of fear on the bailiff's face, fleeting as it was, confirmed Lizzie's guess. He realized it, and his mouth curled into a sneer as his gaze focused on St. Vincent. "At least I won't hang for murder! Everyone in the neighborhood knows you killed your cousin for the estate, before he could bleed it any more."

Lizzie flushed. "How dare you imply—"

St. Vincent laid a hand on her shoulder, silencing her. "What he says is of no moment, my dear. You know how a vicious cur is when it's trapped. He's only striking out in spite."

Coggins ran a hand over his chin. "That's as may be, m'lord. What I wants to know, is, what made him think as he could of got away with it?"

"My cousin enjoyed the acquiring of the collection more than the items themselves, I should imagine. It was packed away in boxes when I saw it, not displayed where it could ever be seen by anyone. I imagine Rycroft could have kept stealing from him indefinitely."

"But His Lordship went and got hisself murdered—and right after that you come." Coggins turned his thoughtful gaze on St. Vincent. "I suppose Mr. Rycroft went and got a bit reckless-like, stealing what he could afore you and Miss Carstairs made it too dangerous with your lists and numbers. Well." He grasped his prisoner's shoulder. "If you'll excuse me, now, I'd like to see this one all safe and secured." He hoisted the bound bailiff to his feet and hauled his captive out the door.

Lizzie's hands encircled St. Vincent's arm, and she clung to him. "He thinks you're guilty."

"Which one of them?"

She considered. "Both," she said at last. "We're going to have the devil of a time proving you innocent."

He cupped her chin in his hand and tilted her face up to his. "He can't take me into custody without any substantial evidence, you know."

"Nor can you touch any of the estate's assets until this is settled."

There was no arguing with that. He picked up the remaining candle Coggins had lit, escorted Lizzie to her bedchamber, then traversed the corridors to his own apartment with heavy steps.

Lizzie went down to breakfast at her usual time the following morning, somewhat tired but by no means done in by her nighttime vigil. The wintry sun shone brightly through the window, bathing the table in a yellow glow. Her heart felt lighter than it had in days. Her demons of uncertainty and worry had faded with the darkness, giving way to a morning filled with hope. Her trap had

290

worked; one less problem now assailed St. Vincent.

She would now concentrate on putting his house in order for his bride—her last service to him. That thought subdued her.

She selected a roll, spread it thick with butter and marmalade, and took a large, meditative bite. The tea steamed in her cup, wafting the delicate aroma of orange into the room. St. Vincent liked a floral scent.

Coggins, his eyes red-rimmed with lack of sleep, stuck his head around the corner of the door. "There you are, Missy. His Lordship's still abed. Just wanted to let you know I'll be off now to Leicester, where there'll be a coach to take our fine gentleman to Bow Street."

"We did a good job." She forced a smile to her lips.

A reluctant grin spread across his face. "That we did, Missy. I only hopes as we can settle the rest of this here matter as easily."

"You mean tracing the pieces of the collection? I doubt you can, after all this time. But you will have Mr. Rycroft's finances investigated, will you not? It would be a blessing if anything could be recovered for the estate."

"I imagine he'll have invested whatever he gained." St. Vincent strode into the room. Strain showed heavy in his face as his gaze rested on her.

"They'll find something," she said.

He nodded without answering and went to the sideboard. Coggins excused himself, but Frederick didn't so much as look at him. He poured himself a tankard of ale, sank into a chair, and stared pensively at the brew.

"Frederick?"

He didn't answer, so Lizzie subsided. Had he counted on the thief also being the murderer? Mr. Rycroft had been correct in at least one of his comments; they would never be able to prove him guilty of that.

She sipped her tea, her gaze resting on the viscount's frowning face. What occupied his mind? Wondering what could be recovered? If the collection were awarded to the entailed estate—which was more than likely—he would gain little immediate advantage from the recovery of any of the stolen items. That still waited on solving the murder to the satisfaction of the solicitors.

St. Vincent looked up, caught her watching him, and managed a smile. "Well, Lizzie?"

She leaned her elbows on the table and rested her chin on the backs of her locked fingers. "I think you have an estate to run and no bailiff."

The corners of his eyes crinkled in sudden amusement. "Ever the pragmatist, my dear."

"Of course. Adrian will do for the interim, but you'll need someone permanently."

"You can have no idea how I look forward to hiring someone when I have not the wherewithal to pay his wages."

She shook her head. "By then we'll have settled all this. Here's Adrian now."

Her brother stalked in and fixed an accusing eye on them. "You didn't wake me. What happened?"

Briefly, St. Vincent filled him in on the night's excitement. "Which leaves me without an estate agent," he finished.

"I ought to refuse, as punishment for your not letting me help out last night." He picked up a plate and began heaping slices of ham on it.

"But you won't." Lizzie watched him fondly. "You can't resist the challenge, and you know it."

He joined them at the table. "This doesn't solve your main problem, though, does it?"

"No. Nor do I look forward to facing Mr. Winfield today, either. If you'll remember, I promised him the proceeds of my cousin's necklace, which I never intended to sell."

"I'll break it to him," Lizzie offered. "He'll understand."

"That we considered him a suspect?" St. Vincent raised a brow that was more mocking than quizzical.

"I have more tact than to mention that."

"You haven't, you know. You—"

She ignored him. "I shall see him at once. *You* may break it to your cousins their trusted bailiff has spent the last few years stealing the few valuable things they possessed."

As soon as she had donned a warm pelisse and boots, Lizzie set off for the vicarage with an enthusiastic Cerb bounding at her side. In the garden, she tethered the protesting hound to a tree, then hurried across to the study window and peered inside.

Mr. Winfield was not alone. In a comfortable chair across the fire from him sat another man: Mr. Wesley Burnett. Lizzie rapped lightly.

The vicar started, turned to peer at her over the rim of his glasses, and stiffened. He exchanged an uneasy glance with his companion, who shrugged in a manner that intrigued Lizzie at once. Mr. Winfield unlatched the French windows and let her in.

"What have you two been talking about?" she demanded at once. "I've never seen such guilty expressions."

"Nothing—well, that is to say—I mean, it's not the least bit improper," Mr. Winfield began, uncertainly.

Mr. Burnett gave his head a rueful shake and positioned a chair for Lizzie before the blazing hearth.

With a word of thanks she settled in it. "I never thought it was, you know. You were talking about St. Vincent, were you not?" she hazarded.

Correctly, it seemed. The gentlemen exchanged another glance.

"We were merely saying how much we appreciate his efforts on behalf of his tenants," Mr. Burnett explained. "It is the greatest pity his cousin could not have been of a similar mind. The money he will bring our good vicar today will save many a family from freezing this winter."

"Yes. Well," Lizzie plunged right in. "That's what I'm here to tell you about. There won't be any money until St. Vincent's man of affairs can send some. The bit about the necklace was all a sham, to set a trap for a thief."

"Was it, now?" Mr. Burnett's eyes narrowed.

"I *am* sorry," Lizzie added, "but he really cannot sell the emeralds when they belonged to Lady St. Vincent's mother."

Mr. Winfield nodded, albeit sadly. "So that is what they were. I did wonder at something of such value being found in His late Lordship's chamber."

"It wasn't," Lizzie admitted. "St. Vincent is sorry to have included the rest of you in his ploy, but it was the only way he could catch Mr. Rycroft in the act of looting."

"Rycroft?" Mr. Burnett raised an eyebrow. "Do they believe him responsible for the murder, then, as well?"

"No. Disgusting, is it not? You'd think a man who would steal from his own employer would be capable of anything. But Mr. Coggins—" Her brow darkened. "He has the nerve to still believe St. Vincent guilty."

Again, her two companions exchanged glances.

"There, now, Miss Carstairs. You are not to worry about him." The vicar patted her hand.

"No need at all," Mr. Burnett added, somewhat dryly. "The entire neighborhood is prepared to stand buff."

"What do you mean?" Lizzie looked from one to the other, suspicious.

"Nothing! I mean—" Mr. Winfield broke off, and cast an appealing look at Mr. Burnett.

"We mean, my dear Miss Carstairs, that not only the tenants, but also the other landlords of the district feel that—" He broke off under the compelling force of Lizzie's gaze.

"Yes?" Her voice dripped with deceptive sweetness. "You mean everyone in the neighborhood thinks St. Vincent guilty of murdering his cousin?"

Mr. Winfield expelled his breath in a sigh. "That's it, Miss Carstairs. No one can help but feel the act justified, though."

"The local people only regret it is too late to provide

evidence to the Runners that St. Vincent was miles away at the time," Mr. Burnett added. "But never fear. No one will permit him to hang for doing the neighborhood such a notable service—even if it means the entire village confessing to the crime *en masse*."

Mr. Winfield, his expression earnest, nodded. "I intend to preach a sermon this Sunday on the occasional necessity of acting against the law for the greater good."

Lizzie stared at the fire for a long minute. "*Everyone* thinks him guilty?" she asked at last.

"They won't let him hang," Mr. Burnett repeated. "He's something of a local hero."

"Oh, confound it!" Lizzie flung herself to her feet. "You really believe him capable of—of *murder?* And his own cousin?"

"Let us say rather the old viscount was a somewhat exceptional case, shall we?" Mr. Winfield suggested.

"I won't believe it!" She slammed out of the room, retrieved Cerb who strained at his tether, whimpering piteously, and stomped off along the path to the Grange. Not until she reached the terrace did it dawn on her she had said she "wouldn't" believe St. Vincent capable of murder, not that she "couldn't."

She found Frederick and Adrian hard at work in the estate room. The dowager viscountess sat near the fire, setting her delicate stitches in the altar cloth that neared completion. She smiled a greeting as Lizzie entered.

"It's such a dreadful business about Mr. Rycroft," she declared, "but at least we may now banish our fears that it was our good vicar who stole that epergne. I have had a thought, St. Vincent."

The viscount looked up from the desk. "Any will be welcome."

"Mr. Winfield may keep the epergne to aid the tenants. And I shall bestow the other upon him, as well."

St. Vincent's hands twitched, and the quill with which he wrote bent in half. "I cannot permit you to use your personal belongings on behalf of the estate."

"Nonsense. If it bothers you, you may pay me back when affairs are settled. I never liked those epergnes above half. This provides an excellent excuse to rid myself of them."

And so it was settled. When Mr. Winfield called later that afternoon, epergne in hand, distress on his countenance, he found himself faced with the prospect of lugging the other back to the vicarage as well, instead of returning unencumbered. Adrian, taking pity on him, offered to drive him into Leicester in the morning, where the heavy silver atrocities might be disposed of at the most advantageous price.

Dabbing at the moisture that sprang to his eyes, Mr. Winfield accepted. "I never dreamed—," he broke off and gazed at the atrocity he held with eyes of love. "When I'd sold the last of my own plate—" He recovered somewhat. "If Mr. Carstairs will assist me, I will see about procuring lumber and nails, or whatever repair materials are most urgently needed, while we are in town."

With that, the two men of the cloth repaired to the stable to procure mounts, and set off on a tour of the tenanted farms.

"That's made them both very happy," Lizzie remarked as she watched her brother escort the vicar from the house.

St. Vincent nodded. "We'll do more, soon," he promised.

"All we have to do is discover the murderer," she agreed.

"It's a pity I'm the odds-on favorite."

She gripped his arm in a comforting gesture. "*I* still like Mr. Rycroft. I think your cousin caught him stealing."

"There was only about an hour between the time I left and the time Hodgkens found him." St. Vincent shook his head. "Rycroft would not have been such a fool as to attempt anything while my cousin was awake."

Reluctantly, Lizzie granted the truth of this. "I

suppose he wouldn't do anything to endanger his lucrative thieving unless he had no choice," she added.

With the apparent removal of Mr. Rycroft from the running, she decided to concentrate on the others. With this end in mind, she went in search of Georgiana.

She found the girl in the Music Room, seated at the pianoforte where she had apparently been practicing. At the moment, though, she was not alone; Mr. Percival Needham stood before her, his expression an odd mixture of consternation and relief. Lizzie halted just over the threshold and Georgiana hurriedly averted her face. Mr. Needham swung about to look at her, and his color deepened with embarrassment.

Lizzie, intrigued, looked from one to the other. "Is something amiss?"

Mr. Needham's flush deepened. "It does not concern you, Miss Carstairs."

"Oh?" She crossed the room and seated herself near Georgiana.

The girl studied her hands, a delicate blush lending very pretty color to her pale cheeks. "He—he has been kind enough to renew his offer for my hand."

Mr. Needham glowered at them.

Lizzie's eyebrows rose. "Would it not be more proper for him to approach St. Vincent? He is your guardian, is he not?"

Georgiana nodded.

Mr. Needham muttered something, of which "dashed hopes" and "cruel beauty" were all that were distinguishable.

Georgiana flared. "Cruel indeed! You positively ordered me to marry you! That is hardly the way to offer for a lady."

"Did he threaten you, too?" Lizzie's interest perked up.

Georgiana nodded with relish. "He did."

"I didn't!" Alarm caused Mr. Needham's voice to crack. "I only—"

297

"You said if I did not marry you at once you would move from the neighborhood and settle elsewhere. That's a threat, isn't it?" She appealed to Lizzie.

Mr. Needham glared at her, his expression sullen. "No need to make a mockery."

"No need, indeed." Lizzie contemplated him a moment. "If I were you, I would make a dignified exit at this juncture. Which is difficult," she added as the door slammed behind him a minute later, "when he insists on wearing those ridiculous coats. What prompted his offering for you?"

Georgiana rose and walked around the pianoforte, fussing unnecessarily with the music sheets. "I don't know. He did not seem to me to be suffering from uncontrollable passion." She sounded offended.

"No," Lizzie agreed. "Quite the opposite, I should guess."

"What do you mean?"

"Do you suppose he counted on your turning down his offer as an excuse to leave the neighborhood?"

"Why should he need—" Georgiana broke off, her expression arrested. "You mean you think he killed Papa, then— No. His only motive would have been Papa's refusing his consent. As you observed, his lack of passion does not bear that out."

"He might be a descendant of our Samuel."

Georgiana stared at her. "Do you really believe there is one? It *could* be he. But then why would he want to *leave* the neighborhood?"

Lizzie leaned forward, elbows on her knees, her chin cupped in her folded hands, lost in thought. "Do you suppose he could have placed papers at the Dower House which prove his connection with the Ashfields? Then if he left, someone else would find them and bring them to light."

"That's a lot of supposition," Georgiana pointed out.

"I know." Lizzie shook her head. "Really, I'm not thinking at all clearly these days. If Frederick *does* have

298

an heir, it could be *any* of our suspects. Or some outside intruder, for that matter. Oh, the devil!''

Georgiana's hand flew to her mouth, but her eyes sparkled with repressed laughter at Lizzie's language.

"We're getting nowhere," Lizzie exclaimed, "and Mr. Coggins is positively breathing down poor Frederick's neck! If we don't figure this out soon, that fool Runner will probably arrest him and *create* the evidence, just to close the case!"

Chapter 23

Two days later, repairs commenced in earnest. St. Vincent accompanied Mr. Winfield and Adrian on a tour of inspection, determined the families in greatest need, and ordered work to begin. Only a few laborers had been hired, but the tenants themselves pitched in eagerly. When the vicar returned to parish duties, St. Vincent remained at the farm, himself overseeing and directing the repairs.

Lizzie, riding out to the site the next morning with her brother and Georgiana, found the viscount deeply engrossed in learning the fine art of driving a nail into a board so it not only didn't bend, but actually held the plank in position.

"He's enjoying himself," Georgiana commented, surprised.

Lizzie nodded, and watched as he helped carry more lumber to where the carpenters worked. Already, great gaping holes waited where the rotten wood had been removed. "He loves this estate."

"Papa didn't." She urged her mount closer. "Cousin Frederick belongs here, though, doesn't he? I don't think I ever thought of it before."

"He does." Lizzie's heart swelled—then gave an uncomfortable lurch. He labored right alongside his tenants, doing work no gentleman would consider for so much as a moment, yet obviously taking great pride and satisfaction in it. He loved the land, all right—but that didn't mean he'd kill to save it! "It's a pity he didn't inherit fifteen years ago!" she declared with savage force.

"He would be a very different person if he had."

"An ideal country squire," Lizzie agreed. One who would want a wife like her. But he wasn't. He was worldly-wise—world-weary, actually. He had indulged himself in every excess, lived exactly as he pleased, and grown cynical and bored. Once the novelty of his inheritance wore off, he probably would return to London and seek the company of polished society ladies.

Word of St. Vincent's eccentric personal involvement spread throughout the countryside, and offers of assistance trickled in from the neighboring estates. Lizzie dove wholeheartedly into the project of organizing donations of blankets and food, and seeing to it that they were delivered to those in greatest need. Assisted by the dowager viscountess, she sorted through shelves of preserves, tisanes, and effusions, checking stocks of remedies for the onslaught of colds, influenza, and other illnesses that plagued the estate every winter.

"You will make an excellent lady of the manor," Georgiana informed her as they packed a basket to take to the retired butler.

"Don't be ridiculous." Lizzie added a freshly baked loaf of bread on top. "I doubt the wife Frederick chooses will have the least notion how to manage here at first. I want everything ready so it will be easy for her."

Georgiana busied herself with the jars of peas and carrots they had taken from the pantry shelves. "You must be a tremendous help to your sister, the duchess."

Lizzie shrugged that off. "Nell manages very well on her own. There really isn't enough to do at the Castle." She hoisted the heavy basket and carried it out to the waiting gig.

There would be more than enough to do here, and for years to come. *Would* a wife of Frederick's choosing be

301

able to manage? So far, Lizzie had thought only of his finding a bride who would adorn her position, be a hostess for elite society in town, who would be witty and gay and entertaining. That might be the sort of wife he wanted—but was that the sort of woman he *needed?*

No! the answer came at once. She, Lizzie, was what he needed. And he hadn't the sense to realize it! Well, she'd see about that.

Thoughtful, and more than a little perturbed, she climbed into the seat, waited for Georgiana to settle at her side, then gave the horse the office.

They remained with the elderly retainer for half an hour, then drove back by way of the farm where the carpenters worked industriously. St. Vincent, Lizzie noted with sudden amusement, had drafted not only Adrian and Mr. Winfield, but also Mr. Burnett, Squire Stellings, and even Mr. Needham into the effort. How had he ever prevailed upon that dandy to sully his hands? Or was the estate of interest to Mr. Needham?

St. Vincent saw them, waved, and strode over, his step lighter than she had seen it in weeks. Definitely, this work agreed with him. He lifted her down from the gig, set her on her feet, then assisted his cousin.

Georgiana huddled in her pelisse and cast an anxious glance at the sky. "Do you think it will snow?"

"It can be a blizzard if it likes, as long as it waits for us to finish the roof of the barn." His enthusiasm would have suited a man half his age.

Lizzie's spirits lifted in response. This was far better than his customary languid drawl.

He caught an arm of each of the ladies and led them to a vantage point out of the way of the workmen. "There is only that last stretch there, on that side, then we can begin transferring feed and stores."

Mr. Wesley Burnett, his face smudged, joined them, smiling. "Miss Carstairs, Miss Ashfield. Do not tell me you plan to take hammers in hand, as well."

Lizzie laughed. "No, though it's tempting."

302

"You certainly seem to be having an excellent time, Mr. Burnett," Georgiana said.

"I am," he admitted. "Cultivated indifference is well enough when among polite society, but there is nothing like assisting one's fellow man to give one a satisfied feeling."

"It does not appear to have rubbed off on Mr. Needham," Lizzie remarked.

That gentleman glanced in their direction, then returned his concentration to directing a tenant farmer in the sawing of a board.

Mr. Burnett shook his head. "I have no idea what he's doing out here. He spends much of his time following St. Vincent about."

Lizzie didn't like the sound of that. Did Mr. Needham merely resent feeling the obligation to help? Or did he covet the property for himself? Almost, she would think him nervous, as if he plotted something devious. . . .

At the far end of the barn, three tenants balanced precariously on ladders, raising boards over their heads to the workmen who stood on the partially repaired roof. The tenant highest up slipped, caught himself, but the board crashed to the ground—narrowly missing Mr. Winfield, who scuttled out of the way. St. Vincent muttered something under his breath, excused himself, and strode to their aid.

Mr. Burnett waited until he was out of earshot, then turned to Lizzie. "How does your Runner do with his investigation?"

"He doesn't confide in me," Lizzie said, regretful.

"He was out here this morning, asking more questions," Mr. Burnett said. "Making a confounded nuisance of himself, too. I will be very glad when he finally makes an arrest."

"So will we all," Georgiana declared.

"I wish the whole matter could be forgotten!" Lizzie started back to where the horse and gig waited. Georgiana followed.

Mr. Burnett fell into step beside them. "The entire neighborhood would agree with you on that, Miss Carstairs. The present viscount is far worthier of the title than his predecessor," he added, apparently forgetting Georgiana's connection with that gentleman. "The means of his inheriting is best ignored. *This* St. Vincent is a good man."

Lizzie gritted her teeth. "He didn't kill his cousin," she averred.

She did not see St. Vincent again until evening, when she came down the stairs dressed for dinner. He stood at the pier table in the hall, his elegant coat and the firm set of his squared chin reflected in the gilt-framed mirror above. The day's post lay scattered before him, and he perused one letter with a concentration that Lizzie found fascinating.

"What is it?" she asked, coming up behind him. "Frederick?"

He lowered the sheet slowly but gave no sign of having heard her. He stared at his own image in the mirror, his eyes unseeing.

"Frederick?" Lizzie, amused but curious, shook his arm. "What does it say?"

He glanced down at her, an irritatingly unreadable expression on his face. "A great deal—and very little."

"Are you going to be inscrutable?" she demanded. "I do not take it very kindly in you, if you are."

"I fear I must, my Lizzie. Where is that Runner of yours?"

"In the servants' hall, most likely, having his dinner. Why, do you need him? Have you learned something?"

"Something," he admitted, and his lips quirked into a slight smile. "Ah, Hodgkens." He hailed the butler, who emerged from the corridor leading to the dining room. "Will you extend my compliments to our Mr. Coggins, and ask him to join me in the library?"

The butler bowed and continued on his way.

Lizzie tilted her head to one side and eyed the viscount

narrowly. "What are you going to tell him?"

"*Sad stories of the death of kings,*" he quoted.

Lizzie wrinkled her nose. "Your cousin wasn't a king," she said, then frowned in an effort to remember *Richard II*. "And you'll never get me to believe he was poisoned by his wife!"

"No, that he was not. Nor *sleeping killed*. But I wonder if our villain will be *haunted by the ghosts they have deposed.*"

"Deposed," she repeated. "You know who Samuel's descendant is, don't you?"

"I believe I do." He tapped the letter he held with deliberation. "And now if you will excuse me, I must speak with our good Coggins."

"If you think for one moment I'm not coming, too—"

"I do. You will join the others and convey my apologies for me. You may start the meal without me."

"*They* can. I—"

"You, my dear Lizzie, will for once do what you are told with no argument." His stern eye fastened on her, brooking no opposition.

It came anyway. She stuck her tongue out at him. "You're going to tell me eventually, St. Vincent. Why can I not come now?"

"Because I am *not* going to tell you."

"You're—" She broke off, too indignant to voice her opinion.

He rested his hands on her shoulders. "The evidence here is all circumstantial. Not definite proof at all. I may well be wrong."

"But why—?"

"I don't want you giving away my suspicions."

She swallowed, digesting this. "That means he's someone here, in this neighborhood." His hesitation proved answer enough, and she surged ahead, not wanting to give him a chance to recover. "Is it Mr. Needham?"

Only the slightest flicker crossed his countenance, but

305

she crowed in delight. "So it *is* Mr. Needham."

"I did not say it was, but if you wish to believe it, that will suit me very well. Excuse me, my dear."

"Frederick—," she began, her tone threatening.

"Lizzie!" he mimicked. "No, listen. Knowing my heir is actually in the vicinity and proving him guilty of murder are two different things. He might very well not even know of his relationship with my family—though the possibility may have occurred to him."

He left her, and her face fell. Did that mean she had guessed right? Or was he merely content to let her jump to the wrong conclusion? *Confound* St. Vincent! Irritated with him, but more with herself for not being able to ferret out the answers, she stalked off to the Green Salon where the others gathered before the meal.

St. Vincent did not join his family until the last course had been brought in. He took his seat with only a smiling apology, and steadfastly refused to offer an explanation. Lizzie glared at him, but found to her growing exasperation that this treatment only amused him. He had come to some decision, of that she was certain. Perhaps she could get it out of Mr. Coggins.

The Runner was nowhere to be found that night, so she went in search of him as soon as she rose the following morning. She ran him to earth at last in the stable, where he handed a letter to the undergroom. The lad took it, along with the coin the Runner offered, and hurried off on his errand.

"Dispatching your information?" Lizzie asked as she joined him.

"That's right, Missy. That, and asking for more."

She nodded. "A very wise move. At least we shall finally see the end of this business."

"Well, now, Missy. I can't say as it's all settled yet, not all right and tight, leastways. Ideas and hearsay is one thing, but solid facts? That's what we're needing. Solid facts."

"We know who St. Vincent's heir is," she tried.

The Runner shook his flaming red head. "Now, Missy. His Lordship warned as you'd be trying to fiddle that information out of me. Mum's the word, though." He winked at her. "Just like my sister's Sarah, you are, always wanting to know everything."

Lizzie muttered something uncomplimentary about Coggins's sister and her numerous offspring, and stalked off.

Not for one moment did she believe this mysterious heir would have come into the neighborhood without being aware of some connection with the family. Once he arrived, he would have discovered quickly enough the lack of candidates for inheriting. The fact he was one of only three direct male descendents might well have proved too big a temptation for one with neither worldly status nor fortune. Both obstacles in his way could be removed by a single murder, for Frederick would surely be blamed.

She called Cerb to heel from where he scrabbled in a corner, attempting to dig mice from under the stalls by way of the cobbles, and took him to inspect the refurbishment of the herb garden, instead. It would be spring—and she would be long gone—before the seeds could be planted, but the design was hers, reminiscent of a medieval knot garden.

With the help of a potboy—one of the few male servants who did not work on the barn—she rearranged a few rocks into a neat border. By the time they completed this to her satisfaction, mud liberally splattered her pelisse, but she had greatly improved her temper—and come to a decision. She would ride out to the farm to see how the barn progressed, and watch St. Vincent as he dealt with Mr. Montague Winfield, Mr. Percival Needham, and Mr. Wesley Burnett. Surely, he would betray his suspicions!

After sending a message to the stable to saddle her horse, she ran up to her room to exchange her dirtied garments for her riding habit and cloak. As she descended the stairs, she saw Coggins in the Great Hall, standing with Hodgkens. The post, it seemed, had arrived.

She hurried down and eagerly took a folded sheet that bore the scrawled frank of Halliford in one corner, and was addressed in her sister Helena's neat copperplate. She broke the seal, then paused. Mr. Coggins, perusing a letter of his own, seemed pleased.

"What is it?" she asked, as usual not wasting time with old-fashioned and unproductive notions of propriety.

"Well, now, Missy, I can't see as there's any harm in telling you. It seems our Mr. Rycroft invested some money on the 'Change, regular-like, over the past few years. There's no one as will say it doesn't rightfully belong to the estate."

Her spirits soared. "Will St. Vincent get it at once?"

"That's a might tricksy, Missy, that is, but there just might be the chance—seeing as how *some* money has to be spent on the upkeep of the estate, even if he can't inherit everything all right and proper yet."

"He will. Soon." Lizzie held the Runner's eye.

"Well, it does begin to look that way," he conceded. He winked at her. "*That* ought to cheer up His Lordship."

It also set the final panache on Lizzie's soaring elation. Now she had another reason to seek out Frederick. Coggins entrusted her with the letter to show him, and took himself off on errands of his own. Lizzie hurried on her way, barely able to restrain herself from shouting with glee.

The groom had saddled Patrick, but the highbred horse did not stand waiting. He paced about the lad, pawing the cobbles with one shod hoof, throwing his head as if to free himself from the restraining bit. Lizzie knew exactly how he felt. As soon as the groom threw her into the saddle and she hooked her knee over the pommel, she gave the animal his head. He crow-hopped twice, then shot forward through the arched gateway.

They followed the drive only a short distance. As soon

308

as they neared the first pasture, Lizzie headed her hunter toward the stone wall. They cleared it flying, landed without so much as a break in stride, and tore headlong cross-country. Lizzie leaned low against Patrick's neck, laughing. St. Vincent's success lay so close; they could make the needed repairs, make the farms profitable once more, restore the estate to what it should be— They? She laughed again. It was *she* Frederick needed, not some languishing beauty. And so she would make him see.

She breathed deeply of the crisp air, and found it laden with acrid smoke. Surprised, she slowed her mount and looked up. Almost straight ahead, a black cloud billowed up from beyond a line of yew trees, folding back in on itself, then shooting skyward. Patrick veered sideways, but she kept her balance and urged him forward once more.

Fire—and the farm where Frederick and the others worked lay just beyond those trees! Her heart blocked her throat, making it difficult to breathe. Patrick reared under the force of her clenched hands, and she released the bit just enough to spur him on.

She could not reach the farm by the fields, now; the spreading line of smoke revealed all too clearly where the flames would cut her off. Instead, she angled toward the lane, cleared the hedge fence and landed on the verge, and rode around the longer way. She turned down the narrow cart track leading to the farm, and caught her breath.

Flames engulfed the barn, destroying the hard work, what little money Frederick had been able to find.

Patrick stopped dead, throwing his head, refusing to go closer. Lizzie jumped down and abandoned him. Everywhere in the yard figures scurried, some fetching water from the well, others racing to throw it on the raging fire. Four of the men attacked the great door, swinging something—axes.

She hadn't realized she had started running, but now she redoubled her pace.

Mr. Needham and the vicar helped with the water. Adrian—there he was, with Mr. Burnett, both wielding axes. She couldn't see Frederick.

Everyone shouted; nothing distinct reached her, because a terrified voice rang in her ears. It broke on a sob, and it was her own, screaming his name.

By instinct, she ran to Adrian. He grabbed her; she barely recognized him through the soot and grime that covered his face.

"Where is he?" she cried.

He dragged her back. "Stay out of the way!"

"*Where is he?*"

"We're trying to get him out, Lizzie. Let me get back. We've—"

He broke off. The door collapsed under the onslaught of the other three men. The wall shimmered in the heat, then swayed with an eerie creaking. With a trembling shudder, the side collapsed inward, showering debris and sparks across the yard.

Chapter 24

Gushing smoke filled Lizzie's lungs, choking her, stinging her eyes. Dashing the back of her hand across her face, she tore free from Adrian's hold and ran forward. She tugged at the flaming timber, all the while screaming Frederick's name.

Adrian tried to pull her away, then abandoned the hopeless attempt and instead concentrated on the more urgent need to find and free the viscount. Water splashed over them as the workers threw buckets on the blazing wreckage, and black smoke enveloped them. Sparks and cinders burned through Lizzie's cloak, and she dragged the garment off and beat at the raging fire with it.

Mr. Burnett, his face grim, joined them, and he and Adrian managed to shift the heavier debris. Lizzie, coughing and bleary-eyed, continued her onslaught on the flames, beating them out only seconds before the two men grabbed the still-smoldering planks and hauled them away.

Lizzie raised her cloak once more, saw the dirtied and scratched leather of a black boot, and a strangled cry broke from her. "Adrian, he's here!"

In an instant, her brother and Mr. Burnett were on their knees, lifting the remaining rubble carefully. Lizzie stood back, afraid of getting in the way. If all that had landed on his head. . . . She dashed away the tears that filled her eyes, leaving streaks of soot and grime across her face.

Mr. Needham and two other workers ran up, and Adrian directed them in pulling away boards. Behind her, she could hear the splash and sizzle as others threw water on the remaining flames. She concentrated on that black boot heel.

Then Adrian lifted the last of the fallen planks from where Frederick's head must be, revealing a beam half-propped across another. Her breath escaped in a shuddering sigh, and for a moment her knees gave way beneath her. He had come so close to being crushed. . . .

"My God—," Mr. Needham's voice shook. "Had that beam fallen an inch farther to the side—"

Adrian knelt next to the viscount and felt his arms and legs. Lizzie shook off her dizziness and went to his aid. "Have someone go for a doctor, Lizzie." He didn't even look up from his examination. A red stain seeped about a jagged tear in his coat sleeve, but he seemed oblivious to it.

"Your arm—"

"Never mind that. Get a doctor!"

Still unsteady, she looked about and spotted the vicar, who helped fill pails at the well. "Mr. Winfield!" Gathering her wits—and her more customary determination—she ran over to him. "We need the doctor."

The vicar turned sharply. "Is he—?"

"I don't know. Please, someone must go for the doctor!"

Mr. Winfield nodded, the light of battle kindling in his bright green eyes. He took off at a run, and a minute later he dashed past again, this time mounted on a startled, nervous cob. The vicar urged the poor beast into a gallop and departed. Lizzie could only hope he knew where to go.

Afraid of what might await her, she started back to where she had left the others. Adrian and Mr. Burnett had not been idle in her absence. Her singed and filthy

312

cloak covered a wooden pallet, and her brother, his face, hands, and clothes covered in grimy soot, directed three workers as they carefully transferred St. Vincent's body to it.

Lizzie bit her lip and kept silent until they completed the delicate operation. "How badly is he hurt?" she asked finally, her voice quavering.

Adrian slipped an arm about her and gave her an encouraging hug. "I couldn't find anything broken."

"Then why does he lie there like that?" To her consternation, tears started to her eyes once more. She turned, trembling, and buried her face in her brother's shoulder.

"He must have been overcome by the smoke."

With an effort, she pulled herself together. "Will he be all right?"

Adrian hesitated. "I wish I could say for certain, Lizzie. We got him out as quickly as we could."

She nodded, knowing he could tell her nothing more.

Mr. Burnett shook his head, as if dazed. "I've never seen anything go up the way this did. We couldn't control it—" He broke off.

Under Adrian's guidance, the workers hefted the pallet on which the viscount lay and carried it to where others hastily emptied a farming cart of its load of building supplies. Silently, Lizzie followed, her gaze never leaving St. Vincent's ashen face.

The cart bore him back to the Grange, where the alarmed Hodgkens ran to greet them, then stood wringing his hands in dismay. Adrian, in spite of the blood that continued to seep down his ruined coat sleeve, took charge and ordered the footmen, along with the two grooms, to carry St. Vincent to his bedchamber. His expression set in grim lines, Adrian, assisted by the viscount's distraught valet, firmly excluded Lizzie from the room. Reluctantly, she went.

By the time they permitted her to enter once more, they had removed St. Vincent's clothes, washed the dirt

313

and soot from him, and gotten him into a nightshirt and between sheets. Only bruises, burns and cuts remained, bearing their mute testimony to the day's catastrophe. Adrian had taken the opportunity to clean himself up a little, as well, and a clean bandage swathed his arm.

Lizzie hesitated on the threshold, staring at the motionless form of St. Vincent. Her worried eyes moved to her brother, then back to the viscount, where they remained fixed.

Adrian didn't waste time on platitudes; he merely drew a chair for her next to the bed, and she sank into it.

Another hour passed before the doctor put in his belated appearance, with Mr. Winfield hurrying in his wake.

"Is St. Vincent—?" The vicar's question trailed off as he looked from one to the other of the occupants of the room.

The doctor brushed past him. "Well, now, if the young lady will leave us, we'll see what we can do."

Lizzie glared at him, but held her tongue. She directed a speaking look at her brother, then took herself off to see whether Georgiana and the dowager viscountess had yet returned from their visit to Mrs. Stellings. They would want to know at once.

As she reached the Great Hall, the butler, somewhat recovered, greeted her with relief. "Mr. Burnett has called, miss. Will you see him?"

Glad to have something constructive to do, she made her way to the drawing room, where their neighbor, still covered in grime, paced the length of the narrow apartment.

He came to her at once and took her hands. "How is he?"

"The doctor has only just arrived. Will you not be seated?" Her calmness—or was that propriety?—surprised her.

He shook his head. "I dare not. My clothes—"

She poured him a glass of wine, then another for

314

herself as she saw how her hands shook. "Is the fire out?"

"Yes. They were throwing water on the last embers when I left. All that work—" He broke off.

Lizzie nodded. But if Frederick were all right . . .

"I suppose you wish me at the devil," he said ruefully. "I just can't seem to interest myself in anything at the moment. Do you suppose they'll be long?"

"You are quite welcome to keep me company. Otherwise I'll just sit here and worry." Lizzie drained her glass, saw that Mr. Burnett had done the same, and refilled them both. She sipped from hers and stared at her hands, not wanting to raise her eyes to the fire that crackled cheerfully in the hearth. It brought too-vivid images to her mind.

On impulse, she rang for a deck of cards and a sheet to cover a chair. When these arrived, Mr. Burnett made himself comfortable, and she shuffled and dealt without asking his preference. They were finishing their eleventh hand of piquet when Adrian entered the room, poured himself a glass of the dark red wine, and sank onto the sofa at Lizzie's side with a sigh. Lizzie lowered her cards and bit her lip.

"He'll be all right," he said at last. "He breathed in too much smoke, as we guessed he had. With rest he'll recover. But Lord, what I wouldn't give to know how that fire started."

Mr. Burnett let out a deep, relieved sigh. He swept the cards into a pile and straightened the edges. "I don't see how it could have begun. There were scraps of wood and sawdust lying about, of course, but I don't understand how they could have ignited."

Lizzie clenched her teeth before she could blurt out the obvious. Not until after the departure of their visitor, who professed several more times his pleasure with the viscount's prospects for a full recovery, did Lizzie round on her brother. "Did someone set it deliberately?"

He took her hand and eased her fingers from the sleeve

315

of his coat. "I wish I could think of another way it might have happened."

Lizzie flung away from him, then stopped before the window and stared out. "Someone is still trying to murder Frederick."

Adrian could not deny it.

The return of Lady St. Vincent and her daughter a half-hour later interrupted Lizzie's unpleasant thoughts. Even though she assured the two ladies their relative did not lie at death's door, nothing would do for them but to be shown into his presence at once. Lizzie accompanied them and stood at the foot of the bed, gazing down at him.

His face, in repose, appeared serene. Almost angelic, she mused—a sharp contrast from his tainted reputation. In silence she studied him, from the blond hair that curled away from his high forehead to each classically handsome feature. She had never noticed just *how* handsome. No wonder ladies succumbed to his charms. She preferred his devilish wit and devious sense of humor, his deep chuckle when they argued over some ridiculous point, the never-fading challenge in his keen blue eyes that dared her to broach another subject for their mutual enjoyment.

Lord, she couldn't bear it if anything happened to him. He was too much a part of her life, a part that had felt like an empty void during his five-year absence.

St. Vincent regained consciousness late in the evening, but Adrian, who had taken charge with his usual quiet efficiency, did not permit her to speak with him until the following morning. By then, she had reached a conclusion and determined to follow through on it at the first possible moment.

As soon as her brother admitted her to the viscount's chamber, she strode to the side of the bed and fixed him with a compelling gaze. "Who is your heir?" she demanded.

A faint spark of amusement lit his eye. "I'm much better, thank you, Lizzie."

She waved his irony aside. "Of course you are. But you haven't told me who Samuel's descendant is."

"I don't know." He reached out to her and she took his hand.

"Cut line. It said in that letter."

"All I learned was who it *might* be."

"Well? Under the circumstances, that sounds fairly certain to me!"

"To you, it would," he murmured.

She regarded him in suspicion for a moment. "If we don't know who is trying to kill you, then how can we keep you safe?"

"Even if he *is* Samuel's descendant—which I am by no means certain—there is no proof he is trying to kill me."

Lizzie glared at him. "You're being idiotish, just asking to be murdered. How many enemies do you have? No one else has any reason to want you dead."

His grip tightened on her fingers. "Do you think me so lovable, then?"

"Certainly not murderable. I know you're a rake and a libertine, but you would never do anything that would actually hurt someone."

"Wouldn't I?" He stared at her for a long moment, then dropped her hand and turned his head so he stared out the window. "You're right. I wouldn't."

Lizzie rearranged the pillows to give him greater support. "I've told your groom to help your valet stand guard over you."

"No, Lizzie." He gazed at her, his expression troubled. "I am in no danger in my own bed."

"Do you mean you've checked the canopy?"

His jaw tightened. "Actually, Adrian did. I meant, though, that my death must appear to be an accident."

"Then you *do* believe it's your heir. You're being thickheaded about this—as usual. If we set abroad the fact we know the truth, then he'll have to quit trying!"

St. Vincent shook his head, firmly but with care. "We will do better to let our villain think we accept these

317

attempts to kill me as accidents, or he's like to come up with something more devious. So far, he's been content to bide his time and seize opportunities with no certainty of success. A direct provocation on our part might make him resort to more subtlety that might work."

Lizzie sank into the chair and glared at him. "We can't let him keep trying! One of these days he might get lucky."

"Thank you, Lizzie."

She wrinkled her nose. "You know what I mean. You can't tell me you *want* to die."

"I have the Grange to live for, at least." He closed his eyes.

Lizzie left him shortly to take Cerb for his morning run. She was not in the least content to allow matters to remain as they stood; she wanted everything settled right now.

In one point, at least, though, she had to admit St. Vincent was right: they needed proof, not just logic and strong suspicions. She slowed her steps, her brow creasing. If she wanted results, and fast, it would be best if they forced the murderer's hand. But how?

A trap had worked in discovering the thieving Mr. Julian Rycroft; perhaps one might work for their murderer, as well.

She tugged a bare twig from a tree and fingered it. The killer wanted St. Vincent convicted of the old viscount's murder, thereby removing both obstacles between himself and the title. What if St. Vincent were publicly cleared of having any connection with the crime? Then the man would have to redouble his efforts in staging "accidents."

That was too risky. Even if she could convince Coggins to pretend to arrest an innocent man, the murderer might wait weeks—even months!—before trying again. No, she needed something that would work now, that would make the murderer throw caution to the winds and make a

318

reckless attack on St. Vincent, one which they could predict and control.

She threw down her twig and paced on, momentarily stymied. What would make him—of course! She stopped dead, triumphant. If Samuel's heir thought St. Vincent were on the verge of marrying, he'd have to act quickly to prevent another heir from entering the picture.

She turned abruptly, called the wandering Cerb to heel, and marched back to the house.

Half an hour later, St. Vincent leaned back against the pillows. "No!"

"But, Frederick—"

He drew a deep breath. "Do you have any idea what you're asking?"

"Of course I do. What's wrong with it?"

"Everything." He frowned at her. "For your harebrained scheme to work, I would need a young lady foolish enough to pose as my betrothed."

Lizzie fiddled with the cord that knotted about the bed hanging. "I'll do it, of course. I know you don't like the idea, but it's not as if we'd actually have to go through with a wedding."

"Do you think anyone would believe it? I'm almost twice your age."

She studied the new knot she had added. "There's nothing wrong with that. We're known to be old friends."

"Friends," he repeated, emphasizing the word. "I'll not be accused of seducing a young innocent."

"It's your own fault for earning such a shocking reputation. Have you any other ridiculous arguments?"

"I doubt I have the strength. You'll do as you please, as always, I suppose."

"That's settled, then. We'll hold an engagement party as soon as possible, and I can cry off right after we've captured our murderer."

She left before he could object. He didn't like the idea

of entering into even a sham betrothal with her. Well, she was not one to give up easily. She would bring him to see the advantages, yet.

Her first impulse, which was to advertise the engagement abroad, she stifled. That put St. Vincent at risk at once. For her trap to work, she needed to surprise the guilty party, make him panic, make him act without proper reflection.

Their first step, therefore, would be to send out invitations to a small ball. Surely there must be enough people in the neighborhood to make up such an event. She didn't really enjoy dancing, but that was a sacrifice she would have to make. It was a pity they couldn't hold an engagement card party, but that wouldn't be proper. If they were going to do this at all, they might as well do it right.

After serious thought, she decided not to tell Georgiana and Lady St. Vincent the truth. They might be surprised the viscount would marry a chit barely twenty and lacking in any social graces or ambitions, but they might suppose their cousin to be thinking of an heir. He'd been out of the country for five years, after all; his old flirts must have found new diversions.

The reaction of St. Vincent's female relatives, though, was not quite what she expected. She walked into the salon before dinner to find the two ladies there before her. Never one to waste time in unnecessary explanation, she went straight to the point. "St. Vincent wishes to hold a ball as soon as possible. How do we go about it?"

The dowager lowered her embroidery and regarded Lizzie in consternation. "A ball? St. Vincent?"

"Just a small one."

"It's not quite proper," Georgiana ventured. "Under the circumstances, I mean."

"It *is* the most appropriate way to announce our engagement, though, is it not?"

Georgiana stared at her for a moment, then squealed.

She sprang to her feet and threw her arms about the appalled Lizzie. "Oh, I knew it must come to this. I am so happy, Lizzie! I would dearly love you for my cousin!"

The dowager went to embrace Lizzie as well. "I wish you the greatest joy, my dear. I feel certain it will be yours." She dabbed at the corners of her eyes and sighed in real pleasure. "In truth, I had begun to fear Cousin Frederick would never get around to it."

"I doubt he did," Georgiana giggled. "This is your doing, isn't it, Lizzie?"

"It is." A rush of comforting warmth washed over her. At least *someone* didn't think the idea of Frederick's marrying her to be ludicrous. Now, if only she could convince Frederick. He could be so irritatingly stubborn, though, and the devil was in it she didn't know how to change his mind.

"When will you wish the ball?" the dowager asked.

"As soon as possible."

"And will the duchess be attending?"

Lizzie considered Helena's probable reaction to her sham betrothal, and shook her head firmly. "No. Adrian will represent the family."

"I will?" Her brother strolled into the room. His expression, Lizzie noted with dismay, was grim.

"Of course you will. You may even perform the marriage immediately after."

He opened his mouth, then shut it tight. White lines formed about his lips. "I don't care for this, Lizzie," he said at last.

She held his gaze. "You have an objection to St. Vincent?"

"That's not what I mean, and you know it."

"It's the unseemly haste, I suppose. Really, Adrian, I hadn't thought you would stand upon ceremony. If ever you marry, I don't doubt for a moment the knot will be tied in a trice, before even you realize yourself what is happening."

Pointedly, he returned no answer.

Lizzie dropped her gaze. "It will be best to do the thing in a simple manner. We will write at once to obtain a special license," she added.

Adrian cast her a glance that should have withered her in her tracks. "I only hope you may both live not to regret this," he informed her, somewhat cryptically.

Chapter 25

Lizzie tapped the tip of her quill on the invitation card, splattering ink across its once-clean surface. "We'll be able to muster ten couples."

"You make it sound like an army." St. Vincent, who lay on the sofa beside the desk in the library, opened his eyes, and let a pained expression cross his features. "I just sharpened that the other day."

She looked at the ruined pen. "Sorry. Where's the knife?" She rummaged in the drawer he indicated, found it, and went to work paring the quill tip. "This is the last thing to take care of. We have everything else organized."

She heard the soft hiss of his brocade dressing gown brushing against the satin of the sofa cushions as he sat up, and she turned to fix him with her compelling eye. "You're supposed to stay down."

"Am I not to be permitted to take part in planning my own engagement ball?"

"It's just a sham." She studied her work on the pen as if she found it fascinating.

"I don't like being left out." He sounded distinctly like a quarrelsome little boy.

Lizzie smiled. "All right, what would you like to do? Approve the list of refreshments we've ordered? Take over addressing the cards, perhaps?"

"I'll take charge of the wine, thank you."

"Certainly. Adrian has—"

"Damn it, Lizzie, this is *my* house and *my* engagement party, however fake it might be. Do I have nothing to do?"

"Only stand around in some secluded spot and hope your heir tries to murder you."

He rose, then rested a hand on her shoulder to steady himself. "He's come near to succeeding already." He turned away. His walking stick lay against the side of the sofa for his convenience, but he scorned it. "I suppose you've already hired the musicians, as well."

"Of course we have. Lord, Frederick, you've been lying abed two whole days. You didn't expect me to be idle, did you?"

"You, Lizzie? Never."

She fell silent as she carefully inscribed the name and direction on the first invitation. "It will be quiet when I return to Yorkshire, after so much excitement here," she said at last.

"I'm glad we've kept you so well entertained." He returned to his seat.

She shook her head, annoyed, and wrote several more cards. He'd been at such pains to recreate their former bantering relationship since she'd suggested this betrothal. Which of them, she wondered, did he seek to convince that his feelings for her were purely avuncular?

"When will your Runner's men arrive?" he asked presently.

"The day before the ball, I hope. That will give them time to become familiar with the house and grounds. And to pick the best spot."

"For my execution?"

She swiveled about in her chair and regarded him with her impish grin. "One might almost think you have no taste for our little plot."

"I suppose you would enjoy waiting about for someone to try and murder you."

She considered. "If I knew he would be prevented, yes,

324

I suppose I might." His deep chuckle sounded and she smiled at him. "Quit trying to gammon me, Frederick. I know perfectly well you wouldn't miss this adventure for worlds."

"Well, no, I wouldn't." He crossed to the hearth and extended his hands to the warmth. "You're never going to tell me our Mr. Coggins has any faith in your plot?"

A slight frown creased her brow. "He agreed," she said at last.

"He thinks we're trying to fool him, doesn't he? To make him believe I'm innocent."

"You are!"

He swept her an exaggerated—and cautious—bow. "Thank you, Lizzie."

"As soon as he arrests the real murderer, you may settle down and become a model landlord—and father, of course," she added in revenge for his mocking. "You'll need a whole brood of children."

He shuddered, but to her utter amazement, the idea appealed to her. She might have to take drastic measures to convince *him*, though.

She was interrupted from her work directing cards a half-hour later by Georgiana, who swept into the room in the whirlwind fashion that so suited her. "Lizzie, your abigail says you haven't a ball gown with you!"

Lizzie set down the quill she had just dipped, and the ink puddled on the card. "No, I don't suppose I have."

Georgiana laughed and hugged her, much to her consternation. "Goose! You must have one at once. And Mamma says so must I, as Papa never let me have anything suitable before."

St. Vincent looked up from the list of confections he studied and directed an evil grin at Lizzie. "What a delightful prospect. You must go to Leicester and spend the entire day shopping. Of course you must have a ball gown."

"And a wedding dress," Georgiana added.

Lizzie nearly knocked over the bottle of ink.

Georgiana laughed merrily. "Oh, you *are* in such pucker, Lizzie. I never thought I should see the day yo *weren't* practical. You are to be married the morning afte the ball, are you not? Then you must have something t wear." She sighed. "How can you contemplate *not* havin an elaborate trousseau?"

"We shall be at pains to rectify the matter as quickly a possible," St. Vincent assured his cousin. "Lizzie, m love, you had best make haste into a carriage gown and b off to Leicester."

She threw him a speaking look, set down the pen wit an audible click, and stalked from the room.

The ladies did not return until evening, when th growing darkness and threatening rain caused th dowager Lady St. Vincent to cast anxious glances a the sky. Lizzie, who could ride or walk all day withou tiring, found herself exhausted by just a few hours c standing still while determined dressmakers pinne with enthusiasm. This was not, she decided, somethin to which she would care to subject herself again, whic opinion she voiced to St. Vincent when she encountere him in the drawing room before dinner that evening.

He raised a finely arched eyebrow. "Do you not car for shopping?"

"You know I don't. How could you subject me t hours of—of torture?"

"But you *must* have a trousseau, my dear. Everyon would be shocked if you did not."

"We're only trying to fool one person," she informe him through gritted teeth.

Smiling, he poured her a glass of wine and handed over. "This will make you feel more the thing. You're a put about, I shouldn't wonder."

"Thanks to you," she muttered, but took the win "What will they say when they find this is all a sham?

St. Vincent stared at the dark liquid as he swirled hi glass. "Our villain is no fool. Do you think he would n

326

see this for what it is if we neglected so important a detail as your bride's clothes?"

"Could we not simply say I am ordering them in London?"

A soft laugh escaped him. "So my cousins already believe. Do you think you would have gotten off so lightly today otherwise?"

Lizzie rolled her eyes. "Lightly," she muttered.

He grinned, but his reply was cut short by the entry of the other two ladies into the room.

"Cousin Frederick!" Georgiana exclaimed even before she was through the doorway. "It was of all things the most delightful day I have ever spent! I have purchased the loveliest gown, the very prettiest I have ever owned, and I owe it all to you and my dearest Lizzie! Oh, Cousin Frederick, you will love her dress! It is all white silk and silvered lace."

"Oh, Lord!" Lizzie exclaimed, and retreated with alacrity.

The next week passed in preparations for the ball and the subsequent wedding. Georgiana and her mother could talk of nothing else, and appeared bewildered by Lizzie's grim expression and refusal to enter into their excitement. Whenever she could bear no more, she took Cerb for a long ramble through the parkland. She would have preferred it if St. Vincent had accompanied her, so they could have enjoyed a rousing argument, but that, Coggins ruled, was out of the question.

"Now, Missy," he cajoled. "Either he's *not* in any danger whatsoever, or he is."

She bristled. "What do you mean?"

"Whispers of this here engagement of yours have spread about the neighborhood, they have. If this supposed heir of His Lordship's really *does* want him dead—"

"He does!"

"Well, Missy, that's as may be. But if—and mind

you, I'm still saying *if*—he does, you're right about him having to act fast-like if'n His Lordship goes and gets hisself caught in parson's mousetrap."

Lizzie digested this. "You mean I've just sentenced St. Vincent to a week-long stay in the house."

He beamed at her. "That's the ticket, Missy. Don't want no harm coming to him, do you?"

"No."

St. Vincent, not much to her surprise, took an even dimmer view of the prospect than did she. He fixed her with an accusing eye and demanded: "Not even out to the stable?"

Lizzie sank onto the chair opposite him. "Only consider, Frederick. You cannot expose yourself to a possible assault until Coggins has his men ready. What good will it do you to prove yourself innocent of murder by being killed?"

After that, Lizzie divided her time between her long rambles and curling up in the library with St. Vincent, playing piquet. As diversions from her ever-increasing worry, though, neither activity proved effective. By the night of the ball, she had worked herself into a mass of nerves. She paced about her chamber, every bit as agitated as the bride she purported to be.

For the fifth time, her maid begged her to be still. Lizzie settled at her dressing table, but her fingers nervously creased her handkerchief.

She didn't feel like herself. She didn't even *look* like herself! She regarded her reflection and wrinkled her nose in disgust. Almost, it might have been Augusta who stared out of the mirror at her. She didn't like her hair all done in ringlets.

What would Frederick think? That she tried to entrap him by aping the toasts of London? He'd be revolted—and with good cause.

Impulsively, unable to sit still another moment while her abigail fussed with the unfamiliar occupation of arranging artificial roses amid the curls, she broke free, thanked the maid for her efforts, and ran downstairs.

She entered the drawing room a full half-hour before dinner would be served. Restless, she rang the bell, and when the flustered Hodgkens arrived, she asked that Mr. Coggins be sent to her.

The Runner entered five minutes later, talking as soon as he opened the door. "Now, now, Missy. No need for you to be all in a pucker. You just relax and enjoy this here ball. My men and I, we'll do our work, never you fear. If anyone does takes it into his mind to have a go at His Lordship, we'll get him, all right and tight, we will."

"But what if *he* gets St. Vincent first?"

He shook his head. "There, now, Missy. We won't go and let nothing happen to him, we won't. Five men I've got, and the grooms and footmen as well. Even His Lordship's valet wants to help out, he does. Very popular with the household is the viscount, Missy. Very popular indeed."

She thanked him, and let him return to his preparations. She had barely resumed her pacing when the door opened once more. St. Vincent strode across the threshold, then came to an abrupt halt, staring at her.

"Is something the matter?" she snapped.

"Nothing. My dearest Lizzie, you are a vision."

She rolled her eyes. "If you're going to make a May game of this, St. Vincent, I warn you, I'll—"

"I am not. You look absolutely delightful this evening. Can I not pay you a compliment?"

"You don't often," she pointed out.

"That's because you fly into an indignant passion whenever I try."

"I am well aware I don't resemble the ladies with whom you normally associate."

"No, you don't." He spoke curtly.

Her heart sank. Their engagement really was nothing but a sham. She had never known Frederick to choose the practical over the more enjoyable.

"You should wear this, this evening." He caught her hand and slipped a large but simple sapphire ring over her gloved finger.

She examined it critically. "It's very nice, Frederick. I like it." Too much, in fact. If only this were real! For the first time in her life, emotional tears of longing sprang to her eyes.

She looked away quickly, glad he hadn't noticed, and groped for her handkerchief. What exquisite agony, to be in love with him and tied in a sham engagement that would be broken in only hours. By helping to clear him of the murder charge, she freed him to find a *real* bride, one who would be to his taste, who would flirt with him, know how to please him. But she wouldn't give up without a fight!

"Lizzie?" His voice, suddenly gentle, tugged at a heart she had never realized could be so fragile or foolish. "You're not afraid, are you? We can call this off at any time."

She turned slowly and looked at him, really studying him. "No. I'll see this through. With you." She breathed the last words. Lord, if Augusta were here, she'd go off into whoops to see her prosaic sister in the grips of a romantic passion!

And what would St. Vincent say if he guessed? It would take every ounce of courage she possessed to find out, she supposed. But find out, she must.

Lady St. Vincent and Adrian joined them, and Georgiana tripped merrily in only minutes before Hodgkens announced dinner. Lizzie tasted little of the excellent meal. Her situation was absurd—that she, of all people, should fall in love. Yet she didn't find it amusing in the least. If Frederick remained stubborn, she wasn't at all certain she could bring him about.

If she couldn't . . . She would get over it, of course. No one with a modicum of common sense died of a broken heart. Maybe she would set herself up as Adrian's housekeeper, once he settled in as a don at Oxford.

At last, Lady St. Vincent rose, and the others followed suit. "The guests should be arriving at any moment," the dowager announced.

St. Vincent drained the last of his glass and met Lizzie's worried gaze. "Time to face the enemy, my girl. Are you ready?"

Chapter 26

St. Vincent gave Lizzie a reassuring smile and a wink, but she didn't respond. She bit her lip and tried to keep the strain she felt from showing. If anything went wrong, if they had made one mistake . . .

St. Vincent appeared quite at his ease. Confound the man, one might almost think he *didn't* expect anyone to try to murder him this night. At least he wouldn't betray their plans. She had better try to emulate his calm.

St. Vincent glanced across the table and met Adrian's frowning gaze. "Everything is in readiness," he assured his friend.

Adrian nodded. "Lizzie? You look pale. Are you all right?"

"Yes." She hoped. "Let's—let's get this over with."

Georgiana's merry laughter rang out. "One would think you dreaded the ball, Lizzie. Do not worry so. Everything will be quite delightful. You know almost everyone who will be here."

Lizzie managed a smile that apparently satisfied the girl. St. Vincent offered her his arm, and she took it; her fingers tightened involuntarily on his sleeve.

As they walked to the ballroom, she mentally reviewed their preparations. Nothing should go wrong; they had taken every precaution to assure success. Even if Frederick's unknown assailant was *not* among the invited guests, he would have every opportunity to enter the grounds this night. They hadn't overlooked the possibility of a hired thug to do away with him.

They entered the ballroom, and she scanned the simple decorations once more. They had achieved just the right effect, befitting this unusual entertainment for a family in mourning. The vast chamber stretched away from her, half again as long as it was wide, with a balcony along one side for the orchestra. The chandeliers glittered, and candles illuminated every corner of the room. Bunches of ribands gathered folds of the long velvet drapes that normally lined the walls. No one could hide behind these to strike a deadly blow.

They strolled about the room together, pretending to admire while in fact taking the opportunity to check that the French windows remained securely locked. In mid-December, it was unlikely anyone would wish to step out onto the terrace.

A scuffling from the balcony above announced the arrival of the musicians. Chairs scraped, a violin string plunked and voices murmured. Papers rustled as the players set music on their stands. One of the members of Mr. Coggins's patrol would be with them, overlooking both the players and the dance floor.

"Frederick!" She clutched his arm. "You will be careful."

His fingers closed over hers. The intense blueness of his smiling eyes wrought pleasant sensations within her. Almost, she could forget what might lie ahead this night—and the risk she herself had to take later.

"That reminds me," he said, as if he echoed her thoughts. "There is still one last detail we must take care of, or our elaborate trap might yet fail."

"What?" She gazed up into his handsome face. Was it her imagination, or had the old telltale signs of dissipation faded? Now, all she saw were lines of concentration, and a complexion tanned and healthy from outdoor living.

"You asked me whom I believed to be my heir. It's Mr. Percival Needham."

She drew in a deep breath, then let it out slowly. "I was right."

"I want you to keep an eye on him this evening for me. If he disappears, though, you are *not* to follow him, is that understood? You might ruin everything if you do. Instead, tell me, or Coggins, or Adrian. Will you promise me that?"

"But what if—"

"No! You are not to follow him, under any circumstances. Alert someone—even one of the footmen—but don't you do anything else. Just watch him. Don't take your eyes off him for a moment, if you can avoid it, until we're ready."

"I won't," she vowed.

His lips twitched into his more usual smile. "Good girl." He touched her cheek with his finger, then took her arm. They continued their tour of the ballroom.

She clung to him, dreading the moment they would separate—and he would become vulnerable. She couldn't sit in his pocket this evening, though; he wouldn't like it. He preferred his ladies to behave with propriety—which was difficult enough for Lizzie at the best of times.

"Cousin Frederick!" Georgiana waved to them. "Someone has arrived."

St. Vincent led Lizzie back to join his cousins in the receiving line, where they remained for some time. Mr. Winfield and Mr. Needham arrived together, followed closely by several families from the neighboring estates and hunting boxes.

As more people entered the ballroom, Mr. Needham eased himself away. He looked distinctly uncomfortable, Lizzie noted. She would see to it he became more so. If he made any attempts on Frederick's life this night, at least he would not do so with a steady hand.

Mr. Needham edged his way toward Georgiana, but

Lizzie cornered him before he had taken a half-dozen steps. With a gleam in her eye that should have warned that gentleman had he known her better, she said: "Tell me about the Dower House. I've never been there, you know."

"Oh, it—it's much like the Grange. Only smaller, of course." Mr. Needham inched away.

Lizzie followed. "Does the ivy cling to every window as it does here?"

"Never really thought about it." He looked about, as if seeking an excuse to escape her.

She remained firmly in his path. "What brought you to this neighborhood in the first place? I should have imagined you would prefer a house in a larger town."

He managed a ghastly smile. "Wanted to rusticate." He took a sidling step away.

Lizzie followed, continuing to bombard him with aimless questions. The poor fellow looked on the verge of panic, she noted, pleased with her success.

Out of the corner of her eye, she saw the Reverend Mr. Winfield seize his opportunity; he begged Georgiana to bestow a dance on him. The girl blushed prettily and nodded. Lizzie nodded in satisfaction, then smiled as St. Vincent, not far away, raised a musing eyebrow at the pair.

At last, there seemed to be enough couples to begin. St. Vincent signaled the musicians, who immediately struck up a cotillion. He strolled over to Lizzie, and Mr. Needham heaved an audible sigh as the viscount drew her onto the floor.

"Mr. Needham is nervous," she whispered smugly as they came together, hands raised between them.

Frederick stepped back into place. "By the time you're done with him, he'll be a complete wreck." He glanced about the floor, to where Mr. Winfield had edged out Mr. Burnett for Georgiana's hand.

Lizzie followed his gaze. "Our vicar has hidden depths," she murmured.

For the country dance, which came next, Frederick led out Mrs. Stellings, the lovely wife of the Master of Hounds. Lizzie bullied Mr. Needham into partnering her. Another hour to go, before they could make the announcement. . . .

Frederick, she noted in growing concern, appeared to find little of his usual pleasure in dancing. He sought each new partner with reluctance, and performed his part in the set mechanically, as if only years of enacting the amused rake carried him through. He kept glancing toward Lizzie, toward Percival Needham.

An unfamiliar rush of protectiveness surged through her. She wouldn't let him down! She would keep that gentleman in sight, no matter what, just as Frederick had asked. She wouldn't—couldn't—let anything happen to him.

At last it was time. Mr. Winfield, her current partner, returned her to her chair, where Frederick waited. She took his arm, wishing they didn't have to go through with this. Adrian, who must have been watching, joined them, and St. Vincent signaled the musicians for the pre-arranged fanfare.

Silence fell over the ballroom as all turned to the trio standing near the door. In a clear, carrying voice, Adrian announced the betrothal, and the immediate marriage, then with great formality laid Lizzie's trembling hand in St. Vincent's.

Frederick squeezed her fingers, but before he could speak, they were surrounded by well-wishers. "Keep your watch," he murmured, then turned to receive the enthusiastic congratulations of the vicar.

The musicians struck up a waltz, and in relief St. Vincent caught Lizzie and led her onto the floor. Other couples joined them, and they swept into the open steps. Lizzie performed them with all her usual *verve*, and hoped she concealed her trembling.

St. Vincent drew her near for the few closed steps. "Not much longer," he murmured in her ear. They

336

separated, and it was a minute before they closed once more in the repeated movements. "Are you ready?"

"Of course." Scorn sounded in her voice, but to her annoyance, so did a slight tremor.

He gave her an encouraging smile, which she doubted she matched.

The dance ended and he placed her hand on his arm and led her toward the door. Once outside in the Great Hall, he said: "Only a little longer, Lizzie."

She nodded. Together, they walked across the tiled marble floor, the music following. That eerie sensation of someone watching assailed her, but she forced herself not to look back. Eyes, only eyes, bored through her back, not daggers or shot. Only a few feet farther. . . .

St. Vincent threw open the door into the library and she had to force herself not to run inside. A warm fire crackled in the hearth, welcoming, but no other lights illuminated the room.

"Frederick—"

He placed his finger on her lips.

"All's quiet, m'lord." Coggins's hissed words came out of the dark shadows. "No need to go alooking for me, I'm behind your desk."

"Glad to have you with us." He turned back to Lizzie. "In another minute or two I want you to hurry back to the ball. Run, if you like. When you get there, find Needham and don't take your eyes off him. If he's already gone, tell Adrian at once. Is that understood?"

She bit her lip. "Do we have to actually let him *try* to murder you one more time?"

"Nothing less will do for our good Coggins—or for a jury, I shouldn't doubt. I have no desire to remain a suspect to the end of my days."

"Which may not be long, if anything goes wrong."

A slow smile lit his eyes. "I have little fear of dying this night. Come, Lizzie. It's time for you to go back." He turned her about and gave her a push.

She went to the door, hesitated, and looked over her

shoulder at him.

"Go," he repeated.

She went.

She hurried into the ballroom and looked about. Nowhere did she see Mr. Percival Needham. Her heart constricted painfully, and she raced along the length of the room, her frantic gaze scanning the dancing couples. No, he wasn't among them. He had gone.

She started for Adrian, then instead sought out the footman James and entrusted him with the information. Adrian would have stopped her. He still might. . . . She couldn't let Frederick face this alone. . . .

She escaped into the hall once more and closed the heavy door behind her. Somehow, she had to slip back into the library, to be with Frederick without upsetting their plan. . . .

She ran down the hall, paused at the library to steady her ragged breath, then inched the door open. He stood before the hearth, his back toward her, his tall, imposing figure silhouetted against the flames. He made a perfect target. The hinges creaked, and he stiffened.

"It's only me," she whispered, then ducked quickly behind the desk. The Runner made what room he could, considering his bulk.

"Get her out of here," she heard Frederick breathe.

"Now, Missy, this here is no place—"

"It is! Mr. Needham was already gone. Do you think I could stay away?"

Frederick muttered something she didn't catch, then added: "We may not have long. Needham should be in place soon. Not another word out of either of you."

Minutes passed; Lizzie counted them by the unnaturally loud ticking of the mantel clock. She longed to straighten from her cramped position. Around the corner of the desk she could barely see the tails of Frederick's coat. He remained before the fireplace, staring into the flames.

A log snapped in the grate and she jumped, then eased

her position. Frederick never moved. He just stood there, as if contemplating—perhaps regretting—his betrothal. It would be impossible for Mr. Needham to miss. . . .

Coggins coughed and shifted his position, and she saw St. Vincent's hand clench, then relax. The waiting was unbearable. . . .

"If this has all been a hum, m'lord—," Coggin began.

"Your men had better be in position," she hissed back.

A slight sound reached them, of a latch being softly lifted, and Lizzie's heart beat in her throat. The French window opened a bare inch. St. Vincent stiffened but remained facing the fire. The door swung wider and Lizzie eased herself into a crouch.

A gust of cold air filled the library, sending sparks shooting from the hearth. Frederick turned, and Lizzie launched herself across the space between them as a deafening explosion filled the room. Burning pain seared Lizzie's shoulder. She clutched Frederick's arm, her fingers went numb, and she fell.

Chapter 27

Coggins dove from the cover of his hiding place and shot past, achieving an amazing speed for such a bulky individual.

Lizzie stared after him, dazed, then struggled to a sitting position. Her shoulder stung and she stared at it, bewildered. A deep red stain beaded along the torn edge of her sleeve.

Frederick dropped to one knee beside her. He gripped his own arm, and blood trickled between his fingers. "Confound it, Lizzie, what the devil do you think you were doing?"

She blinked, and her mind began to function once more. "You were hit—"

"The ball grazed us both. Damnation! Can you never do as you're told? You might have been killed!"

"Me! I like that. *You're* the one he was aiming at! You were just going to stand there and let him shoot you! I tell you, Frederick, I won't have it! I—" With a strangled cry, she threw herself into his arms. His good one closed tightly about her.

A commotion sounded on the terrace, and St. Vincent stood at once, then assisted her to her feet. She clung to him for a moment until her head stopped reeling. It was no more than the merest scratch! she told herself, disgusted by her weakness. It must be the shock of having

340

been hit.

Frederick, his arm still about her, led her to the French window. Outside, three men grasped a fourth, who struggled for a moment, then stood still. On the ground at his feet lay a dueling pistol. St. Vincent stooped carefully and picked it up.

"One of a matched pair that belonged to my uncle," he said. "Last time I saw them, they were in a case in the gun room. Did you leave the mate with Mr. Needham?" He looked directly into Mr. Wesley Burnett's haggard eyes.

Lizzie stared at the gentleman, nonplussed.

"I didn't shoot to kill," Mr. Burnett declared. His voice cracked on the last word.

"I know you did not. I must suppose you to be a better shot than you are a knife-thrower. Or did you count on the second pistol providing incontrovertible proof against Mr. Needham?"

Mr. Burnett made no response.

Frederick turned to the Runner. "Have you found Needham?"

"That hound of Missy's did, m'lord. He was just about where you thought he'd be, behind them shrubs over there, lying as if he'd a-run into that overhanging branch. Had the other pistol in his pocket, he did, too. Two of my men are carrying him inside right now. There's a nasty blow on his temple, but nothing he won't recover from. Miserable headache he'll have, o'course."

Lizzie pulled away from Frederick and stared from Mr. Coggins to Mr. Burnett and back again. "But—"

"I fear I misled you somewhat, my dear. Mr. Burnett, not my long-missing heir, murdered my cousin."

"You can't prove that!" Mr. Burnett declared.

St. Vincent shook his head. "I think perhaps we can."

The door behind them burst open and Adrian rushed into the library. He stopped, drew a deep breath as he took in the situation, then leaned against the jamb, watching.

Lizzie gave her brother a shaky smile, then turned back

to Frederick. "I don't understand. Why would *Mr Burnett* want to kill you?"

"He didn't. Did you?" He raised questioning brows toward that gentleman.

"Of course not." The man glared back at him, then added savagely: "Perhaps I should have."

"Oh, no." St. Vincent's lips twitched into a wry smile. "It's much better this way, I assure you. When, bye the bye, did the delightful idea of staging these attempts occur to you? No? Well, I can't blame you for not answering." He turned to Mr. Coggins. "I believe we brought it on ourselves, with our determined search for my possible missing heir."

"There had been two—no, three!—attempts on your life before we caught on," Lizzie protested.

"Not exactly." He tightened his arm about her—then released her abruptly. "The first—that shot in the woods—I believe to have been nothing more than a careless tenant. My cut girth and the collapsing bedframe were most likely presents from Mr. Rycroft. If we hadn't taken such an interest in the collection, he shortly would have been a very wealthy man."

Lizzie nodded, frowning. "That makes sense. If you were seriously injured or killed, he'd have time to remove the rest of the pieces and be gone without a trace before the rest of us noticed. If he just stole it—"

"We'd have been after him afore he could be out of the country, we would," Mr. Coggins finished.

"Quite so." St. Vincent's mouth tightened. "We were convinced, though, my heir must be out to murder me and make it appear an accident. And there was Mr Needham, so afraid we would assume it was he. I don't believe it mattered to our Mr. Burnett whether Needham was really an Ashfield or not—the fact Needham believed it was sufficient."

Lizzie glared at the man. "Setting that fire was a terrible thing to do. All that work, the supplies—"

Frederick caught her hand. "You have to remember he

was desperate. Mr. Coggins's investigation was thorough, yet he turned up very little information on Mr. Burnett. It would not have been much longer before he received an answer from America and discovered no such person existed."

Lizzie stared up at him, brightening. "You mean a false identity?" She turned her fascinated gaze on the man. "Why? Unless *he* is your heir?"

"Really, Lizzie, are you forgetting my cousin's penchant for blackmail?"

"We only found evidence against Mr. Winfield—" She broke off. "You mean Mr. Burnett already retrieved whatever your cousin held against him—the night of the murder?"

"I doubt he'd have dared take the time to search for the hidden panel then. More likely he found it the night Hodgkens was attacked in the library."

"But *why?*" she demanded.

Mr. Coggins coughed. "Do you remember that story I was telling you, Missy? About the cove what sold faked works of art and was transported?"

It only took Lizzie a second to make the connection. "He escaped and returned to England under a different name," she breathed, delighted. "Frederick, do you mean you've known this and not told me?"

"It's still a guess, based on information Coggins received. But it's one that can be easily proved, I should imagine. It's been almost eight years, but I doubt he's changed so much no one would recognize him. If any evidence existed, you may be sure my cousin would have discovered it and planned to put it to some use."

The pure hatred of Mr. Burnett's expression proved all the confirmation Lizzie needed. She turned away and shuddered. "What of Henry? I suppose he must have seen something that night. And then he gave himself away at dinner when he spilled the wine—" She huddled against St. Vincent's shoulder.

Coggins nodded briskly. "Never you fear, Missy. We'll

settle this case, all right and tight." His gaze rested on her, and a slight smile just touched his grim mouth. "Begging your pardon, but I thinks as it's about time we was off. Bring him along, then, men. I'll be back to see you in the morning, I will," he added to St. Vincent. His party set forth.

Adrian, who had been lounging against the door frame all this while, straightened up. "It may have escaped your notice, St. Vincent, but it's freezing out here. Lizzie hasn't even a shawl."

St. Vincent stepped away from her. "Forgive me." He bowed in an exaggerated manner and waved her indoors.

Adrian closed the French windows behind them and adjusted the drapes to block the cold that seeped around the glass panes.

Lizzie went to the fire, then turned her back to it so she could face St. Vincent. She stared at him, dismayed. "You're still bleeding!"

Frederick glanced down at the torn patch on his sleeve, and the blood that seeped from his cuff over his gloved hand. "It's only a scratch. No worse than yours. He didn't mean to kill me, you know. I doubt either of us would have been hit if you hadn't interfered."

"If that isn't the outside of enough! I didn't interfere with his aim—I was just going to push you aside."

"If you two can stop arguing for a moment? I think you should both be bandaged." Adrian rang for the housekeeper, then thrust Lizzie into a chair.

She ignored her brother and fixed her compelling gaze on St. Vincent. "You will kindly explain why you didn't tell me the truth of your suspicions."

"*After* we have you two tended," Adrian declared in a tone that defied opposition.

"I'm not hurt," Lizzie snapped, but she leaned back against the cushions and closed her eyes. Her arm did sting so. Frederick's must hurt dreadfully, though he didn't betray it by a single sign.

Both wounds proved to be no more than grazes.

344

Relieved, Adrian assisted Mrs. Hodgkens in the bandaging, and forcibly restrained Lizzie from herself inspecting Frederick's deeper scratch. When the housekeeper at last retreated with the bowl of dirtied linen, Lizzie perched on the arm of the viscount's chair.

"Now," she ordered.

"Unfeeling wench," he murmured. "Have you no pity? Or concern for yourself?"

"Only rampant curiosity."

He sighed. "Mr. Percival Needham is indeed the descendant of your Samuel."

"Does he know, do you think?" she asked.

"I'm quite certain of it. Do you remember his paying Mr. Rycroft for information? I imagine that's where the page from the Bible went."

Lizzie digested this, and a soft chuckle escaped her. "Poor Mr. Needham. He must have realized how guilty he appeared. No wonder he's become so nervous." She sobered abruptly. "It really wasn't kind of Mr. Burnett to throw suspicion on him like that."

"Kindness is not one of his virtues, my dear. But to give the devil his due, I doubt he would have thought of it had we not made such an uproar of discovering my missing heir."

Her brow puckered. "Me, you mean. I suppose I shall have to apologize to Mr. Needham."

"My poor Lizzie. Will you survive the experience, do you think?" He drew back in his chair, as if he found her nearness not to his liking. "You've bled all over your pretty dress."

Lizzie looked at the gown critically. "Did you like it?"

Adrian, who leaned against the edge of the desk, straightened up. "One of us had best return to the ball. I left Lady St. Vincent with orders not to permit anyone to leave."

"Why don't I—" St. Vincent started to rise.

Lizzie pushed him back. "An excellent idea, Adrian. Either pack them off home, or send them in to supper."

A sudden smile lit Adrian's eyes. "I leave you in good hands, I make no doubt."

"You do. The best possible." She met her brother's gaze and managed a shaky smile. "If I can just make him believe it."

Adrian took his leave.

Lizzie mustered her courage, then turned back to Frederick. "There is a little matter you and I still have to discuss."

"No, Lizzie." His voice was firm, but an infinite sadness lurked in his eyes. "I will not—"

"You're just being mule-headed! I—"

A light rap sounded on the door. St. Vincent looked relieved, but Lizzie called: "Go away."

The door opened, and the Reverend Mr. Winfield hesitated on the threshold. "I am so glad to see you are well, my lord, Miss Carstairs. Your brother explained—"

"Obviously not enough," Lizzie murmured.

Frederick silenced her with a look. "What may I do for you?"

The vicar cleared his throat. "I—that is, Miss Ashfield—" He broke off.

Lizzie glared at him. "Can it not wait until morning?"

"No! That is to say, Miss Ashfield would be most displeased—I mean—"

"Out with it, Vicar!" Lizzie ordered.

The man colored to the roots of his sandy hair. "I—I have come to you upon a matter of greatest urgency, my lord, to my future happiness and well-being," he pronounced, as if reciting a memorized speech.

"Yes?"

Georgiana's head appeared in the doorway. She whispered something to Mr. Winfield and pushed him forward.

The vicar turned back to St. Vincent. "As—as the official head of Miss Ashfield's family, and—," he checked with Georgiana for guidance, "—her guardian by law, I wish to make formal application to you for her

346

hand in marriage."

A sad smile touched St. Vincent's lips. "Very well, if somewhat slowly, said. I take it this meets with my cousin's approval?"

"Your cousin," Georgiana said from the doorway, "most humbly begs you to hear his suit with favor. It's taken me the better part of an hour to screw his courage up to the sticking point, you know," she added with a rush of candor.

The vicar turned an even deeper shade of red. "Miss Ashfield, it is highly improper—"

"Oh, bother impropriety!"

To Mr. Winfield's further consternation, she threw her arms about him. Over his shoulder, she said: "Have we your permission, Cousin Frederick? I should like to marry him of all things."

"No more doubts?" Lizzie asked.

"None. I've always relied on his judgment, you must know, but until recently I thought that was the *only* reason I found such pleasure in his company. I know better, now." She directed an adoring look at Mr. Winfield. "To think, all this time, he kept his true feelings hidden from me."

St. Vincent nodded. "You have my permission."

"On the condition you take yourselves off on the instant," Lizzie added.

Mr. Winfield, who by this time had ventured to enfold her in his embrace, started and pulled back.

Georgiana, not the least backward, giggled. "You are quite right. There are some things best discussed in private, are there not?" She winked at Lizzie and, taking the stammering vicar by the arm, drew him from the room.

"She will run his life for him," Lizzie commented, pleased.

"He'll steady her, and she'll give him confidence," Frederick agreed. "They should suit very well."

"Indeed they will." She looked down at the ring that

347

sparkled on her gloved finger, and the fear of real uncertainty shot through her. She stood to lose everything she loved in the next few minutes, if she couldn't overcome his stubbornness.

"We had better return to the ballroom and admit our own engagement is a hoax." He started to rise.

She pushed him back, and fixed him with her affronted gaze. "Are you going to jilt me?" she demanded, pretending outrage.

"Lizzie—" He sounded tired, as one goaded beyond endurance.

"I won't have it!" She rushed on, before she lost her nerve. "To be engaged for no more than an hour or two. You'll make me the joke of every club in London."

His hands clenched. "Our engagement is nothing but a sham, Lizzie—as you well know."

"*Too* well," she muttered. She bit her lip, then plunged on. "Do you know, I've been thinking about that. You really won't be safe until you have an heir. Or several of them, for that matter. Five," she added, staring at her hands, "seems like an excellent number."

"Mr. Needham is not trying to murder me, remember," he pointed out.

"Well, how can you be certain this hasn't given him an idea? If you were to meet with an accident *now*, no one would ever suspect him. Not after all this fuss. He might think it the perfect time to act."

"You need have no worry." Frederick spoke through gritted teeth. "I know my duty, and I intend to marry."

Lizzie shook her head. "The sort of wife you have in mind would be a mistake. She'd never be happy here, not with all the work that needs to be done. You need someone who enjoys a challenge—someone like me." She held her breath.

He ran his fingers through the orderly waves of his blond hair. "You don't want to marry me, Lizzie."

"Why not? It seems to me exactly what I should like."

"I'm twice your age."

"Which means you've had your youthful sprees and now you're ready to settle down. That will be much more comfortable than being tied to a young, flighty gentleman."

"My reputation—"

"I've known about it any time these past eight years, and it's never bothered me before. Why should it now?"

"I won't take advantage of your innocence!"

"Stop being so pig-headedly noble! I—"

She broke off as the door swung open. With a muttered expletive, she rearranged herself more decorously on the arm of the chair, but couldn't manage a smile for the uncertain dowager who hesitated on the threshold.

"St. Vincent? Lizzie? Are you both all right? Mr. Carstairs assured me your injuries were quite minor, but you haven't returned to the ballroom, and I couldn't help but worry."

"We'll be there in a moment, Cousin Isobel." Frederick straightened, taking the opportunity to move farther from Lizzie. "We have another announcement to make."

"No we haven't." Lizzie's chin thrust out. "Do get rid of everyone for us, would you, Lady St. Vincent? Before Frederick does something I'll regret."

She regarded them in uncertainty. "I don't see how I could end the ball, my dear. It would be so very rude. And Squire Stellings has been asking for St. Vincent."

"I'll be with him in five minutes," Frederick assured her.

"Make it fifteen," Lizzie pleaded. Her hand tightened on his arm, and she turned her intent gaze on the dowager. "Or twenty? Please," she added.

Lady St. Vincent nodded, relieved, and withdrew.

"Five minutes or twenty, Lizzie, it isn't going to make any difference." Frederick loosened her hold, finger by finger, on his arm.

"Not if we keep getting interrupted," she agreed. She rose, went to the desk where she rummaged through the top drawer, and drew out the key. She locked the door,

349

then turned back to Frederick with a smile of triumph. "Maybe *now* we can settle this," she said, and returned to her perch at his side.

He shook his head. "I am no fit husband for you."

"Why may *I* not have any say in the matter?"

He took her hands between his. "It's for your own good, Lizzie. Let me behave in an honorable manner, just this once."

"Honorable!" She glared at him, frustrated, then inspiration struck. She drew her hands free of his hold, then leaned forward and slid one arm behind his neck. Gathering her nerve, she kissed the lobe of his ear.

He stiffened. "What are you doing?"

"I'm trying to seduce you. *Then* we can talk about your precious honor."

"Lizzie—" His voice shook with his effort of control.

Nerves fluttered in her stomach as she sensed his inner conflict, the nearness of her victory—or defeat. She moved closer, but her innate honesty won out. "The devil's in it, Frederick," she sighed. "I've never tried to seduce anyone before, and I haven't the faintest notion how to go about it. Have I started right?"

His longing showed clearly in his eyes, but he continued to resist. His unwavering gaze met hers. "You mustn't, my dear. Please, Lizzie—"

"*Have* I?"

"It would be unforgivable—"

"Can you never stop arguing with me?" she demanded, exasperated. She smoothed a finger along the line of his jaw. "Should I be doing something else?"

"Yes! Finding a gentleman worthy of you!"

"What a bore that would be. And you know perfectly well that wasn't what I meant." She ran her fingers through his waving hair, and allowed her lips to just brush the nape of his neck. "Am I doing it right, *now?*" she breathed.

He gritted his teeth. "Exactly right."

"Good." This time, it was his mouth she kissed.

350

Strange sensations, which she had the distinct feeling she was going to enjoy exploring, shot through her.

With a low groan of surrender, he dragged her onto his lap and held her tightly. "I shouldn't," he murmured against her hair, "but confound it, Lizzie, a man can only take just so much. Are you sure you won't regret this?"

For answer, she threw her arms about him and kissed him once more, with every ounce of the joy and enthusiasm that filled her.

"Oh, my love," he murmured when he could speak again. "My dearest, dearest love." With a tentative hand, he stroked her hair, shaking his head as if unable to believe she really wanted him.

The tenderness of his expression brought an unaccustomed lump to her throat. With a soft cry of happiness, she buried her face against his neckcloth and clung to him.

He rubbed his chin along the top of her curls. "And to think I was actually sorry you had grown up." His voice shook with repressed laughter and wonder.

She looked up. "You don't mind now?"

"What do you think?" His fingers caressed her cheek and he kissed her forehead, then closed her eyes with his lips. "Were you serious about those five heirs, by the way?"

"Yes, I was." She wrinkled her freckled nose. "I think it will be rather fun. And it won't be so *very* long before we can teach them to hunt and fish. *You* won't mind, will you?"

A soft chuckle escaped him. "If Halliford can survive fatherhood, then so can I." He gazed at her, and his smile slowly faded. The passion he'd tried so long to deny flickered into a glowing flame in his eyes. "As you say," he murmured, "this just might prove rather enjoyable."

"Of course it will." She rubbed her forehead against his chin and curled even closer against him.

A sudden frown creased his brow. "Speaking of Halliford, he—or rather Helena—will have something to say about this, I fear."

"Undoubtedly. You can ask them when they get here tomorrow. They're bringing the Special License."

"The devil they are!"

"Well, when I wrote to Nell, I was *hoping* . . ."

"And I suppose Adrian has already agreed to perform the ceremony for us?" he demanded.

"No, he's being stubborn. He says he refuses to take part in a forced marriage, and won't do anything until you've assured him I'm not constraining you."

"You've arranged everything?" Frederick asked, his tone ominous.

"Not quite. I thought I'd better let you pick the wine for the wedding breakfast."

He struggled for a moment, then his deep chuckle broke from him. He hugged her as if he'd never set her free. "You'll never change, will you, my love?"

She opened her eyes wide and fixed him with her bright, candid stare. "Well, why should I?" she demanded.